FROZEN

AND DEATH MAGIC

OF FIRE & FAE 1

Frozen Hearts
and Death Magic

DAY LEITAO

SPARKLY WAVE

MONTREAL, 2022

CONTENTS

Fernick

Karsal

Formosa

Vastfield

Varana

Royal Manor

Haven

Umbrar

Eaglehold

Greenstone

Wolfmark

Wildspring

Mount
Prime

Iron Citadel

Ironhold

Frostlake
Castle

Frostlake

N

I

SECRET IN THE WOODS

Naia's toes were freezing, and she still had no idea what insanity had made her leave the warmth of her bed, no idea what had compelled her to climb out of her window, no idea why she was out in the rain in the middle of the night. An odd feeling, a hunch, a weird, unscratchable itch.

Pity that the hunch had forgotten to warn her that these slippers would get drenched outside. But then, did she really need to be reminded of the obvious? Common sense wasn't her companion tonight. At all.

It was as if something called her, pulled her, but whatever that something was, it was perhaps going too far, as she was now leaving the manor's garden and stepping into the Shadowy Woods. If she kept going, eventually she'd come across one of the royal guards stationed in the forest around the property, and then she didn't even want to think about all the explaining she'd have to do.

When she pictured herself sitting across from her father, the part she dreaded the most wasn't making him angry or worried, but the fact that he'd learn that she could bend the iron bars from her window. He'd probably put some wooden trellis there or something, meaning no more random strolls at weird hours, also known as *bye, freedom*.

That was a horrible thought. But she did wonder how come he'd never guessed that *iron bars* wouldn't contain an *ironbringer*. Right. As if he thought her magic was worth anything. At least being underestimated had its perks. Wow, freezing outside, what a magnificent perk.

The worst was that now everything was getting hard to see, considering the light from the garden lamps was fading into darkness, and any different sound would be drowned by the raindrops falling on the trees and leaves rustling with the wind.

Alone in dark woods in the middle of the night, her feet wet, unsure why she was even here, this would be the time to turn back to her warm room and some dry socks. Oh, the wonder of dry socks. And yet, there was something out there. Something... Nothing that she should fear, rather something calling her.

With eyes closed, she reached for her magic, but couldn't feel any type of metal other than the faint traces of iron deep within the earth. She took a few more steps into the woods, trying to sense what was out there—then tripped on a root and almost fell. She should have paid more attention to where she was going.

Naia looked back. Too light to be tree bark. As she reached out and touched it, she realized it was soft and smooth, like... skin. This was a person. A person, lying on their stomach, wearing no shirt, unconscious—or dead.

Naia checked for a pulse. Still alive. But the hand was so cold. She was about to yell for the guards, yell for someone so they could get a healer, when she noticed the nails. Pointy, dark nails.

A chill ran down her spine. It couldn't be. But then, the

long hair was not white or pale blond. Even drenched and muddy, it looked brown or at least dark blond. She moved some of it away from one ear—and sucked in a breath.

This was her enemy.

Sure, she'd only heard of them in stories; the dreaded race that had razed cities to the ground, killed her grandparents, almost rid Aluria of humans.

Until they disappeared.

Her father had always thought they would return one day. Here was the proof that he'd been right.

With dark nails and pointy ears, this was a fae.

She touched the top of his head and found pointy, backward horns. Fae, for sure, but these creatures in Aluria were supposed to be monstrous, with blond-white hair, claws, and red eyes. Well, the hands had pointy nails. But at the same time, there was something so human, so vulnerable about this fae, unconscious in the woods, perhaps dying. A young man, based on the size of his arms and back and what she could see of his face.

Naia swallowed, her heart thrumming in her chest. She should call the guards. And then what? The fae would be beaten, perhaps worse. But he was an enemy. Or maybe not. So much time had passed. This could be a sole survivor or maybe someone who had nothing to do with the past war. Or perhaps a different fae race from across the sea.

Maybe, maybe. Every second she spent thinking was a second he remained on that cold ground. Naia was no healer. But calling guards or her father could seal his fate, and she didn't know if she would want that blame. She had a choice to make.

Naia got up and ran back to her room, then tiptoed down the hallway to the kitchen. There, she took the biggest tray she could find, one meant for serving whole boars. Sometimes she used her metal magic to transport animals she hunted, and this was the only way she could imagine herself bringing that fae inside.

Perhaps she should call Fel to help her. No. Her brother would definitely want to tell their father, and for now, she wasn't sure if it would be a good idea. Yes, her twin's outrageous metal magic would probably be helpful, but... The fae was her secret, and perhaps she wanted to keep it that way.

Carrying the tray and also a blanket from her bedroom, she returned to that place in the forest, almost afraid that someone would have found him or that he would have disappeared somehow, but he was still there, still unconscious. She placed the blanket over the tray, then, with some effort, rolled the fae over it and wrapped him. Hopefully that would prevent the iron from hurting him. If it was true that iron hurt them. If he was really a fae.

She hoped that he was not a white fae, that this didn't mean they were returning, didn't mean another war would start. Still, for now, she just wanted to save him; otherwise she'd never know why she'd been drawn to him, who he was, or what he was doing here.

Moving him all the way to her bedroom wasn't going to be easy. Naia sighed. The weight over the metal should make no difference, except that she always felt that it did, and then had trouble moving heavy objects. Fel would be able to get this fae inside without even blinking or breaking a sweat.

Yeah, yeah, yeah. Perhaps that was how her magic had gotten so shitty; by relying so much on her twin. She sighed again, then reached for her connection with the iron. It wasn't that it called to her, but that she could feel it, as if it were an extension of her own body that she could touch when the need came.

Naia floated the tray with the fae on it, carefully bringing it to the gardens. Thankfully there was nobody there. She approached her window, moved the bars again, then opened the glass panes wide, to make room for the unconscious fae.

Getting him in was going to be the hardest part: a mistake could make him fall and break his neck. If fae even got broken bones.

For now, she raised her hand, even if she knew that it made no difference for the magic, and guided the tray through her window. Her arm was trembling, and, feeling she'd be unable to hold anymore, she dropped the muddy tray, blanket, and fae on her bed.

What a mess.

Naia climbed in, closed the windows, and moved the iron bars back to their original place.

The room was chilly, so she put more wood in the fire, and only then turned to look at the bed. It was a young man, regardless of his pointy ears, which were not even that visible under his wavy brown hair, which hung past his shoulders. The two horns on top of his head made a difference, but somehow it was as if they belonged there. He had a square jaw with delicate lips and no facial hair. This was the furthest away from a monster that she could imagine. Now, white fae, as far as she knew, had light hair, so she wasn't sure what to make of him. His skin was much lighter than hers, but his hair was brown, also lighter than her own black hair, but definitely not pale blond.

Carefully, she pulled the metal tray from under him, then took another blanket and dried his hair, torso, and pants, avoiding the weird parts. He had no visible wounds and no fever. His only issue was how cold he was. She warmed a blanket by the fire and wrapped it around him. The room was no longer as chilly, so that should also help.

Naia got up, stood by him, then checked his pulse again. Still alive. Hopefully his problem was only cold. For a so-called monstrous creature, he was quite vulnerable, quite...

human. She touched one of his horns. The texture was different from what she'd expected. Despite its smooth appearance, it was rugged and rough. She ran her finger over it, fascinated by it. This would probably be the only time she'd be so close to a fae. And then, perhaps this was also the only time she'd be close to a beautiful young man, at least if it depended on her father. His voice echoed in her mind, saying she didn't need to get married, that she was so lucky, so strong, so independent.

If romantic wishes and dreams of kisses were weaknesses, then she was far from strong. She was seventeen, and had no idea if she was normal or not, no idea what a girl her age would be doing or thinking. No idea about anything, just some odd wishes. And perhaps that was why she was keeping the fae a secret. It was nice to look at his pleasant face with delicate lips, alone where nobody would know what she was doing. It was nice to look at him while he couldn't see her, couldn't judge her. Even if he was probably her enemy and likely to have horrific red eyes, at least she had this moment.

More and more droplets, then drops of water hit the windowpane and the roof as the drizzle turned into thick rain, the loud noise outside a quiet comfort in case one of her thoughts escaped her head and turned into words. Thoughts. Nonsense.

The scent of rain was taking over the room, a scent so intoxicatingly wonderful that she closed her eyes for a moment to bask in that feeling. Odd how she'd never noticed what rain smelled like. Perhaps because she'd never brought in a wet, muddy young man.

A young man that hopefully would survive. He had to. Even her heart was starting to tremble with worry. So much worry for him... Well, of course. She had to figure out who he was and what he was doing here. In fact, as a princess, getting that information was her duty.

And so was telling her father.

But she could ignore that part for now. After all, she'd been the one to find him. And the one to get her feet wet.

Speaking of that, only then did she remember her numb toes, so she took off her shoes and sat by the fire, imagining how horrible it would be to have her entire body cold like that. After a couple minutes, when she felt her feet had thawed, she got up. When she was about to turn, something pushed her.

Naia found herself face down on her rug, the fae above her, with a hand around her neck, as if about to choke her. Before she could even process what was happening, she called an iron poker and hit his arm, then between his legs. Her brother had told her that men were fragile there or something, and it seemed to be true, as the fae yelled in pain and let go of her. Naia took the opportunity to push him and roll away.

Enemy. Monster. She should have known he could be dangerous.

Naia got up, still pointing the poker at him. "Is that how you thank me for saving your life, you ungrateful prick?"

Trembling on the floor, his pointy nails holding the blanket around his torso, he turned to face her, his eyes wide. Those eyes. They were not red, but rather a warm brown. Mahogany eyes, now moving about as if to check the room, check where he was. And no sign that he had even heard her question.

"Do you speak my language?" she asked.

He looked at her and frowned. "No."

Great. She was wondering how come he had answered her, when he added, "*You* speak my language."

She rolled her eyes. Aluria had its own language. It was old, yes. She had never thought about its origin. But that wasn't even the point.

"Why can't you answer me, then?"

"I just did, didn't I?" He remained on the floor, a casual expression on his face as if he were relaxing there.

"I meant the first question. I saved your life, and I can still decide whether I tell anyone about you, so if I were you, I'd make an effort to be nice."

He frowned, as if thoughtful, or perhaps in disbelief, then chuckled. "Saved... me?"

Naia shrugged. "Well, is it a fae thing to lie half-naked outside in the rain?"

An edge of a smirk appeared on his pretty lips. "Well... Maybe not in the rain. Not—" He lifted the blanket wrapped around him and peeked underneath it. "Half-naked, you say?"

"And unconscious. I brought you here. I won't accept anything less than life servitude as thanks." She was joking. Or maybe testing him.

He blinked slowly. "Life servitude?" He looked away, as if thinking, then ran his dark nails through his hair. "I would need to agree with that."

Naia scoffed. "I wasn't serious. But I do want an apology for attacking me. And keep your voice down. You don't want my father finding you here." Neither did she, in fact.

He got up, towering over her, which was odd because she was tall herself and it meant he was even taller than her brother. Her first reflex was to step back, but she stood her ground. She wasn't going to let him think he could intimidate her.

But then the fae bowed slightly, put his hand on his head, between his horns, as if dizzy, and sat on the bed, eyeing her with curiosity. "I didn't mean to hurt you, and didn't know you had... brought me in... with good intent." His words were careful, as if he were measuring them.

She stared at him. "You don't want to admit I saved you?"

His expression was relaxed, bored even. "We can't know what could have happened."

She moved to the window and touched the latch. "It's all a matter of experimenting. You can go back outside and see. It won't be fair because you're conscious now, but it's worth a try." Of course she didn't want him to leave, but she didn't think he was ready to go anywhere, and it was annoying that he wouldn't even thank her.

"Still won't prove anything about the past. Unless you want me gone." He tilted his head and narrowed his beautiful eyes. "But you don't, do you?"

"Not before I know who you are and what you're doing here."

He looked up, an amused expression on his face. "But those are such big questions. Do you know who you are and what you're doing in this place?"

She scoffed. "Of course I do."

There was a knock on the door. Naia stiffened, then threw another blanket at him and whispered, "Lie down and hide."

The fae frowned but got under the blankets. Funny how he didn't argue when it was something that benefited him. Hopefully it was just her brother and he hadn't heard the fae's voice. With that much rain outside, he shouldn't be able to hear anything.

Naia moved the door just enough to see her twin standing in the hallway, his long black hair messy for once.

"Fel? Something wrong?"

"I..." He craned his neck as if trying to look inside the bedroom. No way he'd see the bed from this angle, and even if he saw it, it would just look like it was messy, but it still unnerved her. Fel frowned, thoughtful. "I thought I heard... Are you all right?"

Naia faked a cough. "Yes. Fine. You probably heard the rain." She fake-coughed again. "Or me."

Her twin narrowed his green eyes as if suspicious, but then smiled. "Are you hiding something?"

She scoffed. Or maybe it was a nervous laugh. "What am I even going to hide?"

Fel shrugged. "You tell me. But you need something for that cough." He then turned around and walked away without even saying goodnight or anything. Weird. Well, at least he wasn't going to stay and chat or check her bedroom.

Naia closed and barred the door, then walked back to the bed and removed the extra blanket.

The fae seemed curious, and cocked his head toward the door, almost as if pointing at it with one of his horns. "That's... metal magic?"

Right. He didn't mean Naia's magic, which had brought him inside and saved his life, but her brother's. On the upside, at least this was a piece of information. "So you know about our magic."

His eyes were quite captivating when looking up, thinking. "I'd say... no. I was under the impression that only royal families had magic among humans."

Naia clenched her fists. "And what in the world do you think we are?"

He narrowed his eyes. "This is... a castle?"

"A manor. Comfortable enough for us. We don't have an obsession with showing off."

"Interesting." The fae took a deep breath, his eyes scanning the room with even more curiosity than before. "And this isn't Ironhold." That was the metal kingdom, and it meant he knew Aluria quite well, to know about their magic and even a kingdom's name. His eyes narrowed, again looking around the room, then setting on her. "Where are we?"

She crossed her arms. "I don't know. What if we exchange an answer for an answer?"

His lips formed a hint of a smile. "You could lie."

"So could you."

He rolled his pretty mahogany eyes. "I'm an Ancient."

Ancient. That was what the white fae called themselves. So he *was* the enemy. Naia had to tread carefully. "Not fae?"

He exhaled, as if annoyed, then shook his head. "Ancient. But you're free to call me whatever you want. And we don't lie. It doesn't mean I have to answer anything."

"So you aren't going to thank me or answer my questions. You know, I might call my father, who'll put you in a dungeon."

"And then chain me in iron and torture me until death." His eyes narrowed. "Are you proud of that, little human?"

"I haven't yet done anything to be either proud or ashamed of, little *fae*."

"River." The word made no sense, until he added, "My name."

Somehow, the honesty and softness in his voice made her tremble, but it wasn't fear, it was something... she wasn't sure what it was. Naia didn't want him to notice her reaction and chuckled. "Isn't there some big deal about knowing your name or something?"

He shrugged. "Who knows? Who knows if the name is real? But you can call me River." He then stared at her with an amused smirk. "Now, who is my beautiful aspiring human savior?"

Naia felt a slight flutter in her stomach, but ignored it. "Not yours. Not aspiring."

He blinked slowly, perhaps to show off his long lashes. "Forgive me. I was under the impression you assumed you had saved my life. Is that not the case?"

"It's not an impression. I *saved* your ungrateful skin. I'll tell you my name if you tell me what you are doing here."

River nodded. "That's a fair deal." Like that? So easily? He then said, "Your name first."

Of course it wouldn't be *that* easy. But if it was a trick, at least she would learn whether he could lie or not. "Naia. Short for Irinaia."

"Naia," he repeated slowly, as if savoring a drink. "Sounds like music." He smiled. "I'm sitting on a bed, not sure where, talking to an unusually gorgeous girl."

What he was doing here. It was a correct answer, by all means. Prick. And it was the second time he was calling her beautiful, probably expecting some reaction, which she wasn't going to give him, even if it was the first time in her life anyone was calling her that—other than her brother, which didn't count. She knew that it was just a polite way to get a woman's attention and didn't mean anything. Of course it didn't. Still, it was interesting to learn that fae also did that.

Naia smiled. "Enlightening. I could never have guessed it."

He returned the smile, as if satisfied. "My pleasure."

Another knock on the door. "Hide," she whispered. This time, she noticed a hint of fear in his eyes. This was good. It meant she could threaten him for answers.

Again she opened the door just a little, and saw Fel, this time holding a cup. She always admired how well he did that.

"Yes?"

He extended his gloved hand, a movement he did so graciously. "Mint tea. For your cough."

Her twin was a treasure, even if his perfection was sometimes annoying. Naia shook her head. "You didn't have to."

"Always support each other."

Their father had hammered that sentence in their heads. Naia hated it. For her, it meant one day seeing her brother become king while she'd need to settle with being just his advisor. For her twin, *supporting each other* meant making tea in the middle of the night.

She took the cup. "Thanks. I'll try to sleep now, if you don't mind."

Fel pushed the door open before she had time to stop him.

For a moment she felt a chill in her stomach, fearing he'd see what was on her bed, but all her brother did was kiss her forehead. "Sleep well, sis. I won't bother you, but call me if you need anything."

"I will." She smiled, then watched as he walked away. He was indeed a treasure.

This was the first time she was lying to her brother, and guilt gnawed at her. Up until now, she had shared everything with him, and it felt odd to hide something. Fel made it very hard to dislike him. Or resent him. Or lie to him. Still, she shut the door, then pressed her ear on it, to make sure his steps were receding down the hall.

Perhaps she could have told him about River. But she hadn't. Naia turned—and saw the fae eyeing her attentively.

"What?" she asked.

He turned away, a bored expression on his perfect face. "Nothing."

Naia sat on the bed and offered him the cup. "You should drink it. Warm tea is good when you're cold."

River grimaced, staring at the cup as if it had poison. "I don't want any."

"My brother prepared it for me. You do realize he doesn't want me dead, right?"

He raised an eyebrow. "One can never know. And it stinks of metal magic."

Naia rolled her eyes. "Metal magic doesn't stink." She truly hoped so, or else he would think her smell was dreadful. "It's just mint. Which I like." Naia shook her head, took a sip of the tea, then put the cup on a corner table, while River still eyed it with disgust.

He took a deep breath, then his face got serious for once. "Ask me something."

"Why? Now you're going to answer?"

"Not a question. Something. You think you saved me, and I can't convince you otherwise, so ask for something in return."

"Eternal devotion." The words popped out of her mouth again. She knew he'd never agree to it, but she wanted to see his reaction.

River sucked in a breath. Again a flash of fear crossed his eyes, but then he laughed. "Not that. Something simple."

That fear... it meant something. She had room to maneuver, had an opening to get what she wanted, but needed to make sure to do this right. "I'll think about it. But before that... You saw my brother, right? I could have told him about you, and I didn't. Now, I'll keep your presence here a secret, as long as you answer my questions."

He managed to look confused. "I haven't refused to answer anything, you know?"

There was no teasing, mischief, or defiance in his face, as if he were the most helpful fae in the world. But since he wanted to pretend to be nice, she'd better seize the opportunity. "Why did you come to this house? What were you doing in the woods?"

He paused, then answered slowly, "I intended none of those things, therefore I cannot give you a reason, Naia. I'm wondering as much as you are."

She took a deep breath, then decided to ask something different. "Why did your people disappear?"

He bit his lip and had a thoughtful expression for a second, then shrugged, as if unfazed. "We didn't disappear. I'm here."

She frowned. "Are you planning to return?"

"You mean my people. Well, do you know everything humans plan?"

"We're many kingdoms in Aluria. You're just one."

River shook his head. "It doesn't mean I know everything."

His eyes locked on hers, and it felt as if it was raining

inside her, but more like a cool, comforting feeling of summer rain. She didn't think he was trying to deceive her. There was openness and honesty in his beautiful red-brown eyes lined by long lashes. His face was so perfect, like an unrealistic drawing or sculpture, and it was calling to her. His lips were calling to her.

Naia looked away, trying to focus, but even the scent of rain was overwhelming her senses. *Focus, Naia.*

She looked back in his direction, making an effort not to pay attention to his astonishingly compelling looks. There was a lot she wanted to understand, and she couldn't afford to be distracted. "You're the first fae to be seen in Aluria in many years. There must be a reason."

He stiffened and his eyes widened, then he looked away. Or maybe it was an impression, as he turned back to her and chuckled. "We also live in Aluria."

"But you weren't seen," she insisted.

He shrugged. "Maybe your kind didn't look." He then stared straight into her eyes. "Ask me something, Naia. I can give you anything you want." His voice was a soft caress in her ear.

Anything? Her attention was again drawn to his lips. She swallowed. It was unlikely that she'd ever again see any man half as good looking as him. It was unlikely that she would ever again be alone with someone like that. The idea that was coming to her was so strange and scary that she didn't even dare think about it.

"What do you want from me, Naia?" he insisted.

There was an entrancing softness in his voice. He'd managed to make her name sound like music, a lullaby soothing her into wanting. It would be bold and wrong and inappropriate. Bold and wrong. Her father would be furious if he learned she did that. His pure daughter, meant to be single forever. Perhaps that was a good reason to ruin his absurd wishes. Undisturbed in her room, she could have wishes of her own.

"Kiss me." She didn't feel embarrassed, afraid, or ashamed. The voice was hers and wasn't. It was the voice of a different Naia, one that had been imprisoned, gagged, and bound. And it was free now.

River's face got even more beautiful as it relaxed into a happy, relieved smile, as if that had been his wish too. That smile made her heart leap—and speed up.

He wrapped an arm around her, and pulled her close, so that she was sitting right beside him, her legs to the opposite side as his. It felt so good to be this close to him, to feel his touch. There was still a blanket around him, but it no longer covered his arms and chest. He turned her towards him, so that they were facing each other, then caressed her hair slowly.

Her heart pounding in her chest, she closed her eyes. He smelled like grass and rain, but there was also something unique, mysterious, magical, and sweet. A reminder that he was not human. Naia sucked in a breath as she felt his lower lip touching her chin, then moving up to meet hers. Such a pleasant softness. He pulled her even closer, so that she felt his chest against hers, her thin nightgown the only thing between them. He opened her lips with his, and then his tongue was caressing the inside of her mouth.

Naia had no idea that a kiss would be like this; luscious, moist, thrilling. She would never have imagined that tongues would touch. Or that it would feel so good. She caressed his hair, then moved her hands down to his back, the pleasant feel of his lips and tongue like water reviving dry soil. And she was absorbing, absorbing, absorbing it, a thrill of life going through her. It was more than just the two mouths moving together, it was an energy moving down her body. She was kissing him back too, lost in the feeling of his lips. Was it seconds, minutes, hours? An eternity perhaps, if it could have been condensed in that moment.

Suddenly, he unwrapped his arms from around her waist, pushed her back, and stared at her, trembling, his eyes wide. Naia was trembling too, but there was something odd in the way he looked at her. Perhaps she'd done it all wrong? But it had felt real and powerful. It seemed that he had enjoyed it too, that he had wanted it as much as her. She had felt it in the way he had pulled her closer and closer, in his movements. Why was he looking at her like that? Why had he pushed her away?

A shiver ran through her body. "River?"

There was no mistaking the horror and shock in his eyes. "What have you done?"

Naia had no idea. No idea what to say or what to think. His face and hair darkened as she stared, unable to understand anything, unable to do anything. At first it was as if his body was emitting black smoke, but after a few seconds, only smoke was left where the fae had once sat. Only smoke remained in place of the lips she had kissed. Only black smoke, without even a smell. The scent of rain was gone.

"River?" she asked again, moving her hands around her, searching fruitlessly for something solid, for a sign of him.

There was nothing. *What have you done?* She had no idea.

2
THE NECROMANCER CASTLE

Blood covered the walls and floor of the ballroom. That and bodies, bodies everywhere. Leah's feet were bare, stepping on granite tiles now viscous and red. She stopped walking, then tried to put her hands together. They crossed through one another.

The feeling of blood on her feet was gone. This was a dream. At least it wasn't one of those weird ones—or a nightmare. Blood and death she could deal with.

Her father's voice came to her. *Necromancy is life; a wisp of it, condensed and returned to the dead, to give them one last chance.* And necromancy in dreams was different, much more powerful than in reality. Leah made her way to the great window. Around her, blood disappeared, wounds healed, bodies became whole again, people got up. She didn't dare look at anyone too close, didn't want to see whose bodies were there, didn't want to let the dream control her. All she wanted was to get to the window and look at the sky. There was always solace there, always an escape from even the most dreadful horror.

She reached her destination, ignoring everything behind

her as she stared through the glass. There, flying in the sky, was the silver dragon. *Her* silver dragon, always present in both her dreams and her nightmares.

Long, wingless, with iridescent scales, it was the most beautiful thing she'd ever seen. And it brimmed with power, so much power that she could sense it even from a distance. But its beauty and power were nothing compared to how she felt when seeing it. Her pain, her fears, her worries all disappeared, as if the sight was a balm to her soul. Her chest brimmed with love—such an amazing feeling—until she opened her eyes.

The curtains of her four-poster bed were closed, but some light was coming through them. This was it; the day the remaining royal delegations would arrive. The gathering was starting. Leah should be happy, should be excited. She did pretend it, especially in front of her mother, who'd been preparing her for this occasion for so long. But the truth was that Leah wished she could turn around and hide in her dreams, even with the blood, bodies, and everything.

No. Nerves were normal. She shouldn't listen to her fears, no matter how much her heart pounded in her chest, no matter how much her stomach felt strange and cold and hollow. The kings and queens would discuss the mysterious attacks, and they would find a solution. Plus, she was indeed looking forward to the balls. Real balls, right here in the castle! And she was curious to meet the other princes and princesses from Aluria. Perhaps she'd even make a few friends. And perhaps there was a nice, handsome prince among them.

And then perhaps there wasn't. Her mother would pick a husband for her regardless.

THE PEBBLED road was a lot smoother than Naia had imagined. It was strange to cross the portal into such a white world. Even in the carriage, wearing a fur coat, she felt her face and hands getting cold, and wished her gloves hadn't been tucked deep in her trunk. She could probably use her magic to get warm, but wasn't in the mood for a scolding from her father.

As she watched the snowy landscape through the window, she considered the upcoming festivities. She and her brother would finally be introduced to the other royal families in Aluria, and she was curious to see in person everyone who apparently hated them, including her mother's family and some cousins who pretended that she and Fel didn't exist. And then there was another reason that made her excited to visit another kingdom for the first time: knowledge. Having access to a different library and to more people, perhaps she could learn more about the fae.

What have you done? The question still echoed in her mind, had never faded, even after almost a year had passed.

A meeting with royals from all over the kingdom could be an opportunity to seek an answer. For now, she appreciated the white landscape; the trees covered in snow as if embraced by clouds, except that the windows of the carriage were getting foggier and foggier, and she eventually gave up trying to see beyond them.

As she turned back inside, a sight surprised her: her father was looking down, his legs restless. She glanced at her brother to see if he noticed it too, but he was playing with his hands, oblivious. Naia took another look at her father. It wasn't an impression; he was nervous.

Strange. She had never seen him even flinch, and would actually have liked to see some emotion from him a few times, like when a wild boar had almost run her over. She had been only seven, terrified, and her father had waited until the very last second to kill the beast, all the while keeping his expression placid and calm. Perhaps it was because he was such a strict father, like when he'd sent her and Fel to the cabin by the manor, to live off whatever they could hunt and gather, without any help. She'd been fourteen then, and had spent some tough six months with her twin. True that at the end of it, they had learned to trust each other, had improved their magic tremendously, and were much stronger. Still, there had been no worry or any hint of fear from his father.

Perhaps he was calm only when dealing with his children? Not really. He could recount tragic events in the war against the white fae without showing even a trace of emotion. On the few occasions he got angry, he kept his voice steady, his composure calm, which made him all the more terrifying. Then, he was a deathbringer, wielder of the most dangerous magic in the eleven kingdoms. Naia had always thought that nothing could rattle him.

But she had been wrong.

Here he was, looking like a common man, dreading something. The question was what.

"Dad?" she asked.

He stopped fidgeting and raised his green eyes. "Yes?"

"Something wrong?"

"Nothing." He rested his hands beside him on the seat and crossed his legs. "I mean, we need to remain alert, of course. It's enemy territory." He said it matter-of-factly.

Was that why he was anxious? About meeting representatives from other kingdoms? "But we're not at war. Even when there was a war, all human kingdoms were allies, right?"

Her father raised an eyebrow. "Just because we joined forces to defeat the fae, it doesn't mean our interests align. And you know they all hate Umbraar."

"Yet you always come to these meetings." Her father had been to all the gatherings, held every three years or so, each time in a different kingdom. Never in Umbraar, of course, since everyone hated them or maybe because her father had no intention of hosting other royals. Well, they didn't even have a proper castle to host anyone.

This year, the gathering was in Frostlake, which was the southernmost kingdom in Aluria, frozen a good part of the year, and far from Umbraar, which was much farther north. Naia was happy it was here because she got to see snow for the first time, but she also knew that her father hated the Frostlake queen and king more than anyone, except maybe for the Iron-hold family—and the Wolfmark family. Well, he hated a lot of people.

Her father took a deep breath. "It's never a good idea to give your back to your enemies. Or to give them reasons to conspire against you. They're all pretending to be friends, and I can pretend too." He pointed at her and Fel. "And so can you." Only then he noticed that her twin was spinning his iron phalanges in the air. "Isofel. I've already told you to keep your hands always gloved."

Fel stopped spinning his fingers, leaving them floating in the air, and had a mocking smile. "Why? Afraid they'll notice I'm a *cripple*?"

Their father sighed. "Don't say that. Still, you don't want to reveal your magic."

That didn't make sense. "But everyone knows we're iron-bringers."

"Still. Never show your true power to your enemies."

Fel snorted and rolled his eyes. "I'm pretty sure they'll be terrified of spinning fingers. But don't worry, I'll hide them when we get there."

Her father grunted, and Fel put his hand back in place; metal pieces mimicking hand bones, kept together with iron-bringing. It was what made Fel so powerful. He had to use an insane amount of magic just to perform ordinary actions, such as holding a fork, drinking from a cup, buttoning his shirt, or brushing his hair—and she was pretty sure he spent a lot of time brushing it.

Naia still remembered her twin as a child, trying to use a solid metal hand, frustrated that he couldn't hold anything. He asked for hands made of more and more pieces, trying hard to mimic normal hand movements. Naia had sat with him as he made an effort to copy her gestures, often feeling defeated, sometimes angry, but never at her. A few times she had heard him crying in his bedroom, but pretended she hadn't noticed, as nothing brought him more shame than being caught in tears. But the tears had been worth it. Eventually he asked for metal pieces that looked like hand bones and, with a lot of training and persistence, mastered his control over the pieces to the point he could mimic hand movements.

Then his magic took this gigantic leap, a leap Naia could never reach no matter how much she practiced. She was happy that her brother was so powerful, but felt weak and incompetent in comparison. That until recently, when she'd found her own magic. Not that her father cared for it.

The air got warmer, so Naia rubbed her hand on the window and noticed they had entered the dome, a colossal metal and glass structure surrounding the Frostlake capital like a gigantic greenhouse.

She turned to her brother. "You could destroy this dome without even blinking, couldn't you?"

Fel looked out the window. "Wow, it's huge. I'd need to get closer, I think."

Their father rolled his eyes. "Great. Our hosts will be delighted to hear you can destroy their city."

Fel chuckled. "Just because I can, it doesn't mean I will."

He then glared at his son. "You think a gathering is a joke? You'll need your wits, you'll need to remain alert. There are princesses from other kingdoms, and they might try to snare you."

Naia pushed back her laughter trying to imagine a horde of young women throwing themselves at her brother and asked, "Don't they hate us?"

Her father was still serious. "Hate is meaningless when they might see a chance to extend their influence to another kingdom." He turned to Fel. "Guard your heart. It's the most precious thing you have."

The funny part was that he didn't give Naia the same advice. Right. He obviously didn't think she had a heart.

Fel rolled his eyes. "We'll spend four days there. What kind of nitwit has their heart stolen in such little time?"

Such little time. Was it possible to steal a heart in four days? What about in an hour? Or in a few seconds? Was her heart still whole? She didn't want to think about it.

A dark shadow crossed her father's eyes. "Young people get carried away by their fancies, they don't know the difference between reality and illusion."

"Noted, father." Fel's voice was still mocking. "What's the next advice? Don't jump from a cliff?"

Naia's father grunted. "We'll also go over treaties, and I want you two learning how to deal with those royal snakes. I fear the Ironhold king will try to extend his power, using the fae as an excuse."

Naia stiffened, even if she'd been practicing acting normal whenever she heard that word. But she couldn't shake her guilt. Guilt for not telling anyone what she'd seen, then even more guilt for perhaps hurting or even killing River. Her father's magic could kill someone easily, and she couldn't stop wondering if that was what had happened.

But if River was alive, where had he gone? How come he had disappeared? What exactly had she done? Then there was the memory of a kiss that would never leave her lips, a taste that had never left her tongue. Did it mean that her heart had been compromised?

"The attacks. You truly don't think it's the fae?" Fel asked.

Attacks. In different kingdoms, a few villages had been targeted by some mysterious magic that left everyone dead. Not yet in Umbraar. She felt guilty for that too, wondering if it had anything to do with the white fae, wondering if she could have somehow prevented this by telling someone that she'd seen one of them.

Her father shook his head. "If they had returned, we would have known by now. Someone would have seen them. This is something else. I don't know what, but it's not the fae."

Naia wished she could disappear in her seat, even if she hoped her father was right and none of it had anything to do with the fae—or her secret. So far she'd wondered how come neither her father nor brother had suspected anything, but then, the idea that she had rescued—and kissed—a fae was so outrageous that there was no way something like that would ever cross their minds.

Fel snorted. "Perhaps the attacks were planned by heart-breaking princesses. That's the real danger."

"Isofel." Her father's voice was low and calm, a warning, as he glared at his son, who stared back.

Naia's father had eyes the green of dried leaves, while her brother's eyes were more like brilliant green jewels. They both had brown skin, but her brother had straight black hair and sharp features, while their father had wavy brown hair and a softer face. It was unsettling to see them staring at each other. In fact, in theory a deathbringer could kill with a stare, so she always felt terrified when her father looked at her brother like that.

"You're sure I shouldn't display my magic?" Naia asked. She knew the answer, but all she wanted was to get her father's attention away from her brother.

It worked, as her father turned to her and sighed. "How many times have I explained it? First, you're not looking for a husband. Second, I won't have my daughter on display like cattle."

She looked away. Cattle, what an exaggeration. To be honest, she wouldn't mind showing off, wouldn't mind impressing everyone with her own, unique talent: fire magic—like nobody else in the kingdom.

It had started about a year before, but she'd been practicing it as much as she could. She was sure it was a manifestation of her deathbringer magic, which was powerful and complex, and still not completely understood. Her father's magic, and he should be proud that at least one of his children had it, but no. Every time she showed any fire magic, it was as if she'd grown a second head or something. She had wondered if maybe... She had asked and read about fae magic, and never found anything associating them with fire, so she couldn't have gotten it from River. It was deathbringer magic, she was sure of it, even if this specific manifestation was unheard of.

And she wouldn't mind astonishing a bunch of condescending royals. Naia lit a flame on the palm of her hand. "I bet my fire would make quite an impression."

Her father frowned. "Stop it. Do you want to burn down the carriage?"

Naia did quench her flame, even if it was unfair. Fel had been playing with his hands a good chunk of the way, and had gotten no scolding.

Her father then added, "Don't give anyone an excuse to start whispers, to wonder why you have that magic."

"It's deathbringer magic, dad. What else could it be?"

"Irinaia. Don't. Hide your power, especially something so exceptional." At least he had a positive word about her magic. "It's strategy; never show your full potential to your enemies. If you do want to be part of the young ladies' introduction, use some mild ironbringing, but I would rather you didn't participate in it, lest anyone think you're looking for a husband."

Naia looked down. It had been just a silly idea, but still, her father's words bothered her.

Fel then asked, "And what if Naia wanted a husband?" He wasn't mocking, but rather curious, voicing a question she hadn't dared ask.

Her heart sped up as her father turned to him. "Why would she, if she doesn't have to?" He chuckled, his expression amused, as if hearing the most ridiculous idea ever, then asked her, "Do you want to get married?"

The question surprised her. "I... I don't know." She had no idea if she'd find someone. All she knew was that she definitely didn't want to watch her brother become king while she remained cast aside, watching, as a mere advisor, without a life of her own, but she didn't want to say that because it sounded as if she envied Fel, and it wasn't really that.

Her father waved a hand. "Nonsense. You'll help your brother, make sure Umbraar is in good hands. That way you can be free, a master of your own destiny. You can be much more than a wife. I raised you two equally, so that you wouldn't succumb to feminine fancies and vanity."

Her father always insisted that she and Fel were equal. But they weren't, were they? He was going to inherit the throne, not her. Naia looked down, as she never knew what to say, and didn't want to sound as if she didn't wish the best for her brother.

Her father seemed satisfied, and turned back to Fel. "And you, sir, next year you'll find a wife: a healthy, honest commoner from Umbraar."

Fel smirked. "How are you going to choose? Line them up, measure them, and examine their teeth?"

"How else would you have it?" He matched his son's smirk. "Pick the one who best pretends to fall in love with you?"

Naia's twin looked out the window. "Obviously not. Who's gonna love a cripple?"

"Fel!" she protested. "Who wouldn't love you?"

He looked at her, his green eyes definitely looking like cold, hard gems.

"Stop saying that word," her father told Fel. "You're perfect. But romantic love is a silly illusion."

Her brother cocked his head, staring straight into his father's eyes. "Is it that you regret eloping with our mother?"

Oh, no. Fel was stepping into forbidden territory.

Her father stared at him for a few seconds, then, in a slow, threatening voice, said, "I have no regrets, but I don't want another word about it."

Naia looked at her brother, pleading with her eyes for him to remain silent. Fel exhaled, bit his lip, then looked out the window. Talk of their mother was absolutely forbidden in their family. Perhaps it caused their father a lot of pain. He still wore the two interconnected wedding rings, and had vowed never to marry again. But it was odd to have only emptiness and silence where her mother's memory should be. So much emptiness.

Naia looked outside and noticed that they were approaching the Frostlake castle. It was all white, with tall spires. Weird. She'd rather imagined that the castle of the necromancer king would be black with huge skulls or something. But then, even the kingdom's name didn't allude to their magic, and the white looked like frost. Frostlake, right? Not Necrokingdom, Deathland, Grimhold, or anything like that. Such a wasted opportunity.

The castle was beautiful. Being under the dome, it had no snow or ice around it, but its whiteness felt like it brought some of that dreamy white landscape to the heart of the kingdom, into that beautiful, majestic building.

Her father always said that a castle was pointless ostentation and a big target for their enemies, but it was also an imposing symbol of power, which Naia found fascinating. This would be her first time in a real castle, her first time wearing a fine dress, her first time attending a ball. So many firsts. And yet the first that mattered most had been in the past; her first kiss. A part of her feared it would be her last. For now, all she wanted was to understand what had happened, and maybe... She even feared to think it, afraid of wanting too much, but maybe there was a chance she'd meet River again. Not in Frostlake, of course. How would a fae reach a city surrounded by a metal dome?

FOR THE FIRST time in her life, Leah hated being in the library. Yes, it was her favorite place in the castle—but not when everything interesting and exciting was happening outside this room. Her mother had even locked the door. The horror. Leah felt like a prisoner in her own castle.

The delegations were arriving from the other ten kingdoms, and Leah wasn't supposed to meet them before the introduction ball. This was the first time she was going to participate in the gathering, now that she was finally seventeen, so she had never seen the other royal families. That was why she wanted to take a look, just a look. Her heart sped up, wondering what the princes were like. Leah wanted to see them, just to feel more at ease knowing they weren't... What? She didn't even know what she feared. Perhaps she feared the unknown, and if she made it known, the fear would be gone. That made sense. Or maybe not.

She thought back to her dream and her dragon, which brought her a soothing feeling of peace and calm. Dragons were said to be the creators, guardians, and arbiters of all the magic in the world. But if they had ever existed, they were gone now. Except in her dreams—and sometimes nightmares.

Her dragon felt so real. He had to be real, somewhere. Unfortunately not in this library.

But there was no point lamenting being locked up. Surrounded by books, she could easily find escape and solace in one of her favorites. Not that all the stories she liked were here. Kissing books were forbidden, but she'd found a few of them hidden within other covers a few years before. Unfortunately, they had eventually disappeared, and as much as Leah had looked, she had never found them again. Well, her mother always said that those books were immoral, that they would give her unrealistic expectations, and that a proper lady shouldn't read that material. Leah didn't think they were that bad, and she did not expect a dashing hero to save her, but her opinion made no difference if the books were gone.

Still, she had other favorites. *Rudolf the Mighty*, with more than twenty books, had been her faithful companion in her days of solitude. She loved reading about his adventures, even when he killed commoners, and he killed a lot of people, sometimes ten or twenty at a time. He also killed evil dragons, and her favorite book was the one where he had to face the three dragon kings who had imprisoned his betrothed. Yes, there was some romance in *Rudolf the Mighty* too, except that there was no kissing. Still, the stories were fun.

In some books, the enemy was a necromancer, King Skeleton, but he was evil, unlike Leah's father. Sometimes she wished she were Rudolf, slashing and killing, getting rid of all her problems. True that she didn't even know how to hold a sword, but it didn't matter. Sometimes she wished she were King Skeleton, raising armies from the dead to smash her enemies, even if she knew necromancy couldn't do that, even if she knew that she would never want to kill or harm anyone. Plus, King Skeleton was pure evil. But they were just stories, filled with comforting power and fearlessness.

Yet Leah was feeling the opposite of powerful as she

grabbed *The Might of Rudolf,* when then the door opened. She thought it was her mother, but turned to see Kasim coming in, and was glad to see her father's closest advisor and best friend, someone who was like a second father to her. She was even gladder to notice that he had a mischievous smile on his dark brown face. That smile was always good news, and often meant he was about to let her do something her mother had forbidden.

Leah beamed at him. "You came to open the door!" Then she added, "But my mother..."

Kasim waved a hand. "If she comes looking for you, I'll find an excuse. But she is too busy planning the festivities."

"Thanks. I was hoping to try to see some of the princes."

He cocked his head. "Try, Leah? You underestimate me so." He put a hand over his heart. "I'm wounded."

"You..." This was almost too good to be true. "Have a plan?"

"A great one, in fact. You do like ice-skating, right?"

"You know the answer." She wasn't sure where he was going with this.

"Guess who's going to visit Sunset Lake right now?"

"I don't know! You have to tell me!"

"The young princes and princesses. Including you, of course."

This was amazing. Or maybe not. "But my mother was very specific that I shouldn't be seen before the ball."

"Oh, dear, but this is such a great opportunity to get to know them." He sighed. "If you truly want to obey Lady Ursiana, you can only watch them. Wear a hood, keep your head down, and pretend you're a servant. Nobody will look at you. You'll be like a little fly, listening when nobody knows you're there."

The idea sounded amazing, except for one small problem. "But then I can't skate or they'll see me."

"Maybe. Maybe you can introduce yourself today, after enough listening. Or maybe it will be your chance to see who they truly are. It's such a great opportunity. I don't know why your mother..." He cleared his throat. "I mean, it's not my place to say that."

Leah chuckled. "Yet it's your place to help me break the rules."

He winked. "Always."

"Let's see these princes, then."

She followed him out of the library, leaving behind those written stories, excited and at the same time terrified to live her own, unsure what to expect from the visiting princes, and trying to forget the pressure of having to make such an important choice in such little time. Unable to forget it, in fact. Her hands were sweaty and her heart was racing.

3
ICE-BREAKING

Three carriages were going to transport the young royals to the Sunset Lake, then three more would follow with guards. The gatherings always had some informal activities to entertain the young royals. Leah's mother had told her that it was common for princesses not to attend them, as the young ladies needed to protect their virtue. But Leah couldn't fathom what was unseemly about skating, and she was glad that Kasim was bringing her along.

Wearing a coat, a scarf, and a hat because of the cold outside the dome, she doubted anyone would notice her. She stood by the last carriage with the guards waiting for the young foreigners to arrive. Kasim stood beside her, ready to tell her who was who.

Leah had three cousins from Greenstone, and she was hoping to meet them. In fact, she couldn't wait to meet her cousin Mariana again, still remembering her short visit when they had been just little girls. The kingdom where her mother had been born had greenbringers, with magic related to growing plants, which was very useful to make sure crops were healthy. That wasn't the only kingdom with green magic, though, as there was also Vastfield and Haven. Speaking of greenbringers, the two older princes from Vastfield were the first ones to get into a carriage. Leah wanted to watch the younger one, since he was one of her potential matches, but it was hard to see much under his hooded coat.

The reason her parents wanted her to marry a younger brother was that she was Frostlake's sole heir, and the idea was to make a strong alliance but marry someone who would be willing to live here and help her rule, instead of taking her to another kingdom. That was why she wanted to watch the younger brothers rather than the crown princes.

The next ones to arrive were the three Ironhold brothers. While in theory the younger ones could be good suitors, the truth was that Ironhold never made marriage alliances, apparently because they wanted ironbringing contained to their kingdom, so Leah knew that neither of them would be a potential husband.

The last ones were the Umbraar twins. Now Leah paid a lot of attention, but it wasn't that she thought the prince could be a potential match, but that she wanted to know why her mother had warned her so much to stay away from them. She hadn't explained much other than saying that they were rude, ill-mannered, and lived in poverty in a kingdom crumbling apart. Some of it was likely exaggeration, but there should be a reason why her mother hated them. Leah had also heard that the twins' mother was from Ironhold and had eloped with their father against her family's wishes.

The Ironholds hated him so much that they had forbidden anyone to trade with Umbraar, and so the kingdom had become isolated. The kids seemed normal, though, and in fact it was good to see that at least one princess was also coming with them.

Minutes went by and nobody else came. Kasim went in to check if the others were late, but returned soon, telling the drivers to move. He took the reins of the last carriage himself, and Leah sat beside him.

"Where are the others?" She knew that all the families had arrived, and yet there were no wildbringers or anyone from the non-magic kingdoms.

Kasim chuckled. "Afraid of the cold, I'd assume."

Well, it was still a good opportunity to get to know the younger Vastfield prince. She almost wished she could go in the carriage with him and his brother, but it would be too obvious—and inappropriate. Apparently a woman's virtue was something that could be snatched from her at any moment if she spent time unattended with a man. At least that was what her mother seemed to think. While she wasn't sure what exactly could be stolen, she doubted anyone would do anything with Kasim here. It meant she wasn't unattended, though, so she wasn't contradicting her mother's advice.

They left the castle and took the road to the Southern Gate. When they were almost crossing the dome, one of the carriages stopped, and a guard came running towards Kasim.

He bowed slightly. "Master. One of the Vastfield princes feels indisposed, sir. They wish to return."

Kasim's expression was grim. "Does he need immediate assistance?"

The man shook his head. "It doesn't seem to be the case."

"I'll see," Kassim said, then told the guard, "Stay here."

The guard looked at Leah, then bowed. "My lady."

She nodded, slightly annoyed that he was making it obvious who she was, then looked at the carriages. The Ironhold princes were getting out of theirs to see what was happening. This was so unlucky. Her chance to get to know one of her potential suitors was gone. Not to mention that having a visitor getting ill during a gathering could be horribly problematic and cause all kinds of talks of poisoning and sabotage. But then, they'd arrived this morning and perhaps hadn't even eaten in Frostlake. It could have been the trip or going through the portals.

All the kingdoms had a portal hub, through which they could visit other kingdoms easily. In Frostlake, it was somewhat far from the dome, for security reasons. Leah had never traveled through one, but she'd heard that the experience could make someone dizzy and indisposed. It was very old magic bringing Aluria together, and likely explained the issue with one of the Vastfield brothers.

Kasim came back and sat beside her. "The Ironhold brothers are returning too. Do you still wish to go to the lake?"

She smiled. "Better than being locked in a library." Perhaps she was also curious to see the Umbraar twins up close, and maybe looking forward to getting some fresh air and spending time outside.

The carriages made their way out of the dome into the Southern Road, then turned into the path leading to the part of the Sunset Lake where they usually skated. The weather was cloudy with a few flurries, and not very cold. It was a perfect day to be out, and it was a pity that almost nobody had come.

Leah watched from a distance as Kasim and a guard led the twins to the benches by the lake and helped them put on the borrowed skates. The girl was tall and beautiful, with brown skin and wavy black hair. Her brother... Leah avoided looking. His hair was black, straight, long, and very shiny. The little she'd seen of his face was quite nice, and that was why she didn't want to look too much, didn't want anyone to think she was admiring him.

Still, Leah was curious to observe the twins better, so she got closer and sat on a bench behind them.

"Want to bet who's going to fall first?" the prince asked his sister.

His voice was deep, and sounded oddly familiar, comforting, even. For the first time, Leah realized that magic was something she could feel, like a smell, but not really a smell, a different sense, and the prince was brimming with magic so strong that if it were a light, it would be dazzling.

The Umbraar princess was trying to lace her skates, doing a poor job of it. "I can see you're confident that it's not gonna be you. But falling doesn't scare me, you know? I'm perfectly capable of getting up." Her tone was playful.

He chuckled. "I'm glad we agree you'll be falling more than me." He got up and walked towards the lake, put his feet on it, and started gliding. His movements were a little odd, as if the skates were being pulled by something.

His sister was after him in no time, her skates horribly laced. Leah understood that neither Kasim nor the guards wanted to lace them for her, but they could have at least told her they were too loose. The princess glided a little, then fell on her butt, but laughed, and yelled at her brother, "How come you're doing it so easily?"

He chuckled and approached his sister. "Not hard to guess, is it? What are the blades made of?"

Metal. His skating was not really skating, but magic.

"Cheater!" his sister yelled. Then, in a lower voice, added, "I thought someone was going to teach us."

Leah felt bad that the twins were getting no help, so she pulled down her hood, walked to the edge of the lake, and addressed the girl. "Come here, let me help you tie your skates. And I'll put on mine and teach you."

The princess struggled to get up, but her brother helped her. That was when Leah noticed his eyes—and face. For a moment she felt as if she had no air in her chest, then she quickly looked away. Those were some bright green eyes. The Umbraar prince was better looking than she thought anyone could be. Leah knew that looks didn't matter—and that she wasn't supposed to notice him. And yet her heart was beating with twice its usual strength, as if it had awakened from a slumber, intent on getting her attention. She would need to find a way to silence it.

NAIA'S FACE HURT. The landscape was beautiful, but she hadn't imagined that the cold air would prickle her skin. But she had always wanted to skate on a frozen lake and wasn't going to quit just because it was freezing. Which was the point, right? Or there would be no ice.

She couldn't help noticing that the girl caught a breath when she saw Fel. It was weird to think of her own brother as beautiful, but he did have amazing hair and unique eyes, so perhaps there would be a horde of young princesses after him —if they ignored he was from Umbraar and didn't mind the fact he was... a little different. Naia felt something cold inside her, fearing that nobody would take Fel seriously as a match. And sure, he wasn't supposed to find anyone, but still, she'd hate for him to be ignored or perhaps even humiliated.

But at least one girl was flustered and embarrassed, as she gestured for Naia to sit, then tied her skates. But that wasn't an ordinary girl or servant. The guards seemed to defer to her, and she'd been sitting by the advisor. Her hair was brown with gracious curls, her skin a little lighter than Naia's, with contrasting blue eyes. Beautiful. Naia glanced back to see if her brother had noticed, but he was fake-skating away from them. Odd.

She turned back to the girl. "Thanks. That's very kind. I'm Irinaia, from Umbraar. You are..."

The girl paused, then said, "Leah."

"Princess Leandra?"

The girl's eyes widened, but then she nodded. "Yes."

"I'm glad to meet you. You can call me Naia." She pointed at her twin. "That's my brother Isofel, or Fel."

Leah glanced at where he was, then looked down quickly at her own skates, which she proceeded to put on. The guards were far, circling the area around the lake, and even the advisor was now sitting at a distance.

The princess seemed friendly, so Naia decided to ask a question. Perhaps it was blunt, but she didn't know when she'd have such a chance again. "Do you know why everyone hates us?"

The girl bit her lip. "I... don't know. I'm sorry." She truly sounded apologetic.

Naia shrugged. "At least you're being honest. Most people would say something like: 'Oh, hate? Of course not. Where did you get that idea?'" She chuckled. "They even turned back, I guess not to be contaminated with evil Umbraar company."

"Perhaps it wasn't that."

"Maybe. I know that some people think my father killed my mother. Do you think that's true?" It was a weird question, and one she didn't really believe, and yet... Naia wanted to know more, and this was the way she found to try to dig some of the past.

Leah shook her head. "Of course not. My father was there when you were born and your mother said he never did anything wrong."

That was a surprise. "Truly?"

The girl's eyes widened. "You didn't know that?"

Naia was still trying to process the information. "So your father spoke to my mother?"

"Just a little." She looked down. "After she... Not when she was alive. You must know she died in childbirth, then he... asked her some questions. He does that in cases where there's a suspicious death. So you can be certain your father didn't kill her. I don't know why some people still insist on this cruel rumor."

Naia nodded. It probably still had something to do with the fact that her father had eloped with her mother, and that Ironhold had never accepted their wedding—or their children. Yet she knew so little of what had happened, so little about her mother.

Leah said, "I'm truly sorry for your loss." She then stared at her feet, as if unsure what to do for a moment, but then she got up. "Shall we go? I'm sure you'll learn in no time." She had a playful smile. "With no cheating."

She held Naia's hands and helped her onto the ice, ignoring Fel, which made sense, since he was also ignoring her.

Naia then remembered her father's instructions that they should be polite, so she turned to her brother. "Fel! Come here and introduce yourself to the Frostlake princess!"

Leah shook her head. "It's fine."

He was beside them in a couple of seconds. "Apologies, my lady." Naia had to hold down her laughter at seeing him acting so formal. He took Leah's hand and kissed it, and for a moment she feared the girl would notice something was off, but she didn't, perhaps because they were both wearing gloves. "Isofel, at your service," he said while looking down, as if avoiding looking at her.

"I'm Leah." She pointed to his skates. "Nice magic you have. I didn't know you could do that with ironbringing."

He smiled and floated above the ice. "I can do a lot." Show off. He probably had iron in his inner shirt or vest.

"You can fly!" Leah sounded impressed.

He got back on the ice and shrugged. "Just float a little."

Leah turned to Naia. "What about you? Are you also an ironbringer, or do you have your father's magic?"

Fel seemed disappointed that he was no longer the center of attention and was now looking away.

Naia considered the question. "I... uh." She couldn't mention her fire. "Ironbringer, like Fel, except he's better. What about you?"

She smiled. "Necromancer. Like my father." Somehow she managed to say it with pride, not with any of the awkwardness or shame Naia would have expected, considering it was the creepiest magic in Aluria.

Fine, deathbringing could be deadly, but it also had many advantages, like allowing someone to travel through the hollow. Necromancy... was about dealing with the dead and there was no getting out of it. But then, if it had been necromancy that had cleared Naia's father's name, perhaps there was something good about it.

Leah explained to her how to move her feet, and slowly, Naia got the hang of it and stopped feeling cold and uncomfortable. She was glad they had come. Being here, in this lake surrounded by snow and ice, felt peaceful. And perhaps she'd make a friend.

Her father didn't have female servants, other than an old cook who worked only a few hours a day, and Naia often wished she had some feminine company. Perhaps she wanted to talk about kissing and love, and all those wishes she never mentioned to anyone. But then, she had no idea if this princess even thought about those things or if she was just cold-hearted and manipulative, like her father claimed all princesses were. Naia was pretty sure she couldn't confess having kissed a fae, couldn't try to figure out if they always disappeared after a kiss or if it had been a problem with her. So many questions.

Fel kept a distance from them, but he did observe their movements enough that he was now actually skating, even if he was also using his magic. Naia was not using ironbringing.

If anything, she thought she'd fall even harder if she tried to control the blades. For Fel it was different; his first instinct was always to turn to his magic, and she didn't blame him. She wondered if there would be malicious whispers about him. The Ironhold family had seen him and Naia when they were born and should be aware of his condition, but she didn't think it was a subject they'd want to mention.

Naia closed her eyes as she felt her feet gliding on the ice. Leah was way ahead of them, further into the frozen lake, speeding with grace and skill.

Fel was near Naia, but his eyes were locked on the Frost-lake princess, which he did whenever the girl wasn't looking at him. Sneaky. Then his eyes widened in shock.

Naia followed his line of sight, and noticed something disturbing the surface of the ice. Then it broke, and a gigantic watersnake emerged from the water, its huge blue scales glinting in the sun. The creature was right beside Leah, who then fell, surrounded by broken ice, the creature advancing on her. Watersnakes were usually seen only near the ocean, and were associated with magic and the fae. It was strange to see one in a lake like that, and in a frozen lake.

Naia felt the fire in her begging to come out, and lit two flames in her hands.

Fel was also rushing to the creature, but his eyes met hers, and he shook his head slightly. "Let me deal with it." His expression was calm except for the warning in his eyes.

Right, she wasn't supposed to let anyone see her power. But if she couldn't use it in an emergency, what was the point? Naia quenched the flames in her palms, but still skated toward the creature, right behind Fel. He ungloved his hands and sent his metal fingers flying towards the monster, hitting the scales around its huge yellow eyes. The creature recoiled and dove back under the water. Leah was sitting, probably about to perform some magic, as her eyes were turning completely black, but the ice she was standing on was already cracking.

Everyone would hate the Umbraar royal family even more if a princess died while skating with them. That was a horrible, selfish thought. Leah had been friendly and nice to them, and didn't deserve to get hurt. But what was Naia going to do? Her fire could only melt the ice, not put it back together. It could have maybe hurt the watersnake, but now it couldn't fix any of the damage.

Then she noticed silver pieces floating towards Leah. Fel's hands. Of course. He could control them from a moderate distance. The hands held Leah and lifted her in the air, while the ice underneath her cracked. He'd done all that without even flinching. Of course; Umbraar men didn't flinch.

Leah was brought close to them and landed beside Fel, her eyes turning blue again, but wide with surprise. Fel pulled the metal pieces that made his hands, reformed them, and put them back in the gloves.

The advisor with the dark brown skin was beside them, a sword in his hand. "Let's go back," he said with some difficulty, as he was almost breathless.

Leah moved quickly to the border of the lake, Naia and Fel following them at a distance.

Naia turned to her brother. "Good job."

Fel grunted, which was what he did when he didn't know what to reply, then said, "Wasn't it an interesting coincidence?"

Naia wasn't sure where he was going with this. "The watersnake?"

He nodded. "Right when the royal families were supposed to be here."

"You think someone enchanted a watersnake? I mean, a powerful wildbringer could do that, but it would be a lot of work."

"I don't know."

Neither did Naia. A planned attack? But who would do it? And why?

NEITHER THE ICE breaking nor the watersnake had scared Leah as much as her magic. For a second she'd been in one of those awful nightmares, macabre figures reaching for her, about to suffocate her—until brilliant hands caught her and pulled her out of that horror.

Kasim was saying something as she put on her boots, but she ignored him and turned to see Fel rushing to her. Fel, who had saved her.

He didn't look worried or even smug. If anything, he had what looked like an apologetic smile. "I'm so sorry. Only later I noticed you were also doing something with your magic. Naia gets furious when I ruin her plans, and I hope you forgive me."

He thought he'd interrupted her? Leah shook her head. "I have no idea what my magic was doing, and I doubt it was going to do anything useful." And it had been terrifying, but she wasn't going to tell him that. She smiled. "You did well. Thank you so much."

"Oh. Good, then." He sat and started unlacing his skates with the same hands that had floated towards her, or were they different?

Leah pointed at them. "How do they work?"

He paused, then took off one of his gloves. What was underneath was like a hand made of silver bones, but then the pieces floated and formed a sphere, spinning in the air.

"That's amazing," she said. Well, everything about him was amazing, and he was so beautiful that looking at him almost hurt. Still, that was some incredible display of magic, and he did it so naturally.

"I guess." He looked down, put his hand back in place and

into the glove, then resumed taking off his skates and then putting his boots on.

Leah couldn't take her eyes off his fingers. "You're using magic now."

He bit his lip, then nodded. "I use it most of the time, barely even notice, I guess." He then stared at her. "You don't find it... odd? Or creepy?"

"Why? This is marvelous." *He* was marvelous, and the thought made her tremble. She then smiled. "And I'm a necromancer. What most people call creepy doesn't faze me. But your magic is the opposite of creepy."

He smiled again, this time showing cute dimples. "Well, my father's a deathbringer. Your family is not the only one with death magic."

Leah smiled, then their eyes met, and she looked away quickly. It took her a moment to steady her breath.

When they all had their boots on, they walked back to the carriage. Kasim sat outside, in the front, Leah and the twins inside. That was how she found herself beside Fel, which was scary in a way, but also good because she was curious about him.

When the carriage started moving, she gathered her courage and asked him, "Do you also have some of your father's magic?"

Fel shook his head. "None. He says it's a good thing. Sometimes he speaks of it almost like a curse."

"But deathbringing can be good, right? Your father could teleport wherever he wants, without a portal."

He nodded. "In theory, yes, but he says it's not that simple. I guess it does something to his mind, gives him nightmares or something."

"Doesn't everyone have nightmares?"

That dimpled smile again. "Maybe. What about you? Your mother's a greenbringer, right?"

"Yes, but I only got my father's magic."

"What's it like? To be a necromancer?"

She enjoyed talking about the magic she loved. "There are two types of necromancy: you can re-awaken a dead body, but for a limited time, and you can communicate with the spirits of the dead, when they allow you to. My father uses it when the dead need to speak, and I sometimes accompany him. I'm still learning necromancy, but I can do it, yes."

Fel raised his eyebrows. "You can re-awaken a dead body?"

"For a few seconds."

"Is it true that a necromancer could raise an army of the dead?"

Leah chuckled. "Like King Skeleton?"

"You read *Rudolf the Mighty!*" he sounded surprised.

"Well, yes. They're popular books."

He then went on to ask her about her favorite character, and they ended up discussing King Skeleton and his completely unrealistic necromancy feats, then moved on to talk about everything absurd in the series. The funny thing was that he enjoyed the books just like her, even if he also knew they were absurd. She felt at ease talking to him, no longer intimidated by his looks.

Fel then asked her, "What about *Adelia's Secret*? Have you read that?"

She swallowed. That was one of those kissing books forbidden to her. She'd read half of book one before it disappeared. "No. I... I don't think we have them."

"I can send them to you. I think you'd love them." He paused. "If it's deemed appropriate, of course."

Leah looked down. "My mother doesn't let me read those books."

He smiled. "I could change the covers. If you wish."

Leah chuckled, but then the carriage stopped. They were already behind the castle and their conversation was cut short.

So soon. It was a pity, as she could spend forever talking to him about books, about anything, really. And his sister was nice too. Leah even felt bad for ignoring her, but she had a friendly smile and didn't seem upset.

They said goodbye, then Kasim took Leah to the rose path in the garden. It was a spot without trees around it, allowing good visibility. While it was a horrible place to hide, it was a great place to talk to someone and be sure not to be overheard.

Leah thought he was going to scold her for almost accepting a gift from a young man, but he just smiled. "You had fun?"

"So much. They're so nice."

He nodded. "I'm glad you're making friends, but I need to warn you against any romantic aspirations towards the Umbraar boy."

He was not a boy. And she wasn't having any romantic aspirations. Not yet, at least. "We were just talking!"

"I know, and it's why I didn't mind it, but he's not for you, Leah."

"Because of his father?"

Kasim sighed. "I won't even tell you my opinion about his father because those would not be appropriate words before a young lady, but I would never judge children for their parents' mistakes. Except in this case."

"But what's the problem? Is it whatever happened between them and Ironhold?"

"Not really. One day you'll learn it all. This is just a warning. I trust you and know you're smart and level-headed. I know you won't make a foolish choice."

Leah nodded, but wished she understood why he was saying that. Kasim was the greatest rule-breaker in their family, and for him to forbid something meant it was pretty bad. But what? What was wrong with the Umbraars? Even Naia didn't know.

Kasim then added, "Also, I'll tell your father about the watersnake, and I'll omit your presence there."

Watersnake. She had forgotten about it—and had many questions. "I don't understand how it showed up at the lake."

"What do you think, Leah?"

"I... it doesn't make sense. It's a lake. Aren't they sea creatures? It's as if someone put it there. But why?"

"I'd say the question would be *by whom*? Then we get the answers."

"But who could perform that kind of magic? I don't think even a wildbringer could." She shivered with dread. "The white fae?"

"I don't know."

"And why?" She paused. "Hang on. If it was on purpose, it could be targeting the twins."

"It could be targeting any young visiting royal. A lot more people were supposed to go there."

"Except they didn't."

"Indeed." Kasim sighed. "And why we'll keep it quiet for now."

"What about the twins? And the guards? They might tell others."

"I'll take care of the guards. As for the Umbraar kids, I don't see them talking to anyone. They would want to hide the boy's magic."

That didn't make sense. "You think they're ashamed of it?"

"I think he's too powerful."

"And yet somehow he's a horrible match."

"Leah." Kasim had a warning in his voice. "It has nothing to do with his magic or even his character. His behavior today was irreproachable. It's his family. Please don't think about him as a potential suitor. I know he's dashing, but looks don't matter for a marriage."

"I wasn't thinking about him like that, I was just wondering why he's so horrible."

"He's not horrible, Leah. He's just not someone you should ever consider marrying. Can I trust you on that?"

She felt as if she were swallowing something bitter, but she didn't want to disappoint him. "Of course."

He raised an eyebrow. "Plus, if your criteria for enjoying someone's company is that they've read *Rudolf the Mighty*, I'm pretty sure there are plenty of candidates."

4

GOLDEN STRANDS

N aia was stunned as she stared at her own image in the mirror. She was part giddy, part surprised at seeing herself wearing a huge, brilliant purple dress, so huge that a maid had to help her get into it. As much as she feared it could be exaggerated, she'd always dreamed of dressing like that, except that she would need to get used to that enormity.

Now, she knew that dresses were often an unfair disadvantage when hunting or running, but she wasn't planning on doing any of that tonight, and it felt good to look so extravagant. People would notice her from across the ballroom—which wasn't necessarily bad, but would be new to her.

Her hair was down, though, as she hadn't let the maid style it. Naia liked her hair too much to keep it in some bun or braid, and she found that the contrast of her black hair with the dress was beautiful. She looked like a princess from one of those stories her brother loved, in that glittery purple that reminded her of the sky right before night.

Speaking of brother, she saw him behind her reflection.

His smile broadened as his bright green eyes set on her. "Wow, look at you."

"Great. Now you're going to mock me."

"I'm not mocking." And yet his face was still playful. "I've never seen you in a ballgown before, and... it's... interesting." Was he trying to keep his laughter down?

She rolled her eyes. "Interesting? I love how you're so encouraging."

"It's beautiful, Naia." There was no trace of mockery now. "It's just that I need to get used to seeing you like that."

Naia shook her head and looked at her brother, who wore all black, his hair seeming to dissolve into his clothes. He looked so elegant, so princely.

She chuckled. "I need to get used to wearing it. And you look great too."

Fel grunted. She really needed to have a talk with him and make a heroic effort to prevent him from becoming a copy of their father. But that was for another time. There was a glint in his eyes, and she had no intention of ruining his happiness. Naia smiled. "She's beautiful."

Her brother's eyes widened, but then he cocked his head casually. "Who?"

"Who, Fel?" She snorted. "Don't give me that. You know who I'm talking about."

"The Frostlake princess. Yes, extremely beautiful," he said matter-of-factly, his voice level.

"Wow, that's some excitement. You're talking about her the way you describe a piece of furniture or something."

He shrugged. "Why should I be excited?"

Naia, who had been talking to him through the reflection, turned. "You don't have to do everything our father says, you know that?"

"That's quite funny coming from you, sister. You never speak for yourself in front of him."

She looked down. It was true. But then, he had no idea what she'd done behind their backs. "Fair enough." She faced her brother. "But this is about you. If you want to fall in love, you should."

"You don't choose to fall, you know? I'm pretty sure you didn't choose to drag your behind on the lake today."

"You were standing."

His eyes had an amused twinkle. "Unlike you, I wasn't taking any risks but rather relying on my magic, something familiar. I'm not sure that's a good way to live." His face then got somber. "Still, as to the Frostlake Princess, I'm not dumb to want what I can't have."

Naia hated hearing that hard edge in her brother's voice. She wanted to tell him that it wasn't true he couldn't have the princess, but feared it would make matters worse, as he would dig himself in a bigger hole by arguing why he shouldn't want her.

She decided to change the subject. "The watersnake, what do you think?" They had told their father, who had dismissed the idea of a wildbringer enchanting the snake, but had no idea what could have caused it. After that, there had been no time to discuss it with her brother.

"If watersnakes were common in this kingdom, they wouldn't have taken us skating. Something doesn't..." He sighed. "I think the fae are returning, Naia."

Naia trembled, then had a nervous laugh. "An odd choice for them, don't you think?"

"Maybe. But just think how many princes and princesses could have been there. They could have reached the heart of Aluria's royal families all at once, with one simple stroke."

"But if they're powerful enough to materialize a watersnake in a frozen lake, they wouldn't still be hidden, don't you think?"

Fel tilted his head. "Who do you think it is, if not the Fae?"

"An accident, maybe? I don't know." When she thought about the Fae, the only image that came to her mind was River, accompanied with guilt and so many questions. She didn't want to think of them as possible enemies, as a threat, didn't want to think whether her silence had put people at risk.

Her brother raised an eyebrow. "I guess we'll see."

LEAH WAS afraid she'd get cramps from sitting for so long while two attendants braided her hair and weaved threads of gold through it. The result was a complex, brilliant bun that she'd describe as a crown tilted back, almost as if it was falling. She didn't mention that it looked like a slipping crown, though, as she knew this hairstyle had been her mother's request. She also had gold powder around her eyes, which looked nice.

Her dress was light blue, with a low neckline held by thin straps, so that her shoulders and the area below her neck were visible, making her feel exposed, but she liked that the skirt had thin, transparent layers that looked like blue feathers.

The thought that came to her most often throughout the ordeal was whether Fel would think she looked ridiculous. It didn't mean she was thinking about him like *that*. She was just curious about his opinion, but then, she thought her hair was ridiculous, so if by any chance he felt the same, at least they could laugh together. Hopefully he'd ask her to dance, and they would have some time for themselves. She wondered what it would be like to look at him up close, to hold his magic hands for a long time. She wondered how he'd react to her pretty dress, to her low neckline. The thought of his eyes on her exposed skin made her shiver, but it wasn't dread or fear. She wasn't sure what it was. For a brief moment, she wondered what it would be like to kiss him, which only meant that her thoughts were going off the track, meandering, and lost.

Leah focused on getting her mind straight again. There would be other princes at the ball, many of them handsome, many of them friendly. The thought made her nauseous.

"Leah, darling." Her mother's voice.

She turned and made her best effort at a smile.

"You look so beautiful," her mother said. She also looked good in a dark-red dress, up to her neck, her curly hair in an elegant bun, kohl lining her youthful brown eyes.

A genuine smile now lit up Leah's face, happy to see her mother looking so pretty. "So do you."

Her mother scoffed and shook her head. "Nonsense." Addressing the servants, she said, "You can leave." She then sat by Leah and took her hand. "I can barely believe you've grown so fast. You're a young woman now. I know I might seem harsh sometimes, but all I want is to see you happy, my darling."

"I know." Leah tensed, sensing that this was unlikely to be a pleasant conversation.

"You will meet some young men today, so I must beseech you to keep your guard up at all times. They will steal your honor, darling, if you let them."

"I..." She didn't want to ask what was possibly a stupid question, but she had to. "Could you explain a little more about it? About what they can steal?"

Her mother paused, then took a deep breath. "I'll tell you a story. There was once a young princess who attended a gathering for the first time. She was young and naive, and perhaps not that smart. There was a prince there, and she thought he was the most handsome man she'd ever seen. They danced, they talked." She had a bitter laugh. "She thought they were in love. He visited her bedroom at night, and she let him stay. So yes, very, very foolish girl, poor thing. He took what he wanted from her."

"What did he take?" Leah didn't like to interrupt her mother, but she wanted to understand the story.

"Her honor, darling. One day you'll understand."

Hopefully. But it still didn't make sense that something would have been stolen so easily. "Couldn't she have called the guards?"

Her mother sighed. "But that's the problem: she thought they were in love and didn't think there was anything wrong in letting him in her room, didn't realize she was being corrupted and ruined, didn't realize he was stealing anything. She did not know. Men can entrance silly girls, make them think it's all love. It's what happened to this princess. Then, the next day, when she was sure he was going to propose to her, do you want to know what happened?"

"He didn't propose?"

"Not only that, he looked at her with loathing and disgust. Now that he had used her like he wanted, she was worth nothing to him. The young girl was ruined, and no man would want her for a wife."

"But how would they even know?"

Her mother eyed her seriously. "There *is* a way to know. And men talk." She got up and fiddled with a comb over the dressing table. "And well, she died of grief." She turned to Leah again. "Perhaps I'm not being fair saying she was foolish. You'll think, 'well, I'm smart, I'll never do such a thing,' but the only way to be smart is to keep your guard up. Always. Always, Leah." There was sadness in her voice.

"Was she your friend?"

Her mother shook her head. "She was nobody and her name has been forgotten. When women do that, they become nobodies, rejected even by their own families. So never spend time alone with a young man. Never, Leah, no matter how nice he seems, no matter if he claims he wants to marry you."

Leah didn't quite understand her mother's words, but it was clear that there was a real warning there, there was some real pain about something in the past. She looked down, wishing she could understand more. "I'll be careful."

Her mother sat by her again. "I didn't mean to upset you with this gloomy talk, just warn you." She ran a rand over Leah's hair. "We have good reasons to celebrate. Tonight we'll find a prince for you, and I want you to have a say on that."

A say. Well, she'd been thinking about it for a while. "Shouldn't we... wait? Give it some time for me to make a choice, to get to know my future husband?"

Her mother took her hand again. "Darling, marriage is not about choosing the right person, but about learning to love and respect the one you chose. It doesn't end when you get married; it starts. And this is an alliance for Frostlake. You will be queen one day, and as a queen, you'll serve your kingdom. A strong alliance will protect both you and your people. And that's what you need to look for. You're smart, Leah, so you'll choose with your head, not your heart. People think that a fast-beating heart is love, but it's fear. Your heart always betrays you, always leads you astray. You need to ignore it."

Despite a cold chill in her stomach, Leah shrugged. "I don't have anything to ignore."

"Ignore the fear, then. Everything will go well." She smiled and got up. "Come. I want you to see your cousin, Mariana."

That was amazing news. "She's here?"

"Of course. Show her the top hallways, that way you can check the guests before you come in." Her mother winked.

Mariana was a little older than Leah, but she had visited once and the girls had played and run around the castle. Leah wished her cousin could have stayed or at least visited more often, wished she could have been her sister, but those were obviously pointless wishes. Leah had written many letters to her, but had never gotten any reply. Her mother claimed Mariana had trouble reading, and Leah eventually stopped writing. Still, she had never forgotten their moments together, dreaming about balls and parties and princes. Now that it was all about to become real, they would be together again.

Indeed her cousin was standing outside her door. She had become quite a pretty young woman, with light brown skin and brown eyes and hair, and was also wearing a dress with thin straps, but hers was pink.

Leah hugged her. "So glad to see you."

The girl broke the hug, and stared at Leah with a polite smile. "Yes. You are?"

"Leah. We played together when you visited, remember?"

"You mean..." She frowned, as if trying to remember something. "When I came here? I was just a little girl."

Leah smiled, glad that her cousin remembered her. "Yes. I was seven. I think you were almost nine. That was ten years ago."

Mariana nodded. "Quite a long time."

"Sure." Leah looked down. She had been expecting a warmer reaction. But then, her cousin had more siblings, lived in a kingdom in the middle of Aluria, and probably had seen many more royal families. She wasn't a lonely weirdo with no friends like Leah, who had only her family and maid for companions. Wow, that was a depressing thought. But it was true. Leah used to play in the kitchen with the cooks' children, but eventually her mother had decided it was not appropriate, so her recent friends were only books. It wasn't Mariana's fault.

Leah smiled. "Want to see the guests before everyone?"

"Sure." Her tone was cold, though, like a stranger.

Still, perhaps they could become friends if she had time to warm up. Leah led her cousin up the stairs until they reached the top hallways surrounding the ballroom. This was the perfect place to look at what happened downstairs, as the halls were surrounded by windows that looked like mirrors from the other side. There were also real mirrors, which multiplied the light from the chandeliers on the ceiling. Leah had been here many times as a young girl, dreaming of the day the palace would be full of joy and dancing. This was the day. And it was terrifying.

There was a band in a corner, and circular tables along the walls, with some empty room in the middle. Servants brought pretty glasses with drinks, and many royal families were already coming in.

They stopped at one window, and Mariana asked, "Do you know who your match is?"

"Not yet. I want to talk to them before choosing. What about you?"

"My father wants me to marry Cassius, from Ironhold."

"And you're fine with that?" It sounded so simple.

The girl shrugged. "Well, I want to be queen, and he's the crown prince."

"Nice." It was good to see someone so calm about it. "But I thought they didn't want their magic out of their kingdom."

"I would go there. The magic wouldn't leave Ironhold."

"True. I need someone who would be willing to come here, not a future king." That was another point against Fel, not that she was thinking about him that way, just that she had been trying to understand why Kasim had warned her so strongly against him, and wondering if there was a solution for that.

"It must be nice being the sole heir." Mariana's tone was wistful.

Leah shrugged. "It's all I've ever known."

She looked back to the ballroom, but couldn't quite recognize the people entering it, until she saw a tall figure with long black hair, and felt like her heart jumped in her chest. The heart she was supposed to ignore.

"Wow, he truly is handsome," Mariana said.

Leah felt her stomach getting cold, annoyed that someone else was admiring Fel.

Her cousin then added, "But they say he vowed never to marry again."

That made no sense. "What?"

"The Umbraar king never married after his wife died. You didn't know that?"

The king, oh. He had an elegant figure, but his hair was brown, and he didn't look much like his children, who likely resembled their mother, except for the skin tone, perhaps, or maybe Fel's eyes, but then they were a different green. Leah relaxed knowing that her cousin was talking about the king, but then was overcome by revulsion. "Yuck. He's old enough to be our father."

Her cousin shrugged. "But he isn't. And it's a chance for a crown. Plus, he's not even forty. That's not old. But I'm just saying."

Leah found it extremely awkward. "How did you even know it was him?"

"The gathering was in Greenstone last time, and he was there. I didn't get to see anyone, but some of the waiting women spent *a lot* of time describing him. Green eyes, dark skin, messy brown hair, a small scar on his right cheek."

Scar, yes, only then she noticed it. All Leah could think was that he was Fel's father, and the idea of finding him attractive filled her with revulsion. Then she realized that her cousin would soon notice that there was another potential king right there. Despite Kasim's warnings, the truth was that many people would consider Fel an excellent match.

And then it was as if Mariana heard her thoughts. "Wait. Is that his son? He looks like the Great Smith."

Most of Aluria worshipped gods related to iron and smelting, the Great Smith the king of them all. Frostlake still worshiped deities related to cold, birth, and death, even if more and more the beliefs from the rest of the land were bleeding through. But what Leah hated was her cousin comparing Fel to a god. Or noticing him.

"Let's go downstairs." Leah pulled her cousin's hand. "I'm sure we'll have to enter the ballroom soon."

As soon as she got to the bottom floor, Leah heard the first chords of *Summer Dreams*. She'd loved this song as a child, and this time it would be even better, since there was a full string set and percussion for the ball. She wanted to mention this to Mariana, but her cousin had already walked away. Perhaps they would talk more later, but then, it was true that the girl wasn't exactly like Leah had imagined. But then, nobody was perfect.

Still, Leah wanted to listen to the music, so she slipped into a side door to hear it better. From across the room, her eyes met Fel's. To her surprise, he got up and advanced toward her. Her hands felt sweaty, the room felt hot, and her heart was definitely speeding up, that stupid heart she wasn't supposed to listen to.

He smiled when he got near her. "Good to see you."

"I'm..." What was she even going to say? Perhaps the truth. "Happy to see you too."

"Do you dance?"

She sucked in a breath, wondering if he was going to ask her. "Yes."

He cocked his head, gesturing to the dance floor. "Would you like to?"

"I'd love to."

Like that, he was holding her hand, then they were standing in front of each other and she was looking into his eyes up close. Well, a lot more up than close. Up, up, up, as he was much taller than her. His eyes were a much brighter green than his father's, a shade she'd never seen before, but then it was true that she hadn't seen many people from outside Frostlake. It was unfair that she wasn't allowed to have any romantic thoughts for him, when he was obviously the best-looking prince of all kingdoms. Sure, she hadn't seen them all, but she didn't have to. Didn't want to.

"Something bothering you?" he asked.

"No. Random thoughts."

"What do I need to do to bring you here, to this moment?"

"Nothing. I am here. Glad to be dancing with you." Perhaps it was a bold confession, but she didn't want him thinking she was ignoring him or something.

His smile lit up his whole face, especially his already bright eyes, which were luminous and entrancing. "Then that's another confirmation that our tastes match, Leah."

She tried to return the smile, except that she was having trouble breathing, and she didn't think her own smile would match his.

A hint of worry crossed his face. "Are you going to present your magic in the introduction? Is that what you're worried about?"

"No. I mean, yes, I'm going to do it, but I wasn't even thinking about it." In fact, she wasn't thinking much at that moment. She managed to laugh. "With everything that happened, I had forgotten it." More like she couldn't have coherent thoughts and stand in front of him at the same time.

He smiled, showing cute dimples. "I think I'd be looking forward to a chance of showing off."

"It seems you enjoy it."

"Maybe." He paused, as if thinking. "How are you going to do necromancy... I mean... I guess you can't—"

"No, no." She chuckled. "That would be morbid. I won't do any magic. I'll just play the flute. I know it's beneath mediocre, but..." Her mother had told her that nobody would pay much attention to her introduction when she had a kingdom, but she didn't want to talk about her marriage prospects. Didn't want to think about them. She stared at her feet, so close to Fel's and yet so far.

He put a hand under her chin and lifted her face softly. "Leah. You were so proud of your necromancy earlier when we spoke. If that's what you want to show, you should show it. Nothing you do can be morbid. You could revive a dead rat, and I'm sure it would be beautiful and graceful."

"Oh, that would be gross." She laughed. He'd misunderstood why she'd felt sad, but he had managed to cheer her up all the same. "Flute is nice, too. And I don't really care for the introduction."

"Not looking to catch the eye of a promising husband?"

Leah felt something cold inside her. "Well, I don't think my performance in the introduction matters that much."

"No. Unless you do some King Skeleton type of necromancy, then I'm pretty sure everyone will be at your feet."

She laughed again.

Fel shook his head. "I'm just kidding. You don't need any magic to..." He looked away, then back at her. "Have you ever met someone and felt as if you already knew them?"

"Maybe."

"That's how I feel about you, Leah, as if we've met before, and I'm not feeling scared or awkward. Well, maybe a little. But it just... feels natural to talk to you. Am I being too forward?"

"No." She felt the same, in fact, if she ignored her difficulty breathing and speeding heart, and was glad he was saying it.

"But I am. It's something I just realized. I used to think that it made no sense to like someone you just met, but it's not like that at all. It's recognizing someone. And I realize I definitely overstepped."

Leah stopped dancing, her jaw dropped. Was he saying he liked her? Well, it didn't necessarily mean anything. "I... also enjoy talking to you."

"So... are we going to have some resuscitated rats for the introduction? You may find it morbid, but then you'll scare away all your potential suitors."

"Except you."

Fel paused, and it was as if even the air shifted around them, like the electric charges before a storm, then his eyes turned even more brilliant. But then he chuckled, his tone playful. "Are you saying I'm on your list, Leah?"

She was still so stunned that words were failing her, and perhaps she had said too much. All she did was shake her head. "There's no such list."

"And where do I fit, then?"

"There's only you." Only after she said it did she realize the meaning of her words. He widened his brilliant eyes, and she cleared her throat. "On a... unique list. A list just for you." Perhaps she was making it worse. Then again, there *was* a list just for him, the "do not consider" list, which was wrong and unfair.

His eyebrows furrowed, a hint of worry in his eyes. "A sad list, based on your face."

"It's not sad. It's the best list."

He took a sharp breath and looked at her lips.

Leah felt heat rising to her face, and tried to change the subject. "Do you think I look ridiculous?"

Fel looked down at her dress, then back to her face, and smiled. "You don't want to hear my opinion."

"But I do."

"Telling girls they are beautiful at parties is a sign of a dull mind and lack of creativity. But lying is bad form. You're putting me in a difficult position."

"I'm asking about my hair and my dress."

"They're pretty. Even so, you could wear a living snake for a necklace and it would be enchanting because of you. Not that anything you're wearing is odd or weird or ridiculous." The song then stopped. "That's it," he said, then gave her a heart-stopping smile. "I'm looking forward to hearing about this list of yours, where you have my name."

"What about you? Do you have any list?" That was a bold question, but she had to ask it, and her heart was now definitely wanting to leave her body and run away.

He was serious now, staring at her. "I didn't. Had no intention. But you see, our tastes match, and now I also have a one-name list. And it's the best list." He took her hand and kissed it. "Talk to you later."

Leah felt as if her legs were wobbly and the floor was moving as she left the ballroom. She could barely believe that he had come straight to her, could barely believe what he'd said, could barely believe the way he'd looked at her.

Before reaching the hallway, her mother grabbed her arm. "Do not do that again."

Leah trembled. "What?"

"Disappear."

So her mother hadn't seen her dancing. Leah exhaled, relieved.

"Don't be nervous. Tonight will be fine," her mother said. "Oh," she pointed at Leah's chest, "and ignore the nonsense there. You'll need to choose with your head."

"I know." She felt as if her heart growled at her words, which was proof of her insanity; hearts didn't growl or have wills of their own.

ALTHOUGH NAIA HAD LOVED her dress when she had put it on, by now she wished she could rip out those flashy purple sleeves. Nobody else wore anything even slightly similar to that. She also reconsidered her decision to keep her hair down. All the ladies had intricate buns, braids, or both, and as much as she didn't want to be like them, it didn't feel great to stand out like that.

Sure, she should ignore their opinion, but the truth was that by now she wished she had deathbringer magic and could walk into the hollow, disappearing from this ball. At least the men in her family didn't seem to have noticed anything and wouldn't feel embarrassed for her looks. Good for them. But then, her father's ignorance of court fashion was to blame for her situation in the first place.

He was just sitting and scowling, and Fel... Where was he? She scanned the room and found him... dancing in a corner? Naia took a better look and realized his partner was Leah, except that her hair was weird, as if it had a gold, brilliant bird's nest on the back of her head. Fel didn't seem to find anything strange about it, though. In fact, they seemed quite at ease with each other. Perhaps it meant nothing. And then perhaps... She glanced at her father to check if he had noticed anything, but he seemed oblivious. He should be the one wearing the puffy sleeves, if he was going to act as if he wasn't there.

Naia kept scanning the room, realizing that there were probably some other nobles or maybe advisors, as there were a lot more people here than just the royal families. She recognized the Ironhold and Vastfield princes only because they had been among the ones supposed to go ice-skating with them. Considering all that had happened, she was glad they had turned back. Unless they had something to do with that water snake. That was an interesting idea. Interesting and likely nonsensical.

The Ironhold princes stood by a well-dressed older man, likely their king—Naia's uncle. Not that he had ever tried to communicate with her or Fel. The princes were both tall and broad and had medium brown hair, their skin a little lighter than their father's. They must have brought a large entourage, as there were four young men around them.

Then Naia's heart jumped in her chest. It couldn't be. Perhaps she was seeing things. Among the Ironhold entourage, she saw River. River, a fae, in the Frostlake castle?

5

MUSIC AND MAGIC

That was definitely River. Naia would never forget his sharp eyes or his jaw with those delicate lips. And here he was talking to one of the Ironhold princes. Unless she was seeing things. She closed her eyes and looked again. Same hair, same face, except that he had no horns, and she couldn't see the shape of his ears.

Naia decided to walk to where Fel was dancing, just so she could get closer to the Ironholds. Her eyes—or mind—could be playing tricks on her. As she passed them, her eyes met River's, which were normal brown, not reddish brown like before. And they didn't show a hint of recognition.

She almost bumped into Fel, who held her shoulders. "Where were you going?"

Her mind was elsewhere, wondering if that was really River and if he'd forgotten her. If it was him, it meant he was alive, it meant she had never caused anyone's death. But then, what was he doing there? With the Ironholds, of all people?

Fel was staring at her, expecting a reply, so she mumbled, "Uh. Circulating. We should circulate in a ball, right?"

Her brother glanced at their father and chuckled. "I think

you're supposed to sit in a corner and mope." Then he got serious. "I know it's not funny."

Naia was having trouble getting her thoughts together. "It's tragic, I suppose." She then noticed the glint in her brother's eyes. "At least one of us is happy."

He raised an eyebrow. "What makes you say so?" Naia thought he was going to deny the obvious, but then a huge smile appeared on his face. "Don't say it. Perhaps I *am* happy, so let me be and not worry or wonder."

"Then don't worry." Naia was happy for her brother, but her mind was still worried about what she'd seen. She glanced at the Ironholds, and again saw River talking to one of the princes.

Fel must have noticed where she was looking, as he asked, "Wishing to say 'hi' to our cousins?"

"Sure. They look so friendly." She sighed, then whispered, "But I do wish our uncle would talk to us, tell us a little about our mother." And also about who was in their entourage.

"Our father would be furious if we tried to speak with him."

"I know. I'm not planning to. I just wish."

And also wished so much more, most of it knowing whether that was really River. So many questions. But it just didn't make sense for him to be with the Ironhold family. She doubted a fae could even step into their kingdom, as there was iron everywhere. Even their palace was supposed to have metal walls.

Perhaps it was just someone who looked like River— exactly like him, but human. Nothing made sense. The only way for her to figure out anything would be by trying to speak to him, but she had no idea how to do that, as she wasn't allowed to initiate communication without being introduced first. She could try to break the rules, but not in front of the

Ironholds. She'd need to be discreet. Right, with two huge purple sleeves.

As she and her twin walked back to their table, Fel said, "I'm glad you're in the moping spirit of the celebration."

"I hate my dress."

"You look so beautiful, Naia, don't say that. True that it does seem a little uncomfortable."

"Very."

Everything was strange and uncomfortable about this ball, this place, and seeing River. Human-looking River who glanced in her direction and yet didn't seem to recognize her —or even see her. Perhaps there was something wrong with her mind.

They sat at the table with their father. She tried to find River again, and saw him leaving the ballroom. For a second, she almost ran after him, but that would be inappropriate— and pathetic. She wished she knew if it was really him and what he was doing there. Perhaps he'd come back.

Naia took the chance to observe the other people at the ball. The advisor who had taken them skating sat by the Frost-lake king—Leah's father. His face had scars, as if an animal had clawed him, and he looked a lot older than most kings. His skin was fair and he had light blue eyes, lighter than his daughter's. That was the necromancer king—who had spoken to Naia's dead mother. Perhaps eventually she could ask Leah if she could talk to him. But the Frostlake princess was no longer in the room, and now the orchestra stopped playing.

This probably meant that the introduction was about to happen. Naia still sort of wished she could go up there and show her fire, but her consolation was the idea that her magic had to be hidden because it was so amazing. That was what she told herself. That was what she hoped her father thought.

Her father, who sat as if this was the last place he'd like to be. She wondered why he didn't use his deathbringer magic and disappear. In fact, he almost never used his magic, claiming it was too dangerous. As she watched him, she noticed that he drew a sharp breath and widened his eyes, looking at something as if it were a ghost. Naia followed his gaze and found just the stage. A young woman directed servants to bring a chair and a table. Not any woman. She was wearing a silver tiara contrasting to curly dark hair. With that tiara, and organizing the introduction, that had to be the Frostlake queen, even if she seemed a little young to be Leah's mother.

The woman looked in their direction and her expression hardened. There was loathing there—and perhaps even disgust. She truly hated her father, and wasn't pretending he didn't exist, like the Ironholds or other families. But a second later, she turned around, her face serene again.

Naia's father got up.

"Dad?" Naia asked.

"I'm going outside."

"You'll miss the introduction."

He rolled his eyes. "I've seen it before. It's all the same."

When he was gone, Fel turned to Naia. "What do you think got into him?"

The look that woman had given her father had been engraved in her mind. "It can't be comfortable being in a room where half the people hate you."

"I wish we knew the reason," he whispered.

A reason? Naia paused. "You think they're justified in hating him? Hating us?"

"Hate is never justified, Naia, but something causes it."

"It's because he married our mother, and you know that."

"Yes, but..." He lowered his whisper even more. "It's just that we've only heard one side of the story. Have you thought of that?"

Naia was about to reply when a bell rang.

On the stage, the queen said, "Welcome to Frostlake. We're so glad to have the gathering here. As is tradition, tonight our daughters will exhibit the best of Aluria's magic and talents."

She then left the stage, and a man took her place, announcing, "Our first princess is Mariana, from Greenstone."

She was a pretty girl, wearing a pink dress with straps, like every young woman in that ball except Naia. She introduced herself, then put a pot with earth on a table, and moved her hands around it. Nothing happened. After a dull eternity, a miniscule sprout appeared on the earth, and was received with a round of applause. Perhaps they were clapping because they were glad it was over.

The next girl was a wildbringer from Wolfmark. She opened a container with butterflies. The creatures landed on her arm, then went back into the container. The clapping was more enthusiastic this time.

Another greenbringer, from Vastfield, sang instead of making any magic. It was a lot less boring than taking forever for a sprout to appear. Still, Naia whispered to Fel, "This is cheating. Since when singing is magic?"

"Music can be magic. Leah is playing the flute."

It made... some sense. And indeed the next princess was from Karsal. They had no magic there, even though they had tried many times to obtain magic through marriage. For some reason, it never passed on to the newer generations. The girl played the harp, her dark brown hair in a bizarre braid over her head. Naia was starting to agree with her father that they were on display like cattle. It wasn't about magic, or nobody would sing or play a musical instrument. Perhaps Naia should be thrilled she wasn't part of that. She looked back at the Ironholds, who were now sitting. No sign of River.

Another wildbringer freed a bird from a cage and it flew away and out the window. It seemed that something had gone wrong, but the girl curtsied, smiled, and got some applause.

The last one to step on the stage was Leah, carrying a box. It didn't look like a flute box. Despite her weird hair, she looked very beautiful with some golden powder on her skin that made her blue eyes stand out.

She looked tense as her eyes scanned the room, but then they found Fel and she smiled. He also smiled at her, showing those dimples that he never showed at home.

On the stage, Leah took a deep breath, then said, "I'm a necromancer, and proud of it. Ours is the magic of life. Brief life, but enough to give someone a second chance."

The girl focused on Fel again, as if there was nobody else in the room. A girl of taste, of course. He, for his part, was completely entranced by her. Naia was starting to think her brother was doing exactly what their father had told him not to do.

Good for him.

Naia could almost see a golden thread bringing the two of them together even if they were so far apart. She was happy for her brother, happy that he'd get the crown and the girl and everything he wanted. Her father would eventually accept the truth, and Fel deserved the world. And yet, Naia had a bitter taste in her mouth. She wished she'd also get at least something, instead of having to live in her brother's shadow.

Leah took a tray out of the box with something under a white cloth, which she put on the table. She looked back at Fel, smiled, then pulled the cloth.

A few people screamed. Naia took a while to understand the reason for that reaction, until she realized that the brown, hairy thing on the tray was a rat. A dead rat.

Leah's eyes turned black, then the creature moved and walked a few steps. More screams. This was hilarious. The rat then collapsed and stopped moving. Leah covered it, put it back on the box, then walked out of the stage.

Naia chuckled, amused. "Well... she's got style."

"She does." Fel's voice was distant and his eyes bright, as if he were contemplating something really good.

"I guess you liked it."

He smiled. "You have no idea how much."

LEAH WALKED off the stage feeling as if she were stepping on clouds, a warm feeling in her heart, but when she saw her mother scowling, her stomach lurched.

Her father was also there, in an elegant white suit, and unlike her mother, he looked happy. He walked to Leah and hugged her. "That was beautiful."

She felt emotional that he appreciated her magic. In a way, she had chosen to display her necromancy to honor him, and was glad that he understood.

Her mother shook her head. "She could have chosen a cute butterfly or something."

"She showed her pride in being a necromancer," her father said.

"She scared half the room." Her mother snorted. "People will fear necromancers for years to come."

"You know that won't happen, Ursiana." His voice was calm and his eyes kind.

One thing Leah liked about their parents was that there was always affection and respect between them, even when they disagreed.

Her mother shook her head and turned away. Leah then sat with her father and Kasim. She glanced at Fel, so far away, hoping he didn't come and ask her to dance, as she'd be obliged to refuse. He did smile at her from a distance, which warmed her heart, but then he looked away, probably knowing he had to be discreet, and turned to his sister.

Oh, Naia looked so pretty! She was definitely the most

beautiful girl in the ball, with her black hair down and dressed in a magnificent purple dress. As Leah admired Naia, her eyes met Fel's again, and he winked at her. There was something playful and flirtatious about that gesture that sent a shiver down her spine. Plus, he was so outrageously good-looking she could barely believe the wink had been for her.

Still, this was so unfair. In books, the romantic couple danced all night long. Books. The ones her mother always told her not to read. And she and Fel weren't even a couple. Yet. No, they wouldn't be. Couldn't. Shouldn't. Oh, dreaded confusion.

At least the dead rat seemed to have worked after all, because only three princes asked her to dance. One was a wildbringer from Wildspring, the other a greenbringer from Haven, and the third, a prince from Ironhold. Very different from what she'd been expecting.

The wildbringer spent the whole time either telling her how beautiful she was, or gawking at her chest, making her feel uncomfortable. It was true that her neckline was low, but he had no right to look at her body like that, to look at her like that. She was counting the seconds for the song to stop and the torture to end.

The greenbringer spent the whole time boasting about his amazing hunting skills. No, she hadn't asked about hunting and wasn't the slightest interested in it, but he didn't seem to notice. She figured he wouldn't care if she were replaced by a wooden figure. But then, at least he wasn't gawking at her, which was a big improvement.

The Ironhold prince had a pleasant smile and could actually carry a conversation. He also enjoyed reading, but wasn't quite as enthusiastic about *Rudolf the Mighty*. At least he liked to play cards and board games, which she also enjoyed. Dancing with him was nice because she didn't think he was interested in proposing. But that left her only two bleak marriage prospects, unless more princes decided to propose in the coming days, which she knew was unlikely.

And yet there was only one person in that ball that she wanted to spend time with, but she wasn't supposed to even think about him. So unfair.

Leah wanted to listen to her mother, to listen to Kasim. She had kept an open mind, but still. Perhaps in normal circumstances it was easy to ignore the heart, but hers was banging on her chest—and screaming.

NAIA HAD ALWAYS THOUGHT that a ball would make her excited, delighted, or some other amazing feeling. Instead, it was an odd kind of torture, as she became more and more aware of how much she stood out with her dress, and how much her family was cast apart. Nobody had spoken to them. Nobody had asked her to dance. Nobody even seemed to notice her.

Not that she wanted the attention of any prince—well, actually, she did want it; just some attention, not a marriage proposal or anything. She didn't want River to see her cast aside like that—if he had even noticed her. If it had been him.

But of course she'd get no attention, considering her father was unlikely to allow anyone to dance with her. That was life.

Fel didn't seem too bothered. As a prince, he could ask a noble to dance, but if he wanted to dance with a princess, he'd need to speak with her parents first, meaning that he'd breached decorum earlier. Not that he seemed to care. Well, why would he? In fact, quite a few princesses and nobles had been walking by their table, glancing at him.

Naia turned to her brother. "You're making all the girls swoon tonight."

"Yes." He sounded annoyed. "And if I remove my gloves, I'll make them faint."

"Leah didn't faint."

"Of course not." He smiled, his eyes brilliant.

Naia wanted to ask him what was going on, what had happened when they danced, but she feared breaking this fragile magic that was keeping him happy.

She wished she could feel the same. River, the person who looked like River, or her illusion, never returned to the ball. Could her mind be cracking?

When their father got back from his walk outside, he was tense, fidgety, and touched his wedding rings often, reminding Naia of the way he'd been in the carriage. Could it be that the gathering brought him some painful memories?

Naia didn't want to bother him, didn't want to disobey him, but perhaps this was an opportunity to learn something. "Did you meet her at a gathering?"

"Yes." His voice was dry. "Wait, who?"

"Who? Mother, of course."

He frowned. "She's never been to a gathering."

"Then why—"

"Let's go." Her father got up. "We've stayed long enough to be polite."

Naia didn't mind leaving early. In fact, she was relieved to get out of that tortuous place, but his behavior was odd. Regardless, she stood up and followed him, and so did Fel, who was still in good spirits despite not being able to talk or dance with Leah, and Naia knew he wanted to. Her brother had been discreet and avoided looking at the Frostlake princess, but the yearning was still clear in his eyes.

They climbed two sets of stairs to the guest wing. A servant approached her father, but he waved her away, grumpy and annoyed. Naia had a room for herself, beside Fel's, and was relieved to enter it and finally be alone with her thoughts and worries. The room could be barred from the inside, with an iron latch, but also a wooden locking bar. Her father had requested that their rooms could be locked from the inside with something other than iron. Perhaps it was an exaggeration, but Naia wouldn't feel safe if her door was locked in a way that even she could open easily. Sure, there were guards in the hall, and she doubted any ironbringer would try anything, but still... After the episode with the watersnake, being careful couldn't hurt.

The room was humongous, with a four-poster bed covered with ornate engravings. It also had a fireplace, but it hadn't been lit, as the temperature was comfortable in the castle thanks to the dome surrounding the city. This was so much more sophisticated than her room at home. Naia was starting to realize that there was a huge difference between her family and the other royals. She knew she was supposed to ignore them, that their opinion didn't matter, but it didn't feel good to be excluded. Then there were Fel's words: *we've only heard one side.*

What if her father was the horrible person there? But it didn't make sense. As a deathbringer, he was extremely powerful, and yet, he never used his magic, never threatened anyone. He cared deeply for his subjects. But that didn't mean he hadn't offended the other families somehow. Or maybe it was still because of her mother, because of that unwanted marriage. And it felt horrible knowing that these royal families wished she and Fel didn't exist. Well, that made *them* horrible and should quench the flames of her doubts about her father.

Naia wanted to lie down and rest, except that first she had to get rid of that purple froufrou she was wearing. She reached out to open the back of her dress, but it was harder than she'd predicted, as the back didn't have buttons, but rather hooks and eyes, quite tight. Going out in the hall and asking for a servant would be the peak of humiliation, considering her father had dismissed them. Well, she could try to use her ironbringing. It would be tedious, but maybe she should look at it as an opportunity to exercise her magic. Fel had gotten amazing after doing tons and tons of tedious, dull tasks; she could do the same—except that it would be incredibly boring.

Unless Naia used her fire, which burned other things, but not her. Perhaps she should incinerate that purple thing. Right. Then she'd probably torch the castle with it, and she was pretty sure that wouldn't be a good act of diplomacy.

Where was her mind going? She took a deep breath and sat on the bed. What she most wanted was to find out whether she'd truly seen River. She could still recall the taste of his lips, even after a year. But it was nonsense. If he was alive, he'd obviously forgotten their kiss. And even if he hadn't forgotten it, what could happen?

Naia shook her head and lit a flame on the palm of her hand, then moved it to the other palm. She loved the ticklish sensation of the fire, the buzz from the power flowing through her.

"River, where are you? Are you alive?" she whispered, then closed her hand and quenched her little flame. The candle went out as well, by coincidence, or perhaps also affected by her magic, leaving only silvery moonlight illuminating the room.

Then there was an odd smell of rain, not any rain, it was an exhilarating, specific smell... She got up, meaning to walk to the window, when something caught her eye beside the fireplace, a shadow that shouldn't be there. Naia lit a flame in her hand again—and her heart jumped.

Someone stood by the fireplace. Not anyone—River.

6

BEHIND DOORS

Naia magnified her fire and walked towards River, unsure if she was dreaming or hallucinating. But then there was that amazing smell of rain. A smell, she realized, that was his.

He raised a hand with dark nails. "No need to set me on fire."

His eyes were reddish brown, like before, and, on top of his head, there were two horns. It was him—unglamoured.

"You're alive?" Naia wasn't sure if she was furious or relieved. "Alive? And never bothered to tell me? I feared I had killed you." That fear had been her ominous companion for a year.

He stared at her fire as if curious, then smiled. "Except you didn't."

"Why didn't you tell me?"

He ran his fingers over the fireplace. "Hum... let me see. That's a hard one." He turned to her, his face so beautiful in the faint light coming from her flame. "Why would anyone not talk to the person who tried to kill them?"

That didn't make sense. "I didn't try to kill you. I have no idea what happened. I felt guilty for a year."

He stared at her for a moment. "Why did you ask me to kiss you, then?"

Oh, did he want her to answer that? She swallowed. "Curiosity. Why did you kiss me?"

"Because you asked! What were you curious about? Whether iron magic would kill a fae?"

Naia frowned. "I didn't use ironbringing on you. To transport you to my room, yes, but it was because I thought you were going to die out in the rain and you're too heavy for me to carry. You can't seriously be thinking that I tried to kill you on purpose. You were unconscious, River. I'm sure you realize there are much easier ways to kill someone who's not awake."

"You're glad I'm alive?" His voice was soft.

"I'm glad I didn't kill you. And what is it you're saying about my magic? That my ironbringing hurt you? How can that be, considering the company you've been keeping? What are you doing with the Ironholds?"

He set his reddish-brown eyes on her. "If you could spy on your enemy, wouldn't you?"

"Is that what you're doing?"

His eyes traveled down her face and he sucked in a breath before looking her in the eye again. "I'm doing many things."

She couldn't shake the memory of the kiss, but she couldn't shake her doubts either. "The attacks. Is it the fae? Are the fae returning?" She realized he didn't call himself a fae. "Or the Ancients or whatever?"

A corner of his beautiful lips lifted. "Give me one reason to answer you."

Well, that was obvious. "I saved your life."

He tsked. "But then you almost killed me, so that doesn't count."

Naia frowned, trying to understand his words. "Is it true what you're saying? I almost killed you?"

He considered her for a moment. "Hmm. You really had no idea."

"You thought it was on purpose?" She couldn't hide her indignation.

"I did." There was an openness in his face.

"Do you realize it makes no sense? I can hunt. I can kill a wild pig with a knife or an arrow. I can most definitely kill an unconscious fae."

"Maybe you wanted to ask me some questions first." He shook his head. "It's what I thought. Your iron magic, Naia, it's what almost killed me. Somehow when we kissed, I absorbed some of it." He took a poker from beside the fireplace and ran his hand over it. "But then it made me stronger."

"You're immune to iron now. That's how you got into Ironhold. How you're here. But how did you hide your horns and your eye color?"

He shrugged. "That's quite easy glamour."

"And how did you get into my room?"

"We're Ancients." He rolled his eyes. "We can go to many places."

She exhaled. "True. You can move through the hollow. Like a deathbringer."

"Death." He waved a hand. "Such a dramatic name for the magic that's closest to ours."

"Can you kill someone with your stare?"

He chuckled. "Can a deathbringer do that? Or are those just stories? You know, it pays to make people fear you."

"My father says we shouldn't show the true extent of our power."

"If you plan to use it, you might hide it." He looked at her. "Is that why you hide your power?"

"This?" She pointed to the flame still burning in her hand. "It's because nobody else has it."

River shook his head. "Either your father or mother had it." He frowned. "I had no idea humans... You said you're the only one with fire?"

"Magic manifests differently in different people. This has to be deathbringing."

He stared at her flame for a moment, as if unsure. "If you say so."

Naia was getting angry. Angry that he'd disappeared and had never sent a word, angry that he was in her bedroom and wasn't even giving her any proper explanation. "Why are you here? Are the fae returning?"

He put the poker back in its place. "We never left."

"You know what I mean. War. Is there a war coming?"

He waved a dark-nailed finger in the air. "There's always a war brewing somewhere, not always related to the fae."

"The attacks in the villages. Do they have anything to do with the fae?"

He paused for a few seconds, and looked up, as if thinking. "Having anything to do is a very broad concept." He stared back at her. "But if you're wondering if Ancients caused these attacks, I'll say no. But you might be right that there could be a war brewing. I have a proposal for you. Leave this gathering and go back home. There are dark times ahead."

Naia felt her stomach lurch. "So the fae *are* going to attack."

River ran his hands through his hair, revealing the pointy tip of his right ear. "I didn't say that. I'm just saying... You can choose to be safe."

"Was it the fae behind the watersnake?"

His eyes widened and he stiffened. "What watersnake?"

"In a lake. Outside the dome. I was there."

From surprise, his face turned into horror, but then he

relaxed again. "You think that the fae who are hiding in their underworld are behind a watersnake? Unlikely, Naia."

"So you do remember my name."

He chuckled. "I remember more than your name." He got close to her. "What about you? What do you remember?"

She had to look up to talk to him at that distance. "Your name. River. If that's really your name."

"What about our kiss?"

She could see his red-brown irises, even if the pupils were so large, and focused on his eyes, avoiding looking at his lips. "Of course I remember it. I feared it had been a deadly kiss. It seems it was."

He tilted his head, as if examining her, and ran his hand over her face. "You could be so much more, you know?"

"More than what?"

He snorted. "At the ball tonight, I'm not sure you noticed it, but all the women looked the same, as if they had all come from the same mold. Same hair, same dress, same style. And yet you stood out like a queen."

Exaggerated compliments like that were extremely suspicious. "And?"

"I'll confess; I was angry. I felt betrayed. I thought maybe you tricked me into kissing you knowing it would hurt me, and I wasn't sure what to do about it."

"What?"

"I did." He looked down, then back at her, his voice even softer. "I see now that I was wrong. But also time... passes differently for us when we're... not here." He was so close, smelling like rain and water, and fresh dew, and yet like something else, so magical, so his.

"Where were you?"

He shrugged. "In the hollow, then the underworld."

Naia stepped back, remembering where she'd seen him

tonight. "Until you somehow joined the Ironhold delegation. I'm pretty sure it didn't take a day."

"A month, in your time." He raised a finger. "But that is a mission. I didn't know I was going to see you here. I should have known, of course..." He took a deep breath. "I have a proposal for you."

She rolled her eyes. "You said it already: go home. Since when is that a proposal, River?"

"It isn't. I mean, it could be. You haven't heard my side of the bargain, but I have a better one."

"I'm listening."

"Marry me."

She choked in a breath. No, that had to be a mistake. His words made no sense. "What?"

"I'm asking you to marry me."

He *was* breathtaking. The proposal should make her heart speed up, but not out of nowhere like that. It didn't even make sense. "Why?"

"What kind of question is why? I have to ask, you know. I can't just abduct you. I mean, fine, I could, but that's not how we do things."

She moved away from him and sat on the bed. "River, people who get married usually like each other."

He sat by her. "You haven't seen many royals, then."

Naia laughed. "But then it's different, it's an alliance."

"Got a better alliance than humans and Ancients?"

"Right." She rolled her eyes. "As you've noticed, all the humans bow to me."

"Well, they should. Now, marry me and I'll make sure you're safe. And you'll go to the underworld with me." He paused, then added, "I can ask whoever we see to bow to you. And... I can do my best to keep your brother safe."

She'd been looking down, but the mention of her brother got her attention. "Safe from what?"

He shrugged. "From whatever comes."

"River, you know something and you're not telling me. I can't marry someone I don't trust."

He frowned and tilted his head. "You haven't seen many married couples, have you? Wait." He paused. "You've *never* seen a married couple up close, Naia."

"Of course I have. There are married people in the village near my house, and some guards are married. And it's in poor taste to mock me because my mother died, you know?"

He bit his lip and looked down. "I didn't mean it like that. I meant no offense."

"Then you shouldn't have said that. But that's not even the point. What are you hiding?"

He shook his head. "Never hiding. I'm sure you're aware that the Ironholds can't be trusted."

"You found out something?"

He looked away. "Not anything specific. Yet."

She decided to ask a different question. "What do I get if I marry you?"

He moved a lock of her hair away from her ear and whispered in it. "Tons of kisses."

His voice gave her goosebumps, and she hoped he didn't notice it. "Won't the kisses hurt you?"

"I don't think so. Not anymore."

"What else do I get?"

He got up. "Greedy, you. Here I am offering you my heart, and you're looking at it like some kind of negotiation."

She snorted. "Offering your heart? You're asking me if I want to marry you as if you were asking whether I'd buy your cart of mangos. Of course I want to inspect the cart."

"You know, I wouldn't mind being treated like a mango."

Naia shook her head. "It's not romantic."

There was a glint in his eyes. "Would you marry me if I were romantic?"

"Maybe I would consider it. But then, let's agree my father will not approve, and I don't know about your family but—"

"They don't tell me what to do."

"Can Ancients even marry humans?"

"Sure." He shrugged. "Nothing wrong with it."

"But why? I mean, you certainly don't care enough for me to send a word that you're alive, so what's the point?"

"I already explained. I was angry. And your house is quite protected—in the hollow. It's not a place an ancient can venture into."

"But you were there."

"Yes. And I'm not sure you noticed it, I almost died."

"Why did you go to Umbraar?"

He looked at her, as if thinking, then smiled. "Marry me, and I'll answer you."

She rolled her eyes. "You don't even sound serious."

"I'm an Ancient. I never sound serious. And perhaps I don't know much about your mating rituals. I don't know anything, in fact. The offer stands, but my pride is getting too scratched with your insistence in saying *no*. I'll give you two days. Think. You won't get another chance."

"Wait," she said, but it was too late, as he'd already disappeared, only black smoke where he had once stood.

Her head was spinning. She'd imagined meeting River again many times, and she'd never have guessed it would be like this. Fine, she had imagined they would kiss, and sometimes even imagined they would do whatever people did after they kissed. But a cold marriage proposal? He was doing it for a reason, she was sure of that. And she didn't even know if it was true. If by any chance it was serious, her father would be furious. Somehow, the idea of her father fuming didn't seem that bad. She was losing her mind.

Naia focused on the metal hooks on her dress, then ripped them all out at once. There.

LEAH SAT QUIETLY while her maid, Siana, undid her braids. It was late for her to still be awake, but on the other hand, it would be awful to sleep with that hair. Siana was much older than Leah, and still single. She'd been her only friend and confidant other than her parents. True that she worked for Leah's family, so she wasn't a true confidant, since she always told her mother everything. And yet. It was company.

Siana's fingers were swift as she pulled out gold threads from Leah's hair. "Looks like you are happy with your marriage prospects."

Involuntarily, Leah smiled, but because she remembered Fel. "I don't know."

"It's in your face, your highness." She had never lost the habit of addressing Leah like that. "You found someone who caught your eye."

"It's hard to know in one night. I danced with them so briefly."

"But you can know. You'll have a banquet tomorrow, won't you? When there are five or six main dishes, how long do you have to look before you choose?"

Leah chuckled. "It has happened to me that something looked quite appetizing, and then in the end it wasn't. I'm not sure your example works."

"Of course it works. How many bites did it take?"

"Well... I didn't bite any prince tonight."

"Aye." There was a mischievous glint in Siana's eyes. "You'll wait until your wedding night."

Leah frowned. "What happens on the wedding night?"

"My lady. Your mother forbids—"

"I know. But I'm asking."

She lowered her head. "I don't know either, as I don't have

a husband. Did you know that all the servants were talking about your rat? Where did you get that idea?"

"I guess..." Even she wasn't sure how she'd gotten the nerve to actually use a rat for her introduction. "I wanted to do something different."

"You certainly did. I think it was smart. Show them that you're no fragile little flower."

Leah smiled. "I hope that's the case."

Siana then helped her out of her dress and left.

It had been such a long night. Leah didn't know if she wanted it to end, afraid of the next day and whatever marriage talks would come. Afraid of the official meetings and what would happen, what they would say. Perhaps the fae were returning, perhaps Aluria was approaching a new war. Funny how she'd never thought it would happen in her time. Her parents had gone through a horrible war, and one war should be enough until forever.

Something tapped on her window. A bird? When she looked, she almost fell back in surprise. Fel was there. But how? Her room was high up in the castle.

She rushed to the window and saw him touching the iron bars. She would be lying if she said she wasn't glad to see him, but what a strange place.

"How did you get here?"

He let go of the bars and she almost screamed, until she realized he was floating in front of her window.

"A little magic. I just wanted to talk to you. Can I come in for a minute?"

"But the bars..."

He rolled his eyes. "Iron bars, Leah."

"I..." She wanted to talk to him, wanted to have a moment alone with him, but her mother's words about a ruined princess still rang in her ears. "It's... not that I don't want to talk to you, but it might be inappropriate."

His smile faded for a moment, but then he brightened up and said, "Come out with me, then."

"Out?"

"Your chance to fly." His smile was inviting, but...

"What if your magic fails? If someone sees us?"

"It won't fail. And nobody is looking up here. If they do, they'll think we're birds."

"Floating birds?"

The bars bent so that there was enough room for her to step out, and he reached out his hand. "Are you going to tell me you never dreamed of flying?"

"You don't want to know my dreams."

"Of course I do."

She shook her head. "I have too many nightmares." Still, she held his gloved hand, then realized she wasn't really holding him. "Are you sure it's safe?"

"I'll hold you. The lights of the city look so good from up high."

That was the kind of thing she'd never forgive herself if she didn't do. She stepped on the windowsill, avoiding looking down, then felt Fel's arms around her as they floated up and away from the castle.

Perhaps it was too late to realize she feared heights, as she leaned her head on his chest and closed her eyes. "How does it work?"

"Don't ruin the magic. Look. It's beautiful, I promise."

Leah dared look and noticed they were almost touching the top of the dome. The lights on the ground looked like glitter. "It is beautiful. But you got my heart racing."

His chest vibrated in a soft chuckle. "Says the girl who scared half the ball tonight."

"It's their fault they're afraid of a dead rat who can cause them no harm."

"Do you think it worked? Did it scare away your suitors?"

"I wish it had." She didn't want to let go of him, so she was still leaning against his chest, which made talking a little odd, as she couldn't see his face. "Aren't you afraid of heights?"

"Fear is not something I yield to. It's useful, and it's good to listen to it, but it's not meant to stop anyone. It's just a warning."

Leah wondered what he could be afraid of, and didn't think she could come up with anything. "A warning against what?"

"A wild animal can be dangerous, for example. Social and political situations can be dangerous. But you're right. That's not really fear. Perhaps I would fear other types of things. Opening up can be scary, as you never know how the other person will react."

"Sometimes you do."

"Maybe." He held her tighter. "Everything worthwhile in this world carries some risk. But the funny thing is that avoiding them won't prevent the pain. My father says you can't fall in love in two days. Or one day. But then how's that supposed to work? How long does it take you to know if a melody pleases you? How long does it take to feel if the weather is hot or cold? How long to know if something fits you? It takes seconds, Leah. My father also says that if falling in love was good, you wouldn't fall. Well, then, I'm flying in love."

Leah could barely believe his words, but she was unsure how to answer. Basking in the smell of his clean hair and skin, the feel of his magic, and his arms around her, she wanted to keep on holding him, but she was also getting dizzy and having difficulty getting her thoughts together.

His forehead leaned against hers. Unwittingly, she raised her face and soon felt his lips meeting hers. Such a soft, delicate, pleasant touch. She kissed his lips, he kissed hers, and then there was nothing but kissing, their mouths entwined.

Leah would be floating even if her feet were on the ground, and now her heart was hammering with twice its usual strength, blending the fear of the height and the ecstasy of kissing the only prince she had ever wanted to kiss.

She moved her face away and confessed, "I'm afraid of heights. Can we go back? But... I liked it."

He chuckled, but guided her back to the castle. The window was still open and the bars bent, so she stepped in, glad to have something firm under her feet. Fel was still floating outside.

"Come in," she said. "But just don't..." She wasn't even sure what to say and felt like her cheeks were burning. "I trust you, but let's not... do anything that would ruin me."

"I would never, Leah. But I can talk to you from here, if you're afraid."

She reached out her hand and pulled his elbow. "I'm not afraid of you."

Fel came in and Leah shut the window behind him. Only now she realized she was wearing only her nightgown, and it was odd that it hadn't bothered her earlier. But then, it covered more than the dress from the ball.

Fel stood by the window, as if hesitant to step inside, perhaps uncomfortable because of her words, but then, her mother's warning... Perhaps this was her chance to understand it all better. "What is it? That ruins a lady? What happens? It can't only be getting in her room."

Fel took a deep breath, bit his lip, and looked away, before turning back to her, somewhat flustered. "It... would involve getting some clothes off."

"Then what?"

His eyes moved down, as if checking her nightgown for the first time, then he looked away. "You'll find out." He smiled. "Once you're married, right?"

Leah was torn between her curiosity to learn more,

knowing that he'd probably answer her if she pushed him, and the fear of where that talk could lead his mind. She ended up just nodding. "Yes."

Fel crossed his arms and leaned on the wall. "Did you consider any of the hopeful suitors?"

"Sure did. Then I let you take me out the window and kiss me, now I'm letting you into my room. What are you thinking?"

He laughed again, such a relaxed, easy laugh. She wouldn't mind hearing it forever. "Considering is not saying yes, Leah. I was just asking." He tilted his head. "Did you consider me?"

Her heart was beating fast in her chest as if she were still up in the air, except that this time she didn't have the comfort of his arms around her. She stared into his bright green eyes. "You need to ask..." Leah was trembling, her voice thin and almost cracking. "Me. To consider you."

Fel blinked and sucked in a breath. Had her words surprised him? Before the disquiet could settle in her mind, he breached the distance between them, held her hands, and kissed her cheek. "Would you marry me?"

"Yes." The word popped out of her mouth on its own before she even thought about the answer. Perhaps it had come straight from her heart.

Her reward was getting the most breathtaking smile ever. She let go of his hands and wrapped her arms around him, then he was holding her close together and they kissed again.

When they parted, he was smiling. "Marry me now, Leah, right now."

She laughed. "You know I can't." For so many reasons. Some big, complicated reasons that smothered her laughter at once. "And I'll have to convince my mother."

Fel's smile also faded, his lips now forming a stiff line. "She hates me, right?"

"I think she hates your father, not you."

They were still so close that she could feel his chest expanding in a deep breath. "And what if she says *no* and doesn't budge, what will you do?" His green eyes were set on her.

"I'll try to convince her first." She had to, and there was no logical reason why her mother would oppose the union. "If she doesn't change her mind, then we'll see."

He nodded. "I'll talk to her tomorrow. Personally. I don't want her issues with my father to get in the way."

"Also..." This was a minor thing, but it was something her mother would question. "I'm supposed to rule Frostlake. But you're the Umbraar heir. How would we make it work?"

He shrugged. "I could leave Umbraar to my sister. I know she wants it, and she's capable. That way you could still rule Frostlake."

That... was perfect. Leah smiled. Everything was so easy with Fel. But perhaps not that easy. "Your father would be fine with that?"

"Maybe not. But when it's time for a new ruler in Umbraar, I'm assuming he won't be around to be upset."

"Those are dark thoughts."

"It's the truth." He brushed a lock of her hair away from her face. "And we can't live tied down by our parents' fears."

She hugged him tight. "We won't."

He kissed her again, a kiss that soon became breathless and urgent, and she wanted more and more and more of it, until he broke the kiss all of a sudden. "Leah, I'd better go. You're right that I shouldn't be in your room. I wouldn't have come, but I had no other way of speaking to you."

She didn't want him to leave, so she kissed his cheek then neck. His breath was getting harder as she ran her hands over his chest. Fel was usually so calm, it felt good to see him so flustered, feel the control slipping from him. "I trust you," she said. "You wouldn't ruin me."

His eyes closed for a moment, but then he pushed her away and climbed on the windowsill. "I would. I want nothing more than to get that nightgown off you, remove your undergarments, then kiss every part of you. But I also know we need to wait." He was so breathless he could barely speak. "Let me stay longer and I'll forget it. And if you forget it too, I'll take every piece of you, make you all mine. And I don't want to wait a month, a few days, even a second."

Leah swallowed. She would like to see his bare chest, touch it, feel more of him. She would like him to take her clothes off, to kiss her everywhere. Those were some strange, surprising thoughts. But it was true. She could be his. Right now. All she had to do was invite him in. Then perhaps there would be no problem in convincing her mother to let her marry him, as it would be too late for her to marry anyone else.

That if he didn't change his mind after he got what he wanted. There was that. Her mother's warning echoed in her head.

He chuckled and shook his head. "Leah, you're considering it. But I promise you we can wait. Think not of tonight, but of tomorrow morning."

Leah was horrified that he noticed her absurd, immoral, depraved thoughts. "I'm not considering it." The idea was so indecent, so wrong. "It's just... I wish you'd stay longer, but your point is fair too."

He nodded and smiled. "I know what I'm going to dream about. Nothing is forbidden there. Perhaps I'll be in your dreams."

She shook her head, still in disbelief at what had just crossed her mind. "My dreams are weird, Fel."

"I hope I can make them better. Tomorrow I'll speak to your mother. I know love grows with time and care, but there's a love seed for you here already, Leah."

"You have such pretty words, I can never match."

"Your smile beats my words." His eyes were sad. "I'd better go. But you said yes, so remember you're engaged now, Leah."

He put the bars back to normal, then floated up and disappeared. She wished he'd stayed. Perhaps she even wished he had stayed and ruined her, whatever that meant.

All she did was lie down on her bed, where she could imagine he'd stayed, imagine him undressing her, kissing her body, doing everything that was forbidden. She let her mind go to a dark, hidden place, a place she wished he'd visit. But it was just a matter of time.

Then she was in a cave crammed with some kind of red-eyed, gray, hairy creatures that looked like gigantic rats but without tails. She screamed but no sound came out. As she tried to put her hands together and they crossed, she realized it was a dream, and yet she was locked in it. Two gigantic rats licked her body, while two more held her down. She told herself that it wasn't real, it wasn't real, it wasn't real. She wanted to reach the silver dragon, but how was she going to do it, inside a cave?

Then fire burst through the walls and the creatures scurried away. The dragon was there, and what had been a horrific nightmare turned into a dream as his scales touched her, then his tongue licked her, healing her wounds, quieting her fears, lulling her into a sleep within her dream, away from her dream self, true self, away from her body and mind. There was just bliss.

7

MEETINGS AND MATCHES

F el knew that he had a mountain ahead of him, but he could deal with challenges. He sat in his father's room for breakfast, as only some dinners would be served in the main dining hall with all the guests. Some allies were perhaps eating together, but his father obviously hadn't been invited to any of these smaller gatherings.

Naia was distracted and pensive, even if it didn't change her appetite. His sister always ate well, and for his part, the worried thoughts crossing his mind were no substitute for proper nourishment.

As his father finished eating his last piece of bread, Fel took a deep breath, hoping it would give him the courage to speak his mind.

"I'm going to propose to Princess Leandra, and I hope you don't try to thwart my efforts." He'd practiced his phrase in his head, but saying it still felt strange.

His father stared at him for a moment, a mix of sadness and pity in his eyes. "Fel... You're not under the illusion you're in love, are you? Or that she's in love?"

This wasn't the reaction he'd expected. Fel had been prepared to see his father angry, upset, arguing, but not pitying him.

"What does it matter?" Fel spat. He hated when people felt sorry for him, hated that.

His father sighed and didn't change that ridiculous, pitiful look. "Isofel... You have no chance with the Frostlake princess." His tone was slow, as if explaining something to a four-year-old.

"He has a chance," Naia intervened, which didn't really help.

Fel glared at his father. "I asked, and she said yes. If her parents don't allow it, I'll take care of it myself."

His father shook his head. "Don't say nonsense, son. You elope with a girl, you ruin her life, you isolate her from her family. You think that's what she wants?"

He couldn't be serious. Fel chuckled. "Funny you say that. Isn't that what you did to our mother?"

"And how did that turn out? Is she alive? Happy? Tell me."

"Her death has nothing—"

"She was poisoned, Isofel." His father's voice was harsh. "I believe the Ironholds poisoned her."

Naia frowned. "You never told us that."

"What's a supposition without proof?" His father snorted. "And don't you see what's happening to you? How your cousins and grandparents love you so much? And yet you should be glad it didn't start a war." He stared at Fel. "You take the Frostlake princess, you don't know what might happen. Just don't. It's not worth it."

Fel sighed. "I'm going to talk to her mother. Nobody has forbidden anything yet. Unless you want to pose another obstacle."

His father raised a hand in the air in frustration. "I'm not opposing. I'm just trying to open your eyes. Think. Her daughter is the sole heir of an entire kingdom. Everyone will be proposing."

"Almost nobody danced with her."

His father exhaled. "Then it's all set up. Whoever is the most powerful bidder told the other families not to get near her. A kingdom is worth killing for. This is not a fight you can win, even if we lived in a world where her mother wasn't a two-faced snake."

Fel scoffed. "Well, maybe if she hadn't shunned you, you wouldn't be so bitter." It was a low blow, and based on a vague assumption, but his father was getting to his nerves.

His father narrowed his eyes. "Who said anything about shunning?"

"I saw how you looked at her, dad. Was our mother your second option?"

"You're imagining things." He laughed. "The Frostlake queen hasn't been to any gatherings since we were young, and she looks a lot like she did almost nineteen years ago. For a moment it was like turning back time, and I was surprised, that was all."

"Why do you hate her, though?" Fel asked. "I understand you hate the Ironholds. But why do you hate her?"

"Why do you care?"

"She's my future mother-in-law."

His father sighed. "Isofel. You need to face reality. And there are girls in our kingdom, you don't need to—"

"Regardless." He didn't want to hear more of that nonsense. "I'll have an audience with her mother. All I'm asking is that you don't stop me."

"Go. Words don't teach, do they? You want to experience the pain."

"Dad," Naia said. "I saw how Princess Leandra looked at Fel. She's in love."

"Oh, love." His father rolled his eyes. "You kids are so adorable." He paused. "Wait. When did you last speak to her?"

"At the ball."

"Don't lie to me."

Fel had nothing to hide and decided to tell the truth. "Fine. I went to her room last night."

"Her room?" There was alarm and fear on his face. "Did you..." He glanced at Naia, probably realizing he couldn't finish his sentence. "Did you...?"

"No." Fel grimaced. "What kind of pervert would do that?"

"What did you do in her room, then? Read stories?"

"I proposed. She said yes. Are you against this match?"

His father snorted. "Against it? It's like being against you being nominated supreme king of Aluria. How can I be against something that has no chance of happening?"

"But you're not against it."

"If her parents approve, I approve. Otherwise, don't elope with her, don't ruin her life and her children's lives, especially if you're under the illusion you love her. You're young and think love is enough, but love is fickle. They say love is like a flame, and that's exactly what it is. All it takes to quench it is a tiny gust of wind. Don't trust it. Don't put your heart out there, Isofel. People will step on it. Marriage is about trust and respect, it's not about a fickle flame."

Fel frowned, tired of hearing the same drivel from his father. "What do you even know about it?"

"Nothing. Absolutely nothing. But children shouldn't repeat their parents' mistakes."

"Was our mother a mistake?" Naia asked, her voice thin.

His father eyed them both. "You two are my joy, my pride, my life. There is no mistake there."

"Great. Then there's no mistake to be repeated." Fel got up and left quickly before he heard any more foolishness and grim warnings.

The funny thing was that Fel had lived under the illusion that the reason his father had defied Ironhold had been love for his mother, one of those romantic stories he usually only found in books, tragic ending and all. And yet more and more his father's refusal in talking about her seemed to be less out of love and more out of indifference. But then the question was why he had eloped with her. It made no sense.

But Leah, Leah loved Fel. He could see it in the brightness of her eyes, in her smile, her kisses. Beautiful Leah, who'd presented a dead rat for her introduction. She'd said she wasn't good with words, but that moment had been the only love declaration he needed. She'd been willing to alienate and scare away everyone else, and that meant she didn't want them. She didn't want any other suitor. Fel didn't want anyone else either.

THE FIRST ROYAL meeting in Leah's life. Such an amazing moment, and yet her thoughts were partly elsewhere, hoping to hear from Fel, wondering what her mother's reaction would be.

But it was still early. Any news would likely come after the meeting, when the kings would discuss the future of Aluria. That was what the gathering was really about. Kings could communicate using distance mirrors, but it didn't work for such a large group at once.

She sat behind her father, like all the heirs who attended the meeting, in a position where she could hear well but not see much, as there were wooden panels separating each king from the others. They could still see everyone, since they were sitting in the front, but the panels hid the heirs behind them.

Fel was probably there too, and she wished she could see

him again, wished she could know that her night hadn't been a dream, that they had really flown together, that they were truly engaged. Private words didn't carry the same meaning as public words, and she wanted to be sure he had truly meant them.

Perhaps she wanted a confirmation because it was hard to believe it was true, hard to believe that the most powerful and best-looking of all princes wanted to marry her, that one day they'd share a castle, a bedroom. She should really stop thinking about that and focus on the meeting. One day she would be sitting in her father's place, having to make decisions that would impact thousands of lives.

They started by discussing the mysterious attacks in small villages. All the people and animals had simply died and had no visible wounds. The vegetation was untouched. Four different kings described it the same way. In many cases, these attacks had only been found out days after, when it was too late to do anything. Leah's father had gone to some of these villages and used his necromancy to contact the dead, but even they didn't know anything.

More than half the kingdoms thought it was the white fae returning. Some kings disagreed. Someone suggested that it was some kind of poison in the air, some kind of weapon. It made some sense. But who would use it? And why?

Her father said that every theory should be given due consideration. Then the Ironhold king spoke, offering to provide support to each and every kingdom, sending his best weapons and some of his soldiers.

"And you'd do that from the kindness of your heart?" someone asked. Leah could see only part of his face from where she was sitting, but recognized Fel's father, the Umbraar king. Odd how his voice was different from his son's.

"No, no," the Ironhold king said. "Not kindness, but

caution. The fae is our common enemy. If they take one king-dom, they'll take us all, including Ironhold. Since I don't want the fae to have Aluria, I'd rather do something before it's too late."

It would be a good idea to do something, for sure. But should Ironhold be the ones doing it?

"And what guarantee do we have that you won't turn your soldiers against our kingdoms?" That was Fel's father again. He was as outspoken in this meeting as he'd been silent in the ball.

A laugh echoed in the room. It was the Ironhold king. "Oh, King Azir, if you're speaking for Umbraar, let me be clear. First, I have no interest in your shabby kingdom. Second, if your guards can't contain a small force meant just to support you, then all it means is that you are definitely unequipped to deal with the fae." He laughed again, and was joined by some of the other kings. "All I want to do is help."

"Great, then. You can help the ones who want your help. I don't need it," the Umbraar king said.

"Aluria needs unity." This was another king speaking. Greenstone maybe? Leah couldn't see. He continued, "It needs a united army to fight the coming threat. This won't work if each of us makes their own decisions. It's not about you or your kingdom, it's about the entire land."

They kept arguing. Her father was silent, and she wondered what he was thinking. What would *she* do? Accepting help from Ironhold could be good, but it could also hurt their autonomy. It could also mean putting potential enemy forces in their kingdom. But Ironhold couldn't want to conquer the entirety of Aluria; it was too big. Also, it was true that a small force sent to support local armies wouldn't be enough to overcome them. And if they moved against one kingdom, all the others would be on alert. And yet, it would give Ironhold immense power over the entire land.

On the other hand, refusing Ironhold's aid could be seen as an act of defiance. Perhaps a good solution would be to accept the help and keep an eye on them. But then again, if the fae did return, these squabbles would matter little, and misplaced pride could put Aluria at risk.

Leah didn't know what the right answer was and apparently neither did most of the kings, as they postponed the matter for further discussion.

Now Leah's heart was truly speeding up. Fel was going to propose. And then what? What would her parents do?

FEL ASSUMED that Queen Ursiana wouldn't attend the council meeting. If she hadn't been in any of the previous gatherings, she likely didn't have an active role as Frostlake Queen, at least concerning inter-kingdom matters.

He let Naia watch his father at the meeting, and took the opportunity to request an audience with Leah's mother. To his surprise, it was immediately granted, and that was how he found himself stepping into a study with bookshelves on one side, a large window with a view of the city, and chairs around a small table. Two guards stood on the corners, and the queen wore a daytime dress. Fel was wearing the shirt and pants from the ball, without the coat, hoping to make a good impression, hoping that his instincts had been right.

Queen Ursiana got up and raised her eyebrows. "You wished to see me?" It was odd to see her from up close. Her face resembled a lot Leah's, except that she had brown eyes and her complexion was a little lighter. Fel wondered if she had indeed rejected his father in the past. Perhaps it was a pointless suspicion.

Fel nodded. "Indeed, your majesty."

She gestured to the chair in front of her. "Well, have a seat."

So far she'd been friendly, and yet his heart was thumping against his chest like a caged animal.

Fel sat down, took a deep breath, then said, "I know that your majesty and my father have had disagreements." There was a flash of fury in her eyes, but very brief. Fel tried to appease her. "No, I mean, perhaps my father has offended you. I wish he had apologized, but what I can say is that I'm sorry, and if I can do any reparation—"

"Skip your pity, boy." She waved a hand, as if dismissing him.

This wasn't going well. "My apologies. I meant no pity. I meant to say that I am not my father. Whatever faults or mistakes he's made, they are not my fault, and if I can, I will do everything possible to repair them."

She arched an eyebrow. "Is that why you came here? Your talk is tedious."

"My apologies. I'm here to request your daughter's hand in marriage." He wished he'd worded this better. He wished it didn't sound as if he were begging, and, most of all, wished he didn't need anyone's permission.

The queen's disgusted grimace was a horrible response. She then closed her eyes and sighed. "You do realize she has other suitors, I assume."

"I do. But I'm also sure your majesty loves your daughter and will let her choose."

She tapped her fingers on the arm of her chair, as if thinking. "Prince Isofel, I have no quarrel with you. However, you must be aware that Leah has better matches. That said, you're right that it's up to her to choose, and I'll pass on your proposal. You'll be notified of her reply."

While her voice had been cold, the words were great. They

were just great. Fel made an effort not to smile too broadly. "Thank you so much."

"Good luck." Queen Ursiana's voice was clipped.

Like that, Fel left the room with the certainty that his father's gloomy warnings had been exaggerated and unfounded, and glad he hadn't listened to any of that.

8
NOTES

Leah sat across from prince Venard, from Ironhold, a challenge board between them. They were in her mother's tearoom, where Leah's suitors should come and visit her, except that nobody else had shown up—or sent any news.

The visit from the Ironhold prince surprised Leah, as she'd always thought his family wasn't interested in marriage alliances. Under her mother's close scrutiny, all they did was play in silence, which was for the best. It was uncomfortable to spend time with a young man to whom she had already decided to say "no". To be fair, he didn't seem that enthusiastic about his proposal either, and kept his eyes on the board, as if embarrassed. He played like a ten-year-old—and still won, as Leah was so distracted that she barely played.

She wished she could ask him about Ironhold's plans to support Aluria, but customs dictated that matching meetings should not include politics, and Leah wasn't going to breach decorum and annoy her mother for no reason, especially considering what was coming.

When he left, Leah finally breathed again. No, that made

no sense. Of course she'd been breathing during all that time, except that now it felt as if she had been suffocating.

Her mother stared at her, a glint in her eyes and a smile on her lips. "So?"

Leah swallowed. "There are more, right?"

Her mother sat by her and held her hands. "Leah, darling, after your disgusting display last night, are you surprised?" Her tone was gentle, though.

"There should be more proposals." Especially Fel. She'd been waiting to hear anything about Fel. Even screams of indignation from her mother would have been more welcome than that silence—strange, uncomfortable silence.

Her mother narrowed her eyes. "Are you thinking about anyone specific?"

Of course she was. Did her mother suspect it? Regardless, she wasn't going to tell, not before he proposed. "Maybe. Maybe not. Venard wasn't the only one I danced with."

"Why worry, if he's a good match?"

"Good?" Leah wanted to scream. "I don't understand why you don't go to the meetings. They want to put their army in each and every kingdom in Aluria. They might want to conquer us all. That's evil."

Her mother shook her head and tsked. "Nobody is evil. Everyone just looks after their own interests. That said, if their interests and yours align..."

"I'm not supporting a war."

"Leah, you think I don't know anything, but I do. Much more than you. I *lived* through a war. If the fae return, and if they attack, war is inevitable. Nobody will ask you if you support it or not. We'd better be ready."

"What if they don't attack? What if the fae are dead or something? What if it's just a sham for Ironhold to grab more power?"

"I don't think so. Still, marrying their prince doesn't mean you support everything they do. It means you will be in a much better position to have a say, to negotiate your own interests, and your kingdom's, too. That if these horrible suppositions are even true. I'll tell you something: I wasn't at the meeting, no. Your father hasn't told me about it yet, but he will. Still, I can tell you who exactly opposed the Ironhold king." She wrinkled her nose. "King Azir Umbraar, wasn't it?"

That was true, but Leah didn't want to admit it. "I... don't know. I couldn't see who was speaking, and many kings weren't sure if it was a good idea."

"Ironhold has always been our ally, and it's unlikely to change. Are they the most powerful kingdom in Aluria? Yes. But there's nothing wrong with power. It's all about how you use it, and you can use it to do good, which seems to be exactly what they're planning on doing. Plus, the prince is polite, gentle, and smart. Remember you need to choose with your head."

Leah swallowed, took some courage, and asked, "What about Prince Isofel?"

Her mother paused, thinking. "From Umbraar. Yes. What about him?"

That was strange. Leah had been expecting at least a stern warning, but not that blank expression. "Hasn't he proposed?"

"It would be a pitiful spectacle. I mean, who are they? But no, he hasn't contacted me."

Leah looked down. That was odd. He'd guaranteed that he would... Unless he'd been lying. But it made no sense. Perhaps he would still talk to her mother, perhaps something was happening.

Leah would need to find a way to contact him. Her mother kept watching her, but at some point she'd need to place her attention elsewhere. Leah's plan was to take the opportunity and write a message to Fel. Then she would need to figure out how to get it to him.

It took a long time, but her mother eventually left the room and Leah took a loose piece of paper quickly and wrote:

Did you have the chance to speak to my mother? Did you try it? Did something happen? Please let me know. Leah.

She stared at the paper. Did it sound desperate? Well, she just wanted to know what was happening. But what if he had changed his mind? He wouldn't. Not Fel, he wouldn't.

After a deep breath, she put the note in an envelope and sealed it, then stepped out of the room. A messenger was walking by, which was quite lucky.

With the most neutral and confident voice she could muster, she gave him the envelope. "A message for the Umbraars. Please deliver it right away." The boy bowed and disappeared down the hall.

Leah sighed and got back into the room, her heart thrumming in her chest. She wanted to hold Fel again, kiss him, hear his voice, his laugh. Happiness was so close, so simple, all she needed was for him to propose. Perhaps she'd even run away with him if her parents opposed the match. But she had to know that he was serious about it, that he had meant it when he'd asked her to marry him. She had to know.

After some time, her mother came in, smiling, Mariana with her.

"Any news?" Leah asked. That was silly. It was way too early for him to have received the note and done something.

"Yes. I brought your cousin here to keep you company, darling. I think the visits are over for today."

"Maybe not," Leah said.

"We'll see." Her mother smiled and left.

At least Mariana Greenstone did not look in great spirits. That was an awful and selfish thought, but Leah would feel even more wretched if her cousin were leaping with joy. Selfish, selfish, horrible thought.

"How's the day been treating you?" Leah asked.

"All right."

"Any proposals?"

"Three. Now I have to choose."

"You should be happy. Especially if your parents are allowing you to choose."

Mariana shook her head. "They said no to one of them. Didn't even let me see him. And the ones they approved, well..." She sighed.

"Who was it?"

"They want Carl, from Haven, but I would rather have someone with another magic, not greenbringing, you know? And he's not an heir. Then there's the crown prince from Zarana. No magic." She looked away and took a deep breath. "I could go there and be a queen and see my magic wither and die, I guess."

"It doesn't sound bad, Mariana. Are they nice?"

"A little. But..." She looked down. "I don't know."

"Do you..." Perhaps it was too bold to ask that question, but Leah was worried about her cousin. "Do you love someone else?"

Mariana chuckled and shook her head. "Love is silly. But I wanted to be a queen in a kingdom with magic."

"Do you have to decide now? Maybe someone could still propose."

"My parents want to settle it now, while we're all together."

It was tough to make such a decision in such little time, but it had become a tradition of the gatherings. Leah tried to console her cousin. "Maybe one of them will make you happy."

Mariana sighed. "Maybe. I just wish.... I mean, why can't it be Cassius? And then, if Ironhold is too hard, why not the Umbraar prince, for example?"

Leah's heart sped up. "Did you talk to any of them?"

"No, but my family could have pushed for it, you know? To make me a queen."

"But Greenstone doesn't get along with Umbraar."

"Who wouldn't want to have influence over another kingdom, Leah?" She then whispered, "But then, I heard that Prince Isofel is a cripple. Can you believe that?"

"He's not a *cripple*. How can anyone say that?"

"My mother said his hands are false and he probably can't have healthy children."

That was absurd. Leah glared at her cousin. "What does one thing have to do with the other? That's beyond stupid—and cruel."

"I don't know why you're angry at *me*. I'm telling you what they said. From my part, I wish my parents had tried to match me with him."

Leah's throat was tight. "Would you pick him?"

"Who wouldn't? What about you? Any proposals?"

So Fel had more options. Of course he had, and Leah wasn't the only one entranced by his looks. Well, obviously not; the other princesses weren't blind.

"So?" Mariana insisted.

Leah took a moment to recall the question, then said, "Prince Venard, from Ironhold."

Her cousin smiled. "Quite impressive, Leah. I'm happy for you."

"But it was only him."

"Of course. They would have warned the other families to back off."

Could it be that Fel's family had been warned or threatened? It made no sense. They weren't allies with Ironhold to start with. "What if I don't want Venard? Nobody else will ever propose? Am I going to stay single forever?"

"I think that if you say *no* to him, other families might step up. But why would you say *no*?"

What an idiotic question. "Because I don't love him?"

Mariana rolled her eyes. "Perhaps you *are* going to stay single forever."

N AIA SAT with her brother in what was her father's allocated office. An untouched challenge board lay on the table. Her mind was elsewhere, and it seemed that her brother was having the same issue.

River's bizarre marriage proposal kept circling in her mind: spinning, spinning, not going anywhere. How could she leave her family? But then, how could she stay and watch Fel get everything while she got nothing? There had never been a future for Naia, and now she had the chance to at least try something different. Try to make a difference. No, what was she thinking? River was probably tricking her.

What Naia wanted to do was tell her brother everything, or at least some of it, then ask for his opinion. She started with an innocent question.

"Fel, would you be upset if I got married and left you?" He gave her a questioning look. She added, "And went to live far away? Even if it was someone who's... hmm... not really an ally?"

"Who is it?" He smiled. "I mean, I can't believe you found someone right under my nose and I didn't notice anything. Who is it?" His tone was a lot more excited than she had expected.

Naia held a wooden piece in her hand and stared at it. "It's just an idea... A maybe. There's nobody."

Fel chuckled. "You don't fool me, sister. But if you don't want to say who it is, I'll respect your choice."

Her brother was a precious jewel, always too kind. She then asked, "And you wouldn't mind it?"

"If you're happy, I'm happy, Naia. You know that."

"We both need to be happy."

"I know." He smiled his non-dimpled, grown-up smile. "And we will. Don't be afraid to go where your heart tells you."

"You mean the opposite of our father's advice?"

Fel shrugged. "How's that been working for him?"

"I think he regrets some of his choices and that's why he doesn't want us making the same mistakes."

"But there's no proven path that is guaranteed to be pain-free. We can always make mistakes, but not doing anything won't help."

Naia laughed. "You read too much, brother, then get all tangled up with pretty words whose meaning you don't understand."

He laughed as well. "Of course I understand. I know you do too."

"Maybe. It's just... it feels like unearned wisdom, unlived wisdom, like a tree without roots."

"See? Now it's you who's digging up the metaphors."

"I guess." She smiled and shook her head, then tried to steer the conversation back to where she wanted it to go. "You wouldn't be angry if I did something our father doesn't approve of?"

He stared at her, those brilliant green eyes open and clear. "I wouldn't even be angry if you did something that *I* don't approve, Naia. Perhaps I'd be worried, but not angry."

But that was exactly what she feared, and it was wild to be actually considering River's proposal, to consider going who knows where with him. But the alternative was staying and wondering.

Her twin stared at her. "But if you're planning something, I do hope you'll tell me." His voice was soft.

She shook her head. "I'm not planning anything, Fel."

"Uh-huh." He nodded sarcastically.

Someone then knocked on the door and Naia rushed to open it. It was a young messenger with an envelope. Naia barely had time to notice that the sender was Princess Leandra, when Fel snatched the envelope from her. At least one twin was on his way to happiness.

Or maybe not. Fel opened the envelope, then stiffened and sucked in a breath. His face was impassive, but that was the face he made when he was hiding his pain, his shame, his fear.

"What is it?" Naia asked.

He crumpled the paper and threw it in a basket. "Nothing."

The messenger boy, who was still standing by the door, said, "My lady requests an answer."

"An answer?" Fel glared at the boy, then pulled a sheet and ink from the desk with so much fury that he dropped a small statue from the table.

"Fel, think before you write," Naia said. "Tell me what it is."

"Quiet," he snarled, while moving the feather as if he were stabbing a threatening beast.

Before she could even see what he'd written, he'd given it to the messenger, then slammed the door and stared at the window, his face impassive.

"Fel, what happened?" she insisted.

"Nothing. Absolutely nothing." His voice cut like the wind outside the dome.

"What's in the note?"

"Nothing, and I don't want to talk about that princess anymore. I'll go for a walk." He turned to leave, but then reached down towards the basket to get the note.

Naia was faster, though, and took it. As much as she hated Fel's look of hurt, she had to know what was there.

But she could barely believe the words.

· · ·

Dear Prince Isofel,

I truly apologize for giving you false hope. Nevertheless, I trust that you will find a good match soon, perhaps even in this gathering. As the sole heir of my kingdom, I had to take my suitor's health and physical integrity into consideration, as I'm sure you'll understand.

Wishing you well,

Leandra

NAIA GLANCED AT FEL, who shook his head and left. Now she understood his reaction. How dare Leah mention his disability? How dare she? The letter combusted in her hand, and she had to check if she hadn't set anything else on fire by accident, furious as she was.

As LEAH WAS STILL ENTERTAINING her cousin, the same messenger returned with a reply. From Fel. She hid it because she didn't want to open it in front of Mariana, and it took a lot of self-control not to try to at least peek and see what was written in it.

A note. That was so romantic. And it probably explained why he hadn't tried to talk to her mother. Or perhaps he *had* tried.

But her mother wouldn't lie. She was the type of person who would get angry and yell at Leah rather than hide something like that.

When Leah finally retreated to her room, to get ready for the grand banquet, she took the chance to open Fel's note. She had to read it twice. It made no sense.

. . .

Dear Princess Leandra Frostlake
I'm glad you have wonderful marriage prospects and I wish you much happiness.
Prince Isofel Umbraar

Did it mean that he wasn't going to propose? That he had never meant to? He hadn't even bothered to answer her question. Perhaps all he had wanted were those kisses, and maybe even more. Her mother's warning came to her mind. But Fel wasn't like that.

Part of her was sure this was a misunderstanding, while another part of her was sure he'd been deceiving her. The two parts were arguing while the attendants did whatever nonsense they wanted to do with her hair. At least she'd have the chance to see him. One look was all she needed to know how he felt. Unless he could pretend. Ah, she couldn't stand those contradicting, conflicting thoughts driving her crazy.

This time Leah's hair was arranged in a less exaggerated style. There was just a top bun with curls cascading down from it, but she didn't even care about it, as anxious as she was.

Her hands were sweating and her heart thrumming as she walked to the dining hall with her mother, and she wished she could become invisible, unnoticeable, that she didn't have to hide her worry. The guests were already at the table. The Umbraars were sitting by the Karsal family, from one of the two kingdoms with no magic in their royal families. Fel was sitting by their pretty princess, talking to her. Leah's stomach lurched.

Perhaps he flirted with many girls in his kingdom. Perhaps he took many of them flying. Perhaps he insisted on leaving so that the girl would plead for him to stay, knowing well what it meant. Or perhaps Leah was imagining all that. Still, when the

Frostlake family was announced, he didn't look at her, even if he was sitting at the opposite side of the table, from where he could see the door. His sister glanced at Leah, but there was no friendliness there. But why? Tears were threatening to burst through, and Leah took a deep breath to quiet them down and keep them where they belonged.

When Leah sat down, she realized her table neighbor was Venard. She wanted to ignore him, ignore everyone and everything, but he called her name. At least turning in his direction gave her an excuse to look at Fel, who was down the table, also to her left.

"This sitting arrangement wasn't my choice," Venard whispered. "I don't want you to think anyone is pressuring you. Also, I won't be hurt if you end up declining my offer."

"Thanks." That was perhaps a nonsensical thing to say. "I'll confess, though, that I hadn't given any thought about hurting your feelings or not." Now, that was a rude thing to say, but she didn't care.

"Ouch." He laughed. "Straight to the heart. But I like honesty, you know?"

"Don't we all?"

"Of course not. Why do you think polite lies are so popular?"

"People are strange." Fel still hadn't acknowledged her even once. It was as if she were invisible.

Leah had to stop being so silly. She realized then that she had an Ironhold prince by her, and perhaps she could try to pry some of his secrets. After all, one day she'd be the head of her kingdom.

She turned back to him, but in a way that she barely saw Fel. "What do you think about your father's plans?"

He choked on the bread he was eating. "You mean me marrying you? Am I supposed to say he has great taste? That it's a brilliant idea? You might make fun of me, you know?"

She shook her head, annoyed that he was mentioning that. "I mean the stuff from the council meeting."

"Right." At once, his posture relaxed. "Sending support to the other kingdoms in Aluria. Why wouldn't we? We are fortunate enough to be prosperous, to have a strong army, and our magic allows us to develop better weapons. When you have more you give to others, don't you?"

Leah grimaced. "Like charity?"

"Like sharing. We're stronger together."

"And this help comes with no cost, just from the goodness of your hearts."

Venard shrugged. "The benefit is a stronger human land. I think it's obvious. When the fae come, they won't be stopping at our imaginary borders. They won't care for our inner sense of pride or autonomy."

"But why do you think it's the fae? It's just... so random, to attack a few small villages here and there."

He looked around, then whispered in her ear. "My father believes they're testing a magical weapon."

"I see." And then she saw something else.

Fel finally glanced at Leah—but his face looked like stone. He then turned to the Karsal princess and made a knife float. The girl gawked at him, looking absolutely ridiculous. Had Leah stared at him like that?

Venard seemed to notice where she was looking and chuckled. "Silly magic. The poor Umbraars have no clue how to use their ironbringing."

Leah would be curious to know how the Ironholds used their magic, if they thought Fel's was silly. But she said something else. "The twins are your cousins. You surely could receive them in your kingdom and teach them." Not that she cared, but it was something that had crossed her mind before.

"Hmm." He snorted. "As if we hadn't offered. My grandmother even wanted to raise the kids, but the deathbringer took them away."

"They are his children."

"My grandmother says he groomed and kidnapped my aunt, then poisoned her."

That wasn't true. "My father was there when the twins were born. Your aunt said he didn't kill her."

"Dead people can also make mistakes. Still, my family honored her post-death wishes out of respect for *your* father."

"I see." Her heart was falling into pieces, she was annoyed to be talking about the Umbraars, and yet, here she had a pleasant-looking prince sitting by her. One who had actually proposed. She decided to ask a more direct question. "If I marry you, what's it going to be like?"

"Eternal happiness." He laughed. "No. Ups and downs, right? But we'll work through them. I promise I'll do my best to honor you and your kingdom, and to make sure our alliance is not only about politics, but based on trust and friendship."

"No love?"

"Mutual respect, trust, and friendship is like a tree. Love is the fruit. We plant the tree and make sure it's healthy, and the fruit will come and keep coming."

"I like that thought." That was what her mother had told her, and it made some sense.

Could she come to love Venard? He was pleasant and kind, and good-looking too, if she were to compare him to most young men, not the stupid prodigy who'd fooled her. And looks didn't even matter. Perhaps a *yes* wouldn't be that terrible. She imagined a quiet tranquility, where they played board games and discussed matters of the kingdom. It wasn't bad. At all. And yet she felt as if a chain was tying her heart.

9

MIRROR SHARDS

Naia still hadn't seen River again. Of course he wouldn't be sitting at the banquet, since he wasn't part of any family. Still, something inside her felt queasy and anxious. Anxious about his strange request, wondering if it was even true, afraid that it was some kind of joke. But then, what if it *wasn't* some kind of joke? What then?

But there was something else overtaking her thoughts. The words from Leah's note to her brother were still fresh in her mind. Perhaps they would be engraved there forever, a memory that made her so angry that her hand trembled when holding a glass.

Fel was entertaining the Karsal princess, but there was something cold, distant, and artificial in him. She hated to see her twin like that, as if something in him had been broken. If only she could hug him and tell him he was wonderful and deserved all the love in the world. But he hated anything that could be interpreted as pity, so Naia remained quiet, pushing down her worries, her anger, her fears.

Plus, Fel hadn't spoken to her since she'd seen the note.

He'd probably take a while to forgive her. But what could she have done?

Leah, for her turn, despite glancing at Fel from time to time, perhaps guilty for the abomination she'd written, seemed happy talking to one of the Ironhold princes. His magic was probably crap compared to Fel's, so at least there was that.

How could things have changed so quickly? The girl had looked at Fel with adoration the night before. Unless there had been some misunderstanding, something. There was something that didn't quite add up there, and Naia decided to figure it out, even if her brother eventually hated her for that.

She wished she could focus on the food, since she had never eaten so many different things—and so much at once. But then she remembered her father's words that it was shameful for royals to feast while their subjects starved. But maybe nobody was starving in Frostlake? She didn't know.

The other reason she couldn't focus on the food was that she was keeping a discreet eye on Leah, who was now quite at ease with her Ironhold prince. And that was fine, but didn't justify that horrible message. Unless her mother had ordered her to write it, but even then, why be so cruel? Fel was still giving attention to the Karsal princess, which wasn't right, if he wasn't interested in her. On the other hand, it was nice to see him getting the attention he deserved. But then, would that princess eventually prefer somebody with *physical integrity*? And was she interested in Fel, or in his crown?

After the main courses, there would be a cocktail in the ballroom, so that the families could mingle and talk. As people moved through the rooms, Naia fell behind, then pulled Leah aside.

The girl was surprised at first, but seemed interested in talking to Naia, and asked, "What happened?"

Naia didn't have much time, as she didn't want people

noticing them, so she asked a very direct question. "Did you write a message to my brother this afternoon? Of your own will? Sent by a short messenger, a boy?"

"I did." She said it as if it had been the most innocent thing in the world.

Oh, no. Naia had been hoping that it had been a misunderstanding or something, that Leah had nothing to do with that dreadful message, and here she was, confirming it.

The girl then dared look hurt, her voice quavering. "Why did he send that reply?"

Naia had no idea what he had written, but based on his fury, could imagine a barrage of insults—each of them more than well deserved. She snorted. "Why? You wonder why? Now go sell yourself to the most powerful kingdom. That's all you care for, isn't it?"

The stupid princess had misty eyes. "That's not true."

Naia walked away quickly, or else she'd slap the girl—or worse—and rushed towards Fel, who was already in the ballroom. He turned back, probably looking for her, but then he perked up all of a sudden, as if paying attention to something.

Then everything changed at once.

A dazzling bright light emerged in the middle of the room. Naia's first thought was that something had exploded, even if there was no noise. She saw her father jumping at something. No, someone. He was pushing someone to the floor, away from another bright light. Then smaller lights flashed all around the ballroom, and two dozen fae, armed with bows and arrows, appeared. They all had blond-white hair, pale complexion, and reddish eyes that looked more like pink or purple. Naia felt her fire calling to her, but before she did anything, the mirrors by the ceiling broke and shards were flying towards the fae. Fel. Fel was fighting back, before she could even consider what to do. But this was so unreal.

Then the shards fell on the floor and everyone stopped

moving, as if time stopped. But it made no sense. She could still move, and then she took in the scene as if examining a painting. The person her father had dropped to the floor was the Frostlake queen, who was still lying on the ground, shielded by him. True that she would have been hit by one of these bright lights if it weren't for him. Perhaps he hated her, but it didn't mean he'd want to see her dead.

Most people had hands raised, protecting their faces, which were contorted in fear. Fel was serene, looking past Naia. Past Naia, where princess Leandra should have been, except that there was a huge mirror between her and the ballroom, protecting her. Naia felt a knot in her heart, realizing that in the split second her brother had reacted, he'd used it to protect the princess who'd humiliated him. The princess he was probably still in love with.

But why was everyone frozen? Why was Naia unaffected, looking at that scene?

Then she felt a strong, inebriating scent of rain and wet leaves. Before she could remember what that smell was, she heard a single person clap, and saw River walking into the ballroom, unglamoured, looking otherworldly, powerful, and breathtaking. Naia finally felt her heart speed up, something it still hadn't done despite the surprise attack and the strange situation. But River, River somehow set it off.

He stared at her and smirked. "Oh, my. Wasn't that a spectacular display of magic?"

"What's happening?" Her voice was shaky.

He gestured around him. "Don't you have a perfect view of the situation? Fae attacking, royals scared." He frowned. "Someone trying to kill all the fae at once..."

"How did they even get in? Was that you?" She felt horrified that he could be such a dangerous enemy, horrified that she had kissed him, that she had considered his proposal. The worst was that she had considered it. And there was something else she didn't understand. "Are you stopping time?"

"Time can't be stopped. But I can stop people." He placed a finger on a man's cheek. "They look funny, don't they?"

"Don't touch them. Why are you doing this?"

He turned and stared at her, his face open, his reddish eyes beautiful and dangerously fascinating. "I'm keeping my word, Naia, it's all I'm doing."

She crossed her arms, annoyed that he affected her so much, tired of this game, tired of asking questions that went unanswered. Perhaps she should wait and let him speak.

He tilted his head. "I got you frozen, too?"

Naia glared at him. "You're here. Talking to me. I assume you want something. Spit it."

With a chuckle, he said, "Oh, crude words." Then he got serious and eyed her intently, which did give her chills. "What do you think I want?"

She pushed down all her weird feelings about him and yelled, "I don't know! I don't understand you! How did the fae even get here?"

River sighed. "I told you I'll answer your questions only when you're my esteemed wife. Regardless, I'm here to stop this attack. So remember I'm the good guy."

"Or maybe you stopped us so that your fae pals wouldn't get hit by the mirror shards."

He glanced around. "Wouldn't you look at that?" He crouched and picked up a piece of a mirror. "I can see thirteen Ancient warriors in this room, and one shard like this aimed at each of them. Not only any shard, but pointy." It was true; it looked like a knife. "I'm assuming that in less than a second, mind you, someone was able to break the mirrors in the exact shape they needed, and point the shards in all these directions at the same time." He glanced at the mirror protecting Princess Leandra. "And also do some other things. That's quite incredible. Now, who would be this person with such amazing metal magic? Someone from Ironhold? Well, strangely, they're still back in the banquet room. I doubt any of them could do it. Even the best iron-bringer usually only manipulates one piece at a time. Now, hear me out: what do you think will happen to this incredible ironbringer once Ironhold finds out how powerful he is?"

"Nothing." Could it be true? Could Fel be in danger because of his power? "What are they going to do?"

River laughed. "Oh, Naia, Naia, you have no clue just how protective of their magic the Ironholds are. I mean, how are they going to be the strongest kingdom if there's someone out there who can best them in their own element? If they see what your brother is capable of, he's as good as dead."

Perhaps there was some logic in his words, but she didn't trust River. She raised an eyebrow. "So you say."

"So I say. Sure. But I'm sure you're smart, Naia, and can come to your own conclusions."

"My conclusion is that your people have just made a successful attack against Aluria. In our territory, and under a dome. What's happening?"

River shrugged. "Perhaps war is upon you. I've told you."

"You didn't say it was the fae."

"I didn't say it wasn't." He stared at her. "So here's my proposal. I'll make sure these warriors disappear—"

"So they can come back and fight us when we're unprepared?"

"Not necessarily. You don't know." He raised his hand, palms facing her. "Let me finish. I'll make these warriors disappear. Nobody will be sure what they've seen, and, most important of all, they won't realize what your brother has done and the extent of his power."

"And in return?"

"Lovely." He widened his eyes and smiled. "You're willing to give me something?'

"No. But you obviously want something."

"Well, yes." He fiddled with his hair, revealing a pointy ear. "You know I do. I'll take you with me."

Her heart almost exploded in her chest. "Now?"

"When were you thinking?" He had a cute smile as he eyed her, his head tilted.

"You take me now, they'll blame the fae. My father and brother will be furious, and I don't know what they'll do."

"That's not my problem."

Naia shrugged. "Well, don't stop the attack, then. We were winning."

"*Your brother* was winning, and if other people realize what he can do, I doubt he lives even one more week. It was very reckless of your father to bring him here, but then, he probably doesn't realize how truly unique you and your twin are."

She chuckled. "Oh. Me too?"

"Of course. Your first instinct was to fight, wasn't it? Look around. That's not how most people react."

Naia did look, and only then she realized that there was something missing from the ballroom. "Hang on. Where are the guards?"

River shrugged again, looking almost bored. "Someone must have gotten rid of them."

"And you knew it and didn't stop any of that."

He sighed. "You speak as if it were easy to convince someone not to do something. But I can make this attack stop. If you come with me. To become my wife."

"Did you plan this? So you could take me?"

"Naia, I'm *stopping* it."

She tried to think, to understand what was happening, then suddenly a thought hit her, and she chuckled. "Did you think we would lose and planned to come here and pretend you were saving everyone's lives?"

"I certainly had no idea what your brother could do, no. Any enemy will be terrified and he'll be their number one target. I can prevent that."

She still wasn't sure if his words were real, still didn't understand why he was offering to marry her, still didn't understand anything, so she asked a question. "Where do you intend to take me?"

"The part of the underworld where I live." His voice was soft, a caress from her ears to her entire body.

For some reason, the thought was exciting and intriguing. Naia swallowed. No, it was terrible. It was probably all tricks and lies. She decided to test him, to understand what he meant by *marrying* her. "And you'll honor me as your wife, according to your customs?"

"Naia, I'm pretty sure you wouldn't want our customs. I'll honor you according to yours."

"Which you know nothing about. Will I be recognized as your wife by your people?"

"Yes."

He couldn't lie, so this was a true proposal. But then it meant marrying the enemy. And then again, it could be an opportunity for her to spy on them. Depending on what she learned about the white fae, she could even save her people, she could find her own glory. Yes, that made sense. It was a unique opportunity that she shouldn't pass, a unique opportunity to do something that mattered, perhaps even to save Aluria.

"Tomorrow morning." She could barely believe she'd said those words, as if they had come from a different Naia. Then she added, "I have to say goodbye to my brother."

"You can't tell him any of this, though. Can I have your

word? That you won't say anything about me or what we just talked about?"

"I won't. I'll just write a note that I'm leaving, and that it's by my own will, that I'm not being kidnapped or anything. It will be good for you."

"Promise you won't mention what you saw, won't mention where you're going, and won't mention what I am."

She was wondering how much she *would* be able to say, but it made sense that such a thing would be secret. "I promise."

He raised an eyebrow. "Dawn, then."

River snapped his fingers and the fae warriors disappeared. *His* magic was terrifying. He could defeat a small army just by freezing them. She didn't say anything because she didn't want to give him any ideas. Then he disappeared, unscented black smoke remaining for a second where he'd been, before dissipating as well. People around her started to move, everyone looking confused and startled. Some people were running out of the ballroom.

Fel rushed to her. "Are you all right?"

"I am." She was trembling, though.

He glanced at the mirror in front of Leah, then it fell forward and shattered, but he turned away from her before the princess could see him. "I don't understand," he said. "I swear I saw many fae surrounding us. Didn't you see them?"

Naia opened her mouth to confirm what he'd seen, but no sound came. Oh, no. Her promise. River's magic wouldn't let her say anything. She shrugged.

Meanwhile, a king yelled that this was a fae attack. Someone said the castle wasn't safe. People were angry, anxious.

Their father got to them. "Let's get back to our quarters."

"You don't want to stay and argue?" Fel asked him.

"Not when tempers are running this hot, no," their father said between gritted teeth.

"It was the fae, wasn't it?" Fel asked.

Her father nodded. "I saw many fae warriors around the room. If that was the fae or an illusion, I do not know."

An illusion? What if the fae warriors hadn't been real? That would explain how River had gotten rid of them so easily.

"But the light explosions were real," her father added.

"Naia, what did you see?" Fel asked.

"Lots of people scared. Screams. Mirrors breaking. That was you, wasn't it?"

Her brother shook his head. "I don't know. It was all so fast. One moment I was throwing shards, the next, it was all gone."

"Strange times are ahead of us," was all she managed to say.

"There's a war coming, isn't there?" Fel asked.

Their father sighed. "I think it just got here. The question is which war. And against whom."

Naia had the same questions, and yet she couldn't say most of what she thought. And to think that she would be gone by dawn. That would be such a blow for her father, such a blow for Fel. She had agreed with River too easily and now was feeling foolish. But foolish or not, she'd made the bargain, and now she'd need to honor it.

LEAH'S WORLD was falling apart like the mirrors that had once surrounded the top hall. There was so much panic around her, and she didn't understand anything. She'd seen almost nothing, considering a mirror had blocked her view before shattering in thousands of pieces—and considering the tears in her eyes. Where had those explosions come from? This attack was terrible for her kingdom and her parents. Other kings could complain about their poor security, could even accuse them of having planned it all.

Strangely, what bothered Leah the most was not the chaos around her, the danger within the walls of the castle she once considered safe, but Naia's words and Fel's indifference. The discomfort was like an insect crawling under her skin, then there was that cold feeling inside her.

Fel was now rushing out of the room with his family without sparing her a single glance. Not a single glance from him, leaving only emptiness inside her. For a moment she even thought that he could have tried to protect her, that he'd moved the mirror that had been in front of her, but that was impossible, when he wasn't even looking in her direction.

What had happened between them had all been a lie, a lie. Leah had been fooled, and almost done what her mother had warned her against. Her mother. Where was she? Leaving the ballroom, looking distraught. Leah then looked for her father, who was walking towards her, Kasim at his side.

"Are you hurt?" her father asked.

"No." She realized she was crying and took a deep breath, in an effort to stop it.

Her father eyed her up and down, as if double-checking her words. "Kasim will take you to your room. Stay inside until someone comes and tells you it's safe."

She frowned. "You think there are more intruders?"

"I don't know."

As she turned to leave, a quick thought came to her mind. "Dad."

He paused.

She continued, "I think I'll accept Venard's offer." The words tasted bitter but sounded right.

"We'll talk about it tomorrow." He waved a hand and dismissed her.

As she walked up with Kasim and two guards, he asked her, "Are you sure of what you just told your father?"

She shrugged. "How sure does one get?"

"You could wait, Leah."

"How is waiting going to change anything?'

"Decisions are like wine. Some ideas need to ferment in our heads."

She looked down. "You need several options to make a decision. Is it a decision when you don't get to choose?"

"You can choose to wait."

"I can choose to strengthen our kingdom, especially at a time when we might face scrutiny and criticism."

He sighed. "That *is* true. But you don't need to sacrifice your happiness, dear."

"What am I sacrificing? Loneliness?" Or perhaps shame, shame for being deceived so easily. She wanted to wash that shame away, wash that awful feeling, forget Fel's note. Saying *yes* to Venard could be the solution. Could be her salvation.

Naia's plan had been to tell Fel everything—or at least as much as she could, but the words never came, the courage never came, and she was starting to rethink her decision.

Her twin was in her bedroom, as her father had ordered them to sleep in the same room, for security. Hopefully he would be fast asleep at dawn. Lying on an improvised bed on the floor, he stared at the ceiling. It pained her to see him with that hardened face and eyes.

"Fel?"

"Yes?"

I'm about to run away with a fae while you're here, broken-hearted. No, that sounded strange, and wasn't even something she'd be able to say. "You do know you're handsome, right?"

He sat up. "Oh, please. Spare me your pity and your words. I know what I look like."

She looked down. "It's just..."

"No, no. You're starting to be dramatic like our father. He thinks it's such a big deal. It's not. I'm not an idiot, Naia. I don't fall in love in one day. And I don't care what a spoiled princess thinks of me. I don't, Naia. So stop staring at me like that."

She swallowed, hating to see the hardness in his face, hating that she'd make it all worse. "I know you're strong, Fel. But I want you to know that whatever happens, you'll always be my brother. I'll always love you."

He narrowed his eyes. "What's going on?"

She shook her head. "Nothing."

"Is it still your mysterious suitor, Naia? You need to be careful, you know? Men sometimes... they want... they trick you."

Trick. Fae were renowned for that. She looked down. "I'm not doing anything. And there's nobody."

His intent green eyes on her were unnerving, and she feared he could see through her flimsy lies. But he just nodded and said, "That's good to know." He then lay down again. "At least I can have a restful sleep, knowing my sister is safe." There was an edge of playfulness in his tone, but he was relaxed on his bed.

Naia lay down as well, planning on taking a short nap before waking up and getting ready to wait for River, but her fast-beating heart wouldn't let her sleep. She feared going with River, but at the same time, was afraid that he wouldn't be able to come to her room, or that Fel would get in her way. She wasn't sure what terrified her more: the idea of going or staying. Then there were all her questions about the strange attack tonight. But that was one good reason to go, one good reason to take this opportunity. And then there was her worry about Fel, her fear that he would somehow get bitter and hardened like their father. No. Somewhat hardened, maybe, but there was no way her sweet brother would ever become bitter. Besides, whatever happened, she wasn't intending on disappearing forever. She'd still come back and see her brother.

After a long time, Naia sat up. Fel's steady, deep breath was the only sound in the room. She walked up to him to make sure he was sleeping, and indeed his eyes were closed. Asleep, his face was so soft and innocent, reminding her of the kid he'd once been, the brother who had grown up with her—and whom she was leaving.

The thought of going away like that, without even saying goodbye, hurt a lot more than she would have guessed. She wondered if he was really in danger because of his magic, and if she was protecting him in a way. But then, she couldn't imagine what it would take to hurt him—unless they caught him like he was now: unguarded, vulnerable. The thought gave her shivers. But Fel wasn't someone to bring his guard down and sleep where he was unprotected—or at least she hoped so.

Silently, she took a piece of paper and wrote a note for him, letting him know that she would miss him and that she loved him. She took another piece to write a note for her father. Words failed her. She didn't want to apologize, didn't want to explain herself. In the end, she just wrote that this was her choice and that she was safe, for him not to worry, and that this was perhaps her chance to do something that mattered. She should write some nice words too, but nothing came, and it wasn't that she didn't love her father. It was just that she was unsure what to write, unsure what to say.

While she didn't want him to suffer because she left them, she wasn't sure he'd ever tried to understand her, ever tried to look at things from her perspective. She felt as if she had a knot in her throat, full of things left unsaid, things she had swallowed, but they had been there for so long that they had petrified, and now they would never become words again. Naia took a deep breath. One good reason for leaving.

She took her suitcase and put some of her clothes inside. Was she supposed to pack before being taken to the underworld? Would she be allowed to bring anything with her?

Her stomach was fluttering and empty, as she grappled with the thought that perhaps she had agreed too easily, hadn't even tried to bargain more, demand more conditions. In retrospect, that hadn't been her brightest moment. But then perhaps the issue was that the idea of marrying River wasn't loathsome. In a way, it meant freedom, possibility. And yet everything was odd and weird and she couldn't help but feel that he was hiding a lot from her. That he was perhaps even tricking her. No. *Trying* to trick her. If he had any mischievous plans, she'd figure them out.

The sky was still black as she stared out the window. If she were to ever do this again, she would agree on a specific time. Dawn felt like an eternity between the pitch black of the night and the light blue of the early sky, a time that was ambiguous and amorphous. An eternity for her to wait and wonder, and even fear River had changed his mind. That was a bizarre realization that in fact she wanted to go, she wanted to get to know the underworld. She could still hear Fel's steady breath when she noticed that familiar smell of fresh rain over leaves, the smell of roots and mushrooms and all the forest condensed in one place. She turned and saw River standing right behind her, closer than she imagined, more beautiful than she remembered, in his full fae form with horns and pointy ears.

Naia sucked in a breath and whispered, "You startled me."

He smirked. "Expecting someone else?"

She put a finger over her lips and pointed to the bed on the floor.

River widened his eyes and turned, then exhaled and whispered, "Oh. Your brother."

She nodded, then pointed at the suitcase. "Can I bring this?"

He stared at it for a moment, as if thinking, then his eyes locked on Naia's. "What's in there?"

"What do you think? Clothes."

He was staring at it, his eyes curious, but then something pushed him. Two pokers were bent around his neck and pinning River to the wall.

"Who's there?" Fel's voice echoed from behind Naia.

If there was a time to regret not having told her brother the truth, it was now.

IO
THROUGH THE HOLLOW

"**F**el!" Naia pleaded, afraid of what her brother would do to River. She let her magic connect with the bent pokers pinning River to the wall and tried to remove them, but her brother was still using his ironbringing, and the pokers wouldn't budge.

River waved a hand and smirked. "It's fine. I'm quite comfortable here."

She gave up trying to set River free, but then glared at Fel. "What are you doing?"

"Really?" Her brother raised an eyebrow. "You're asking *me*?" He then turned to River. "Who are you and what do you want with my sister?"

Even though River was against the wall and had two iron sticks around his neck, his face and body were relaxed and confident. His horns and red eyes were still visible as he gave Fel a broad smile. "Delighted to meet you, prince Isofel. I'm River, and—"

"River what?" Fel spat.

He paused and his eyes widened for a second, then he smiled. "River Ancient."

Fel frowned. "That's not a last name."

"If I'm saying it is; it is." River shrugged. "And what difference does it even make?"

"I want to know who is here to take my sister. I think I have that right, don't I?"

"Fel." Naia tried to calm him down. The amount of magic in that room felt like heavy clouds, and she didn't want it to become a storm.

Her brother raised a gloved hand. "Let me talk to him." His voice was calmer, though, as he turned to River. "What are your plans? What do you want with her?"

River now looked comfortable standing on the wall. "She agreed to marry me."

Fel stared at him as if he were some disgusting insect. "Do you even know her?"

"Not as much as I would like to." River sighed. "But some knowing needs marrying first, right?"

There was pain in Fel's eyes as he turned to Naia. "Is that what you want? You're leaving with this... This fae?"

"Yes." She looked down, unable to say any more, unwilling to face her twin, to see the hurt in those eyes.

Fel turned to River again, his voice clipped. "Do you promise to honor her?"

"Absolutely." River's voice sounded calm but firm. She dared glance at him, and saw him looking at her brother. No malice, deceit, or mockery in his expression.

For a moment, it was as if Fel was frozen, staring at River, perhaps unable to counter his words, unable to find fault in his promises. Then he glared at the fae. "Listen, if you are playing with her, if you cause her any harm, I swear I'll find you and kill you—slowly. And if you're dead, I'll find the ones you love."

River tilted his head, glanced at Naia, then turned to Fel. "I'm absolutely sure you don't want to hurt the people I love."

Love? Had he just suggested that he loved her?

"Not Naia, of course!" Fel said.

River nodded. "You want her safe and I want her safe." He then turned into black smoke and reappeared right in front of Fel, extending a hand. "We're of the same mind, human prince."

Fel frowned, seeing that River was no longer pinned to the wall.

The fae looked back at the pokers. "Oops," he said, then returned to where Fel had pushed him, smirking behind the bent pokers now surrounding his neck again. "I guess you prefer me here."

Fel shook his head and turned to Naia. "*This* is your choice? *This* was what you were talking about?"

"Fel, I…" Why were these words so hard?

Her twin scoffed. "We might become enemies, you know? Not sure you noticed it, but his kind attacked us tonight."

Naia shook her head. "I'll never be your enemy, ever. Trust me, Fel."

"Do you trust *him*?" Fel's voice was breaking as he pointed at River.

This wasn't a question she could answer *yes* to. But it didn't mean she had to be afraid, it didn't mean she had to stay. She wanted to see what happened, wanted to learn more about the fae, and, more than anything, wanted to see where this road would take her, as she was tired of being locked in her manor, tired of seeing no possibilities. And she had ironbringing and fire magic, knew how to hunt, and was sure she could get herself out of a tight situation if it ever came to it. "I trust myself."

Fel sighed, then advanced towards her, hugged her, and kissed her forehead, while slipping something in her hand. "Don't disappear, sis. And whatever happens, you'll always be welcome back. If you have any problem, don't hesitate to call for help. I'll always be there for you."

Based on the size and shape, he'd passed her a communication mirror, which she put in the pocket of her dress. She realized that her brother had only pretended to sleep, and had planned to pass her this—and to confront her visitor. Quite shrewd. But his support meant the world. The fact that he was letting her go, even if somewhat grumpy about it, made her feel much lighter and happier. Whatever happened, she'd make sure never to disappoint her brother.

They broke apart, and Fel eyed River. "Treat her well."

"That has always been my intention," River said, this time standing by Naia's suitcase. He turned to her. "I'll carry this." Then he turned to Fel. "It was a pleasure to meet you, iron prince."

"Umbraar prince," Fel said.

"Umbraar prince," River repeated. "Trust me that I'll do everything in my power to make sure your sister is always safe."

"And you'll honor and respect her," Fel added.

"Always." River nodded.

Fel then crossed his arms. "I'll let you go, but I hope you are aware that you don't deserve her."

River glanced at Naia. "I doubt any man deserves even the ground she walks on, Umbraar prince. At least I know it."

Fel nodded. Naia wanted to chuckle at the insane exaggeration, but didn't want to hurt her brother's feelings, who seemed to think it was a sensible thing to say.

River took Naia's hand, sending a thrill through her body. In truth, it was the first time they were holding hands, something they should have done *before* she decided to go with him to his underworld.

Everything around her went dark. So suddenly. She didn't

even get a warning, didn't even get a chance for one last goodbye to Fel. River's arms wrapped around her, the only comfort amidst that darkness and nothingness. So much uncertainty. She had no idea where she was going, no idea what would happen, no idea if she had made the right choice —and about to figure it out.

At first, Naia felt as if she was going to suffocate in darkness, that it was a tangible thing enveloping her, getting tighter and tighter. Even River's arms got lost in that strange sensation. This was nothing like when the carriage had gone through the portal, which had been dark as well, and felt as if she were falling, but hadn't felt like this... *thing*.

If River left her here, she'd certainly die. If there was even anything like death in this place. Perhaps it would be just eternal suffering, being lost in nothingness.

The first hint that she was getting out of this darkness was sensing River's smell again. Then she felt his presence and leaned closer, afraid of whatever was out there. For a second, she even feared that perhaps he'd brought her here to kill her. Even then, she held tighter; if he tried anything, she'd bring him with her. Plus, she felt safer with him. Incoherent thoughts.

"Naia." There was a hint of worry in his voice. "We're here. You can look."

She hadn't even realized that her eyes were shut tight. When she opened them, she noticed that she was holding him tight, her head against his chest. She stepped back and felt heat rising to her face, flustered by their sudden proximity. They were standing by a cottage surrounded by a thick forest, much thicker than the forest by her house, made of dense vegetation that would be hard to walk through.

Her suitcase was beside him, which was odd because carrying it now seemed like an impossible feat.

He pointed at the cottage. "This is... our house. For now. Later we can move into something better."

Our house. The thought had trouble entering her mind, as if it were some strange substance that didn't belong there, and plus Naia was still rattled by the journey. "What... how did we get here? What was that?"

"The hollow, Naia. I'm sorry, I should have warned you about it."

"But when crossing the portals between kingdoms, isn't it the same?"

"Those are old portals. Some say they have dragon magic. The hollow, on the other hand, is like a dark, wild, dangerous forest. Ancients travel through old, carved paths, where the forest no longer intrudes. Some of these paths are wide like roads. That's the case with your portals."

"It didn't feel like a path."

He shook his head. "Because it wasn't. I learned how to walk through the hollow. I mean, I traced my own paths, but they're not wide."

"Like a deathbringer?'

"I would think they have an easier time crossing the hollow, or perhaps they have an easier time finding the paths that are there. I do not know."

"My father says it's dangerous to cross. As a deathbringer. That he can't bring anyone else with him or they might get lost." Funny that she hadn't considered this.

River thought for a moment. "If they get in the wild, I can see how it's dangerous. They have the skills to cross, but the other person doesn't..."

Skills to cross... A horrible thought struck Naia. "So I can't leave?" Perhaps she should have known that she would be stuck wherever he brought her, and yet the idea still caused her some discomfort—and loneliness. "And where are your people?"

"You can leave with me, Naia. You're not a prisoner. As to my people, they're..." His hesitation was short, but quite clear. "Here and there."

Naia had been imagining something different, like seeing more of the fae underworld, learning more about them. She swallowed. "Will we meet them?"

"Eventually. Not yet. Come. I'm sure you want to get settled."

Naia followed him, and had to agree that the place was charming. Walls and ceiling were polished wood, with a small kitchen and even a living room with couches, many pillows on the floor, and shelves with some books. Then there was a set of stairs to a mezzanine. Quilts of different colors were thrown over the sofas, bringing happiness and warmth to that place.

He looked at her. "It's temporary, Naia."

"I like it."

A smile lit up his face. "You do? I tried to make it look a little like your house, except that I couldn't help but adding some color. Come, I'll show you what we have."

In the kitchen, he opened many cupboards, showing flour, vegetables, bread, marmalades. There was even a special cupboard with eggs and some meat, in the bottom of the kitchen, carved within a stone.

She wasn't paying attention to the food supplies, as her heart was beating too fast for her to focus on anything. What happened now? Would they kiss? Would they more-than-kiss? But they weren't married yet.

He fiddled with a jar on the counter, then looked at her. "I'll make you something to eat, then I have to go."

"Go?"

"I'm still on my mission, getting to know the Ironholds. I can't just disappear, and I can't give up what I'm doing."

"So you'll leave me here *alone*?"

"I'll be back. I'll always be back."

"You didn't have to bring me here. We could have waited until you finish whatever you're doing. Or you could have brought me somewhere where there are more of your people."

"No, Naia. You have to understand, I want to keep you safe, and there's no place safer than here."

"Maybe you are hiding me, then you'll go and marry someone else."

He raised his hands, showing his palms. "We'll wait to marry. We'll wait for everything. Meanwhile, you're safe, and we can get to know each other. I'll get you something to eat. What do you want?"

"I'm not hungry, and I'm perfectly capable of caring for myself. I can even hunt."

He looked down. "There isn't much in the forest here, and I suggest you don't try to go there. But I'll make sure our kitchen is always full."

"What am I supposed to do during the whole day?"

He shrugged. "I don't know. Royals spend their days doing nothing, don't they?"

"No. I trained with my brother, I went hunting, I explored the forest, I had animal companions. I never spent my days sitting down, doing nothing, with nobody to talk to."

There was a hint of hurt in his reddish-brown eyes, and he blinked. "Naia, what were you expecting?"

"I didn't expect being alone all day, that's it."

He took a deep breath. "Most couples don't spend all day together. You know that, right?"

"In the beginning they do, when they are recently married."

"There are serious issues about to happen in Aluria, Naia. And I told you we'll wait to get married, wait to make sure that's what you really want."

"That's even worse. I'll be ruined and unmarried."

He shook his head. "You won't be ruined. Your brother will take you back, your father will probably do that too. Then you'll even be able to pick another husband. But that won't happen because everything will be fine, and when everything is solved, I'll introduce you to my family, and we'll have a public Ancient ceremony. I'm promising you that, Naia. And tonight we'll have more time."

Tonight. What was he expecting tonight?

He must have noticed her fear, as he said, "I won't touch you. We'll do it if and when the time is right, when you trust me, when everything's settled, when you're my wife. Meanwhile, you're safe."

She was almost asking if the not-touching thing included not kissing, which would be unfair. Perhaps one of the reasons she'd come was in the hopes of more kisses, and yet, she didn't want to beg for one. "Fine."

His beautiful reddish eyes were on her for a long while, as if trying to read her. There was something disconcerting about seeing him almost vulnerable, different from his usual confident, playful manners.

He extended his arms. "Come here." Naia should resist, but she didn't, and found herself hugging him, the feeling so comforting. Strangely, it felt right. Caressing her hair, he said, "It will get better, I promise. And I'll do everything I can to make you happy."

"What about the kisses?" she blurted, regretting it even before she finished the pathetic sentence, but her mouth and mind were unfortunately disconnected.

"There will be tons of kisses," he whispered, then kissed her temple. "I was just planning on going slowly, and I don't know if you want to wait. I didn't want to be, like your people say, improper. It's up to you."

"No kisses." This was her sense of shame finally speaking, but part of her was fuming that she was saying that, when he was so close, when it would be just a matter of moving a little. "Not until it's all official." The upside was that her self-respect had won.

"That's what I thought." He was still hugging her. "I need to get used to a human companion. Let me know if I do something wrong."

"Leaving me alone is wrong, River."

He hugged her tighter. "Did you know I love my name on your lips? But yes, it will get better. This is not forever."

She raised her head to look at him. "Is River your real name?"

"It is." His face was so close.

"What about your last name? I'm sure it's not *Ancient*."

"It is, in a way. What about you? Umbraar? Is that even a name?"

"The kingdoms take the name of their families."

"Hmm." He had an amused expression. "And here I was thinking it was the other way around..."

"What's your last name, River? Your real one?"

He tensed in their hug. "I lost my name."

"You can *lose* that?"

He ran his hands up and down her back, as if to comfort her. "It can be taken away from you, yes. So you can call me whatever you want."

"Hmm... River Annoying. Do you like that?"

He chuckled. "If I'm annoying, why are you upset if I leave you alone?"

"You're annoying *because* you leave me." Naia then remembered one other reason she'd chosen to come here. "And I want answers to my other questions."

"Of course, of course."

"What happened to your name? And what was it?"

He kissed her temple again, and Naia closed her eyes, wishing he'd move his lips lower. "Tonight we'll talk. And we'll spend time together, doing anything you want. I really have to go now."

"Weren't you going to prepare some breakfast for me?"

"Yes." He broke the hug, then took a plate, a cup, some bread, marmalade, and juice, and put them on the kitchen table. He then took a sweet cake and a plate with apples. "Let me know what else you want, and I'll make sure you have it. I'll be back tonight." He looked at her. "Don't go into the forest."

For some reason, she felt that it was exactly what she had to do. Why did people even warn others not to do things, if all it did was tempt them?

River smirked. "I'm serious. It's dark and thick, and there's nothing to hunt there, but if you want to try it, by all means, have fun." He kissed her cheek. "I'll think about you all day." He smiled, then became black smoke and disappeared.

Naia was left staring at the food on the table. She wasn't even hungry, wasn't even sure where her life was going.

Then she took another look at the cottage. It was clean, well organized, but simple. Was River a peasant? A fae peasant? Or maybe fae didn't have classes like humans. She hadn't given it any thought, hadn't realized that perhaps she was giving away all her aspirations, that instead of becoming a king's advisor, she was about to be a nobody's wife. River's wife, though, and when his face and their kiss came to her mind, it didn't sound bad. It was just... perhaps she wanted more from him, more love, more affection, more something. Perhaps tonight. After all, he had sounded sincere when claiming things would be better, when promising he'd make her happy.

And then there were things she needed to learn about the

fae, about the attack in Frostlake, and this was still her best shot. If she ever changed her mind and returned home, she wouldn't do it with empty hands. And yet... she wanted to hold River's hand. Once she was sure she could trust him.

FEL WOULD DO anything for his sister. Anything. He'd face any threat, he'd give up riches, he'd fight any foe. And yet, letting her leave—elope—with a fae was not something he'd ever imagined he'd have to do. Perhaps it was worse than fighting a monster, as it meant letting the monster go, letting his sister, his twin, his best friend, leave with the enemy. And yet, he'd told her he'd support her choices. He wanted to see her happy, and if she and the fae were in love, who was he to get in the way? That if the fae truly loved her, but he'd promised he would respect her, and as vicious as those creatures could be, one thing they did was honor their word.

Nothing made sense. How had she even met him? But then, if his sister was happy, who was he to judge? To interfere? But had it been her choice? Or had the fae tricked her? *River.* Obviously fake name. And Fel let him take Naia.

He touched his end of the communication mirror in his pocket, hoping she would remember it, hoping it would work wherever she went, hoping she'd call him if she had any problem. But another thought was on his mind: his own mother. Perhaps the Ironholds had felt the same way when they found she had eloped, and who knew how much they had interfered? How much of the problems were caused because they hadn't approved her choice? Perhaps it had even caused her death. Fel wasn't going to do the same. And yet now he was bracing himself to face sheer wrath.

Holding the note meant for his father, he walked to his family's quarters with sure steps but an unsteady heart.

He'd barely come in, when he heard, "Where's Naia?"

As expected, that was the first question his father asked. Fel swallowed, then handed him the note in silence. As his father read the first words, his face became petrified, his eyes wild.

Before his father could ask or say anything, Fel said, "I saw him. I let him take her."

His father stared at him for a few long seconds. When he opened his mouth, what came out was an almost intelligible barrage of insults and protests.

Fel himself agreed with a lot of it. *Why hadn't he done something? As her brother, it was his duty to protect her. How could he have been so useless?*

When his father's words quieted down, Fel said, "It was her choice."

"Choice?" his father spat.

"Yes. Like my mother."

His father shook his head, then touched his ear. "Is this pointy? Do I have horns? Red eyes? No, right? So there's a difference there." He wasn't yelling, and yet, every word was laced with fury. "And I have no clue why your mother did what she did. No clue. None of my business. And that's not a behavior I'd like Naia to replicate, or my son to condone."

"I understand."

"You do not. You definitely do not, and I am ashamed of trusting you, of putting Naia's safety in your hands."

"Well, I have no hands. And I respect my sister and what she chooses for herself."

His father was shaking his head. "Foolish, foolish children. Foolish." He stared at Fel with a new resolve. "There's an emergency meeting. You'll go in my place. Return to Umbraar and bring our things. I'll wait for you there."

"Where are you going?"

"Where?" His father narrowed his eyes. "You're asking me

where? I'm getting your sister back." His eyes turned black, then his entire body dissolved in black smoke, which then disappeared.

Fel was left alone, with dread in his already broken heart. There was no way any of this would end up well.

II

DECISIONS

Leah knew this was a dream, and yet she still felt disoriented, still felt a chill through her body. There was blood again, blood on the floor, blood on the walls of a ballroom with gold cornices on the ceiling. Not gold anymore; blood was dripping through them, turning them red. This wasn't Frostlake, this wasn't anywhere she knew, and the place was empty, without even corpses on the floor. And now the blood was rising, about to engulf her, drown her.

The single window was on the opposite side of the ballroom. So far. With more and more difficulty with each step, she waded through the blood until she reached it. Outside, all she saw were black clouds and a storm. No sign of her dragon. No sign of anything she knew, and yet she had to run, escape, or the blood would drown her.

Soft knocks on her door woke Leah up. Her relief in being out of that dream didn't last long, as she soon remembered that this was also a strange reality, a reality where her castle had been attacked, where she had to make a lifetime decision in an insanely short amount of time. The knocks got louder.

She was about to ask who it was, when her mother walked

in, already wearing a day dress, her face stern. "There's a lot to do today."

Leah sat up. "I know." She then noticed the dark circles under her mother's eyes and her demeanor, as if she were carrying a heavy weight. Leah added, "I know everything's really difficult right now."

Her mother sighed. "Everyone's leaving after the emergency meeting. The gathering's over." Her voice was clipped.

Leah knew how much her mother had planned for this gathering, how much she'd been looking forward to it. The closing ball would have been amazing, with more musicians and artists. Now none of that would happen. "I'm sorry."

"No." Her mother shook her head. "It could have been worse." She gave Leah a strained smile. "But you have a wonderful opportunity, and I feel that you might have good news." There was a hint of hope in her eyes.

About what? What could Leah do that would make her mother happy? The answer came to her like a punch. Venard. Leah felt a chill in her insides. "I don't know."

"Leah." her mother's voice was slow. "There won't be as much time for you to make up your mind. But you can strengthen Frostlake. The decision is in your hands."

Leah sighed, and decided to say what she was thinking. "Marriage is forever. How can I choose it like that?"

Her mother took Leah's hand in hers. "You're still under the incorrect assumption that the secret to happiness is choosing well. It isn't. The secret is honoring the person you chose."

"When do I have to make a decision?" Leah felt cold inside.

"Ideally before they leave. If you're smart, before the emergency meeting. We'll need allies, darling."

Memories of the previous night came to Leah. Venard wasn't unpleasant. But then, every time she thought about him, it was as if Fel came into the thought and ruined it. It was Isofel that she wanted. Isofel, who'd told her he wanted nothing with her.

Was Leah going to sacrifice an alliance and maybe even the chance for a happy union because of some silly, pointless feelings for a prince who had turned his back to her? And again, there was nothing wrong with Venard, who was even good looking. And yet all she thought about were Isofel's green eyes. Isofel, Isofel, Isofel, a horrible obsession that would cost her dearly. Here was her mother, wrapped in sadness, waiting for one piece of news that could cheer her up. And Leah had the power to give it to her.

Leah sighed and stared at her mother. "If I agree to marry Venard, you think it will help us?"

"A lot." A smile illuminated her face. "You are so lucky, Leah, that you have a handsome young man interested in you, and it couldn't be a better match."

Young and handsome. True. A thought then hit her: unlike her father, who was much older than her mother. "How did it feel? When you chose to say *yes* to dad?"

She looked away briefly, then faced Leah again. "It was like the sun piercing the clouds after a devastating storm."

Leah smiled. "It sounds romantic when you say it."

Her mother shook her head. "Anything but romantic. Practical, realistic. Thunderstorms are romantic. A safe, dry house is practical. That's what I need you to be: realistic, rational. Things that are worthwhile, things that matter, they aren't romantic. Day-to-day life isn't romantic. Kingdom treaties aren't romantic. But it's going to be your life, and you might as well find joy and beauty in it, in things that matter, in things that have true value."

Her kingdom, her future, it all depended on this moment. Perhaps her father would let her say *no* to Venard, perhaps he wouldn't even mind it. But that would certainly create an added strain between Frostlake and Ironhold—right when they needed allies. And what would it change for Leah? Who would marry her after that? She didn't have much of a choice —and she was acting like a spoiled brat, dreading not having more choices, when the one she had was perfectly fine.

"I know," Leah said. "I know romance is silly. And..." It took some strength to say the next words. "I'll marry Venard."

Her mother smiled. "Darling, I'm so proud of you, so happy for you."

Leah nodded. Her heart was racing. If fast-beating hearts were a sign of love, perhaps there was something to Venard.

A hint of emotion laced her mother's voice, as she said, "All I want is to see you happy, Leah. I want you to have everything: the love, the husband, the castle, the crown, the happy children. I want to see you happy, fulfilled." Her smile was broad now. "And I think I will."

"Yes." Leah wasn't sure of anything. She felt as if there was something rotten inside her, something festering. But that was her heart, right? And she was supposed to ignore it. Still, for now, she wanted to focus on something else. "I... I'd better get ready for the emergency meeting."

Her mother shook her head. "No. I'll be arranging the details of your wedding, and your presence might be necessary. Get dressed, and I'll call you when I need you." She then kissed Leah's face and smiled. "My beautiful girl. So grown up. You're my life, my pride, you know?"

At least her mother was happy with Leah's decision. That made one of them. "I'll... get ready."

"And I'll negotiate a wedding's terms, then be right back." Her mother winked, then left.

Leah stared at the door her mother had closed, feeling as if the room was about to swallow her.

⚜

FEL HAD to stuff down a host of conflicted feelings as he walked to the emergency meeting. The future of his kingdom, the fate of Aluria, it was all bigger than him, than his sister's choice, his father's anger, Leah's hurtful words. And why was he even mixing Leah with his life?

It felt strange to step into his role as heir before the time was right, to sit in the position that still belonged to his father.

Fel scanned the room as the kings took their places. King Herald, from Ironhold, was already there, but Fel couldn't see if he was alone or had a prince with him. Not that it mattered. What did matter was whatever he was going to propose, and how he was planning to expand Ironhold's power. Frostlake's King Flavio was also there—alone. Fel's stomach lurched—and surprised him. He had no idea he'd been hoping to see Leah again. Perhaps it was just that he wanted her to see what she was missing, see that even if he wasn't physically perfect, he was still capable, and could even act as a king. But it was all nonsense. What did Leah even mean to him?

Nothing, nothing, nothing. So much nothingness inside him. And dread for this meeting.

The Vastfield king stared at Fel. "Your father couldn't grace us with his presence? Too scared?"

Fel ignored the jab and gave him a polite smile. "He had to leave. I deeply apologize."

Another king, this one from Wolfmark, sneered. "The most important meeting since the war councils, and he's not here."

Fel kept his composure. "I know how much you all love him and appreciate his presence." He made an effort to hide any trace of sarcasm in his voice. "But you'll have to deal with me today." There was no holding back the smirk, though.

That seemed enough to quiet down the questions, even if he still got weird glances. But then, they despised his father, so why did they even care? Right. To have an excuse to despise him even more. That said, his father was a strong voice opposing Ironhold, and Fel doubted his own voice could carry the same power. Naia, Naia, why had she left today? Now Fel was here, trying to hold it all together, having to be careful and wise despite everything around him—and inside him—falling apart.

The Frostlake King opened the meeting by mentioning the attack from the previous night, then urging the other kings to choose wisely how to react in these extraordinary circumstances. The Wildspring and Zarana kings complained that perhaps Frostlake hadn't cared enough for the security of the gathering, but then Ironhold's king shut them down, defending Frostlake. His defense was a little too impassioned, though, as if he were great friends with their king. They were close allies, as far as he knew, and maybe even friends. Still, Fel felt queasy about it.

King Herald repeated Ironhold's proposal to send part of their army to each of the ten other kingdoms. He claimed it was to help Aluria prepare against the threat of the fae, then asked for a vote. With this, Fel didn't agree.

"No vote," he said, as the kings looked at him with wide eyes, perhaps wondering how come he had dared to speak. "This matter is up to each kingdom. From Umbraar, we deeply appreciate the friendship and support offered by Ironhold, and hope it will lead to fruitful alliances and opportunities, but we trust our own forces."

Someone sniggered, and he wished he could see if it was the Vastfield or Haven king.

King Herold stared at Fel for a moment, then looked at him as if in pity. "You'll be the first ones attacked by the fae, then. And if they take your kingdom, we'll have to protect the rest of the land."

Fel smiled. "Well said: if. We'll communicate with our dear allies, and tell you about any threat coming our way. If it comes." If. Fel knew that the fae were back. And yet, with Naia aligned with one of them, it was so much more complicated. And still, so far he feared Ironhold more than the fae. Perhaps he was wrong, but he didn't want them in his kingdom and knew that his father had the same opinion.

King Herald had his arms crossed and still looked at Fel as if he were a dirty spot on the wall. "There's no if. The fae are here."

Fel nodded. "And we'll fight them when the need comes."

Then they all lost interest in Fel, as each kingdom agreed to receive Ironhold's forces. It was strange. Fel knew that many of them didn't enjoy the idea of having part of a potential enemy army within their borders, but perhaps they were truly afraid of the fae. Or else they didn't want to defy Ironhold, who now had claws all over Aluria. Except for Umbraar, who stood alone, more isolated than ever. Everything about these agreements made Fel's hair stand on end.

Perhaps it was true that Ironhold only wanted to protect their land from the Fae, but it was also true that they were amassing incredible power, and power was inebriating: people who had it ended up wanting more and more. Fel hoped that they would ignore his kingdom, since it was mostly rural and didn't have precious metals or any other riches. Before the fae war, Umbraar had been prosperous, but now its relative poverty could perhaps keep them safe. Hopefully.

But then there were other nefarious possibilities. Ironhold could want to make an example out of Umbraar, to prevent anyone else from defying them. Fel had better prepare for the worst.

As LEAH SAT at the breakfast table with her maid Siana, she glanced at the clock often, but it looked as if it were stuck.

Time seemed to slow down, or perhaps it couldn't keep up with Leah's anxiety, waiting for what her mother would say.

Yes might have been the right answer, but it didn't mean her mind—and heart—had accepted Venard for her future. It was a matter of time, of course. And yet, her mother was negotiating her wedding right now, and it meant Leah would be married in a few months, a year at most.

So soon.

So sudden.

And yet she had always known it would come to this—and always dreaded it. Except when she thought it would have been with Fel. Those silly thoughts.

She also wished she had been to the emergency meeting. They could have blamed her father for the attack, and here she was, unable to do a thing. True that she wouldn't have done much there either—but she wished she were supporting her father. She wished she knew what they were deciding for the future of Aluria. Fel had probably gone to the meeting. Or maybe Naia. The people she should stop thinking about.

Her mother then came in with rushed steps. "There you are! Let's go to your room. Oh, you'll look so pretty!"

Leah got up and followed her mother. "What is it?"

"Your dress. We need to make sure it's all set."

"What dress?"

"You'll marry in your second ball dress, since you're not using it, and there's no time to get a new one."

That made no sense. "What do you mean *no time*?"

"You think anyone can get a new dress ready for this afternoon?"

Leah still had no idea what her mother was talking about. "What's happening this afternoon?"

Her mother stopped and frowned, as if Leah had asked a stupid question. "You're getting married."

Leah felt as if she were falling into a bottomless pit. A pit of despair. And she didn't know how to get out of it.

NAIA STARED at the dark forest surrounding the cottage, stunned that River expected her to be confined to this small clearing, this small house. The truth was that she'd expected that coming to the underworld would widen her horizons, not narrow them.

The sun was now high in the sky, which was something else she hadn't expected. Somehow she'd thought that the underworld would be literally, well, under the world—or ground. Instead it had a regular sky above it. But perhaps this was not the underworld, but some place in Aluria. There was no way for her to know.

The hurt in her brother's eyes came to her mind. Right when he needed her the most, she'd left him. And for what? Naia sighed. For a cute little house and a good-looking future husband. For a chance to learn more. For hope. Maybe she was just annoyed that River had left, but then it meant she missed him. It was all very complicated, and even more so because she didn't know exactly what she was getting into, and didn't know River's motivations.

A sound of steps caught her by surprise. They were heavy steps, definitely not River's. Even before she turned to look, she heard:

"Naia!" Her father's voice. Furious. She turned and saw more fury in his eyes, his face, his posture, his clenched fists. Hopefully he wouldn't murder her by accident—or on purpose—with his death glare.

"Hi, dad." She smiled. What was she supposed to do? Cower? No way.

"We're going home." He wrapped a hand around her wrist and pulled it.

At once, she remembered all the times he had made decisions for her, all the times he had thought he knew what was best for her, without ever bothering to ask her, listen to her. And now here he was again, not the least interested in understanding her, not even making the least effort to try to convince her, as if she had no say in her life.

"No!" She pulled her hand and stepped back. "No," she repeated. The word sounded strange coming from her mouth.

He grimaced. "What do you mean, *no?*"

"It means I'm a person, I have choices. I'm not an object for you to carry around, to control."

"An object?" He looked disgusted. "Since when? I gave nothing but love to you and your brother. I cared for you, fed you, taught you to be strong, self-sufficient, encouraged you to use your magic. What are you talking about? Did that fae brainwash you?"

"Nobody brainwashed anyone. You gave us love, yes, but it was always Fel first. You never asked me what I wanted, and you never cared for my fire, never even had a nice word about it."

He threw up his hands. "Because it worried me! I don't know what it means, I don't know how you got it. I don't want anyone to see it. And perhaps I never asked you what you wanted, fine. I don't think so, but let's assume it's true. Well, then, you never told me! If there was anything you weren't happy about, how was I supposed to guess, Irinaia? I can cross through the hollow, but I can't read minds."

"I'm telling you now that I want to stay here."

"To spite me? To defy me? Why, Naia, why? What are you going to accomplish here? This fae will use you then leave you, they aren't like us. He might even kill you. Don't ruin your life." His tone was now more pleading than angry. "Is it marriage you want? I'll help you find a husband, Naia. Come home. I'm asking you."

His reaction confused her. She didn't expect him to stop being angry, didn't expect him to try to be understanding. But it was true that at first he was going to drag her back home without even asking what she thought about it. And there was another problem. "You can't carry me; it's dangerous. You've always said you can't bring anyone through the hollow."

"Dangerous?" He threw up his hands again. "I'd rather spend years lost in darkness than having a daughter ruined by a fae. Did you forget they attacked us? Did you forget they destroyed Umbraar's most beautiful city? Right, you weren't alive then, so you don't care. Well, they killed my family, my childhood home, they destroyed most of what I held dear."

"And you don't think I can make a difference? I'm here. What better place to learn more about them?"

"So you're here to spy on them? You'll give him your body in exchange for some false, scattered information? Is that how it works? Is that how I raised you?"

He was suggesting that she was selling herself? Oh, no, she wasn't going to let him get away with that. Naia glared at her father. "No." It felt good to say that word. "I'm not exchanging anything. I'm here because I want to." It felt even better to say something that she knew would hurt him. "Believe it or not, I have wishes too."

Her father stepped back, staring at her in horror. "You want a monstrous enemy? I raised you, cared for you, for a *fae* to have you?"

"For a lot more than that, but if that's how you want to see it, that's not my problem." She didn't know where she was finding the strength to defy him.

It was that different Naia, the Naia that had kissed River, the same Naia who wanted to stay, who was going to find out everything she could about the fae, but who wasn't going to back down and return home. Well, she probably couldn't even return home, having given River her word. There was that.

Plus, she didn't want to let her father control her. She wanted to trace her own path. Even if led in disaster, it was her disaster. She wanted to be in control of her life.

He stared at her. "Truly, you choose to stay? To say goodbye to your family?"

"I'm not saying goodbye to anyone. It's you who's doing it."

He stared at her, his jaw set. "Very well, Irinaia. If you don't come with me now, you'll no longer be my daughter. I will disown you. I won't speak to you or about you again. Is that what you want?"

Tears were pricking her eyes. "If I'm only your daughter within certain conditions, then I was never your daughter to begin with."

He glared at her for a moment, as if in disbelief, then said, "You're right. You were *never* my daughter. Goodbye, Irinaia."

Her father's eyes turned completely black. Naia shuddered, fearing he would kill her, but then he disappeared in a cloud of black smoke.

It was as if she was swallowing that smoke, which was the bitterest thing she'd ever tasted. A lot of what she had told him had been stuck in her throat for years. She should have been relieved to say it, and yet, all she could remember was her father disappearing, the sense that she was losing part of her family, part of her identity, that she no longer had a safe harbor to return to and would spend her life adrift. It was freedom, yes, but not the way she wanted.

"Naia?"

She raised her eyes and, to her surprise, saw River, looking at her with concern.

"I'm so sorry," he said, then wrapped her in his arms. "Perhaps he'll change his mind. He's just angry. But I'm here for you now. And you still have your brother."

Naia was stunned at sweet River, but glad that he was here,

even if she would have preferred if he hadn't heard this conversation. "I thought you were gone."

She could feel the vibration of his chest as he spoke. "I know when there are intruders here, Naia. I just didn't interfere because I knew it was between you two. I'm sure you were always a wonderful daughter and he's very proud of you. It wouldn't bother him if he didn't love you, so I hope you know that."

She looked at him. "It's fine. I never liked to have people telling me what to do, and now he'll stop."

River nodded and ran his fingers through her hair. "He will. You deserve your freedom."

She opened her arms and gestured around her. "So much freedom. Look at everywhere I can go!"

He chuckled, then got serious. "It's just for now. Trust me. And this place will keep you safe. I think only a deathbringer could come here, and as far as I know he's the only one."

"Another fae could come, couldn't they?"

He looked up, thinking. "In theory, yes, but they would need to know about this place and know how to get here, so the answer's no. It's safe. And I'm here. And so are you and your powerful magic."

"I don't care about being safe, I care about being free." She then recalled something else River might have heard. "And—I just said I was spying on you —"

"I know. I understand. Nothing you told him was for my ears. And you will be free—and powerful, like you deserve. Just wait, that's all I'm asking you."

"You have to make the waiting better, River. You leave me here alone, don't even kiss me—"

His lips were on hers in less than a second, and then she felt that wondrous connection to him, their energy intermingling, even some of their magic. And at that moment, she knew she'd made the right decision.

12

CHANGING COURSE

Fel's journey home felt empty and lonely. He wanted to deny it, but the truth was that he couldn't stop thinking about Leah. Leah, who'd made it very clear he wasn't good enough for her.

And then there was Naia and her father. The worst part had been packing their things, while his already beaten-down heart was strained wondering what was happening to them, wondering if perhaps his father would want to hurt River, would bring his sister back by force. Would he do it? Fel liked to think that he knew his father well, but the truth was that he had no idea how he'd react in such a situation. And perhaps River or some other Fae could hurt or even kill his father.

He touched his end of the communication mirror still in his pocket. It would be impossible to make it work in a carriage, as he needed a stable surface for it. More time wondering about Naia and his father. So much wondering and anxiety and pain.

When he got near his house, he ran inside—and found his father sitting at the kitchen table, a goblet in his hand.

"Where's Naia?" Fel asked.

"Naia?" His father frowned, as if thinking. "I have no idea what you're talking about."

"My sister. Did you find her?"

"Sister, sister. Yes, she's somewhere, not sure where, by a house."

"Is she well? What happened?"

"Of course she's not well. She's been taken by a fae."

"What did you do to her?"

"I?" He laughed. "You mistake me. I did nothing. Coward, you may say, but hey, she's not even my daughter. What do I care?"

"She's my sister."

"And yet you let her go."

"I didn't *let* her go. She's not mine to tell her what to do."

He shrugged. "Well, she's not mine either."

Fel noticed that his father was drinking spirits, which was odd, since alcohol had always been forbidden in their house. "You're drinking?"

He lifted his cup. "Celebrating. I stopped drinking when I brought you two home, did you know that? So now I'm reverse-celebrating and drinking a little, now that I lost a daughter."

"How's that going to help?"

"Drinking doesn't change the facts, but it changes the eyes that look at the facts, and then when they're not double, they're blurry, less sharp, so the truth won't cut you."

Fel shook his head, and again pressed his point. "So she's fine?"

"No. And so what, right? She said I never listened to her. Is it fair?"

"Perhaps she was upset, depending on what you told her."

"Well, *I* was upset because of what she's done. Not that it matters." He raised his glass and stared at it, as if examining the liquid.

"Right." Of course Fel understood that his father was angry. Still... "But she'll always be my sister. If she ever wants to come back home and you forbid her to return, you'll have to kick both of us out."

His father snorted. "Your thankfulness is touching, you know? You know what the Ironholds would have done to you? You know what they told me?"

"I don't want to hear it."

"Oh, but you do. They said they were going to end your suffering. They were going to kill you, Isofel. Isn't that horrible?"

"Well, aren't you glad Naia isn't marrying someone aligned to Ironhold?" He felt a jab of pain then, thinking of Leah talking to that prince, but she was not his to care for. And yet, he felt uneasy.

His father snorted. "You think that Fae will marry her? And what's going to happen when they attack us? Also, maybe it was him behind the attack in the castle."

"If she's there, maybe they can be our allies." Fel said it half joking, but now was thinking that perhaps there could be some truth to it. "Ironhold is going to send their army to each and every kingdom in Aluria, except us. I doubt they're happy with Umbraar defying them. I wouldn't put it past them to make an example out of us, then blame the fae. Either they're really expecting the fae to attack, or they're planning something."

"So what?" His father chuckled. "You hope your sister will make them spare us?"

"I don't know." Fel had no idea if River was aligned with the others and what his deal was with Naia. He didn't even know if she had any influence over him.

His father rolled his eyes. "Nobody knows anything."

Maybe. But they had to do something. "I'll go to the Royal Fort. I might even sleep there. Make sure our new weapons are metal proof, make sure we're ready. Are you coming?"

His father waved a hand. "It's my reverse celebration day. Leave me."

"Fair. But the kingdom needs you. "

"I know. It's a day. Not a lifetime. I swore never to drink again because of my children. I still have you."

For some reason, his words touched him. Fel approached the back of his chair, wrapped his arms around him, and kissed his cheek. "Thank you. For making sure I lived, for teaching me so many things. I appreciate it very much."

Perhaps the gesture surprised his father, who stiffened and grunted.

Fel broke the hug, then went to the stable to get his horse. His father was not perfect, but he did love him and Naia. Even Naia. Perhaps his words had been cruel now, but if he had left her alone, it meant he also respected her choices. Fel wished his sister had been more open with both of them. Perhaps then this situation could have been avoided.

He also wondered what had happened to his father to make him so bitter, jaded. It was a question Fel had been asking himself lately, and he wished he could find out more, and understand where his mother fit in all that. Even the drinking was strange. He had not known that his father had stopped drinking when they were born. That meant he'd been drinking before, and if his mother was in Ironhold, they'd been separated. But was it because he hadn't known where she was? Or had something happened? Sometimes Fel thought that the past had the keys to unlock the present, except that they were lost somewhere.

He dressed his horse, his thoughts now focused on Ironhold and whatever threat they could pose to Umbraar. Or was he being paranoid? No, he had a queasy feeling about all that, and they'd better be ready. That was why he wanted to rush to the fort.

But then, once he was on his way, another thought wouldn't leave his mind: Leah. He kept remembering Leah with the Ironhold prince, and felt as if he were suffocating. Then he mulled over her note. Those were not her words. If there was one thing that had impressed him about Leah was how natural she was about his metal hands. She hadn't shown any shock or surprise, and didn't seem to mind them.

Then Fel thought about her mother, the way she'd treated him, as if she doubted Leah would accept his proposal. She could have forced Leah to write that horrible note. Yes, Leah should have refused it, but maybe she didn't have the will or strength to defy her mother. But did he want someone who wouldn't stand up for him? Who'd shame him to please her mother? But then, it wasn't easy to defy a parent, and Fel knew that.

These thoughts kept circling in his head, and he decided that he should have talked to Leah to understand the situation. The only reason he hadn't done so was because of his hurt pride. But what was pride compared to his heart? Was he going to become bitter and cold-hearted like his father? Fel changed his course. He was going back to Frostlake. Perhaps it was better to hurt his pride, to face shame, than to keep on wondering. He was going to talk to Leah.

LEAH FELT as if she wasn't in her body anymore, but was watching herself as things happened to her. She didn't know if she agreed with her mother's reasons for speeding the marriage so much, but oh, she had tons of them. *The Ironholds wanted her to visit their kingdom, but no way she was traveling with a young man without being married. These were difficult times, and it was better to consolidate a strong alliance. It didn't matter anyway; marriage was not about choosing, but about honoring the choice made.*

But then, it was true that if it had been decided, it had been decided. Postponing it wouldn't change anything. Leah had also dreamed about a nicer wedding, with more people, a special dress... But even that they said she'd get in Ironhold, that they would have a second celebration there.

If she spoke to her father, asked him to delay the wedding, she thought he would listen to her, but she didn't want to be an immature girl and ruin an important alliance right when things were about to get difficult. And yet her heart heard none of the arguments. The heart she was supposed to ignore. That heart that screamed *Fel* like a spoiled child who didn't want to part with her toy.

And that was how she found herself walking to the rose garden, the same garden where Kasim had told her she couldn't have Isofel. And that was her biggest problem, wanting someone who didn't want her. Waiting to get married wasn't going to solve anything.

Since most of the visiting families had already left, there weren't that many guests. Well, it wasn't too bad. The Wolfmark and Haven families were there, as well as her mother's family from Greenstone, then the visitors from Zarana. Leah wondered if they were all repurposing the outfits that should have been worn at the second ball.

Leah could barely breathe, as her heart punched her chest in protest for this wedding. But she knew it wouldn't be that bad. It was all a matter of getting along with her husband, and he was amicable, so there was no reason they couldn't be friends.

Her father took her arm. "I'm sorry this is so rushed."

Leah shook her head. "No matter." And it was true. Nothing mattered.

And maybe she was just overreacting. Maybe she had been influenced by some unrealistic, lofty romantic ideals, and if she kept hoping for that, she would ruin her true happiness. She walked with her father through a path in the garden. The guests were sitting in a semi-circle around a pulpit where the Master was going to officiate the ceremony.

Then she felt something with the wind. The smell of magic. Fel's magic. And perhaps she was imagining things, since his family wasn't among the guests. No, he was there, he had to be. Leah looked and saw someone on a horse, far away, behind the circle of guards protecting the garden. Fel? Or an illusion? Stupid, stupid Leah. He'd been very clear that he didn't want her anymore. And then the horse and the scent were gone from the garden, but not from her mind.

Leah took Venard's arm and wanted to give him a smile, but her mouth had such a bitter taste that she feared she'd grimace. At least he didn't seem to notice. The Master's words flew by, as she tried to forget that bitterness. The day had been so rushed, she had barely eaten anything savory, except for some rice cakes. Fried, greasy. And then too many pastries instead of real food. That one with the orange feeling had tasted great, but now its pieces were dancing in her stomach. Not dancing. They had formed a mob, about to attack or destroy something, as if somehow they had taken the heart's side and wanted to punish Leah. She took deep breaths, hoping that her stomach would quiet down, that the pieces would remain where they should, but eventually, they won— and came out on her dress and shoes.

FEL TURNED AROUND and galloped away, as fast as he could. He wanted that image to fade away behind him, he wanted his feelings, his silly illusions to fade away.

And yet... A wedding? How could she have moved so fast? She'd given him her *yes,* she had been promised to him. Lies, so many lies, like his father had warned him.

He didn't regret having returned to Frostlake. It was better to accept an uncomfortable truth than to keep wondering. And yet it felt wrong, as if that Ironhold prince was taking away something that should be his. Not something. Someone. Like Naia, she had made her choice. A clear choice, which wasn't him.

All the times his father had told him to be careful, not to open his heart, came to his mind. He'd thought it was nonsense, but it turned out to be true. And how could it not be true?

Fel had been delusional thinking that any girl could truly love him. And he'd made the mistake of setting his foolish hopes on the heir of a kingdom, a princess more beautiful than what any artist could conceive. Some silly fantasy that she'd choose him, defective as he was. Incomplete. All his magic, all his power, didn't change the fact that he'd never have real fingers to run through her hair, he'd never be able to properly hold her hand.

He galloped away, hoping that the pain, the shame, the hurt wouldn't catch up with him, hoping that they would stay all behind. Remain in Frostlake, frozen with his heart.

LEAH WAITED in a small adjacent room by the reception hall, secretly hoping the wedding would be annulled or something. Then what? She was hoping for the impossible, still thinking she'd seen Fel, still... Still wanting him—and knowing she had to stuff down those pointless thoughts, swallow her pain.

The Ironholds and her mother had made such a fuss, as if they had never seen anyone feeling ill before. Sure that she had ruined her dress—and Venard's suit. It had been an awful spectacle, but still... It wasn't as if she'd committed some horrible transgression that justified the horror in her mother's eyes, the disgust in the guests' faces, and those whispers... Whispers that sounded like censure and mockery, and yet low enough that she never discerned the words.

Now her mother and the Ironholds were having negotiations again, which was pretty odd. Were they going to reject her because she'd felt sick? The weird part was that she was hoping that would be the case. Hoping that she wouldn't have to visit Ironhold, hoping... She didn't even know what. But then, the wedding had been concluded. Wedding. Leah was married—and yet it didn't feel like it.

The door opened, and it was her father. His face was calm, which brought her immense relief, after being pushed into this room as if she were some kind of criminal.

"Too nervous, Leah?"

"I think so." She choked back a sob.

He sighed. "Well, this wedding *was* quite sudden. But you do understand why it was so rushed, don't you?"

She nodded because if she tried to speak, she'd break down crying.

His eyes were calm and he even had a hint of a smile. "It's all good, and might be for the best."

Hope lit up in her heart. "Did they annul the marriage?"

"Oh, no, don't worry. Everything is fine and you're set to go to Ironhold with them, to get to know their kingdom. King Harold and the queen won't be there, but you'll get to know the rest of the family. Now, the important thing is that your husband will wait longer for the consummation, which is a good idea."

Leah had so many questions, but one of them stood out. "What's a consummation?"

He paused, as if the answer had gotten stuck in his mouth, then, after a while, said, "Ask your mother."

"What does it have to do with the fact I got sick?"

He bit his lip. "Some nonsense. But your mother will tell you."

But when her mother came, she was in a foul mood and hurried Leah to her bedroom to change, and Leah didn't feel at ease to ask her question. But she had to ask it.

After she changed, when the maids were gone, Leah took a deep breath and said, "Mom, what happens in the consummation?"

Her mother paused, took a deep breath, then bit her lip. "Leah... Just relax and everything will be fine."

"But how? And what happens?"

"You'll lie down together. The first time you can maybe think about something you like. Imagine you're in a wonderful place, close your eyes and just forget about what's happening. That's all you need to know."

Leah swallowed.

Her mother shook her head and hugged her. "Leah, darling, I'm sorry I was angry. I... people talk." She smiled. "But you'll be fine and you'll be happy."

Leah nodded, and before she could even realize what was going on, they descended the stairs and then she was ushered into a carriage with Venard and his grandmother, Lady Celia, an elegant widow with pretty gray hair and piercing dark eyes, which were focused on Leah, making her feel small and insignificant. Venard, for his part, was looking out the window, as if uninterested in talking to her.

Leah was trembling, ill at ease in that small, hostile space which felt as if it was about to suffocate her. Out the window, her castle was getting smaller and smaller, fading away in the distance. This felt very different from when she'd seen her city from up above, when she had still believed in falling in love, when her heart had been young and hopeful, full of romantic dreams. Now everything she knew was behind her, while she moved towards the unknown.

13

NAIA AND RIVER

Naia closed her eyes, moved by the hypnotizing melody River played in his carlay, a small harp, an instrument from his people.

He had spent the day with her, and every second in his company made her more and more certain that this had been the right choice. From the lunch with fish and some weird seeds they had prepared together, to him helping her set up her things, there was a calm normality to it, a special soft, serene companionship. And now this music that dug deep within her, reaching for some buried pain, then transcending it into song.

River stopped. "It makes you sad."

Naia realized she had tears in her eyes. "It's a good kind of sad, emotional. Not sure why." Perhaps she was still hurt because of her father, but she didn't want to think about it.

He sighed and put the instrument away. "Some pains are better left alone instead of stirred. I wish I could play something joyous." He smiled at her. "Maybe someday I will."

"It's beautiful, River."

He sat on the cushions by her and took her hand. "Do you

like it?" He gestured to the house around them. "Us here. It's not going to be here forever, but I mean... This..."

"Is good." She kissed his cheek.

He closed his eyes, then ran his hand through her hair, his long dark nails so close to her face. "We'll have a lot of quiet days like this, and joyful days, and more. But for now... I need to do what I'm doing, Naia."

She stared into his beautiful reddish-brown eyes. "What is it? You need to tell me, otherwise I'll think you don't trust me. Unless you're tricking me."

"You think information is a gift, and it can be. But it can also be a curse, or a heavy load, or even a treasure people will do anything to steal. I can't tell you everything. Yet. But I can tell you a little. Let's do a question for a question. But we can refuse to answer some of them. Does that work?"

"It depends. If you refuse everything, it's pointless. Let me ask you five questions. Yes or no only. You don't need to explain. But answer them."

He swallowed. "Go ahead."

She was surprised that he'd agreed so easily, but then she didn't waste time asking the one thing that had been bugging her for a long time. "Were you targeting me or my family when you first appeared by my house?"

"No." He had a hint of a smile, as if the question had been amusing.

His playfulness made her worry that he wasn't being truthful to her, that he was tricking her, but there was no way to know if it was true or not other than asking questions. And she did have quite a few of them. "Do you have any other lover or, hmm, special lady?" The question sounded odd, but she wanted to know.

He grimaced. "No!"

She sighed, relieved at his reaction. "It was just a question."

"I can't believe you'd think that," he said, sounding offended.

"Fine." But there were so many more things she wanted to know. It was even hard to pick a question, but she did. "Are you truly spying on the Ironholds?"

"Yes."

He sounded certain. This was good. But then, what else could he be doing? There was a big question she'd wanted to ask for a while. "Are the fae returning?"

He paused, his face conflicted. "Ask something else."

"You said you'd answer."

"I don't know the answer, and yet I promised *yes* or *no*, but I can't lie, and I can't give you an answer to that."

She took a deep breath. "You truly don't know if the fae are returning?"

It was as if his eyes were cloudy for a moment. "Yes, I don't know, Naia"

"Is bringing me here part of some scheme?"

He shrugged. "That's an ambiguous question. What's a scheme? Making you happy? Making you marry me? The answer's yes, but I don't think it's in the sense you're thinking. There. Your five questions are over. Now you can ask whatever you want, but I can refuse to answer. I'll do the same to you, even if it's unfair, as you can lie."

"It's not as easy as you think, River, and when you know people well, you know when they are lying."

He rolled his eyes. "A skill I obviously don't have."

"Pay attention and you'll learn it. If you're trying to get information from humans, you'll need to know when they are lying. Now, what do you want to know about me?"

He stared at her. "How did you get your fire?"

It was funny that he was curious about that. "I don't know. It was a few days after you disappeared. I mean, after I rescued you. I felt this new magic pulsing inside me, and it wanted to get out, and then the next thing I knew I had fire on the palms of my hands."

River observed her attentively. "But nobody else in your family has it?"

"Not that I know of. I think it's from my father's death-bringing."

"No." His voice was certain. "Death magic is... cold. I mean, that's not the right description, but fire just doesn't go with it. Maybe..." He looked up, thinking. "Ironbringers can manipulate metal temperatures..."

"They can? I mean, we can?"

He nodded. "Yes. In Ironhold they use it to help with the smelting. So maybe..." He tilted his head. "I don't know."

"Could I have gotten it from you?"

He smiled. "I ignited your fire, Naia?"

"You know what I'm talking about." She felt heat rising to her face.

He was still chuckling, looking so good. "I do, I do. But I don't have any fire. That kind of fire, at least."

She rolled her eyes. "So funny."

"Your fire's a mystery, Naia."

"It's not. My father's a deathbringer, my mother's an iron-bringer. It's one of those two types of magic."

River bit his lip. "Unless one of them had some kind of dormant magic, maybe if one of their grandparents, great-grandparents or something had it."

"Maybe." She stared at him. "You know a lot about human magic, don't you?"

He shrugged. "Gotta study your enemy."

"We're enemies now?"

"Humans. They were. We had a war, remember? And I don't mean you."

Naia looked down, thinking, then decided to ask one of the

questions that had been bothering her the most. "How did you get to my house that day? And why?"

He took a deep breath. "I was lost in the hollow."

She was surprised he'd answered her so easily, but the thought of getting lost there was also horrifying. "That place we traveled through?"

He nodded. "It wasn't... fun. Or pleasant. But it didn't feel that long being there. Weeks or months, maybe. Time passes differently there. But then I saw a light, and I did everything I could to get to that light. Next thing I knew I was in your bedroom."

Naia recalled the dreadful feeling of crossing the hollow and couldn't imagine someone there for weeks. "Aren't you afraid? Of getting lost again?"

"No, not anymore. I... Let's say I found my path again."

"What happened when we kissed?"

"I absorbed some of your metal magic. It's deadly to us."

"How did you survive?"

"I'm not sure. Now it's time I ask *you* some questions. Why did you agree to come with me?"

Naia smiled. "Your beautiful eyes."

"See? It's not fair. You say anything you want instead of answering."

She laughed. "But it *is* part of the truth."

"I thought your kind was repulsed by our eyes."

"Nothing about you is repulsive."

He scoffed. "That's a... *touching* compliment."

"What about me? Do you find anything about me strange?"

"Not strange, just... You're like the night sky when the clouds are gone, when just staring at it fills you with awe and wonder, and it makes you humbled that you're alive to witness it."

She paused, stunned by his words, but then realizing she shouldn't take them seriously. "You truly exaggerate."

"I can't lie."

"But what's the rule about exaggeration?"

"It would be a lie. I don't exaggerate, Naia. Just because your people do, it doesn't mean I do."

She couldn't hold back her laughter. "So you're *humbled* that you get to look at me?"

"I don't know what's funny about it, but go on, mock me."

"I'm not mocking. Your words sound..." She was going to say funny, but then thought better of it. "Odd to me."

"First you complain I'm not romantic. When I do express what I think, I'm odd."

"Being here is romantic. Your music is romantic. Yes, your words were romantic. But you coming into my room saying: *let's make a deal, marry me,* that was awful."

He shrugged. "I don't see why."

"Now tell me, if looking at me is so great, what does it feel when you kiss me?"

"There are places words can't reach."

She stared into his eyes, wondering if he was going to take the hint, but instead he got up suddenly, and said, "I have something for us. A special drink for a toast."

"I don't drink alcohol." Perhaps she should stop being the obedient daughter, but she couldn't shake her upbringing, all the times her father warned her against it... She just didn't want it.

"Not alcohol. It's... a juice. Rare and special." He walked to the kitchen counter and took two cups and a large purple bottle.

She got up and followed him. "Is it some fae drink?"

"Well, yes. Assuming that by fae you mean Ancient."

"No. I mean, will it have some effect on me?"

"You're going to like it." He locked his eyes on her. "You still don't trust me?"

"I don't know."

"You think I'd poison you?"

"No. But, I don't know, it could make me act differently or something." She was thinking that maybe it would make her more open to his romantic advances, but the sad truth was that she doubted she needed a drink for that. Still, he shouldn't be giving her a drink to make her do whatever he wanted to do—if he even wanted to do anything. "Will this juice take away my free will?"

He shook his head. "This is taken from a rare flower, flumenscia. It has deep purple leaves and only grows in our land. I mean, grew. It's known for its unique taste." He smiled. "And it won't make you think or act differently, if that's what you're afraid of."

"Go on, laugh. How am I supposed to know?"

"I wish you trusted me." His eyes were wistful.

"I'm here. Isn't that good enough?"

He nodded. "It's like a dream I never want to wake up from."

Naia felt flustered again, then took a sip. It was sweet, but not like a juice, more like a subtle sweetness and freshness. "It's good. But what do you mean the flowers grew? They don't grow anymore? They're gone?"

He looked down. "I'm not sure. Dormant, maybe. Like some plants in winter, in places where it freezes."

"It gets cold in the underworld?"

He looked down and shook his head. "No. We're in the underworld, and as you can see, it's not cold. It was just an example, or a thought to what's happening with the flower. Or maybe they're gone. So you better enjoy it while you have it. Some things aren't meant to last." There was sadness in his eyes as he stared at her.

"Like what?"

He ran his fingers through her hair. "You're so beautiful."

"You're dodging the answer."

"You're distracting me."

He took the cup from her hand and put it on the counter and gave her a brief, soft kiss, but then stared at her with that sad longing.

Naia didn't know what made him so sad. She caressed his hair, feeling the soft strands through her fingers, then ran a finger over one of his horns, again fascinated by its rough texture.

"Don't." He pushed her hand away and shut his eyes, as if in pain.

"It hurts?"

"They're sensitive."

He still had his eyes shut. When he opened them, there was an intensity there that scared her. He pushed her against the counter, pressing his body against hers, and kissed her.

This was a different kiss, deep, desperate, filled with longing and wanting. He sat her on the counter, then slowly moved his hands up her leg, at first over her skirt, then under it, the feel of his nails on her skin bringing a shiver through her whole body, as he caressed her inner thigh.

There was something thrilling and exciting in the thought of those strange hands, those dark claws against her naked skin, those dark claws that she wished could explore more of her. And then he got closer and closer, Naia getting lost in the feel of his mouth, the heat of his body. He was so close that she wrapped her legs around him, knowing that it was wrong and inappropriate, deliciously wrong and inappropriate. He lifted her then carried her up the stairs, all the while kissing her.

Then she was lying on the bed. Her heart started hammering in her chest, as she wondered what was about to happen, lost in the feel of his kisses, lost in the touch of his hands trailing her body. But all that happened was that she fell into a peaceful slumber.

RIVER STARED AT NAIA, so serene in her sleep. This had been so, so close. But then, when he stared at her, he did feel humbled and ironically lucky that she was here with him, that she wanted him. She was the kind of girl for whom kingdoms were lost, empires fell, loyalties changed, betrayals happened. If anyone told his story, nobody would blame him for giving up everything for her—except that if he gave it all up, there would be nobody to tell his story.

River didn't want Naia to fall for him, not yet at least. And yet he was the one who'd fallen deep into a precipice. Perhaps he'd been gone the moment she'd first saved him, looking at him with kindness instead of hate, with magnificent fascination in her pretty dark eyes. He'd been taken by her contradictory ways: daring but innocent, trusting but skeptical. And so beautiful and powerful.

Perhaps it had been wrong to give her the flumenscia juice, but in the end, it had saved *her* from him.

What had just happened? If she'd been awake for a little longer, he wouldn't have stopped. He wouldn't have stopped kissing her, caressing her, and he'd have gone as far as she would have let him, as far as making her all his on this very bed, this very night.

And it would have been wrong. He'd given her his word that he would wait. Wait for a faint hope that one day this would be real, this would be forever. That one day they would indeed stand before the Ancient council, before his father. Perhaps he'd be lucky enough to make love to her every night until the end of his days. A sweet, idealistic dream. Of course he wanted her, but she had to want him too—and know all the truth to be able to decide.

So strange that he had spent so many years frozen in time in the hollow. For him it had felt like days or at most months, he hadn't even aged, but the reality was that he had spent almost nineteen years lost in that darkness, only to wake up again when it was time to meet her, wake up years later, still young, still the right age for her.

River didn't want to believe in destiny, didn't want to think horrible things had been meant to happen. And still, the fact that he'd been frozen in time for nineteen years, only to wake up and see her... It gave him pause. Perhaps there was something bigger than time itself connecting them, some mysterious magic. And yet, even if they were connected, it wouldn't change the burden on his back.

A drop of water fell on her face. He looked at the ceiling, but it was well sealed, and it wasn't even raining. Another drop, and he realized it was from his eyes—a tear.

Because he knew. Once he did all he had to do, he'd be lucky if she didn't try to kill him. Not try. Kill him. He doubted he'd have any strength left to stop her.

20 years before

RIVER LAY UNDER A TREE, his carlay on his lap, fuzzy memories of the revel dancing in his head.

"River!"

Somebody was angry at him. A day like any other. Based on the voice, it was his cousin, Kanestar. River closed his eyes and pretended he was asleep, then felt a kick on his ribs.

"What was that for?"

His cousin had dark brown hair and two long horns, which

he adorned with rings and even golden tips. Right now he looked like a bull. "Where were you?"

"Here. Didn't you just find me?"

"There was a meeting, you miscreant."

River ran his hand through his hair, painfully aware of the lack of horns on his head, and smirked. "I like it when people use pretty words to describe me."

Kanestar glared at him. "You are a disgrace, River. Irresponsible, drunkard, selfish, careless, immature."

"Why are you naming all my lovely qualities in such an exasperated tone?"

"You think you're funny, River?"

"I'm pretty sure, actually."

"We're at war, cousin."

River mock-shivered. "Oooh, so scary. Humans. I'm terrified."

"Don't be dim. They have weapons, they have iron, they even have deadly metal magic." His cousin was so dramatic and exaggerated.

"Oh, stop it. Their magic doesn't compare to us. And even if it did, I'm sure we can trap them into a deal or something. What horrible nonsense."

Kanestar glared at him. "That's it, then? You're going to act like a spoiled kid and ignore your responsibilities?"

"I'm the youngest brother. Don't you all say I'm just a child? I don't even have my horns."

"You're eighteen. And you know you'll never have horns."

That was probably true. River should perhaps see the healer about that, but then if anyone found out he actually worried about it, the mockery would have no end. He had also considered glamouring fake horns on his head. He was good enough that he could keep the spell all the time, but then, if anyone tried to touch them, it would be the pinnacle of humiliation.

So River just laughed and ran his hand through his hair. "Oh, so that's the problem. You're jealous because I don't have an anatomic hindrance on top of my head."

Kanestar rolled his eyes. "Your knowledge of anatomy is as bad as your fighting prowess."

"Who even cares about that? There are better things in life. And, by the way, if you're going to call me weak, don't blame me for wanting nothing to do with this ridiculous squabble with the pitiful humans."

"Pitiful. Yes. Maybe that's why you look like one of them."

River almost clenched his fists, but stopped himself in time. It was never good to let people know they had reached their target. He chuckled. "Girls like it. Perhaps you should chop off your horns and take life more lightly."

"River." Kanestar's voice was strained, serious. "We used to be friends. Your father might have given up on you, but I haven't. I know you seem lazy and irresponsible, but I think it's an act. I'm not sure why, but there's more to you than partying. And you do have powerful magic." Kanestar was... pleading? That was incredibly awkward.

"So what? I'm not using it. Not for a stupid war." River lay down again and closed his eyes.

His cousin was silent for a while, then said, "That's it, then? You can make a difference and you're choosing not to?"

River sighed and sat up. "What do you want?"

"The humans are poisoning our circles. Our settlements are being attacked. We need to push them back. Join us. Join me." Kanestar was definitely taking it way more seriously than he should.

"I'm sure you'll do fine without me." River smirked. "Got your mighty horns, you know?"

Kanestar sighed and walked away. He had been River's close friend once, before he decided to dedicate his life to their kingdom and some nonsensical yada yada.

Now they were taking humans seriously? It was just an excuse to worry. There were fae living all over Aluria, and they used circles to move to the Ancient City and from settlement to settlement. Now there were more and more humans all over the land, as their numbers had been growing quite fast. Still, most of them were quite useless against Ancients: they were weaker, slower, had no magic, and knew nothing about verbal tricks and bargains. The ones with magic usually hid behind thick walls. He was sure that this war was nothing, and that his family was overreacting.

THIS WAS the last time River saw his cousin, his once best friend.

A month later, his body was brought back to the Ancient City.

Guilt. Shame. They were just words. What River felt was something else, something deep, something eating him inside.

14

THE IRON CITADEL

L eah had expected to feel dizzy or nauseous when crossing the portal into Ironhold, but it felt normal, like passing through a regular arc, except that the landscape changed from frosty to foggy with winter dry trees but no ice or snow.

Venard was still looking outside, while Lady Celia kept staring at Leah with narrowed eyes. The woman was probably going to get some extra wrinkles from that trip—which would be well deserved.

Then, for the first time, the woman smiled. It was a cold smile that didn't reach her eyes, but at least it was something. "We're home. This is also your home now, even if you're here only for a short visit."

Leah nodded. "Yes."

Lady Celia frowned. "Yes? That's what you have to say? We are admitting you into our kingdom, the richest in Aluria, despite your horrible display, despite everyone's suspicions about you."

"I meant—"

"Quiet!" the woman roared. "Don't interrupt me when I speak."

Leah had only wanted to say she had meant no disrespect, but now she thought that she wanted to disrespect that woman, and she had quite a few words that required a lot of effort to be contained.

"We're welcoming you." The woman raised an eyebrow. "For now. But if we find out you're carrying some servant's child, oh girl, you'll regret your lies."

"Lies?" Leah couldn't hold back her words. "How dare you question my honor?"

"Venard."

He looked between Leah and Lady Celia, as if hesitating for a second. Then he slapped Leah's face so hard that it brought tears to her eyes. Before she could even recover from it, he was holding both of her hands, and whispered in her ear, "Please be quiet or it will be worse. Please." His voice was pleading, not threatening.

The woman looked at her grandson with a satisfied smirk. Leah wanted to jump out of the carriage, but she was restrained. She wanted to say that they should annul the wedding, that she hated them, that she wanted to go back home, but his tone gave her pause. Perhaps he was trying to warn her. He had hurt her and she couldn't forgive him for that, and couldn't imagine a peaceful union with him. But that woman... there was clear satisfaction in her face. She enjoyed seeing Leah humiliated, hurt.

"There, there, child," Lady Celia said. "If you want to be part of our family, you need to adapt to our ways. Don't interrupt us. Don't contradict us. Your husband will teach you some manners, so that we can welcome you among us. It will soften you, make you more amenable. Like meat."

Meat? Leah stared at the woman. "I want to go back."

Lady Celia mimic-pouted. "So cute. She thinks she has a

choice. Understand one thing, child: we don't care what you want. Venard."

"Don't hurt me, don't hurt me, or it will be worse!" Leah screamed.

He held her wrists with one hand, then took a thin iron bar, bent it, and wrapped it around one of her wrists.

Lady Celia raised an eyebrow. "If you yell, if you complain, if you scream, it will burn you. Try to run, and it will burn you. And don't think that it will be a soft burn. We'll make sure it cuts across your bone until you're like the Umbraar boy."

Fel. How dare she say that about him? Was that how he'd lost his hands? No, it couldn't be, he'd never been to Ironhold, as far as she knew. Thinking about him made Leah feel even worse, but then, what if he was also cruel? How would she know?

Lady Celia chuckled. "Silent. Much better, isn't it? Now, we wanted to treat you kindly, but you chose this. We can still treat you kindly, mind you, once your behavior is appropriate for Ironhold. And I'll be honest: I don't care what your mother or father says. For me, you are a little slut who let some servant between your legs, and nothing will convince me otherwise. Who was it, darling? A guard?" She tsked and shook her head. "So many guards in the hallways, that's what you get. But I don't care who it was. If there's a child there, it won't survive."

"Don't say anything," Venard whispered in her ear.

Leah had never been so humiliated in her life. In fact, she'd never been humiliated. The taste was bitter, but it mostly made her angry, an ugly anger that wanted to harm and maybe even kill someone. But she remained silent. She remained silent as the woman kept talking about how daughters were poorly raised nowadays, how Ironhold had high standards, how Leah was like a wild animal that needed to be tamed. It was as if this was a test to see how long she could stand being insulted without replying.

At last, the woman had a warmer smile. "I see you're learning better manners, girl. You'll see. Soon you'll become a real princess, worthy of the Ironhold title."

Leah wanted to roll her eyes and tell her that she had always been a future queen, but it wasn't worth it.

Lady Celia raised an eyebrow. "Can you behave when we arrive at the Iron Citadel?"

That was the name of their castle. Leah remained silent.

"Can you behave?" she repeated.

"Yes," Leah said between gritted teeth.

The woman turned to her grandson. "Venard." Leah flinched, wondering what they were going to subject her to, but the woman said, "Release her."

He stopped holding her. Leah hoped that didn't mean she was about to face something worse.

The woman then had a broad smile. "I'm sure we'll be best friends, and I'm glad you're going to be part of our family. I want you to look out the window, girl. This is a sight you'll never forget."

Leah did look out, especially because it meant a break from facing the two horrible people in the carriage. What she saw surprised her.

THE SUN WAS SETTING when Fel got to the fort, darkness settling in, and it felt so appropriate. This time, the journey back to his kingdom hadn't felt lonely and plagued with worry. There was nothing for him to worry about anymore. And yet emptiness failed to numb him, as his heart cracked like the ice on the lake. That lake from a pointless dream.

His solace was that his father and sister were alive and safe, or at least as safe as Naia could be where she was. Safe. Fel feared that this was the calm before the storm, his heart filled with an eerie worry that everything was about to fall apart, that his kingdom would be in danger.

But at least that gave him a purpose, a goal. Perhaps he was breaking down inside, but he had to stand tall and prepare for whatever threat would come their way. He got to the fort, then left his horse in the stable.

Fel hadn't been here much in the last year. His father didn't want Naia there, afraid that some young man would take advantage of her, and Fel didn't want to leave her behind. In retrospect, he should have questioned his father more, insisted that Naia come. Keeping her isolated hadn't worked out that well, had it?

He rushed to the armory, where they now had carpenters working alongside smiths. A gigantic wooden catapult stood outside, by the courtyard where their soldiers trained. A small courtyard, as they had few soldiers, and he hoped they didn't have to change that.

Silvan, their weapons master, greeted him with a smile. He was about his father's age and had been working with them for more than twenty years now.

"Isofel! You grace us with your visit."

Fel shook his head and pointed to the weapon. "All wood?"

"Yes. A piece of art, isn't it?"

Maybe. No. Something was wrong. He could feel magic in that catapult calling to him. And there was only one kind of magic that could do that. He felt what was calling him, then pulled them out of the wooden structure: five large iron nails. He made them fly toward Silvan, stopping them when they were a finger away from his face. The catapult collapsed.

Silvan didn't dare step back, but his face was pale as he looked at Fel. "Your grace, it was just a few nails."

Fel let the nails drop to the ground. "I was making a point. You use that against an ironbringer, they'll use it against you."

"But what if we fight the fae?"

"We do have iron weapons as well, don't we? But we need to make sure we can face Ironhold, if anything happens."

"Would they send their royalty here?"

"We can't bet that they won't."

"Hey, there," someone said behind Fel. "One of these days you'll kill someone by accident."

He turned and saw Ariel, or rather, Arry, their general's son, and the only person Fel considered a friend.

Fel smiled then shook his head. "I'm sure I'll kill someone on purpose." He kept thinking about that Ironhold prince taking Leah's arm, and his imagination made it all end in blood and violence. And he wished he could forget that.

"So now Ironhold is the enemy?" his friend asked.

"Haven't they always been?"

Arry nodded, then bit his lip. "Where's Naia?"

Poor guy. His eyes always sparkled when he mentioned her. Could he have been an appropriate match for her? Could things have been different if she had come here more often?

"Home," Fel lied.

"Right." Arry looked down.

"Fel!" A girl's voice called him. He could recognise that sound anywhere, and now he wished he could disappear. It was quite unfair that he hadn't inherited his father's death-bringing.

Christine was then in front of him. "How was the gathering?"

"I'll discuss it later with the concerned parties." Not with her, he meant. He didn't want to talk to her.

"I'm just asking. As a friend."

Fel shrugged. "It was fine. I... have things to do. If you excuse me."

He turned around and ran to the barracks. Christine. Not long ago, he'd fancied himself in love with her. She was beautiful, and had cute freckles on her face. Since she was Sivan's daughter, Fel had ended up very interested in the manufacturing of weapons, and coming here a lot more often than he should.

Eventually he had kissed her—then it all crumbled away when she flinched. Just a flinch, and all his illusions of love were gone. A flinch when he touched her with his fake hand. If he had thought her voice was melodious, now he found it annoying. For some reason, his feelings turned into repulsion, and it got worse as she kept pursuing him.

That gave him hope. It meant that his illusions of love for Leah should also crumble soon, right? After all, that letter had been much worse than flinching. And yet it was taking too long. Way too long.

MONSTROUS, magnificent, horrid. The Ironhold castle was all these things at once, but if Leah were to pick one description, it would be monumental—or perhaps fearsome.

At a first glance, it looked like the peak of a mountain, but it was a silver peak, all made of some wrought iron, shining in the sun. That thing had to have at least some twenty floors, shaped like a steep hill, surrounded by what looked like a moat from a distance. Perhaps it was a mountain surrounded by the castle. She couldn't believe that it would be just a building, couldn't even fathom how they had erected such a thing. The enormity of that man-made structure made her shiver, such unnaturalness dominating the landscape as if to tell everyone that here humans were the ones who ruled over nature. Ironbringers.

Even then, how long had it taken for a family to build that colossal thing? She had never taken the Ironholds for hard workers, but perhaps they could do it fast. That explained why Venard had said Fel's magic was pitiful. Fel. Just his name was a stab opening a pit of pain for something that would never be true. And yet, Venard didn't exude that magic that the Umbraar prince did. Maybe it was just different. Or maybe it had been buried under their evil ways.

The truth was that any castle would be terrifying for someone arriving there with two horrible people who'd been threatening to hurt her. The very first hours with her new family didn't bode well for her future. Leah had to find a way to undo this, to undo the wedding, to go back home. Lady Celia's hard eyes on her reminded her that it wouldn't be easy. Venard was again looking outside, as if Leah were none of his business.

Lady Celia smiled. "Impressed?"

Leah decided to be polite and play the game they wanted her to play. "A lot. It's... majestic." The word that had come to her mind at first had been *monstrous*, but she was glad she'd fixed it in time.

The woman's smile was warm. "Your new home, darling. You'll be majestic too."

Leah nodded, then looked outside. Friendly Lady Celia managed to be unsettling.

"Look at me, girl," the woman said. Leah turned to her. She still had that warm smile that didn't even look fake. "From today on, you'll also be my granddaughter. Everything I do, it's because I care for you, because I want you to be truly a part of our family. You understand that, don't you?"

"Yes. Of course." Leah tried to smile, but she didn't think the result was great.

"Well, then, behave and be a good girl, and you'll have a lovely, happy life. It's quite easy."

Right. Except for the part where Leah would regret living if by any chance she were pregnant. Unless... could a kiss get someone pregnant? No, that would ruin a girl. It was something Fel had avoided. He had left her room so that nothing compromising would happen between them, so she couldn't have gotten pregnant. He had seemed so respectful, so... It was better not to think about him, or that little glimpse of happiness would only make her current reality even gloomier. This reality where the next day he'd forgotten about Leah and had wished her good luck with her marriage prospects. Eerily similar to the story her mother had told her. The story Leah had thought would never happen to her. Yet here she was, the Iron Citadel looking more and more immense by the minute.

When they approached it, she realized that the castle wasn't circled by a moat, but by a circular cliff, which also looked man made. It didn't look so much like a hill from this distance, as she could see columns and sharp angles in that gigantic castle. A humongous bridge led to the front gate. Leah shivered, noticing that the bridge had no foundations. Instead, it stood suspended in nothingness, and a fall from that height would be deadly. Of course the bridge wasn't going to fall, or it wouldn't still be standing. But Leah avoided looking out the window as they crossed it, her stomach feeling cold and hollow.

Lady Celia had an amused smile. "Scared of heights?"

"A little," Leah croaked.

"We're getting there. Make the right choices, uh? I truly, truly want us to get along."

"That's also my wish," Leah lied.

She wanted to toss that woman from the bridge. In fact, she was wondering if it would be terrible if the bridge broke. Leah didn't want to die, but she wouldn't mind seeing her husband and grandmother-in-law dead. Wild. She hadn't spent a day with them and was already wishing them dead. Those were bad thoughts. Death wasn't something for humans to decide or to wish. She knew that. And maybe all she wanted was to get out of this place, and then nobody would need to get hurt. Especially her.

The carriage stopped, and Leah shivered, now dreading what she was about to face. But then, perhaps it would be fine, perhaps it had been just a stern warning to scare her, perhaps she wasn't going to be hurt or threatened anymore.

Venard was the first one out. He helped his grandmother out of the carriage, and only then extended his arm to Leah, who took it. In such little time, her feelings for him had turned from indifference and some curiosity to disgust and revulsion. But holding his arm wasn't going to kill her.

Two rows of guards wearing gray uniforms lined the way until the main door of the castle. Quite an exaggerated door, as if they were expecting a giant to visit or something. The thought amused her, and Leah figured that if she found little things to laugh about, she could survive until she found a way to go back home.

Venard's two older brothers were there too, waiting for them. Leah recalled her cousin Mariana, who wished she could marry Cassius, the eldest. Sometimes not getting what you wanted was a blessing, and she wished Mariana knew that.

Walking in that path surrounded by guards made her feel threatened again. Or maybe she was overreacting. Again, perhaps it would be fine from now on.

When they were almost reaching that humongous door, a girl came running towards them. She had reddish blond hair and was dressed like a noble. Leah's first thought was that it was some family member who missed Venard or the other brothers, but her face was in tears.

"Venard!" the girl yelled. "It's true, then? You're married? What about us? What about everything you told me?"

Leah felt him stiffening beside her, and was taken by pity of the girl. She wished they could make a deal right then, and let her marry him, if she liked him so much. Let *her* be tortured by his grandmother. His grandmother, who muttered, "Venard."

Leah flinched, having heard that tone twice now. Such a quiet voice, such a harmless word carrying the threat of violence. Venard stiffened even more, and stared at the girl.

Oh, no, Leah didn't want to see her getting hurt, getting beaten. What were they going to do to the poor girl?

The answer came quickly. The girl was wearing a gold chain around her neck, and, in a quick motion, it strangled the girl, who fell down, her face turning purple.

"No!" Leah screamed, then, by instinct, tried to reach out for the fallen girl, wanting to take that chain from her, wanting to do something... even if it was too late, even if the girl was already dead.

Instead she felt two guards grabbing her by the arms, dragging her inside the castle. Hear ears were ringing and everything was blurry. This couldn't be real, but it wasn't one of her dreams. She knew it even if she couldn't try to cross her hands, with her arms being held like that, as she was being dragged like a prisoner. Would they put her in a cell, in a dungeon? Would they hurt her?

The halls here had granite floors and wooden walls, meaning that it wasn't the entire castle that was made of metal. Metal, like the girl's necklace. The girl who likely once had loved Venard, who was Leah's husband. She wished her mother were here, she wished she could ask her if it was possible to make it work with a cold-blooded murderer. Somebody then put a blindfold on Leah and the only reason it didn't make her more scared was that she was probably as scared as she could be.

Leah felt as if she was somewhere moving up, then she was pushed some more, and heard a door closing.

"You can take the blindfold off." Venard's voice, which now felt as if maggots were crawling into her ear.

But Leah did what she'd been told, and was astonished to find herself in a completely pink room. Walls, ceiling, chandelier, rug, bed, beddings, tables, chairs. Her breath paused for a moment, that awful feeling of anticipation as she found Venard staring at her, hatred in his eyes.

He pulled her, then his lips were by her ear. "Do what I tell you, or else I'll make you," he whispered. "Scream now. Yell for me to stop."

Leah truly didn't understand what he was saying. "What?"

"They expect me to punish you for your insubordination. And I will if I have to. I won't if you help me. Now scream, or I'll make you."

The message was clear. The memory of the trip back here, of being hit, then bound, then seeing that young woman murdered all came to her mind at once, and came out in a horrifying scream.

There was a glint of delight in Venard's eyes, as if he enjoyed it. "More," he said.

Leah was nauseous. The idea that she was living with a family that expected him to hurt her was horrific. She yelled again, as tears ran down her eyes.

He nodded. "A little more." He then gave his back to her and kicked a drawer chest. Not only kicked it, but took out a drawer and threw it against a wall. Perhaps it was to make some noise, but then, there was real anger there. He glared at her, and then she started yelling all the words she could come up with. *Please, stop, don't. Please.* And perhaps part of it was true. What she meant was "please let me go back home." "Please nightmare, end." And yet her screams just echoed on the walls, hopefully crossed them, to be heard by some sadistic loony in the hallway. Her new "family."

Fel stared at Arry, standing across from him in the fort vault. This was a room that could double up as a deposit and as a safety chamber for royalty, but the floor was just packed earth, and it was large enough to allow magic practice and, most importantly, wrestling.

That was what Fel was doing. He'd chosen such a secluded place because he wasn't using any magic and wasn't that comfortable being seen without hands by strangers.

His friend had his light brown hair in a ponytail, and stood still, staring at him, both of them waiting for an opening. Sweat was dripping down Fel's neck, even if he had also pulled his hair up, as they'd been at this for over an hour.

Arry tried to trip him, but Fel ended up with the advantage and tossed his friend on the floor.

"Ouch," Arry grimaced. "You're gonna end up killing me like that."

"Not quite. Another round?"

Arry sat and put a hand up. "Give me a break. I need to catch my breath, you know? And why are you so worked up?"

Fel shrugged. "The same. If ever my magic fails I need to be ready. Even if it doesn't, I mean... And it's good exercise." Good to make him stop thinking, stop feeling, stop remembering. Good for him to leave Frostlake and the gathering behind him.

"*Great* exercise." Arry rolled his eyes. "So much that I'm exhausted. And hungry."

"You could have to face an enemy in those conditions. If you want you can try to sleep choke me, then I'll leave you alone for a while." It was a technique to make the enemy unconscious for a couple minutes, but Fel himself hesitated trying it because he feared he could do something wrong.

Arry starred at Fel. "You still haven't said anything, but I know something's wrong. What is it?"

"What's wrong with practicing?"

His friend kept staring at him. "What is it?"

Using his magic, Fel pulled his hands, which had been lying on the ground, then crossed his arms. "I say it's nothing, it's nothing."

Arry was thoughtful, then said, "It's a girl." He scratched his chin. "I know it is. You were there with all the fancy princesses. One of them stole your heart."

Fel chuckled and looked away. "Not quite."

"You think you can fool me?"

The more he avoided the topic, the worse it would get. Arry would not leave him alone, would tease him, would insist... Fel decided to tell him the truth. "Maybe. Yes. I met someone. And then she married another prince. Happy?"

Arry stared at him for a moment. "Sorry. I..."

"Nevermind." Fel shook his head. "I just don't want to talk about it."

If only stopping thinking about it were as easy.

15
THE WOODS

S trange dream. No deaths, blood, or any sinister creature, and it only increased Leah's dread at what new horror she was about to face. She was in a green meadow by a river. Everything too green, too bright, too pretty. And no sign of her dragon in the sky. Agonizing absence.

She then heard a voice behind her, a girl, asking, "But why?"

Leah turned and thought she knew the speaker, and yet she couldn't remember from where. She was with a young man she also knew, and yet somehow they didn't fit anywhere in her memory.

They were sitting on the grass and he held her hand. "Serine, please. There are bigger things at play: politics, family. I'd rather not involve you in any of that."

She looked down, but didn't pull her hand. "With you it's promises and promises. All idle words."

He kissed her cheek. "What about this?" She had a small smile, but still looked displeased. He caressed her hair. "And I love you."

"Words again." She laughed bitterly.

"But I do. Still, love and marriage are not the same. Love is love, it's us together. Marriage, when you're a prince, it's about power. It's something else."

"You said you'd marry me."

"Maybe. One day. I don't know. Not now. It can't be now."

She plucked some grass from the ground, then looked at him. "I'm not going to be your other woman, I won't."

"You'll always be the only one. Can you trust me?" The girl looked down. He kissed her neck and asked again, this time in a whisper, "Can you trust me?"

Leah thought the girl would push him away, but instead she kissed him back, as if a kiss could quiet her fears, quench her worries, as if she kissed him long enough he would marry her. But then perhaps it was just that she wanted this moment, she wanted him.

The couple was now lying on the grass, his hands trailing down her body, then lifting her skirt. Would that count as "ruining" a woman? But Fel had told her the clothes had to come off. If he had been saying the truth.

Leah couldn't look away, even if she knew she should, even if she knew it was an intimate moment, not for her eyes. Was this what happened when a marriage was consummated? But they were not married. And yet here they were, his hands caressing her legs, moving up, up. Leah swallowed as she realized that some of the girl's clothes—and his—were now coming off. And yet she didn't deem it scandalous or immoral. Instead, she wondered what it would be like to feel it, to be this close to someone, not for duty, not as part of a marriage. She wondered what it would be like to be that close to Isofel. Had she let him stay in her bedroom that night, had she been ruined, perhaps she wouldn't be married now.

Married. The truth hit her like a rock—and then she recognized the young man—and the girl. He was Venard, and Serine was the girl he'd murdered. Heavy clouds appeared in the sky, and the scene changed. The girl was no longer living, but a corpse, pale and slightly bluish, her face purple.

Leah finally had to turn away. She didn't even have time to catch her breath when Serine, or rather, her corpse, appeared in front of her.

"You. You killed me." She wrapped her cold hands around Leah's neck.

Leah wanted to scream, yell, knew this wasn't real and yet couldn't stop it. But she would suffocate if she remained there. She had to wake up. Wake up, wake up. If only she could explain to the girl, explain none of this was her fault, explain that this was a horrible mistake, a horrible situation, and if anything, they were both victims. No. Not victim. Leah wanted to be a survivor, wanted to see the Ironholds pay for that.

Hatred did it. Leah woke up, her own hands around her throat. She'd been strangling herself? It didn't make sense. Her father had always told her that the dead could not harm the living, and that dreams couldn't harm her.

She got up, adjusting her eyes to the light coming from the window and the extreme pinkness of the room. There was a full-body mirror on a wall, and she stared at herself. Her neck was already bruising. It had been real. Horrifyingly real. And this: this room, this life, was real too.

The first feeling that overwhelmed her was hunger. Incredible. Her life was falling apart, and here her stomach wanted something so basic, so normal. But she was starving. They hadn't given her anything to eat, and Venard had left right after that fake beating that had been humiliating nonetheless. Were they planning on starving her? No. She knew the answer. Getting food would likely involve more humiliation.

Why had this happened? Her mother had told her it would be fine. Even her father had approved this. He'd been friends with King Harold. Hadn't he noticed anything strange about the Ironhold family? Couldn't he have investigated them some more?

Leah had trusted her parents, trusted their advice. For what? She sighed. Getting upset at her family wasn't going to solve her problem. They likely had no idea about what was happening, and could not have predicted that the Ironholds would be sadistic monsters. If they had known, things would have been different.

That was what Leah had to do: tell her parents. But how? She was pretty sure that every step she took was being watched. Well, not really. She was alone now. And had to use her opportunity.

NAIA WAS ALONE in her bed, unsure for how long she had slept, unsure even how she had gotten here. Her bed. That was an interesting way to call this bed in this strange house. Perhaps it meant she was ready to accept she belonged here.

Her first thought was to call River, but that would make him feel too important. She got up and went down the stairs, where she found food set on the table. Again there was bread, cakes, juice—but no River. The upside was that she wasn't going to starve. The downside? She felt like a pet. Yes, Naia was hungry. But she was hungry for explanations, for information, which she hadn't gotten much.

She tried to recall the previous day, tried to recall why she hadn't insisted on knowing more, then all the memories came to her like a dam being broken. His kisses, the feel of his hands on her legs, and all that want. Want that kept wanting. But now, in the morning, it felt wrong, as if she'd been ready to give River everything in exchange for so little. And yet being with him had felt good, almost as if his kisses could lull her into forgetting she still didn't trust him—but it felt so good being lulled into obliviousness.

There was a note on the table:

I'll be back soon. You'll be in my thoughts all day long.

She felt a flutter in her stomach. But then, perhaps he could lie in writing. Oh, why was she second-guessing everything he did? It would drive her crazy. She was going crazy and confused, but she knew the solution.

Her decision had been made the moment he'd told her not to go into the woods. Perhaps one day, if she wanted someone to do something really badly, she'd tell them not to do it.

The forest had the answers, she knew it, and she wasn't afraid of getting lost or getting hurt, used to spending days and days in the woods surrounding her manor. But then, she'd had a knife and her bow and arrows. Her father's words came to her, clear as if he'd been standing beside her: "Always carry a weapon when going into the woods. You never know what creature you might encounter."

The memory of his words made her heart heavy, now remembering him telling her she was no longer his daughter. But he had never listened to her! She didn't want to become Fel's advisor. And yet it hurt all the same to know she would never be able to turn to him for advice, for a laugh, for a game of cards. Well, he was the one who had chosen to disregard her choice. But it hurt. At least she still had her brother, too good for this world, too good for his sister. And it was true that he would be a better king than her. It didn't mean it didn't annoy her, as much as she loved her twin with all her heart.

But she had to stop getting sad because of her family, and get ready instead. She took a look at the house and found no bow and arrows, but she found two knives, which she strapped to her belt, then went outside. It wasn't perfect, but it was something. And having some metal with her always made her feel more at ease. Silver knives.

Sometimes she wondered why her magic was not called silverbringing or even goldbringing, since they could manipulate these metals as well. But then, perhaps it had been because of the war against the fae, their magic being the deadliest against them. Deadly. She shuddered as she remembered River disappearing after her first kiss. The fact that she had hurt him was hard to bear, the mere thought that she could have killed him. Perhaps she didn't trust him fully, but the idea of seeing him hurt got her all cold inside. Some strong feelings for a fae who had dumped her in this house like a bird or something. Not a bird, as at least it could fly.

So much nonsense. What she had to do was find out his secrets, and she was sure they would be in these woods—or beyond them.

The vegetation was thick and dense, not only with trees but also with bushes and thick undergrowth, but she found a way to step in anyway, soon finding herself under a closed canopy which made the forest dark and foreboding. One thing that made her uneasy was the silence—despite all the greenery, it was as if the forest were dead. No birds, rodents, or much of anything in here.

She felt an odd, slight dizziness for a while, but then it passed, and she realized she didn't want to be here. No, she wanted to go back to her cozy, little house. There was nothing in this forest, nothing.

Naia turned around and went back, then found herself in her kitchen, holding a knife, not even sure if she had really stepped out or imagined it, unsure why she had left. No, there had been a reason, there had been. There was something she needed to find out, somewhere she needed to go. What was it?

LEAH WAS glad that her room had paper and ink, but her heart was racing. She wrote a note relating the trip here, saying she was well and that the castle was beautiful, but there was a secret inside. Some letters were slightly taller than the others, forming the sentence: *I'm in danger. Help me return home.*

Home, home, home, even if she wasn't allowed much company, even if she couldn't read everything she wanted, felt like a dream right now. Her parents *had* made a mistake. Yes, marrying someone you didn't know could work—but it could also be a disaster. It was like tossing up a coin—and Leah had been unlucky. As much as her mother believed that the important thing was to make the marriage work after the wedding, there was a limit to what could be worked on.

Perhaps even Fel would have been a bad idea, considering how little she knew him. That if he hadn't shunned her, of course—which only proved he wasn't right for her, but what a bitter proof. And crazy-dream-Leah thinking she wanted to let him ruin her? Ugh. Him, who didn't deserve her? Well, still better than Venard.

It was as if she conjured her husband, as he opened the door and entered—without even knocking. And then her dream came to her so clearly, her vision of him and the girl, Serine, his sweet words to her, and then her strangled body. He had either loved or lied to her, then killed her as easily as someone tosses an old boot.

He stared at Leah up and down. "How are you?"

"Hungry."

He nodded. "I thought so." His eyes then focused on her neck. "What's that?"

Strangling hands from her dream, or from a dead girl, who knew? But she wasn't going to tell him any of that. "Making it... realistic."

"True. Good call." He frowned. "It's just... No. Yes. Good

idea. Anyway, my grandmother wants to know if you'll behave. To sit for breakfast with us."

Leah wanted to snort, roll her eyes, but it wasn't worth it. She just asked, "What do you think?"

"I'm saying. If you're pleasant, she'll be pleasant too."

"Venard, are you serious when you say you're my friend?'

"Haven't you noticed it?"

"I mean, can I ask you a question? Or will you punish me if it's not something you want to hear?"

He shrugged. "Between us, ask anything. Between us."

Of course. Not in front of his sadistic family. "Serine," she said, and watched as his eyes widened. "How could you kill her like that?"

There was a dark shadow in his eyes and he clenched his fists. "It was her fault. Her fault. She shouldn't have done that, shouldn't. Her fault."

"Did you like her?"

He paced around the room. "What difference does it make?" The words were being spat in anger, even if he wasn't shouting. "If I had refused, if I had tried to protect her, do you think she would have made it out alive?" He faced Leah, his face contorted in anger. "Do you think you'll miss her more than me? Do you think you have any right to condemn me? Do you?"

"No." Her voice was almost a whisper. She wondered if he could eventually be an ally, since he didn't seem happy that Serine was dead. But still, he'd been so cold about it. "I'm sorry," she added, just because he looked as if about to snap at any moment and she wanted to appease him.

He shook his head. "It was unfortunate." There was sadness in his eyes, though.

"Are you upset? At your grandmother?"

He glared at her. "Of course not. It was Serine's fault. All Serine's. If only..." He sighed. "My grandmother might seem...

difficult. But it's for our own good. You'll see. Just make sure you don't step out of line, and she'll be like a mother to you. I'm sure you'll start to like her."

Leah decided that he was definitely not right in the head. Since she didn't want to argue with crazy, she made an effort to fake a smile. "I hope so."

"Yes." He nodded. "Me too. You'll be part of our family."

A chill ran down her spine. And then another chill, as she remembered what she was about to do.

"Here." She handed him the note, her hand slightly trembling. "My parents asked me to write to them once I arrived."

He raised an eyebrow, took the note, then unfolded it, read it, then folded it again. "I'm sure you'll soon be able to talk to them through the distance mirrors."

"I know." By soon he meant whenever they believed she was submissive enough or something. "But for now, I don't want my parents to worry. If any communication is sent to Frostlake, perhaps you could send this as well?"

He nodded, then put the note in his pocket. "Fair. I'll have it sent as soon as I can."

She exhaled, relieved that he was going to take care of it. Her father would notice her message, she was sure he would. He had never meant for things to be this way.

Venard was staring at her. "So, do you want to eat or not?"

"What are the rules?"

He thought for a moment. "Look down, don't speak to anyone unless spoken to, don't contradict anyone." She had asked it partly in jest, but he was serious about it. He then smiled. "You'll be fine. I'm sure they'll all love you despite our rough start."

"Venard. A girl was murdered in front of me. I would call it worse than rough."

"It could have been rougher." His tone was friendly, but she didn't miss the implicit threat in his words.

But it was true that he wasn't as bad as the rest, and she didn't want to change that. "Thank you. For sparing me." Those words sounded awful. Thanking someone for having a minimum amount of decency was bizarre, but if she wanted to survive this place, she had to dance to their song, and shouldn't cross her only partial ally here.

"I'm your friend, Leah. I'll always protect you when I can."

She nodded, knowing that he would also kill her if his family told him to do it. "I hope you'll always be able to."

He shook his head and offered her his arm. "There's nothing for you to worry about."

His arm reminded her of the dream, the arms around Serine, then Serine's corpse. She shuddered, but took it, and they left the room. One thing she realized was that he had probably been planning to keep the girl as a lover. Leah didn't even care. Worrying about that sounded so petty in comparison to fearing being beaten into submission, fearing being killed. Perhaps that was why they did it: to make her scared and compliant. Her only solace was that she would leave this place soon, then none of this would matter.

But they wouldn't kill her. At least not yet. She had the key to a kingdom. And yet, that didn't mean they wouldn't hurt her.

Blindfolded the night before, she hadn't seen this part of the castle. A short hall led her to an atrium with an interior balcony. They were high up. Her first thought was that a fall from that height would be deadly. Venard led her to an iron box, closed a grated door, and then they started to move down.

"What's this?"

"An elevator. Don't worry, it has cables holding it. But it needs an ironbringer to move it."

"Why not just use the stairs?"

"There are none. That way we make sure only people authorized by our family can come up here. It makes it safe."

Leah was almost asking how she would move about when she had no metal magic, but realized the question was stupid before it came out of her mouth. That was the point: her room was a prison, and unless she learned to climb really well, there was no getting out of there. Only an ironbringer could move the cage up and down. Fel. Yes, she was going insane now. He'd never come anywhere near here, and even if he did, it wouldn't be to save her.

She had to smarten up. Now. She turned to Venard and smiled. "That's amazing."

"Isn't it?" He seemed satisfied.

Leah was starting to think that he truly believed she was going to get along with his family and everything would be wonderful. Something wrong with his head, for sure.

They stopped a couple floors below where Leah's room was, then walked to a large silver door, which two guards opened. Somewhat silly to have them open it, if it was made of metal, but she didn't say anything.

Beyond the doors was a large room, all beige, with huge chandeliers and a table long enough that it could fit some sixty people. Large windows on both sides illuminated it. At the edge of the table was Lady Celia, and Leah had to refrain from shuddering. Beside her was the middle brother, Silas. Across from them was the crown prince, Cassius. Leah almost shuddered again remembering that her cousin had been hoping to marry him. At least she had escaped. Unless there were more cruel people in the world, unless marriage was a prison from which there was no escape.

But those were some unwelcome thoughts, when she had to act nice and friendly and oh, so happy to be part of that lovely family.

They sat her across from Lady Celia, between Cassius and Venard.

The woman smiled at her. "How did you sleep?"

Leah was staring at her plate and glanced at Lady Celia. "Very well."

"Feeling calmer than yesterday?"

"Much calmer."

The woman stared at Leah's bruised neck and had a satisfied smile. "That's great to hear. Now I bet you must be hungry." She snapped her fingers. "Servers."

From a side door, three young women brought trays with bread, cuts of meat, fruit, cakes, pastries, and cheese. Leah was going to avoid the pastries this time, even if she'd love to puke on these people.

She took bread, cheese, a slice of beef, and a glass of tea. She made an effort to bite and chew slowly so as not to look like a starved wild animal, even if she was starved. But she got a second serving and a third serving, ignoring the intent eyes on her.

"Got a good appetite?" Celia commented.

Leah swallowed quickly, so as not to speak with her mouth full, and smiled. "These are delicious, that's all." That, and spending so long without food, but she wasn't going to mention that.

The woman took a deep breath. "I was thinking you'd like to send a word to your parents, wouldn't you?"

Leah froze. No, there was no reason to panic, she didn't know about her note. She nodded. "Yes. Of course."

"She wrote a note already," Venard said, then took it from his pocket.

Cold, so much cold inside her. No, it should be fine, the code was very subtle, nobody would notice it. Hopefully.

"Let me see that," Celia took the note and unfolded it. She tilted her head and looked at it. "So lovely. She finds our castle beautiful, had a pleasant trip, and has a beautiful, pink bedroom. That's such a harmless note." She was smiling, but there was something chilling about her tone. Then she glared at Leah. "Why, then, are you so pale?"

Quick, quick, she had to come up with something. "Afraid you'll find some offense in what I wrote." Her voice came out clipped and strained. Well, she was afraid.

Celia frowned. "Oh, but you look so guilty. Something doesn't make sense."

"It's... been stressful."

"Stressful? We've received you in our family, despite your shame, and you dare complain?"

"No, it's—"

"Do not interrupt me." The woman glared at her, but then she smiled. "But now I'm curious. What's in this note? A secret message? You need to tell me, girl, or I'll be wondering until the rest of my days."

Celia glanced at Venard, then her eyes traveled to his brother. "Cassius. Encourage her."

He pulled her hand, then pressed something hot on it. A butter knife. It was getting hotter and hotter—and burning her.

Leah felt Venard restraining her other hand. She tried to pull the hand being burned, but the prince's grip was too strong.

"Stop! Please!"

Celia glared at her. "Say what you did."

"No—" She couldn't stand the pain anymore. "I wrote a code. Stop."

The woman nodded to Cassius, who removed the knife, but kept holding her hand. She needed to put something cold on it, as she felt it burning.

"What code?" the woman asked.

Leah felt the knife close to her skin. "Slightly bigger letters.

I just want to go home, that's all." Tears were pricking down her eyes. Tears for the pain, for the hope lost, for her fear, and yet she was trying to hold them back. "Let me put something cold on my hand."

Celia frowned. "Oh. You think you can demand anything?"

"Please!"

The woman now eyed her with disgust. "Girl. You don't get to ask anything. And you don't get to choose where to go. You're married now. Your choices are no longer your own."

Leah kept her face neutral, as if she were indeed listening and paying attention, as if any of that made any sense.

Celia then looked at the note carefully. No, no, no. Now Leah would never again be able to use that code for her parents. The woman shook her head. "I'm in danger? Danger of what? You're being well treated here. You must have been really spoiled if you can't stand some mild scolding. You want to upset your parents, is that what you want? You want to break our alliance? Do you realize what it would entail? Or are you still a little child, unaware of your responsibilities?"

Anger. So much anger bubbling up inside her. And yet anything she did would only make them hurt her even more. "I meant no offense."

"No offense! You wanted to lie to your parents that you're being mistreated. For what? Missing your dolls?"

"Missing not being burned."

"Cassius."

Oh, no. He pressed the knife against the back of her wrist. It didn't burn as much yet.

"Will you hold your tongue?" Celia asked.

"Yes."

The woman nodded, and the prince lifted the knife.

The woman shook her head. "Just a little scolding. You know why? To put you in line. To make you a good wife, a good queen, a good mother."

Oh, yes, being inflicted physical punishment would make her a wonderful mother. But they wanted her to be humble, so she was going to act humble. "I understand."

"Do you? Really?"

"Yes. I'm starting to understand."

"Let's hope that's the case. I think you need to cool off a little. Guards!" The two men walked in. "Escort her to the calming room." She turned to Cassius. "Take her."

Leah didn't resist or complain or anything. They grabbed her two arms, blindfolded her, and took her away. Her hand was throbbing. She felt that they took the lifting cage again, and descended—a lot. When the blindfold was removed, she was in a room with white walls, floor, and ceiling, some faint sunlight coming from a small, high, round window.

They closed the door and left her there. Alone. This was some kind of cell. Not as bad as she had expected. Nowhere to sit or lie down other than the floor, but at least she wasn't anywhere near those princes or that woman. Those princes. Her dear husband and alleged "friend" hadn't said a word during the whole ordeal. He'd probably have burned her hand had his grandmother asked him to. Leah wished she could tell that to her mother, tell her that it wasn't always possible to make it work.

But more than yelling at her mother, she wanted to see her again, wanted a hug. Leah had to return home. The issue was how. It wasn't going to be easy. But there had to be a way.

16
ATTACK

Fel had checked the weapons and they were actually advancing on the wooden catapult. It felt good to feel useful, to be doing something. He'd missed his friend, missed being here—but he also missed his sister, and worried about what was happening to her. And he also missed Leah, which was absolutely ridiculous. He couldn't miss someone who'd never been his friend—or anything, really. But he felt uneasy and worried about her, which was again ridiculous. She was probably happy with her two-handed, perfect husband.

And then there was someone else Fel was worried about—his father. He was still home, just a short ride away. As much as Fel would like to remain in the fort focusing on planning for who knows what threat, trying to forget all memories from the gathering, from Frostlake, he decided it was better to go back home and check on his father.

The sun was already setting when Fel crossed the huge iron gate and headed back to his manor. He never took the main road, but a more discreet path, sheltered from view by treetops.

As he rode, he kept feeling an unrelenting anguish that wouldn't leave his chest. He was still thinking about Leah, still worried about her. All nonsense, of course. So much nonsense, nonsense like his father had warned him against. He was *worried* about Leah? That was laughable. Even if the Ironholds were evil, she was going to become part of that family. Perhaps she and her lovely husband would sit on a throne and share a sinister laugh about all the kingdoms they conquered. Her choice had been clear, and Fel had nothing to do with that.

And then there was something else, a strange presence in the forest. Not an animal. He stopped and listened—then ducked, as an arrow flew past him, right above his head. Another arrow flew below him, from the opposite direction, and his horse reared. Shit, no. They got Flip's leg.

Fel dismounted and sent his horse away before he got hit again for something that wasn't his fault. But now he was alone, carrying just a sword, without even a shield, and there were at least two archers targeting him. At least he could sense where they were just by feeling how they disturbed the forest.

Fel didn't even have time to unglove his hands as he sent each of them towards the direction from where the arrows had come, while at the same time ducking a third arrow.

Three attackers surrounded him, not two. This was an ambush, there was no question about it, and no time for him to wonder who could be behind it or what their motives were. All he could do was focus all his senses into finding his attackers.

One of his hands found one person and was now strangling them. Their bow and arrows fell from a tree, then the person jumped. The other hand... he could no longer feel it. Another arrow came from that direction, but Fel had already hidden behind a tree, taking cover from the two archers who were still shooting. He ran, to give some distance, and heard steps behind him. They were coming for him, two of them. No, three, as the one who had fallen from the tree somehow had managed to get up.

Fel pulled his sword using his magic and sent it flying in the direction of the first one coming. The weapon met some resistance, then he heard a grunt, pulled back the sword, and sent it toward the second attacker, but then, again, he could no longer feel the sword, as if it had disintegrated or something.

Four daggers came in his direction. Iron daggers. Easy. He turned them around, two towards each assailant who was still standing. He felt one of them hitting an attacker, one missing, but then he lost the two other daggers. One attacker was messing with his magic—and now getting close, a strange dagger in his hand. A wooden dagger. Sneaky. He had medium skin and brown hair, and could be from any kingdom, even from Umbraar.

Fel managed to pull back one of his hands, but the other was lost, as if it had dissolved into the environment or maybe it was just too far. He formed a fist with the hand he could reach, and sent it towards the man running towards him, who stopped and smiled. Fel watched in horror as the man stared at his hand, and it got hotter and hotter, standing still in the air. The man was an ironbringer. Fel shoved down all the questions that this information raised, and took the opportunity to kick a rock towards the man. It hit his shoulder, but with little damage. Meanwhile, Fel's hand had melted and fallen to the ground.

"Ooooh." The man mock-pouted. "Not fun to play when you're not the only one with the tricks." His accent was neutral Alurian, but if he was an ironbringer, it wasn't hard to guess where he was from.

"Just go. And I'll spare your life," Fel said.

The man laughed. "You? Really?" He frowned and

pretended to be thoughtful. "How is that going to work? Without a sword? Without... hands."

Fel had considered negotiating, proposing to pay more than whoever had hired them, but that was always a risky thing to do. And now he was pissed that the man was mocking him, as if Fel were lesser than anyone, and he wasn't. "If you want to die today, it's your choice."

The man rolled his eyes, which only made Fel even angrier. No. This was wrong. Feelings had no place in a fight. He could get angry later. Now was the time to think; think clearly and find an opening. There was always an opening if one cared to see. But he needed time. The man stood still watching him, perhaps also observing, also strategizing.

"I give up." Fel raised his arms. "What do you want?"

"Your life, fake ironbringer."

"Surely there are more things you want."

He shrugged. "They don't matter right now."

Then another man came running, the first archer who had almost been strangled. Fel's compassion was going to be his doom, considering he should have killed him while he could.

As both of them advanced on Fel, he tried to reach for any metal, any iron... The only thing he found were small nails on both men's boots, keeping the soles in place. He ripped them out and poked their feet, then kicked a twig and hit the ironbringer on the head, and kicked the other man, but it didn't do much to hurt them. The nails were gone now, even if the men's shoes were ruined, which hindered their walking. Fel could perhaps take the opportunity and run now, but that would leave both assailants alive and prone to return, perhaps with more help. He had to fight. But how?

His moment of indecision cost him dearly, as the ironbringer jumped on him and managed to push him to the ground. Fel felt his back hitting the hard edge of a rock, sharp pain coursing through him, but the worst was seeing a sharp wooden dagger aimed at his face.

Naia still didn't understand what was bothering her. Everything was lovely and colorful in this house. Perhaps it was just that it missed more warmth and life, and yet she felt calm, at peace—except for something nagging her on the back of her mind.

Her days in Umbraar had been spent studying, training her magic, or walking in the woods. The woods—she missed them. Naia glanced out the window. There was a forest surrounding the house, but it wasn't the same. Something about it wasn't appealing.

But looking outside gave her an idea. She walked out, glad to see that there was an area paved with stones. Perfect for training her fire magic, which was something she always liked to do for at least one hour a day.

She lit two flames and turned them into balls of fire, which she was planning to circle around her, but then a memory came to her so fast that it even startled her.

The woods. River's secrets. She wasn't here to do nothing all day; she was here to find out his secrets, and she knew the woods were the key. How could she have forgotten it?

She even still had a knife strapped to her belt. What had she been thinking? That she was carrying it in case a steak appeared by surprise? No. She hadn't been thinking—but now she was.

With firm steps, she ventured into those dark woods.

· · ·

Naia found herself in her kitchen, unsure of what was bothering her. There was something she wanted, something... Oh, she knew. Some more apple juice.

This would be the moment when Fel should see his life pass by in a flash, but instead his mind was whirling, trying to come up with an idea on how to defeat these two men, especially the one above him, ready to stab him with a wooden dagger. His magic still called to him, as if it had a will, a desire to act, and it was searching, searching. Then he felt some metal, faint but close, dissolved...

He'd never done that, had never done anything even remotely close to that, and had no idea if it was possible, but he reached for the iron moving within the men, within their veins—and pulled it all out at once.

Fel closed his eyes, trembling, as the men collapsed, dead, then he got up quickly and ran toward where the other attacker had been hit with the sword. The man was lying on the ground, still alive, but with a pool of blood forming around him. Fel kneeled beside him, at enough distance to be safe. "Tell me who sent you and why, and I'll spare you."

The man had a bitter laugh. "You think my life is worth it if I fail, fake ironbringer?"

"Everyone's life is worth it. I'm sure you're just following orders."

The man shook his head and closed his eyes. Something blue tainted his lips. Poison. He'd been truly afraid of surviving his failure.

Fel was still trembling, still horrified at what he'd done, but he didn't want to lower his guard, as there could be more attackers. And indeed, he felt another presence, this time in front of him. But there was nobody, or at least nobody he could see—at first. After a few seconds, Fel finally saw someone materializing out of thin air: Naia's fae friend.

The fae had his hands up, as if surrendering, but his teasing smirk was anything but scared or humble. "Don't murder me with my own blood. I'm here to help."

Fel couldn't believe him. "You want to help me *now*? After I almost got killed?"

"No." The fae frowned. "I got here a while ago, but didn't want to interrupt your impressive display."

"Murder is impressive?"

"Martial prowess is always something to be admired. It might be sad and violent, but there's beauty in it. You're quite impressive." His admiration sounded genuine, which only made him weirder in Fel's eyes.

"Are you interested in me or my sister?"

From playful, the fae's face became serious. "How dare you? I've got a loyal heart. And it's Naia's." He sounded offended. Truly. Being offended for that was stupid, but being so insistent on his devotion for his sister was something Fel could get behind.

He smiled. "It was a joke."

The fae frowned, thinking. "A joke. Aren't human jokes supposed to be funny?"

Fel sighed. "It was a bad and stupid joke, all right? And nonsensical. Forgive me. Now, what are you doing here and what do you want other than admiring senseless violence?"

"I don't know why you're angry at me."

"Maybe because you stood there and didn't raise a finger, now you're trying to claim you're here to help me."

"Peace, human. You don't want to owe a fae a life debt. You should be glad I didn't intervene."

Fel shook his head. "And how did you even know I was going to be..." A memory came to him from the ball. "Hang on. I saw you. With the Ironholds. Which doesn't make any sense. Are you behind this?"

"I gave my word to Naia I would protect you. Sending assassins doesn't sound like protecting, does it?"

Maybe. And if that fae wanted him dead, he wouldn't be standing here talking. But Fel still had tons of questions. "What are you doing with the Ironholds?"

"Information. Information is always good, isn't it?"

"But how can you even... Aren't you, uh, allergic to iron and metal magic?"

"If iron magic hurt me, I wouldn't be able to get close to your sister, would I?"

"Maybe it depends how close." And this was not something he wanted to imagine.

The fae shook his head. "Iron doesn't hurt me."

"Oh." Fel had always thought that the metal hurt the fae, then he remembered what he had just done. "But it makes sense, otherwise your blood—"

"Blood is different. When iron is dissolved into something living, like a green leaf or earth, it's different, it doesn't hurt us."

"So does iron hurt you or not?"

The fae shrugged. "Doesn't hurt *me*."

He probably meant that it hurt other fae but not him, and that was quite useful information. "Great. Go get a shovel, then."

River sneered. "You dare give me an order?"

"You're the one who said you were here to help. Well, then help."

The fae stared at him for a long while, then disappeared. Fel wasn't sure if he was going to return, didn't understand why he was here, and was still rattled because of the attack— and what his magic had done.

"Here," the fae said, now standing behind Fel—with an iron shovel.

"Thanks."

River's eyes glinted. "Your thankfulness is appreciated."

"It's always good to have help offered freely," Fel said, before the fae got any ideas about some debt or another insanity. He then moved the shovel with his magic and started digging a grave. So many questions going through his mind. "If blood is different, and I know it is, how did my magic affect it?"

"Magic is not precise. It's living, breathing, evolving. It grows with you and changes."

Fel glanced at the two men he had killed with their blood, but then glanced back, still horrified, and turned to River. "Since you're so helpful today, and since you watched the fight, do you have any idea where they are from?"

The fae shrugged. "One of them is an ironbringer. What's to wonder?"

"A lot. I mean, he's not part of the royal family, and yet... He could be from anywhere, like me and my sister."

River shook his head. "They're from Ironhold, and it's not hard to guess why they want you dead, is it?"

"So many possibilities. I have to pick one?"

"Imagine if you were counting on your unique magic to bend other kingdoms into submission. Having someone else out there with the same magic would be a problem, wouldn't it? Not to mention that an ironbringer could cause serious damage to their castle, for example. They can't have that."

It made sense. A lot of sense. "But then... Naia would also be a target."

"Exactly." River smirked. "And this is the part where you should realize what a genius I am, making sure your sister is safe at a time like this. Aren't you happy about that?"

"They can't get to where she is?"

The fae shook his head. "No. She's completely safe."

"Well, knowing we would be targets implies previous knowledge, which doesn't improve my trust in you."

The fae shrugged. "I'm not big on trust anyway. That's why we make deals—and don't lie."

"So you say. Is your name even River?"

"It is."

"And you don't have a last name."

"You can call me River Annoying."

Fel rolled his eyes. "Fascinating. And what does the illustrious River Annoying want? I'm sure you're here for a reason."

"First was to keep you safe."

"Your help was impressive, *River*." He didn't hide the derision in the way he said his name.

"I'm glad you liked it. I want a deal."

"I'm listening."

The fae then stared at the shovel, now digging the second grave, and frowned. "You're going to do it all with your magic?"

"As opposed to what? Using my *bare hands*?" Fel raised his arms. He was wearing long sleeves, as always, but it was still obvious that his hands were gone.

"Right," River blinked. "Anyway, they sent three men. What do you think will happen when they find out they failed?"

"They'll send more." It was obvious. But there were things he didn't understand. "But how did they even get to Umbraar? I mean, the portals are closed."

"You do realize there are other ways to travel, right? They could have gone through the woods. Getting here is not that big of an issue. The thing is... if you don't do something, this won't stop, and eventually you won't be able to save yourself."

"What do you care?"

"I don't, actually, now that you asked." River tilted his head. "But your sister does. And she asked me to make sure you're safe. So here I am. But see, I can't be everywhere at once, so I want you to make my job easier."

"Do you expect me to hide?"

"Kind of." The amused expression was back on his face. "Pretend you're dead. Make your father announce it. The Ironholds are arrogant, and they won't suspect that their henchmen failed."

"Won't they notice they didn't come back?"

"Committing a crime is easy. Escaping is hard. I don't think they care."

"But one of them is an ironbringer. It has to be someone related to the royal family or something. Do you know anything about it?"

There was a slight hardness in River's reddish eyes. "I'm not here to give you information on Ironhold. I'm here to ask you to pretend you're dead, so that they won't bother you again."

"Won't they try to find Naia?"

"Say you're both dead. Puff. Easy. Problem temporarily solved."

"What do I get if I do that?" Fel knew that fae liked bargains, and he wanted to take advantage of that. "If I announce that I'm dead?"

River stared at his nails, which were ugly and dark. Goodness, how could Naia stand those fingers with those disgusting things? Well, probably better than no fingernails—or fingers. Depressing thought.

"Well, your sister, we... I want to marry her. Truly. But I want to give her some time to think if that's what she really wants. To get to know me. If you pretend you're dead, I'll guarantee she'll keep her... virtue, like you say."

Oh, gross, he couldn't be meaning to make a deal involving that kind of thing. "Naia will always be virtuous no matter what she does, and you can't be such a creep to want to make a deal of that."

"Yes, always virtuous, I agree. We don't use these words, I was just trying to speak the way your kind does. Do you want details on what I won't do?"

Again, gross. "No, no. But I trust your honor. Didn't you say your heart belonged to her?"

"It's not the only part."

"Spare me. I don't want to hear it. Don't want to know anything about it. I'm not making deals on your respect for my sister. If I thought I had to do such a thing, you'd be dead already."

The fae laughed. "You think it would be that easy?"

A day before, Fel would perhaps have had his doubts, but after what he'd just done... "I do, River. It *is* that easy to kill you."

River glanced quickly at the two men's bodies. "Fair, fair. So you'll pretend you're dead because it's a good idea, right?"

"No. I still want a deal."

"What do you want?"

It was that anguish still speaking to him, even if it made no sense. "Do you go to Ironhold sometimes? Do you have any influence there?"

"I'm not going to answer."

Fel chuckled. "You realize that counts as a yes, right?"

River frowned.

Still somewhat in disbelief about what he was going to ask, Fel was unable to stop himself. "Anyway, one of their princes just got married. Leandra is his wife. I... if she needs... I..." He wasn't sure what to say.

River had an amused smile. "Oh, you love her."

"I hate her."

The fae tilted his head, as if genuinely curious. "How does it work when you lie to yourself? Do you actually believe it?"

"Nobody's lying. But I want you to help her."

"Help? The only help she can get is if I get her out of that place." He looked up. "It's... a little difficult. The deal would need to be—"

"No, no. She's probably happy with her Ironhold husband. I mean, I don't know." It had been her choice, and she was probably fine. Fel knew that, and knew that his anxiety was nonsensical. And yet. He bit his lip. "Let's say war breaks. Let's say Ironhold is attacked. I doubt it, but let's assume that could happen. I mean in a life-or-death situation. Save her." The pleading in his voice surprised even him.

"The girl you hate. Right." River was thoughtful. "The problem is that I can't be everywhere at once. I can't protect everyone."

"Do what you can. It's... probably nonsense. You probably won't need to do anything."

"But in a life and death situation, if I can, I will save this Leandra. In exchange, you'll agree to disappear. State you're dead."

"I'll ask my father to do that."

"Indeed." River rolled his eyes. "I wasn't expecting you to communicate it personally."

"And treat my sister well. But no deal for that. It's your duty."

He shrugged. "Not asking for any deal."

Actually, he had asked for a deal involving Naia, but Fel was going to pretend he had never heard it. He did have an important question. "Do you love her?"

"Love is a strange, wild thing, isn't it? It gets caged in such a little word."

Fel didn't like that. At all. "Evading a question counts as a *no*."

"Then you clearly don't understand us, do you?"

"Never claimed to do. Still counts as a no. What do you want with Naia?"

"Keep her safe, for one. Which I was under the impression we agreed."

Fel sighed. There wasn't much he could do in regard to that. He still wished he could change his sister's mind, but then, River was here, apparently doing something he'd promised her, stating clearly that his heart belonged to her. And yet, not saying he loved her. And then, hanging out with the Ironholds. It was a puzzle.

"Fair. Now, for me, I appreciate the amount of looking you did today." Fel rolled his eyes. "Quite helpful. But if the fae or Ironhold attack, I'll be in the frontline defending my people, so your efforts will be fruitless."

River's face was impassive. "Live one day at a time, or a few days at a time. Makes sense."

"Are they going to attack? Your people? Ironhold?"

"I don't know why you ask. I saw you preparing wooden weapons. I think you already have your answer. My advice: keep it up."

That was a confirmation. "Well, Ironhold, after our refusal in having their forces, I think it's a matter of when. The fae... Are your people back?"

River again stared at his horrible nails. "This is quite a complex question, for an answer that wouldn't be satisfactory. Just pretend you're dead for now. The future takes care of itself."

"No, it doesn't." Fel was going to say *you have to plan for it*, but something got his attention.

It was as if darkness settled at once, then a disconcerting quietness hit the forest, after a brief rustle, when the wood creatures had hidden as fast as they could, as if to escape a predator. Fel could feel a growing threat coming in his direction.

River smirked. "My cue to leave. We have a deal, Isofel." He then disappeared.

Alone, sensing the disquiet in the forest, Fel turned—and saw his father galloping fast in his direction. He must have seen Flip arriving, hurt.

His father slowed down when he saw him, and that sense of growing threat started to dissolve. It had been a hint of his magic: deadly, powerful, terrorizing. Strong enough to disturb the forest and cast fear for a long distance around him. Death-bringer magic.

"What happened?" his father asked.

"A lot."

He wasn't going to mention River—at least not yet. He didn't want to make his father angrier than he already was, and didn't want him coming to wrong conclusions about the fae. But the rest he had to tell. Difficult times were coming.

17
VOICES

After an hour in that room, Leah's teeth were chattering, her hands and feet cold. The place wasn't freezing, but it was cool enough that being there for a long while got uncomfortable.

The floor was granite, so that if she sat or lay down, she'd get even colder. But standing there was exhausting, so she was sitting, alternating positions so as not to get any part of her body too cold. What was the Ironholds' plan? To make her hate them? She didn't understand the point of it. Fine, maybe they wanted her meek and pliable, but she couldn't believe that their strategy was the best. Then again, maybe they were just sadistic.

A sound caught her attention, like a strong wind blowing, but it made no sense that she would hear it all of a sudden like that. Well, maybe there was some piping or something amplifying it. But it was like a voice. It sounded as if it was calling her name. Perhaps she was hearing things. But what if... what if the dead were trying to talk to her? It was possible. The dead. Her magic. Perhaps there was a solution there. Perhaps she should turn to her necromancy.

As she tried to pay attention to any other sound, the lock in the door rattled. Leah got up, unsure what to expect, but it was just Venard, alone. Surprisingly, she felt relieved.

"How are you?" He didn't sound concerned, though.

"What do you think?" It took some effort to take out the bite from her words. Defiance wasn't going to help her here.

He shook his head. "I brought you a salve. For your hand. It will help it heal."

Was she supposed to thank him? For bringing something for a wound his own family had caused? A glance at his face told her that yes, that was what he expected.

"That's very kind," she said, then she caught herself before she rolled her eyes.

He stared at her. "Why did you do that? Am I not treating you well? Don't you have all the comforts you want?" That sounded like a nonsensical joke

"Your brother burned my hand, in case you didn't notice."

"But that was after. You could have caused a diplomatic issue. Why would you do that?"

Why? He didn't understand why? She wasn't sure if he was oblivious, dumb, or just truly thought it was all normal. Leah pushed down her anger. "I want to go home, that's all. I don't want to cause any trouble."

"And we will. You're just visiting. You know that." He sounded as if he were calming down a child or something. "Once everyone trusts you, once you get to know us, we'll go back to Frostlake. That was the deal, wasn't it? But you're not helping it."

"Well, it's not acceptable to leave me without food, to burn me, to want to hear me yelling. It's not normal. Can't you see?"

He stared at her and sighed. "There are many types of normal. That's why you're here; to get used to our ways. You're making it seem much worse than it is, truly."

There was no way she'd make him understand, and there

was no point. "Perhaps you're right." No, he was absolutely wrong, but she wasn't going to say it. She wanted to remain on his good side, even if it wasn't that great. For now. "I... I would like to ask something."

"Yes?"

She was about to make up a colorful lie and hoped he bought it. "In Frostlake, my family, especially my father and I, we worship the dead. And it keeps us from being sick, because of our magic." She wasn't even sure if what she was saying was making any sense, but kept on. "From time to time, I need to be near the dead."

He frowned. "Like in a cemetery?"

"A mortuary would be better. Before they're buried."

"Because it's not creepy at all."

"I'm a necromancer. What were you expecting?"

He paused, then said, "This isn't another trick, is it? Please don't tell me you are going to raise the dead and try something stupid."

"We can't *raise* the dead. And I'm not going to do anything. I just need... the energy of death, otherwise I feel weak, I can get sick." Perhaps this was the wrong thing to say, as she wasn't sure if they cared if she was weak or not.

"I'll see what I can do."

"You'll check with your grandmother."

"Once she's in a good mood, and once she has forgotten your offense, yes."

"If your grandmother had asked you to chop off one of my fingers you'd do it, wouldn't you? Without even blinking."

He looked at her for a moment. "No. I think I'd blink."

THE SKY WAS GETTING red when Naia walked outside to practice her fire magic. Strange how she hadn't done this earlier. The day had passed in a blur, much faster than it should have, which was odd. And then there was that feeling that she was forgetting something. But what?

Although she was pretty sure she could control her magic in an enclosed space, she always practiced outdoors. Her father's voice still rang in her ears: "You're going to burn down the house!" Exaggeration. That said, she probably *could* burn down the house—just not by accident.

And yet even if her father wasn't here, she was still walking outside. It was true that it was better to have more room and no flammable objects around her. Her plan was to practice her wall of fire, as she wanted to learn how to keep it steady for longer periods. Her magic *was* awesome—even if nobody seemed to notice it. Except her brother, of course, the broken-hearted brother she'd left behind. No, they'll see each other soon, she knew it. And Fel was tough—or at least she hoped so.

There was no point dwelling on that. She took a deep breath, then felt that familiar, thrilling feel of the magic running through her, as if it had life and will and was excited to be freed, then she raised her hands. At these times she always recalled her brother's voice telling her she didn't need to use her hands to perform magic, and that it gave away her next moves, but she couldn't help it. Easy for him to say hands were not needed. Or maybe hard. That had been a mean thought. She didn't want to worry about her brother, and focused back on her magic.

The moment she lit her first flame, a flood of memories came to her. Memories of that day. She *had* tried to check the woods. Twice. And had forgotten. Either the woods were enchanted or else River had done something, placed some kind of magical barrier to prevent her from going there. Prick. A thousand times prick. Unless it was the woods, not him.

Naia wanted to clear this matter right away, but rushing in

again, especially in the darkening hours, would be reckless. What she had to do was plan better. She'd write herself reminders, so that if she returned, she'd remember what she had tried to do. She would also make sure she was alert when stepping in. There was something in those woods, and it was something being hidden from her, probably on purpose. If it was River messing with her mind, she would be furious. But why would he do such a thing? Why. Stupid question. Because he was keeping secrets from her.

Right as those thoughts crossed her mind, he appeared in front of her.

He must have noticed the flash of anger in her eyes, as his playful smile was replaced by a curious expression. "Your delight in seeing me is touching."

Naia wanted to smack his beautiful head, but that wasn't likely to give her answers. Or was it? She considered it for a second, then decided to pretend she didn't know anything. That way she could try to garner some information from him tonight and then investigate the woods tomorrow, and he wouldn't try anything else to prevent her from going. She smiled. "You startled me."

He looked at her and her surroundings, as if trying to find something, then asked, "Were you just standing outside?"

"I was practicing some magic."

"Really? Show me."

A smile lit his face. That was an incredibly annoying smile, as it made something inside her stir, as it did something to her heart. Why was he so beautiful? Naia wanted to be focused, not light-headed. That said, she would be glad to show him her magic.

She raised her hands, obviously aware that the movement was unnecessary, while River looked at her, curious.

Then she unleashed a wall of fire around him, close enough that he should feel its heat. Well, she was angry.

He didn't flinch or cower, but rather looked amused. After a few seconds, she extinguished all the fire at once, just because it was more dramatic.

River managed to look impressed. "That's amazing, Naia. You're so incredibly powerful."

Naia shrugged, unused to compliments like that, unsure if it wasn't empty flattery. "I bet you also have amazing magic. Why don't you show me?"

"You saw a lot of it already."

True, he'd stopped everyone in the ball in Frostlake, he'd brought them here. But learning about his magic was information. "Show me a little more."

He chuckled. "Fine. Here it goes."

A circle of fire, identical to the one she had cast around him, now surrounded her. Amazing. So she couldn't beat him even with the magic she thought was unique to her. "You also have fire?" She did her best to hide the surprise in her voice.

He shook his head. "Touch it. Trust me."

Naia hesitated, but as her hand approached the fire, she noticed that it emitted no heat. When she crossed it, she felt nothing at all. She frowned, confused, then remembered what the fae were known for: trickery. "It's an illusion."

"Yes. No substance or truth to it."

"Interesting, for someone who claims he can't lie."

"I can't lie with *words*."

This was a good reminder. But why? "You want me to trust you even less?"

His illusion disappeared, and he bit his lip. "I want you to know more of who I am." A corner of his lips lifted. "And show off, even though I'm tremendously outmatched here."

Naia rolled her eyes. "Insanely outmatched. I'm so much more powerful than you."

"With fire, absolutely." He took her hand, and her heart leaped, while at the same time that touch felt comforting and familiar as if she'd always known it. Then he led her inside the house. "You know what I was thinking? A picnic."

"In the woods?" She smiled and managed not to show any reaction.

"Oh, no, they're dark. Instead, we'll sit by the house and watch the stars. I'm not really into being indoors, you know?" He was then in the kitchen, opening a cupboard and some jars. "Are you up for it?"

"Sure. How do you know the forest is dark? Have you been there?"

He chuckled. "C'mon. It doesn't take a genius. One glance and you'll see that it's already pitch black."

"We could light some candles."

He was putting some nuts and fruit on a tablecloth. "Then we'll miss the stars." He paused, turned to her, and smiled.

Naia was starting to think that his smile had some magic, because when he looked at her like that, she wanted to forget her doubts, forget the woods, forget that there was some strange magic affecting her memory. It was as if all that mattered was him. That was a strange and scary feeling.

"Is this good?" he pointed at the food he had gathered, his brows furrowed, some slight apprehension on his face as he expected her reply.

Seeds, fruit, and nuts. They were going to eat like birds— or fae. But she wasn't that hungry, considering that the second time she'd returned from the woods, she had made lunch. And it all looked tasty. "Of course."

Soon they were sitting outside, and Naia was nibbling on some grapes, while he was having hefty portions of seeds and nuts. She wondered where he had gotten all that stuff, but she had more important things to ask first.

"I really like hunting, you know?" she said. "In Umbraar, I always brought something for us to eat, from wild pigs to some large rodents."

River's eyes were bright. "I know. Hunter princess. It sounds... exciting." He was either totally missing the point or just pretending to do so.

"I miss hunting. I doubt these woods are so terrible, and if—"

"There's nothing there for you to hunt, Naia. If you need anything, just ask me."

"I'm going to be bored at home!"

"I know. But there are books, and you could practice some magic—"

"How do you know there's nothing in those woods? Have you been there?"

He shrugged. "They're too thick."

"Perhaps I could go and check what's there."

He paused. "I guess. Did you try to go there?"

"Not that I recall." The words had been chosen carefully, and she observed his expression attentively, but he gave nothing away.

"Well, this is not like your Umbraar woods, I'm sorry."

She decided to be more forward with her question. "Is there any magic in this forest?"

"All forests have magic, Naia, it's why they can be so fascinating, why you can go there and sometimes never want to go back."

River was a master at giving non-answers, but she noticed that his reply was not a *no*. She pressed forward again. "You told me not to go there."

"Well, it's closed, dark, and doesn't have wild pigs. I don't think you'd like it." His reddish eyes were on her. "Naia, I know this is not ideal. There are books inside, but I understand this is not like the life you had. This... is not forever. Think about this place as a safe harbor in turbulent times."

"No harbor in Aluria is safe anymore."

His face was wistful, as if recalling a memory. "Yes. But they used to be."

"River, how old are you?" Yes, she realized she was asking this a little too late.

"I don't know. Truly. I was eighteen when I got lost. A lot of time passed, but not for me. Not the same."

"When did you get lost?"

"Some twenty years ago. But I didn't live through these years, I didn't age in these years, so it doesn't count."

"Don't fae live longer?"

"Not that much. Us, at least. I don't know about across the sea. We tend to be healthier, that's all."

Twenty years ago. "You were alive during the war."

"Yes, Naia, I was. Before you get angry at me, please know that I lost many friends, many people I loved."

She wondered if he had lost a girl he had loved, and felt an odd pang of jealousy. "My kingdom lost an entire city."

A cloud crossed his eyes. "I know. But I don't think it was us."

"If not the fae, then who?"

"A natural disaster. Some magical race from the continent. Another human kingdom. Those are my theories."

"What race? Like other fae?"

He shook his head. "Fae are peaceful."

"Then who? Trolls? Dragons?" She wasn't even sure if they existed, but was asking.

"You mean dragon lords." His voice was clipped. "I doubt it was them."

"*Dragon lords?*"

River sighed. "They're magicians from the continent. Apparently they rode dragons. A long time ago."

"Then who?"

His face was strangely serious and thoughtful. "Either us,

but I knew nothing about it, and it doesn't make sense. Or another kingdom."

"Let me guess. Ironhold. Your pals. But why?"

River stared at her. "Not necessarily them. Still, you should know that humans can do despicable things."

"Fae, too. Or Ancients."

"True."

Naia hadn't expected him to agree with that. She lay down on the blanket, but turned to him. "But how... I mean, how are you in Ironhold? I mean, I doubt they'll just take anyone who walks in and then even bring this person to the gathering. Bring them to a ball."

He had a relaxed chuckle. "Oh, Naia. Am I supposed to feel slighted that you're overlooking my irresistible charm?"

She raised an eyebrow. "I know of your charm. But it doesn't explain how Ironhold let you in their circle."

His expression was still playful. "Of course it does."

"And you're not going to tell me."

"You shouldn't worry about that kind of thing."

"You said you'd answer."

He fixed his eyes on her. "When we get married."

"Yes, and now I'm here and you're stalling."

"I'm nice. I'm giving you a chance to change your mind."

"And what if I change my mind now? What if I want to wait at home until you decide whatever you need to do is done?" She didn't want to go home. At least not before figuring out what was in those woods, but she was testing him.

He was peeling a peach with his bare hands. "You made a deal. A deal is a deal."

"But it wasn't fair."

The corner of his lips lifted. "Tip: if you ever make a deal with a fae, and if you think they didn't swindle you, watch out, something even worse is coming."

Naia couldn't believe herself. "Really? You'll keep me here as a prisoner? If I want to go home you won't let me?"

"For a short while. I like you, Naia, I truly do, and you should believe me. You're powerful and sweet, and you have so much kindness and compassion, but it's not naive compassion. There's slyness and strength behind it. You're a force to be reckoned with, and I like it."

She exhaled and rolled her eyes. "Great. Changing the subject."

"Not really, no. I've thought about it. I'd been lost for so long, then there was that light calling me. I didn't understand it at first. Now I think it was you."

"Maybe. When I forget to wash my face my skin does get shiny."

He laughed. "And you? How did you find me?"

A hunch. Something so powerful that had gotten her out of bed. She hadn't given it much thought, but now that he had mentioned it... Still, no way she would confess this. Naia shrugged. "I was out for a walk."

"In the middle of the night."

"Couldn't sleep." Technically, that was true.

"I'm glad you found me, my beautiful savior."

"What about me? Should I be glad I found you?"

"That...will be up to you." He lay down beside her, and reached out for her. "Come here."

She leaned on his chest, hearing his heart beneath his thin tunic. While she still wanted to figure out his secrets, staying away from him wasn't going to change anything. Unless... she recalled the previous night, the feel of his hands against her skin... It was better to forget it for now.

"It's a moonless night," he said. "Beautiful."

There was a brilliant trail of what looked like silvery dust across the sky. "Funny how the dark reveals the light."

"It does." She could feel his chest reverberating with his

voice, such a lovely voice. He continued, "You see those stars? We Ancients believe that each of them has a whole world in it."

"That's a lot of worlds."

His arm wrapped around her, and she couldn't say she didn't like that. "Imagine the possibilities. Sometimes I wonder if there would be a world like ours, but where things had gone differently. For a long time, I wished things had been different, I wished I hadn't ..." He sighed. "Gotten lost. It makes sense, right? But then I wouldn't be here, and it makes me question so much." There was a sad longing in his voice.

"What would you like to be different?"

"Right now? Nothing. This is a perfect moment. And perhaps that's what life is. We think about it as a journey, as where it's leading us. Maybe it goes nowhere. Maybe all it is are all those tiny, perfect moments. At the end of the day, nothing lasts anyway."

"What we leave behind lasts," she said. "Our lineage, our legacy, things we do that are bigger than our lives." Those were her father's words, explaining to her and Fel what being a ruler entailed.

"We can hope it lasts. We don't know if it does." His chest rose and fell in a deep breath. "But this, this is real. For me, at least."

"Despite all your secrets?"

He ran his hand through her hair. "They don't belong to this moment. Don't belong to us. Let me believe that we're bigger than all that, that nothing can shake us, that this is forever. Let tomorrow worry about itself, take care of itself. Worrying now won't change anything."

Naia closed her eyes, taking in his scent, the feeling of being there. "I want this to last, River." She couldn't believe she was opening up that much.

"Then maybe we have a chance."

Perhaps he was right that worrying wouldn't change the future. She was going to check the woods tomorrow, she was going to find out whatever nefarious secret he was keeping. For now, she could enjoy his warmth, his presence, the close sound of his heart beating. For now, she could pretend this moment would last forever.

THE IDEA of being threatening amused Leah. If only it were true. But apparently Ironhold wasn't sure about it, as they had six guards following her. Her request to visit a mortuary had been granted—quite quickly. Too quickly for her taste. Perhaps they wanted to test her. Unfortunately, she wasn't going to attack anyone or do anything impressive. All she was after was some information, a clue, a lead, something... Her only magic was necromancy, so that was what she had to use.

They had walked through long corridors at the base of the castle, arriving to a room where two bodies were being prepared to be buried. Castle workers or guards, she wasn't sure.

There wasn't any smell of decay yet, but the scent of death lingered in the dark room. That smell didn't bother her, instead it brought her memories of holding her father's hand and learning about his magic, of trying to listen to the dead, seeing how he helped poor or rich, noble or servants, anyone who required his assistance. She missed her father, and couldn't believe he had sent her here, had given her to these monsters. *But he didn't know.* Her own thoughts defended him. No time for regrets or resentment. She looked at the two forms under white sheets.

"Who are they?" she asked the female soldier next to her.

"We're not supposed to answer you."

Leah could insist, but in truth it didn't matter that much.

Talk to me, she thought, directing it to the bodies. *If you have something to say, talk to me.* Nothing. Perhaps it had been foolish to think anyone would help her. The dead rarely had any business with the living.

And there was another problem: Leah wasn't that great in necromancy. Sometimes she had lied to her father that she had heard the dead, when she hadn't, just because he was always so satisfied when she performed any necromancy. Perhaps she'd wasted her chance to learn while she could. Still, she kept trying to ask, to plead, to see if any spirit, either of the people on the tables or anyone who'd been there could help her.

"Your highness." A male soldier said. "Your time is over."

Leah sighed. At least it had been worth trying. Then, right when they were walking out of the room, she heard a voice, and it wasn't her imagination. "At night, child. In your dreams."

18
THE ANCIENT CITY

Naia still didn't understand how River always left before she woke up, or how he had brought her to bed. Well, fae were supposed to be stronger than humans, and he had to be. She'd fallen asleep outside, leaning on his chest, as he sang an old, sad song. So much melancholy, but an odd kind of melancholy, like a soothing balm. And that moment, just being close to each other, had felt so good. Naia could get used to this, even used to spending her days alone, as long as she figured out his secrets, as long as it wasn't anything nefarious.

Sometimes people kept secrets thinking it was for the best, sometimes it wasn't with ill intent. She hoped to return to that rain-scented embrace, to look into those strangely beautiful red eyes without fear, without worries. That was why she had to know what lay in those woods—or beyond them.

Naia ate some nuts and fruit, thinking she was about to become a squirrel, then she took some paper and ink and wrote herself a note: *Going into the forest, ten in the morning. Use your fire magic if you don't remember this.*

Her steps were firm as she walked outside. Twice now her

memories had returned when she lit her fire, so she was going to count on her fire magic to help her make it through the enchantment of the woods. If by any chance it didn't work, she would see her note—and then try again, over and over and over until she broke through the magic messing with her memory.

With a flame in her hand and worry in her heart, she stepped out of the clearing and into the trees. She was still aware of what she was doing, still remembered she had to find out what was in here. The vegetation was thick with undergrowth, and the trees blocked the sun shining above them, so that Naia's flame was bright and visible in that semi-darkness. There were no sounds of birds or any other animal, which was very strange. Step after step she moved, small branches and leaves cracking under her boots. She felt no enchantment yet, and figured her fire was keeping it at bay, but she didn't want to quench it and test her theory.

After a few steps, the very air became thicker, and it was hard to walk, as if she had encountered some kind of magical barrier, pushing her back. She increased her flame and pushed through. Then, suddenly, the feeling went away, like when her ears were blocked then unblocked all out of sudden. But what she saw was horrifying.

The trees ahead of her were mangled and dead. She turned, and noticed that everything was also dead behind her. Dead bushes, dead trees, everything dried. Her heart beat faster. It was possible to cross into a land of the dead in the hollow but she didn't think she had the power to travel there. Unless she had deathbringer magic. Still, the living shouldn't venture there, lest they become lost.

Naia took a deep breath. She wasn't going back. Not yet. Not while she still didn't understand what was in here. And if she was using deathbringer magic, she surely could use it to return.

As she stepped forward, the dead forest was left behind. In its place she found hills with dead vegetation, and a dry bed of a stream, which she decided to follow, so as not to get lost. What was this place? Why was it so dry? So dead?

Gloom settled upon her, with the desire to return to that safe, colorful house surrounded by green grass, where she had watched the stars with River. And yet she had to know what was in here, had to understand what this place meant for him —if it even meant anything.

Beyond the hill, she saw a small building. It almost looked as if it had been made naturally, from tree branches that had bent together forming a circular shelter. Still with fire on her palms, she ran to it, her ears alert for any different sound, for any threat. But there was only silence, desolate silence. She glanced back to make sure that the dead stream and the dead woods were still there, then ran towards the building, her heart racing with dread about what she was going to find.

That place had a wooden door with beautiful carvings of flowers. The handle was also carved wood, and she turned it, expecting it to be locked. Instead, the door moved in, revealing a small, low wooden table beside two pallets. She stepped back when she saw what was on them, or rather, who. An old woman and a child, both white fae, with pale blond hair and short horns. She observed them carefully for any movement of breathing. They didn't look dead, but they were so still... There was a slight, slow up-and-down movement in the woman's chest. Perhaps fae breathed more slowly.

Naia closed the door gently, so as to not make any noise, then walked out. All right. So this was a fae settlement, and it made sense, since that was where River had told Naia he'd bring her: to the underworld. Except that it looked as if the clearing was in an isolated part of it. Perhaps he was hiding her. Her fists clenched in anger and she almost let her flame extinguish, but caught herself in time. Imagine if she got lost in this place? Would River even worry? She remembered the previous night. Of course he'd worry. And yet she had that odd bitterness in her mouth.

From where she was, she could see farther down in the valley. There were more small buildings, perhaps houses as well, and, further down, far away, what looked like a gigantic tree surrounded by houses. She took a better look and realized it was not a tree, but a building, a palace. It was just that it was built as if it were a humongous tree trunk with branches.

Naia could return now, knowing what was beyond the woods, knowing what River had wanted to prevent her from seeing, and yet, perhaps she could learn more about this place. She would have to be more careful, as she didn't know what could happen if a fae saw her. Perhaps that was the reason he hadn't wanted her to come here: it was dangerous for her. But she could defend herself. As she thought that, she felt the fire magic pulsing within her, like a reminder of her strength. She was going to check that palace, doing the best to avoid being seen, but she was going there.

RIVER HAD BEEN SEARCHING the Iron Citadel and still couldn't find what he was looking for. Perhaps it wasn't there. Perhaps it had been a silly assumption. So much uncertainty ahead of him. He wished he could spend more time with Naia. Wished. So many wishes. He wished his cousin had never died.

20 years before

River sat in the ceremony hall by Ciara, his favorite among his siblings. It was funny because she had an identical twin, Anelise, but he didn't get along as well with her. Both girls had the typical Ancient look, with pale blond hair and burgundy eyes.

The place was empty now, as everyone had left after the cremation ceremony, which had turned into ash what remained of some of their best warriors.

Meanwhile, their Ancient City was taking in refugees from all over Aluria, coming for the safety of the underworld. But this was a small city, and connected to Mount Prime, which was still being destroyed. Nature here wouldn't survive long with that destruction, and soon there would be no food for anyone, let alone that many fae.

The Ancients' hopes were dimming.

"What I don't understand is why," he said, realizing his voice was strained. "How? How could humans have killed so many of us? They're so weak."

"They're too many." Ciara stared at the pyre, thoughtful. "But we'll figure a way to defeat them." She then turned to River. "You know, they're so violent and greedy, perhaps we shouldn't bother fighting them. Instead, we should just let them all destroy each other." She said it as a joke, but perhaps there could be some truth in it.

But then, given their situation, it wasn't a feasible idea. "It would take too long. Humans. Sometimes I wish they had never come to Aluria."

"You're forgetting we're part human, River."

He ran his hand over his head. "Indeed. So hard for me to remember it." Just his great-grandmother, but it was enough that some of the royal family had dark hair, and enough that River was hornless, which was a first among Ancients.

Ciara took a long, deep breath. "We'll find a way to win this, I'm sure we will."

That was what he most wished: revenge. He hoped to kill as many enemies as possible, but he wondered if that would ever be enough. "And yet it won't bring anyone back. You know what hurts? Kanestar died and I wasn't there."

"Then you wouldn't be here, River. There's no point regretting the past."

He leaned his head on her shoulder. "I just want this to end."

"It will."

But how? He tried to remember what he had studied, and then recalled some of his father's words to his master magician. "Do you believe the dragon lords truly have a staff that could help us counter the iron magic?"

She paused. "If anyone has something like that, it's them. But I don't think it's that easy to find the dragon lords, and even if we did, I doubt they would just hand the staff to us. As to stealing it... How are we even going to find this thing? I doubt it's going to be standing over a sign saying *metal magic defying staff*. How can you steal something when you don't know what it looks like and where it is?"

River was thinking that such a powerful object wouldn't be put away carelessly. "It's probably under high security."

"Exactly." His sister's tone implied that she thought that was an obstacle. For River, the extra security would be the sign pointing to the artifact. She shook her head. "Trying to steal it would be utterly reckless and foolish."

Reckless and foolish. Reckless and foolish—like River.

LEAH HAD an ominous feeling as she stood in a dressing room, watched by Lady Celia, two servants, and Venard's two older brothers. She would have preferred to be thrown into a giant snake's nest, but her preferences hadn't been heard in a while.

This was the dress-maker's room, and there were many patches of fabric in one corner and a circular platform to step on. Slanted sun rays came through three tall windows, from where she could glimpse some of the valley below.

"Venard says you're calmer," Celia said, that voice grating Leah's insides.

"Yes." Leah managed a fake smile. "I'm getting used to Ironhold."

"That's good to know. Now, do you know why we're making you try on a dress?"

"I'd love to know." Reigning in her anger had been hard at first, but she was getting the hang of it. The issue was that it felt like swallowing poison, something bitter, corrosive, and it was getting accumulated inside her, about to turn into something she had no idea what it was.

"A proper wedding party, child. Like you deserve."

Leah had dreamed about her party, her dress, and now she didn't care about any of it. One of the women opened a huge box and took a golden gown.

Lady Celia then said, "Undress, child."

There was a screen on a corner, and Leah moved to that direction, but the old woman stepped in front of her. "Here. There's nothing to be ashamed of."

The thought of being in her undergarments in front of these two princes made her insides freeze. "Can they leave? Or turn around?"

The woman slapped her face. "Who do you think you are to make demands? To give orders to two Ironhold princes? They're here to ensure your safety. Nothing more."

Cassius snickered. His other brother didn't show any reaction, and to be fair, he wasn't even looking at her.

Leah stared straight ahead and told herself that she was alone, that nobody was seeing her. That was the only way she could keep doing this, and yet her hands were trembling as she unlaced the front of her dress, took it off, then waited, wearing only her undergarments. Her throat felt dry and thick, with swallowed tears, swallowed words, swallowed screams.

"What are you waiting for?" Celia said.

"I'm undressed."

"Silly, stupid, girl. We want to examine you. Get everything off."

"What?" the word escaped from her lips, partly in disbelief, partly in horror.

"I'll count to ten. If you still have difficulty understanding what I told you, I'll get the princes to help you."

The princes. Still in the room. As her eyes met Cassius's, he licked his lips.

This was wrong. Awful. "Seven, eight," the woman said.

There was no choice. Leah pulled up her under slip, feeling cold, vulnerable, feeling mortified at having her nipples exposed. She was trembling as she took off her underpants, dread taking over her as she had never felt before. This time she did focus on a random point on the wall. She didn't want to see their faces as they looked at her, their glee as they savored her humiliation.

Celia approached Leah, then turned to the woman beside her. "What do you think?"

"I need to examine her."

The old woman frowned. "What do you think you're here for?"

"Pardon, your highness."

The woman touched Leah's belly, and then Leah almost screamed, as the woman pinched her right breast. "I don't think she's pregnant," the woman said.

"Let me see." Celia groped Leah's boobs. "Probably." She turned to the woman. "Dismissed."

The woman scurried away, her relief clear. The servants here likely had it really hard. Leah pitied them and wished she could do something. Perhaps everyone pitied everyone, but they were all paralyzed in their own fears, feeling threatened in their own way.

The other woman then brought a different under slip, which Leah was glad to put on, and then the dress, which took longer, as it had to be tied carefully on the back. But just not being naked anymore brought her an immense relief.

Celia stared at Leah. "We're all trusting you, girl. We're betting on your honor, so remember that."

So much honor, stripping naked in front of two men. Still, she lowered her head. "I appreciate it."

"Yes. Good girl. We need good, obedient girls like you, you know? And a party to cheer us up. Forgive me if I'm sour today, but I just learned I lost two grandchildren. Horrible, horrible."

Leah felt as if she had swallowed a huge, heavy stone. It couldn't be... No, it wasn't who she feared it was, or else the woman wouldn't even pretend to be upset.

"Yes," Celia continued. "They think I don't care, but I do. They were stolen from me, taken by that ruffian. Not only did he ruin my daughter, he didn't take care of my grandchildren. Now they're dead. Umbraar scum. Should never have touched those kids, after all he had done."

Umbraar. Umbraar. The woman went on, ranting, but Leah couldn't focus anymore. She thought about Fel and Naia, so full of life, so full of love for each other. How? How could that be? And the worst was that she knew she shouldn't dare ask what had happened. Fel hadn't been nice to Leah, but still, why should this happen to him, when Cassius was here, alive? When this woman was still alive?

Leah bottled down her tears and tried to nod on cue, thinking that at least now she had a chance to talk to Fel, if she found a way to use her necromancy. Perhaps she wanted to understand what had happened or perhaps she just wanted one last chance to see him. That was a selfish wish. The dead should be left alone. She knew it. And yet, and yet... Seeing

Isofel once more was too much of a temptation for her not to fall into it.

Naia was careful as she moved towards the fae castle and the city. There were some trees along the way—all dry, without any leaves—and she moved from the shade of a trunk to another, to make sure she had some kind of cover. The flames in her hands were the opposite of conspicuous, but she didn't dare risk quenching them and maybe finding herself lost there.

She found a couple houses like the first one, but they were empty. So far Naia hadn't seen any fae and she was finding it all very strange. The dried stream bed led to a dry riverbed, with bigger buildings by its margins, where she was sure she'd find someone. Then what? Was she going to ask them something? She stopped, thinking. Well, she could try to hear them, try to glimpse something, try to understand who River was and why he was in that isolated area in the underworld. Right. What were the odds that she would stumble on someone talking about him? Still, she had to gather as much information as she could.

She found a big building made of stones, in a dry grove. Some of the trunks were part of the walls, so that the place seemed to belong in nature.

There was no glass on the windows, and she slipped in—and was shocked. She found herself in a large room with a high, domed ceiling. There were some ten long wooden tables in it, with pieces of weapons on them: mostly bows and arrows. This was a place where they built them.

But that wasn't what impressed Naia. What caught her eye was that there were some thirty fae here, all sleeping on the hard stone floor, as if they had all gotten suddenly tired from working and lay down.

There was something bigger going on than just whatever was happening at that first house. Naia observed the sleeping fae. There were men and women, all wearing simple tunics and pants. Some of them had accessories like belts, bracelets, earrings, but overall, they dressed simply. Most of them had very long silvery blond hair, but two of them had ash blond hair, and one had light brown hair, lighter than River's.

Danger be damned. Naia crouched by a worker that was farther from the rest, quenched one of her flames to free a hand, and tapped on his shoulder.

"Hello? Hello?"

His skin was warm like any living person, so he wasn't dead. With a shiver Naia recalled the day she'd found River and how cold he'd been, dreading what could have happened if she hadn't found him. What had made her go out that night? She did not know, but she was glad for it. Even here, trying to find out River's secrets, suspicious of him, she still cared about him. She did, and it would be foolish to deny it.

For now, she wanted to get answers, wanted to understand what was happening. She tapped some more on the fae's shoulder, but he didn't wake up. If the fact that they were all sleeping on the floor hadn't already been a huge hint, now she was certain that this was an enchanted sleep. But then who had attacked the gathering? So strange.

She left that building and ran towards what she thought was the palace, now much less fearful that someone would find her, as she was starting to think that they were all asleep.

And then the question was: why not River? Perhaps he'd been in the hollow when this happened. It made sense. And then, it still didn't explain the fae she'd seen in the ballroom in Frostlake.

Naia didn't know what else she'd find in the palace, but she had the feeling that she had to go there. As she approached it, she saw more and more houses, mostly made of stone.

The area around the palace was a little city with cobbled streets and many square stone houses, surrounded by dry trees.

Naia found a few fae sleeping on the street. This was odd. She wished she could move them somewhere better, but she didn't even know where to move them and how to do it. Well, she could maybe find some large silver tray or something and use it to move them. Too much work. Perhaps River could do it. Perhaps that was what he was doing. Suddenly, she realized that he could catch her here. Oh, well, perhaps that would be good: a chance to confront him directly.

The palace was built of stones, even if the exterior walls were wood. It had large chambers and the main difference from human palaces was that the walls were less polished, and some places on the floor looked like they used to have vegetation. It was as if even the palace wanted to be part of nature. Dead nature. Her stomach churned. Whatever was happening here was a horrible tragedy. She couldn't fathom what River felt seeing this place like this, so dead.

Naia wasn't sure what she was looking for as she wandered through hallways and rooms, crossing sleeping fae here and there, who were dressed in silk and velvet and wore more accessories than the fae outside.

Eventually, she found a large chamber with two large chairs. That had to be the throne room, but it was empty. Naia's attention was drawn to a tapestry behind the chairs. It had to be the royal family. There was a couple wearing bramble crowns: the king and queen. The king had brown hair and brown-red eyes, while the queen had the typical silvery blond hair. Her eyes looked pink in the tapestry. Surrounding them, there were two identical girls, both looking like the queen, and two male fae with blonde hair and red eyes. A part of the tapestry had been burned, and Naia wasn't sure if there had been anyone there or not.

This didn't explain the sleeping. Well, what had she been expecting? Some written account on how this had happened? If anything, there had been no warning, otherwise the fae would have changed clothes and gone to their beds. At least that was what Naia would have done.

Having come here looking for answers, all she had found was an even bigger mystery. Oh, she was going to make River talk, no matter what it took.

19
ASLEEP

Leah was alone in her very bright pink room—again. They didn't even have a servant attending her, perhaps so that she wouldn't complain or that she wouldn't have anyone to talk to.

She wanted to forget the scene from this afternoon, wanted to forget the shame and humiliation of standing undressed in front of two of the princes, but Cassius look still felt like a sticky slime covering her body, even after a bath. The worst part had been crying. Like a silly ten-year-old, Leah had wept on her bed for a long time.

Crying was not going to help; she had to plan, had to think. She had to find a way to contact the dead—and Fel. True, he had rejected her, and yet, the world felt strange without him, as if a bright star had been plucked out of the firmament. Two stars. His sister had been so beautiful, smart, full of life and joy.

Right then, her door opened, bringing Venard, who was smiling, carrying a book under his arms.

"How was the dress fitting?"

She stared at him. She'd considered telling him what had

happened, but what difference would it make? It would just extend her humiliation further than she wished.

Leah shrugged. "Fine."

"I brought something I think you'll like." He extended his hand, showing her a book. *The Wondrous Rufus.* "That is your favorite, isn't it?"

No. Leah enjoyed *The Mighty Rudolf.* That said, perhaps this imitation would be entertaining, and it would be better than being alone with nothing to do. "Thanks."

He looked at her and sighed. "I know not everything has been perfect. But I want you to know that I want this to work." He pointed at the two of them.

Right. His plan had been to have a lover—or more. But Leah didn't want to argue. She just nodded. "Good."

He took her hands, and she hated the feel of his skin against hers. "Soon we'll celebrate our wedding for Ironhold to see. But it's also our chance to try, our chance to make it real, Leah."

"Sure." She stepped back and ran her fingers through her hair, relieved to break contact with him.

He looked at her up and down. "My grandmother doesn't think you're pregnant. I never thought you were, Leah." He smiled. "It's good news for us."

"I guess."

She looked away, hoping he'd get the clue and leave soon. Instead, he touched her face and turned her head so that she'd look back at him. The gesture was gentle, though.

"Leah. Listen to me. We're going back to Frostlake. You know that, right?"

"When?"

He took a moment, then said, "If everything goes well, the day after the wedding."

That soon? In three days? Her heart got lighter and a smile came to her face.

He nodded. "I knew you would like to hear this news, but keep it a secret. It's supposed to be a surprise. I'm looking forward to it as much as you are. Then it will be just us, and you'll be near your family. It will be fine. My grandmother is happy to see your improvement."

She wanted to punch him. *Improvement?* As if she'd been the one causing problems.

He continued, "You're becoming part of the family now."

She sighed. "I'm being kept in this room like a prisoner, Venard. I'm not even getting fed. They're bringing me just salad and fruit."

"But that's for your own good. You don't want to repeat what you did at the wedding in Frostlake, do you?"

"I was nervous."

"Well, eating light will make sure you don't puke."

"Sure. I could faint."

"I'll hold you, then." He smiled and approached her. "I've been wanting to, you know?"

She wasn't sure if he was trying to be seductive. All she knew was that she felt a chill down her spine—the bad kind of chill.

"Fine." She wanted to change the subject, quickly. "Why then am I left in this room? Without even any books?"

He tilted his head, as if confused. "For your safety. Where do you even want to go?"

What kind of stupid question was that? Still, she only said, "The library, for example."

"Tell me which books you want and I'll bring them to you. And you won't be alone anymore. I'll come every night to see you."

"What?"

"What do you mean what? You're not pregnant." He pointed at her belly. "It means you're ready to have a little iron-bringer in there. What do you say?"

She swallowed, feeling cold all over. "I... Can't we wait?"

"I know you're afraid. But I'll be gentle."

No, no, no. The thought of him touching her made her want to retch, even if she hadn't eaten much. She had to postpone, had to find a way out. "We should... get to know each other a little more, don't you think?" She considered mentioning that they had barely kissed, but then feared he'd want to kiss her and the thought was revolting.

He stared into her eyes. There was kindness there. The problem was that he had a screwed-up version of what kindness was. "That's the whole point, Leah. Get to know each other. Grow closer. This will help us."

No, not tonight. Not ever, in fact. She had to find some excuse for now, some way out. "I think we should wait until... until after the wedding party."

He paused. "Technically, we're already married, but... that's fair, I guess. Enjoy then your last nights alone."

Leah was trembling when he left. She sat on the bed and took slow, deep breaths. She knew this would come one day, knew it even when she had told her mother she agreed to marry him. What had she been thinking? It was all well and good for her mother to say that friendship was enough for a marriage, but they would need to... get close. Get their clothes off and then do whatever they had to do. She recalled Cassius staring at her naked body and imagined Venard doing the same while at the same time touching her. So gross. Perhaps she would retch even while half starving.

She had to focus. Had to find a way out. These were small details that didn't matter that much. His words that they would leave to Frostlake soon didn't make that much sense.

If they got there, the first thing she'd want to do would be to order someone to give Venard a good flogging or something. Great, she was turning into Lady Celia. And plus, it wasn't *him* that she wanted to flog.

Perhaps that was what he was counting on; that she didn't like his family but liked him. Perhaps this was even a strategy planned by the Ironholds, to isolate her and make sure he was the only person offering her "kindness". Perhaps they thought she'd be under his control by the time they went to Frostlake. They had to be insane. Insane, yes, sure. On second thought, it actually made a lot of sense.

So if they were thinking she and Venard were getting along well, that would be her key to going home: pretending she liked him. Oh, no. That would mean eventually doing whatever she had to do with him. She took another deep breath. She'd postpone, postpone, postpone—until she couldn't anymore. Then she would be brave.

For now, there was one thing she wanted: to communicate with someone dead from Ironhold that could maybe tell her a secret, something. There should be at least one person who had been wronged, who could use the opportunity for revenge, who could maybe give her some information that could be useful. At first Leah wanted to try to find a way to escape this kingdom, but now that she was about to return home so soon, she wasn't sure if trying to escape was wise. She had also realized that it would be wrong to try to reach Fel— wrong and useless.

Using her dreams to reach the dead was very different from the way her father did necromancy, but she figured her strange, weird nightmares had to be worth something.

That was how she lay down, trying to forget Venard, forget her humiliation, forget the wedding party, forget what would happen after the party, as she wasn't going to go anywhere if her thoughts kept circling her mind.

With slow, deep breaths, she tried to reach her land of dreams—and nightmares. There had to be someone dead around that castle who would want to talk to her. There had to be.

．　．　．

LEAH WAS STANDING on a frozen lake at night.

"Isofel!" she yelled. "Fel!" Her eyes were wet with tears. She had to find him.

A humongous wolf approached her. It wasn't a wolf, as its hair was all mangled and strange, and it had three red, brilliant eyes.

The creature jumped on her and she trembled with the rush of fear—then woke up on her bed, sweating. Why was she trying to find Isofel? She should leave him alone, let him rest. It wasn't as if they'd been anything special when he'd been alive. Still, his death made no sense, it hurt. She didn't even have any idea how he'd died, but it wasn't as if she was going to ask anyone.

But she had to bury all thoughts of him—and try to find some useful information. This was not time for reminiscing, regretting, or even mourning. *Oh, Leah. Focus.*

EVERYTHING WAS DARK AROUND LEAH. Darkness, so much darkness and nothingness.

"Fel!" she yelled.

A pretty girl, no older than fourteen, with brown hair, appeared in front of her. "Who are you looking for?"

"Isofel. The Umbraar prince. Is this... Are the dead here?"

"Take my hand," the girl said.

For some reason, everything in Leah screamed *no*. "Can't I just follow you?"

The girl nodded and pulled back her arm. "Come with me."

"You know where Isofel is?"

The girl was walking ahead of Leah now. "Come with me."

There was something odd about the situation, but Leah

would like to see Isofel one last time, perhaps to say goodbye, perhaps to understand what had happened, perhaps even to yell at him for having rejected her. That was why she followed the girl, and maybe it had been the right call, as soon she was out of that darkness and walking on a rocky path among mountains. There was something gloomy and desolate about that place, but Leah couldn't put her finger on what it was. This mountain range seemed taller than the one in Aluria, so this was somewhere else, probably the place where the dead went. And still, Leah felt that there was something wrong.

"Where are we going?"

"You'll see," the girl replied while still facing straight ahead.

"Are you taking me to Isofel? Is he here?"

The girl stopped and turned. "Why do you wish to see someone who doesn't love you? Someone who never wanted you?"

"That's none of your business. Maybe I want to yell at him." She did want to yell at him, knowing well it wouldn't make any difference, knowing well it wouldn't change anything or change his mind. And still.

The girl had a smirk. "You're such a sad, unloved girl."

"For sure." She didn't roll her eyes because there was no point. "Are you taking me to Isofel?"

"I'll give you something better." The girl then opened her mouth, revealing teeth as sharp as long metal nails, teeth that didn't belong in a human head, which indeed got distorted as the gap where the mouth should be got bigger and bigger.

Leah turned to run back, but felt arms around her.

"Why run?" the girl asked. "I'll end your pain."

This was a dream, and Leah could control it. She pressed her hands together—but they didn't cross. What? That didn't make any sense. This had to be a dream and she was going to leave it now. The arms were now squeezing her. Pain shot through her body as something sharp punched her shoulder. Nothing made sense, and Leah didn't know how to get out of this. Hopefully this wasn't real and she wasn't going to die, even if the pain didn't feel like an illusion.

Leah shut her eyes, dreading the worst, but then the arms and teeth let go of her.

"Be gone." That was another woman's voice.

Leah opened her eyes and saw a beautiful dark-haired woman standing in front of her. The girl—or creature—was no longer there.

Right when Leah was about to thank her, the woman spoke again. "That was foolish, Leah. You should know better than to try to reach the dead."

"You know my name?"

"I do. And we have to leave. Now." She extended her hand, and Leah flinched and stepped back, remembering the girl from earlier.

"Now," the woman repeated. "Unless you want to join your former company."

Well, between someone who had tried to eat her and someone who was apparently saving her, Leah had to pick one. She took the woman's hand.

Soon she was back in that black place, then in her pink room. It was strange to dream about something as ordinary as her room.

"You're safe now, but don't do that again. And don't try to find Isofel. He's not in the land of the dead, and even if he was, you shouldn't try to disturb him."

That meant... "He's not dead?"

The woman paused. "He isn't."

Leah was surprised at the relief she felt. "Thank you. For saving me. For everything."

"I owed your father."

That made a lot of sense, and Leah was touched and

thankful that her father's necromancy had saved her, perhaps even saved her life. "Do you want me to tell him? Thank him?"

She shook her head. "There's no such need."

Leah wanted to ask more, ask what that creature had been, ask how the woman had found her, but she knew that if she was a spirit, her time was very limited, and every second counted.

"Can you tell me your name?"

The woman shook her head. "Such an old, forgotten word. But it's Ticiane."

Ticiane. Names, even forgotten ones, had power, and if it was her real name, it meant she trusted Leah. "Ticiane, can you help me? I think there might be something wrong happening here in Ironhold. Some secret, maybe. Can you tell or show me something? If you can. Or want to." Leah swallowed, wondering if she was being too bold, if she was pushing her luck too much.

The woman had a bitter laugh. "You think? Something wrong in Ironhold? Do you really want to see it?"

"Yes."

"Then trust me." Ticiane went to the window and unlatched it. "We're going this way."

Leah approached her, and had vertigo just looking down. "How?"

"You've flown before, haven't you?"

With Fel. Her heart jolted with the memory. "Not alone."

The woman took Leah's hand. "Come."

Perhaps the wise thing would be to stay in that awful bedroom, but if this was Leah's chance to find anything, she had to take it.

So she took Ticiane's hand—and jumped out the window.

NAIA WAS tired as she reached the woods surrounding River's house. Coming back from the palace had taken much longer than she had expected, her legs getting wobbly now that there was no more curiosity propelling them.

She wasn't angry at River anymore. Well, maybe just a little, as he shouldn't have hidden this from her. Still, she was mostly worried and couldn't imagine how much suffering he was going through. There had to be a connection between that enchantment on his people and whatever he was doing in Ironhold, but she didn't understand what it was. All she knew was that they had to talk.

Her flames were still lit as she crossed the woods back to the clearing. It was odd how that magic wasn't tiring. If anything, she felt more and more energized as she used it. It was as if it took more effort to repress it than to let it flow.

When she stepped out of the woods, she saw River, disheveled, eyes wide.

He rushed to Naia and then enveloped her in his arms, pulling her close.

"Where were you? What happened?" His voice was hoarse, quivering with emotion, his breathing fast.

Naia looked up at him, surprised at his reaction. "I'm fine."

His eyes were misty. "I thought I had lost you."

He cared. He did care. And she wasn't sure what to make of it. "I'm... sorry. I didn't know I was going to take that long."

He ran both his hands over her hair. "Where were you? What happened? Are you all right?"

"I'm fine." She still didn't understand his reaction. "You're truly worried about me?"

He snorted. "What do you think?"

"I..." She wanted to ask if it meant he liked her for real. Funny how she'd come here without knowing, how she still wasn't sure, but then, he kept all these secrets... "I don't know what to think."

"You don't trust me yet." There was no sadness in his eyes or voice, it sounded like a mere observation.

"It's time we changed that, isn't it?"

"Where were you?" he insisted, his voice urgent.

Naia stepped back and smiled. "Let's do this: I'll tell you what happened and you tell me your secrets." She then added, "And we eat, 'cause I'm starving."

He must have seen that she was well, as his expression relaxed. "I definitely agree with eating. Under the stars again? Or do you want us to sit inside, like humans?"

"Under the stars."

He kissed her cheek and hugged her tight. "I'm so glad you're here."

Naia leaned on his touch, and then he kissed her lips, softly at first, then he pulled her even closer for a deep kiss. Why was it always so magical to kiss him?

He stopped abruptly, and chuckled. "You have to stop me, or I'll let you starve."

"Maybe I won't mind it."

"No. I told you I'd take good care of you." He kissed her briefly, then went into the house again.

Naia followed him, her heart fluttering in her chest. Soon they were sitting outside, in silence for a while, as she was busy eating. River ate too, but more slowly, as he kept his attention on her. There was affection in his eyes, a sweet affection that warmed her heart. Perhaps... perhaps she was falling in love with River.

The bread she was holding fell as she came to this realization.

"What?" He chuckled.

"Nothing." She did feel blood rising to her cheeks, but it felt good. She knew that she was close to figuring him out, that they were close to understanding and trusting each other.

His reddish eyes locked on hers. "You look happy."

"Maybe I am."

"Hmm..." He scratched his chin, as if thoughtful, but his tone was playful. "Am I supposed to assume that all this glee is because you're keeping me in suspense?"

"Got a taste of your own medicine?" She chuckled, then recalled his face when she returned. "I really didn't mean to worry you."

He looked away and shook his head. "You have no idea, Naia."

"So you care about me?"

Instead of replying, River glared at her.

She frowned. "What's that face supposed to mean?"

He rolled his eyes. "Really? Really, Naia? You think I don't care about you?"

"It's not normal to keep secrets from the ones you care." There. She was getting to her point.

He snorted. "You should know that it's not true. People keep secrets. All the time. Even from the ones they love."

Did he love her? But she went back to the subject at hand. "But it means they don't trust them."

He shrugged. "Maybe. Maybe not."

"What's beyond the woods?" There. A direct question.

He stared at her for some long seconds, then he took in a sharp breath, surprised. "Were you there?"

"Why? You think you can read my mind now?"

"No. But you're not asking as if you truly want to know what's there, you're asking it like you're daring me to say it. Did you go there? To the Ancient City? How?"

"I didn't know it had a name, but sure, yes, I was in a place with a lot of fae and a city and a palace."

He got up and put both hands on his head. "You went there? How?"

"What's the difference?" She wasn't going to give him his

answers that easily. "And if you were so worried, how come you didn't try to look for me there?"

"Did you see any Ancients? Are they alive? What's happening there?" His tone was urgent, upset. Could it be that *he* hadn't been there? But how?

Naia wanted to tell him everything, but she didn't want to waste her chance to pry some information from him. "Tell me what you're doing in Ironhold."

"Isn't it obvious? I hate them." He lost his cool composure and started yelling. "I want every single one of them dead, ideally after a lot of pain and suffering. I want them gone from this land, I want them forsaken, hated, humiliated. That's what I'm doing!"

It was surprising and even scary to see him enraged like that. And still, she had to keep pushing. "How?" she asked.

"One question for a question, Naia. Are my people alive?"

"Yes. But they're all asleep. You didn't know that? You didn't go there?"

"I can't. I can't go there! I don't know how you did it, but maybe because you're human, or maybe your iron magic undoes the barrier. I don't know."

It wasn't the iron magic, but for some reason she didn't want to tell him. He was so angry and agitated.

"River," her voice was gentle, "I can help you."

"Naia, can't you see? I'm one. One. A single one. Against an evil kingdom with freaky magic."

"You think iron magic is freaky?"

"No. No. Of course not. But they have more magic. They're..." He closed his eyes, then stared at her, but his expression was hard. "Naia, if you start to think, you'll put two and two together."

"I understand you're upset. Truly. But seriously, you don't need to do it alone."

He chuckled and shook his head. "You're not going

anywhere near that forsaken kingdom, you aren't."

"My magic is stronger than you think."

"I don't care. I want you safe."

"Imprisoned?"

His eyes were hard. "If that's what it takes, yes."

Naia hated the look he gave her, hated what he said, but she decided to ignore it because he was so nervous. "Fel could help you."

"Fel?" River snorted. "He has a kingdom and his own skin to protect, Naia. And I doubt he cares about the Ancients."

"Trust me, then. If you don't want me to fight, I won't." That wasn't true, but she didn't want to contradict him when he was so agitated. "But tell me what's happening and what you're planning."

River's eyes were sad, then he hugged her and whispered in her ear. "I do love you, just so you know. But I'm still your people's enemy."

That didn't make sense.

He kissed her cheek, then whispered, "Sleep."

Naia wanted to say something, ask what was going on, but her mouth wouldn't move. Then she leaned against him, unable to stand anymore. Then there was nothing.

Leah stuffed down the scream coming to her as she felt herself falling, falling, falling. She didn't know if a scream would be heard for real, and didn't want to see what would happen. Then she felt a hand pulling her, as she was getting close to the abyss below the castle.

"You have to fly," the woman said.

"I don't have wings."

"Just float. Or we won't get anywhere."

Just float. Sure. Such an easy piece of advice. But this was a dream, and Leah should be able to control it. A dream. Soon she stood in the air as if it was water.

Ticiane nodded. "Follow me. Don't worry, nobody will be able to see you." She then shot up in the air.

Leah tried to imagine she was in the bottom of a deep lake and had to swim up, and that was how she followed the mysterious woman, who stopped at a balcony in the castle. They were still down below the valley level, deep in the abyss around the castle.

A large patio door led to an inside garden. Leah was about to try to open it, but Ticiane stopped her. "Let's not go in. What do you see?"

It wasn't truly a garden, now that she took a better look, and it made sense, considering that this part of the castle didn't get that much sunlight. There was a large room with a fountain and some fake plants around it, illuminated by sconces, leading to two hallways.

"A fake garden."

"Come to the window."

This meant stepping out of the balcony again, and Leah's insides were about to freeze, but she did it. A window showed a room with a large engraved double bed, and a young woman in it. These could be some kind of servant quarters, except that the decoration was too lavish, with paintings on the wall, silks and velvets. Maybe Ironhold treated their servants well? Now that was an idiotic thought. Of course they didn't.

"Who's she?" Leah asked.

"An iron mother. They are handpicked and chosen to come to the castle to bear ironbringers."

Leah tried to think. "Wouldn't their children belong to the royal family?"

Ticiane shook her head. "Not if they're not married to the princes, not if the children aren't recognized."

"Are they... forced to come here?"

"That's an interesting question, Leah. They come from poor families. This is their chance to give them a better life. So you could say they chose this. But between starvation and this, how much choice did they have? Although it is true that at least they're not dragged here against their will, which is surprising for Ironhold standards."

"Why would the Ironholds want illegitimate children?"

"Take my hand."

They were in that oppressing darkness again, then Leah was above a forest and saw a large stone building with an immense courtyard surrounded by high walls. Some kind of fortress.

"They come and train here."

Even though it was night, a group of some six young men were doing something. Leah had to look twice to be sure of what she was seeing, but they were floating metal bars above them. That was an iron magic practice. But the building was so large...

"How many of them are here?"

"Hundreds." Ticiane kept looking at the fortress, some sadness in her voice. "Ironhold has been doing this since shortly after the Fae War. Their first children are becoming adults now. They can pass for normal soldiers."

Leah was still somewhat incredulous as to how they could have birthed so many ironbringers, but the issue was what she recalled from the royal meeting. "If they send ten, twenty of them to each kingdom, these ironbringers could do a lot of damage, even in small numbers."

Ticiane sighed. "I know not of their current plans. Do what you will with this information. Let's go back."

The woman pulled Leah's hand, then they were in that horrible darkness again, then in the pink bedroom.

She stared at Leah with a serious expression. "I helped you, but don't think that's the norm. Never seek the dead. You, of all people, were raised by a necromancer and should know better."

That was true. But then... "I was desperate."

"Don't let desperation take hold of you, or you'll make foolish choices in your worst hours. I saved you—and I showed you Ironhold's secret—out of respect for your father. But I won't come again. If the dead want to speak to you, they'll seek you, not the other way around. Never, ever, the other way around." Her dark brown eyes were set on Leah.

But the woman's words weren't totally true. "Necromancy lets you talk to a dead person."

"When the body has just died, Leah. There's a very small window where it can be done. Again, I shouldn't have to explain this to you. Seeking the dead is foolish and dangerous. Best case scenario you'll get a lost spirit following you, worst case scenario, they'll trap you somewhere. Am I clear?"

"Yes." Indeed. Of course Leah knew all that. And still, her foolishness had gotten her useful information—but she wasn't going to mention that.

Ticiane eyed her for a moment, perhaps to double check that the *yes* had been sincere, then said, "Stay strong. No torment lasts forever. Now try to sleep again, but don't go seeking what you aren't supposed to seek. I'll stay here until you're asleep, just in case."

"Thank you."

Leah lay on her bed, thinking that it was odd to sleep within a dream, but perhaps that was the way to transition back to reality. She missed her dragon, but tonight she wasn't going to try to find anything or anyone anymore.

What she had to do was try to find a way to warn her parents, warn other kingdoms. Perhaps this ironbringer army was meant to defeat the fae. And then perhaps... The little she knew about them made her doubt any chance of good intentions. But what were their intentions?

20

DEATH SAILS

R iver couldn't believe that his magic had worked on Naia, considering there was something different about her, something that had allowed her to cross into the Ancient City. But she had fallen asleep and now he was bringing her to their room.

He watched her peaceful face, thankful that she was so close, that nothing bad had happened to her. There weren't enough words to explain the fear he'd felt. And yet, he had made her sleep.

But what could he have done? He had to be cautious. On one hand, he didn't want her to risk getting hurt, on the other, he couldn't let her sway him from his course.

Some people compared having a big responsibility to carrying a boulder. River felt like he was juggling boulders. There had been a time when he wouldn't have imagined that he'd take on such a burden. A time when he wouldn't have guessed he'd ever be able to take *any* responsibility. He wasn't sure if he missed those days or if he wished he could go back and do things right. But what did it matter now?

20 years before

HARSH, brash, irresponsible. Those were virtues, if one knew how to look at them the right way. River dressed in a simple white shirt and brown linen pants, hoping it made him look human.

The sun was high and most Ancients were asleep at this time, when he tiptoed out of the palace. He hadn't told anyone where he was going, as some tasks were better carried out alone.

"River."

He shuddered at his sister's voice. Ciara was too shrewd for anyone's taste.

"Yes?"

She stared at him with her dark-pink eyes. "I know what you're doing."

He gave her a smile. "If you mean going for a walk, I will say you're very perceptive."

"Spare your verbal knots, brother." She rolled her eyes. "You're going to Fernick to try to find the dragons, to try to find the staff, aren't you?"

"Why do you want to know?"

She shook her head and extended her hand. "Here." On her palm, there were five blue pebbles.

"The lapse stones?" Their grandmother had given them to Ciara before moving on to the afterlife. The issue was that nobody knew what they did. Or maybe nobody knew how to use them. Or, most likely, a silly combination of both.

"If any of us can figure them out, that's you."

River hesitated. "Our grandmother gave them to you."

"And I'm giving them to you now. Take them."

She had made up her mind, and when she did that, it was impossible to contradict her, so River did as he'd been told, and put the pebbles in his pocket.

She took a deep breath. "But please... come back. We'll figure it out, we'll find a way to win this war with or without that staff. Don't risk your life for it. I know you're feeling guilty because of Kanestar, but if you're still here, it's for a reason."

"I'm trying to find the reason, sister. If I'm still here, I might as well do something useful."

"You do know father is planning a mission to collect that staff, right? You don't need to do this."

"Hang on." He stared at her and tried to keep his tone playful. "Do you want me to go or do you want me to stay? Because you don't give someone a magical heirloom if you don't want them to succeed."

"I just want you to be careful. And to come back."

"If everything goes right, I'll be back before our father and the council even agree on whether they should try to send a mission to Fernick or not."

"That's what I'm hoping, that you'll come back. Staff or no staff. Understood?"

River wasn't going to return empty handed, but thankfully his sister wasn't asking for a promise, but for him to tell her he understood her point, which he obviously did. He nodded. "Perfectly."

"And how do you plan to get there? The path in the hollow across the ocean has been lost for generations."

He ran a hand over his head. "Not for humans. Since I can pass for one, I might as well make use of it."

"Humans can't... wait. You're going to take a *boat*?" She said it as if it was the most horrific idea ever. "With the enemy?"

"Tell me you're astonished at my ingenuity."

She snorted. "I know you're smart, River. It runs in the family. Now figure out the lapse stones. And let's hope for the best."

. . .

EVEN IF CIARA had told him to be careful, even if perhaps she didn't trust he'd be able to retrieve the staff, her words had encouraged him. The lapse stones encouraged him. Perhaps they were just pebbles, but it was his family legacy, a strange family heirloom passed on through generations.

With that recently-found confidence, River moved to one of the circles in Umbraar. Fewer and fewer of these passage-ways were available for his people, now that humans were targeting them, but some of them were still intact in kingdoms with extensive forests, like Umbraar. But the fae settlement here had been abandoned recently, everyone retreating back to the safety of the Ancient City.

He didn't have to walk much until he was in the magnifi-cent city of Formosa. Ciara always said it was powered by greed, but it was also beautiful, with cobbled streets and houses on an uneven terrain bordering a huge cliff, as if it was hidden by a huge wall. A wall housing golden turrets, as if the castle had been partly embedded in the rock. All the ships going to Fernick docked here, as it was the center of trade in Aluria.

A lot of gold left this port, thanks to the ironbringers who could sense the metal in the earth. They would destroy anything and everything for gold and precious stones. Perhaps this city *was* powered by greed. It was still untouched by war, which had been raging rather in the kingdoms of Ironhold, Wolfmark, and Wildspring, but it didn't mean Umbraar wasn't sending soldiers and supplies to kill River's people. The thought that everyone there would like to see him dead made the city ugly, but what mattered for him was that it had ships, and one of them could take him across the sea.

Wearing gloves and his hair down, over his ears, the only glamour River needed was in his eyes, and it wasn't that big of a difference. He had considered turning them blue or green, but brown was the easiest—and was practically his real eye color.

Despite having a body of water for a name, River knew nothing about boats. Even then, he found a job in one of them as a guard. He had a sword, after all. A bronze sword, but it might as well have been a wooden sword, considering how much they checked it. In truth, he'd used his persuasive magic to convince the captain. He'd always wondered why his people didn't just come up to some important humans and convince them to quit this silly war. Or slaughter each other. Or something. His grandparents had told him that he could infiltrate the human courts, but it had always annoyed him to think that his strength was in his human looks. Still, now he was taking advantage of it, on his way to the continent, on a hopeless quest.

LEAH WOKE up and knew two things. First, other kingdoms could be in danger, if Ironhold was sending ironbringers to them. Probably not Frostlake, if Leah and Venard were returning so soon. Still, it was something she would need to tell her parents.

Second, Isofel was alive. Alive! Leah was sure it was true, and couldn't keep her heart from leaping in joy. True that him being dead or alive made no difference in her life, but at least she wouldn't need to pity the fool who had rejected her. Yes. That explained why she was so happy.

Perhaps if she hadn't been so taken by Isofel she would have paid more attention to Venard, she would have realized there was something wrong with his family, she would have made a better choice. What choice? His had been the only proposal. It had been all set up. Since the Ironhold king was her father's friend, it was unlikely that her family would oppose the union. And Venard seemed decent when he wasn't near his unhinged grandmother or sadistic brother.

Then there was a third thing in her mind. Venard's request and what would happen after the wedding party. If she thought too much about it she would eventually puke. She knew that she wanted to return to Frostlake as soon as possible, and knew that it would only happen if his family trusted her. That would be a way to gain their trust quickly—unless she could convince him to lie. Maybe. If he was her friend, maybe he would help her.

She got dressed, which was good because soon her husband came in, smiling.

"Excited for your great day?"

"Yes." What was she going to say?

He offered his arm. "Come. You're to have breakfast with us."

Leah trembled, dreading facing his brothers, her hand still hurt from the burn she'd gotten last time. "Are you sure it's necessary?" Her voice quivered.

"It will be fine. Come."

LEAH SAT between Lady Celia and Venard, glad to be away from Cassius, but then he was right across from her. She looked down at the one toast they allowed her to have, and tried not to gobble it too fast, as wasting a perfectly good piece of bread by puking it would be horrible. Then there was whatever punishment the freaks would inflict on her if it happened, which she wasn't looking forward to either.

Leah nodded while Celia lectured about propriety, modesty, and good manners, congratulating her on having acquired them, as if she had been some wild animal that was now being domesticated. Well, an imprisoned animal, a bird with its wings cut, those were some appropriate descriptions to the way she felt in Ironhold.

But apparently, according to them, Leah was learning to behave and become a decent person. That was good to hear, as outrageous as the whole thing was, as her hope of returning home was alight in her heart. If acting like a submissive bootlicker was what it took, Leah was ready to do it. Especially now that she wanted to tell her parents about the ironbringer army. She had to.

Celia put a hand on Leah's arm. "You've been such an adorable, good girl that we have a gift for you. Cassius." Her tone was different, not a threat this time. It was impressive how Leah had gotten good at decoding the woman's inflections.

The prince passed a box to his grandmother. Inside it was a choker gold necklace with encrusted diamonds, a necklace that made her entire body shiver remembering Serine being killed.

"It's lovely." Leah smiled, hoping the fear wasn't audible in her voice.

Cassius smirked. He knew. Venard was eating and pretending he didn't see anything.

Celia stood behind her. "We'll put it on now, as you'll wear it for your wedding, dear."

Leah almost asked if they shouldn't wait until after she put on the dress, but she knew better and remained silent. She swallowed her anger, hurt, revulsion, swallowed all these words that were now living inside her, festering.

One day she would vomit back all these swallowed words, one day she would, even if she kept them all hidden under a smile—for now.

It made no sense for them to try to threaten her into submission. It was like raising a panther. But then, perhaps they trusted that their leash would never break. And indeed they were giving her a collar. She swallowed as the woman fastened the necklace.

"Venard, dear," Celia said. "Come and close this. So it doesn't come off."

What? They were welding it so it wouldn't come off? That would be awfully uncomfortable, not to mention how dirty it would get. It could even hurt her. Perhaps it was just for now. Leah didn't even want to know, all she wanted was to leave that horrid castle and return home.

"Thank you." Leah smiled again.

"Oh, dear, you're a jewel who deserves jewels." Celia smiled as if she really meant the words.

"It looks great." It was Cassius who said it, and Leah stared at her plate. "You know what looks even better?"

She kept staring down, then felt her necklace getting warm.

"Look at me," he said. "I'm talking to you."

She raised her eyes to him, and the warm sensation in the necklace stopped. Cassius took two peaches. "These look better. Look delicious. And I can't wait to try them. And you know why? Because I get everything I want."

He stared straight at her, then licked one of the peaches. She couldn't believe that he was doing that in front of his brother, his grandmother, but then, neither Venard nor Celia were even paying attention.

"Are you going to like it when I try them?" Cassius asked.

Murder and death. Those were the only two thoughts in her mind then. She was going to kill him, no matter what it took.

"Are you?" he insisted.

"Immensely," she blurted. She hoped he'd choke to death.

Cassius smirked, satisfied.

Lady Celia chuckled and addressed the prince. "Since when are you taken with peaches?"

"Since I saw them." He kept his eyes on Leah.

Venard was looking down, oblivious. No, he was too still. He *was* listening. Leah recognized something in him: fear. Like her, he kept his head down and didn't speak unless spoken to. But it was fear that had turned him into a murderer, fear that kept him from changing anything, that kept him from being a decent person.

But then, here she was, accepting humiliation after humiliation in silence. Would she speak up for someone else? All she wanted was to kill them all. If her father saw her now, he'd be disappointed. Well, no. If he knew what was happening, perhaps he'd be the first to kill them. This was the part that Leah didn't understand. How did the Ironholds imagine she would go home and everything would be fine? Unless they were so deranged that they thought the way they were treating her was normal. Well, they *were* deranged, so that likely explained it.

RIVER WAS in the Iron Citadel, profiting from a rare moment when he was unattended. His glamour allowed him to look like a guard, allowing him to move in the castle, and he could go through most doors—not that it was easy, as everything was so well guarded.

He'd been searching, searching, and still wasn't anywhere close to finding what he was looking for. So much on his shoulders. For someone who once had wanted nothing to do with the duties of the kingdom, this was a big change. Perhaps it was a punishment. It *was* a punishment. Nobody should see that much death in their lives. His thoughts moved to the past.

20 years before

THE GOOD PART was that he was on a boat going to Fernick. The bad part was that he was among enemies. The biggest danger wasn't being found out, although it was a possibility. The danger was no longer seeing them as enemies. He knew that it was an illusion. There had been hybrid human and fae villages in some kingdoms, and yet when war had broken out, many Ancients had been killed by their own neighbors. It wasn't something he liked to think about.

River had used his persuasion to avoid doing any work. It wasn't that he was lazy, although, to be fair, he *was* lazy. It was mostly that he didn't know how to do any manual labor and certainly knew nothing about handling a ship. He'd been hired to save them from thieves or any other threat. That, he thought he could do well, as his magic could come in handy.

The ship was called Death Sails. The sea was full of sea-monsters, and the only reason there was a route to the continent was that the Umbraar king traveled here sometimes, spreading his magic, which was strong enough to keep the creatures at bay. Like most Umbraar ships, it was decorated with skulls and other symbols related to death, as they believed it would help keep the monsters away. Hopefully the king's magic wouldn't fail now. While River could definitely defend the ship from some thieves, he was thoroughly unqualified to face a gigantic sea serpent, let alone more than one.

While he'd been diligently avoiding work, he hadn't managed to skip the card games in the quarters. He'd gotten the hang of them easily, and it was the third night he was sitting with Keller and Antonio. The bizarre part? He was starting to like the men. Keller was about sixty-five years old, his fair skin weathered from the sun. He had a wide smile despite having two of his front teeth missing, and spent a lot of his time working on a small wooden figurine, a little doll for his granddaughter, who lived in Formosa.

Antonio was twenty-five, and had dark brown skin and

black hair. Soon to be married, he often talked about his fiancee to the point the other men were teasing him. River didn't mind it. In fact, he saw something captivating in the man's eyes full of hopes and dreams. Simple dreams, as if one person could hold them all.

When asked about his past, River told them he was an orphan and pretended there were only painful memories that he wanted to forget. The men didn't seem to care much, as it gave them more time to talk about themselves. That was how he was playing another game of dead king in the crew cabin.

"Say, lad." Keller laughed, showing the gaps in his teeth. "You lied to the captain to get this job." He took a long sip of his rum.

Well, no. River couldn't lie. But they couldn't know that. Or that he had indeed deceived the captain. He chuckled. "Did I?"

"Aye. I doubt you ever saw any action with that sword of yours. If anything, I think it's a toy."

River shrugged. "I can defend the ship. But you're free to doubt me. I actually hope I never have to prove my worth in combat."

"Hmm." The old man stared at him. "You're younger than my son. Not even a beard yet. You aren't even eighteen, are you?"

"I'm eighteen. But the captain never asked my age."

"Keller, shush it," Antonio said. "You keep talking about having to save us, you're going to attract danger. The lad is fine. Just too fancy, that's all."

Fancy? River had dressed to look like a dock or ship worker.

Antonio added, "Must have been raised by some noble. They do have free time to learn to wield swords, don't they?" He turned to River. "It's fine if you don't want to talk about it."

He definitely didn't. And the man had gotten awfully close to the truth. River had been drinking rum, dressed in simple linen clothes, wearing his hair all messy to cover his ears, and they still thought he'd been raised by a noble? His disguise was definitely shitty.

Keller still stared at him. "You remind me of my son."

"Everyone does when you're drunk, old man." Antonio laughed.

"True. I just... I thought there was so much more to life. Kept chasing empty dreams in the sea. Meanwhile, my son grew up, and you know what I am? A lonely old man whose only son won't talk to him."

"You have your granddaughter," River reminded him.

"Hopefully." He looked down.

The old man had been trying to communicate with her and was going to bring her gifts from his trip. Older people's regrets were regrets to pay attention to. They had lived enough that eventually they turned back to what truly mattered. In the man's case, it was his family, the family he had ignored his entire life.

River thought about the man's regret over his son and his own relationship with his father. Perhaps River could have cared more, but caring was dangerous. When you cared, you could get hurt. It was so much easier to pretend he didn't want anything to do with his father's expectations. So much easier than letting him down. The realization surprised him.

"Your eyes are *red?*" Keller asked.

Shit. River had lost hold over the glamour for a second, but he fixed it. "What?"

"For a moment I thought your eyes were red, like those evil fae."

River shifted, but smiled. "You're definitely getting drunk."

The man squinted. "We never see your ears, lad."

Antonio snorted. "Stop with the nonsense. If he were fae, we'd all be dead by now."

River pulled up his hair in a bun, first having glamoured

his ears. "There. Happy?" He was going to pull up his hair more often during the day, as the last thing he wanted was for someone to get curious and check him while he slept. He had no glamour while asleep, but with his eyes closed and his hair over the ears, with strands carefully stuck to them, nobody would find out what he was.

Keller looked away. "I'll be happy when I give my little Janet the figurine."

So much pain in his voice. River tried to console him. "I think it's the intention that counts. That you want to be close to her." His own words sounded odd. River had been dodging any and all responsibility related to the kingdom and causing a rift between him and his father. He had never considered if just the intention of helping could have been enough. He'd never considered if he could have been enough.

Antonio then said, "I'll be happy when I'm married." He turned to River. "What about you? When will you be happy?"

"When the war is over." There had been no hesitation in his words. It was indeed what he most wished.

Keller nodded. "Aye, lad. That, too."

Like him, they just wanted the war to end, just wanted their lives to go back to normal. Most people probably wanted the same. And then, if fae and human all wanted the war to end, why was it still raging?

Well, Mount Prime was still being destroyed, and humans gave no sign that they'd ever leave it, despite all the Ancients' pleas. It was humans' greed, destroying everything in their path. And yet humans were also like Keller and Antonio, who just wanted to love and be loved.

"Also," Antonio then added, "I've heard some things. It's... a rumor, but makes sense. The Umbraar king could find that hidden city of the white fae."

River stiffened. The Ancient City was getting overcrowded, as they were receiving Ancients from all over Aluria, and they were not warriors, but regular men, women, and even some children. But Umbraar royals had what they called death-bringer magic, allowing them to move through time and space, to walk through the hollow. They could eventually find even a hidden fae city.

"What would that accomplish?" River's voice came out harsher than intended.

Antonio shrugged. "Then they can't hide."

"That makes no sense." River tried to sound calmer and not that invested in the subject, but wasn't sure he managed it. "If you think they're dangerous, wouldn't you *want* them to remain hidden?"

"Not if they're coming and attacking us." He showed the palms of his hands. "I mean, it's a supposition, and it's just a way to get an upper hand. It doesn't mean anyone's going to attack their city, but it could mean the end of the war."

"Sure." River nodded. Perhaps these men were not that different from him, but they still stood on opposite sides, and he had to remember that.

Most of all, he had to hurry and find that staff. Their sanctuary, where he thought everyone was safe, was no sanctuary after all.

LEAH MANAGED to keep her head down, her mouth shut, and her anger under control for a day and a half. Considering she'd been wearing the equivalent of a collar, that had been an impressive display of self-control. What had kept her calm was knowing that in one day she would be back home. Just one more day.

At least when it was time to get ready, Leah was left alone with three servants and Lady Celia. No Cassius. The gold dress was beautiful, with delicate embroidery and pearls. One day

Leah had dreamed of a beautiful wedding, a lovely dress with a huge skirt, and an unforgettable party. Now it was all a doorway to a prison.

She almost didn't recognize the beautiful young woman staring back at her in the mirror. Well, she wasn't the same person anymore, she wasn't the same person who had left her home just a few days before. So much bitterness and anger inside her, something dark growing there, waiting, biding its time.

With that external semblance of calm she followed Lady Celia to take a carriage out of the castle to Cinaria, the city closest to it. More than fifty soldiers on horses accompanied them, perhaps some ironbringers among them. In the carriage was Lady Celia and Silas, the other prince. At least it wasn't Cassius. The king and queen still weren't back from their travels through Aluria.

"We'll be at the heart of the kingdom," Celia said, after a long time of silence. "And you'll want to behave." She raised an eyebrow and gave Leah a pointed look.

"I will." She had gotten great at not showing any reaction.

They rode until they reached the town, but it was empty, as if it was a ghost town, like a place from nightmares. It felt unreal like a bad dream. She got off the carriage behind a tall building, eight guards trailing her, and four more opening large doors. When she crossed them, she found herself on a platform, a thick glass wall separating it from a plaza where hundreds of commoners stood. So that was where the people were. Why would they be interested in that wedding? Why did they care?

Leah walked to the middle of the platform and stood by Venard, her back to the crowd beyond the glass. Daydreaming about returning to her kingdom, she barely heard the Master's words about union and love and family and whatever nonsense. At the end of it, Venard held her hand and raised it, to tremendous applause. This was a spectacle.

After that, she and Venard paraded on a tall glass carriage. She stood and waved, hopefully in a way that didn't displease lady Celia. But then, she figured that if she did something they didn't like, her necklace would get hot or something.

So many faces, so many people, some of them in ragged clothes. There were even children and parents with babies. Why did they even care? She was never going to be their queen. And then, perhaps all they wanted was to see her pretty dress, to see a prince and a princess from up close, as if they were gods who could bless them. But they were not gods, they were just monsters, unlikely to care about any of the people there. She even wondered if *she* would care. In Frostlake, her father helped even the poor when they needed a necromancer. She'd been in the village and in some distant farms, and the faces were not so hollow, did not seem to be in so much suffering, in hunger even. And yet Leah could barely fend for herself in this place, in this horrible kingdom. How could she help anyone? And then, wasn't that Venard's excuse? That he didn't have a choice?

Those thoughts followed her back to the castle, as she considered that soon she would be able to warn her parents and other kingdoms about their ironbringer army. But then, the Ironholds were awful, but it didn't mean they were planning on attacking anyone. Perhaps it was all to defeat the fae. And then, perhaps the other kingdoms should know about it —just in case.

Venard was also probably eager to escape his family's influence, eager for more independence, so he was probably looking forward to leaving Ironhold too.

Two servants helped Leah undress, under Celia's supervision, then they brought her a chicken soup, which she devoured. When she was left alone, in the silence of her solitude, she noticed that her heart was jumping in her chest. The night. The consummation. She couldn't come up with a way to avoid that. If anything, she needed Venard's trust. She sighed and closed her eyes, a bitter feeling in her mouth.

Right as she was thinking it, he came in. "You did well today."

"It wasn't hard."

"We'll be going to Frostlake soon. I..." He looked down. "It's just... My parents are there now, and they have a good retinue. Quite a few soldiers."

Probably with some ironbringers, making them a lot more deadly than they seemed.

He stared in her eyes. "Please don't try anything foolish."

"I wasn't going to—" the meaning of his words hit her. "Are you threatening my parents?"

"No." He showed the palms of his hands. "Of course not. I'd never. I'm... just warning you, Leah. But you're right that we've been getting along and that's a pointless warning."

A chill ran down her spine. "You think my parents are in danger?"

"No. My father and yours are friends. You know that."

"That's not what you said."

"It was a silly assumption. In case something major happened, like if you tried to run away or something."

"Why would I run away now, if I'm about to go home?" She pointed to the window. "And you think I'm going to climb out?"

He shook his head. "No. Forgive my nonsense. There's nothing to worry. We'll be in Frostlake soon. But we need to be husband and wife by then, so..."

"So you decided to threaten my parents because that's so romantic and will definitely help us grow close."

He shook his head again. "I'm not the one you need to fear. You know that. You know it so much that you're not holding your tongue." He put a hand on his head. "Which is for the best. We need to be honest with each other, and I was being honest with you, that's all. Are you ready?"

She almost asked, "For what?" then his words hit her. "We could wait," she blurted.

Venard nodded. "True. I'm also a little winded from the wedding. Try to relax, and I'll be back in an hour. Oh." He reached out his land and removed her choker necklace, which was a relief. "See? I trust you. Until later, Leah."

Leandra. She hated when he used her nickname. And what did he mean by one hour? No, no. That was not what she had meant by waiting.

She sat on her bed, her heart racing. Had he been saying that if she were difficult to him her parents would be in danger? No, he couldn't have said that. But she wasn't sure. The thought that he would be somehow forcing her to cooperate made her nauseous. She had been planning on cooperating. There were certainly many more women in loveless marriages, and they did what they had to.

Leah could maybe try to relax and do what her mother had told her: imagine she was somewhere else. It still sounded dreadful. And yet now her parents kept coming to her mind, worry taking over her thoughts.

She had to come up with a plan, and she wasn't going to do it while worried like that. Perhaps the answer could be in her dreams. Leah lay down, closed her eyes, and took slow, deep breaths. She could imagine she was somewhere else. Her dragon. Perhaps she could find it in her thoughts or dreams. That would help her calm down.

She closed her eyes, imagining she was outdoors on a meadow, trying to find her connection with her dragon. All she saw were fluffy, white clouds in the sky, but she decided she was going to be patient. Her dragon, her dragon, her dragon. She kept that thought steady in her mind.

The ground in front of her opened, and a huge form emerged from it, his iridescent silver scales reflecting the sun. Brilliant, delightful colors, a soothing feeling in her heart, in her mind. Soothing, soothing, all these colors dancing, reflected in those brilliant, magnificent scales. She followed the dragon, running in that meadow.

Then she was in a dark room with stone walls. A huge map of Aluria was attached to a wall, with some drawings and arrows in it. A small wooden table had some twenty books on history and military strategy, piled on top of each other, some of them lying open facing down. That was a horrible thing to do to a book.

On a shelf, by a window, there were some fiction titles. The sky was darkening outside. She looked at the other side and found a single bed with someone asleep on it. Even turned to the other side, she recognized the hair: that was Isofel. Leah was in her dream world, she was sure of it. This wasn't Ironhold and she wasn't in her body anymore. She approached the bed and he turned.

He smiled when he saw her, a dimpled smile that was delight, surprise, wonder, it was everything. This was indeed a dream, or he wouldn't be looking at her like that, with his eyes so brilliant. She realized that this was the place she most wanted to be, this was what she most wanted. And if it was a dream, then nothing was forbidden.

21

THE HOLLOW

Leah was glad to be far from everything, far from her nightmarish life. Perhaps that was why her dreams were no longer uncomfortable and disturbing, but rather wonderful. And that was how she was here with Fel. It was as if in this dreamscape he had never rejected her. And indeed, the green fire in his eyes was the furthest away from rejection she could imagine.

She sat by him and ran her hand over his hair, feeling its soft texture in the tips of her fingers. He closed his eyes, as if basking in her touch. When he opened them, there was determination in his look, then he wrapped his arms around her and kissed her. It was like the kiss that had been cut short in her room, deep and desperate and hungry, except that this time she had no fear, no guilt, no shame. His kiss was also sweet and tender, but it was a furious, desperate tenderness, a touch that she relished.

Leah ran her hands over his back, realizing, with surprise, that there was no fabric between his skin and her fingers, as she felt his warmth, his softness.

It all felt unreal, magical, wonderful. Leah closed her eyes as he kissed her neck then felt him pulling up her nightgown, pulling down her bodice. As it should be. Now there was nothing between them, nothing separating them. He laid her down and kissed her more and more and more, the feeling of his body over hers pleasant, soothing, the feeling of his chest against hers delightful.

It was all wondrous, even more so as he kissed her breasts, her belly, all the way to that strange place of pleasure and shame and guilt, except that there was only tenderness and pleasure now. It all felt right. His clothes were off too, and then he was staring into her eyes, so much feeling in his look. Dream Fel loved her. And she loved him back, she knew it in her heart. More than just her heart.

He gave a light chuckle, as if coming to the same realization as her. Regret and sadness overtook her when she remembered this was just a dream.

His eyes widened and he tensed. "Leah?"

"Yes?"

"How..." He frowned, confused.

Many silver pieces flew from a side table. His hands. He pinched her shoulder softly. "Are you real?"

A horrible feeling was settling in the pit of her stomach. But it couldn't be. "Are *you* real?"

He sat up, his expression horrified. "Shit, Leah. Of course I'm real. What are *you* doing here?" He was getting dressed and tossed her clothes back. "I mean, I'm so, so, so sorry. You have no idea how sorry I am."

This was strange. But Leah was used to strange dreams. But then, something was off. She tried to cross her hands— and couldn't. But that had happened to her before. He was part of her dream, even if it didn't make much sense.

He continued, "I swear, I thought I was dreaming, I thought... I'm so awfully sorry."

Leah pulled a sheet to cover her naked body. She

wasn't going to process what was happening and put on her bodice at the same time. "You are part of my dream, right?" She really hoped so. "There's nothing to be sorry about."

He covered his face with his metal hand. "Leah. This is real. I'm real. This place is real. And if you're not my very realistic hallucination, then you're here, and it means..." He sighed.

Real? It didn't make sense. "What's this place?"

"The barracks in the Umbraar Royal Fort."

She decided to get dressed. "Umbraar. Then it's obviously a dream." Her fingers were shaky as she laced her bodice. "How would I have gotten here?" It was bizarre to argue against someone imaginary.

"How do *I* know? I was sleeping. I saw you. What did you expect me to think?"

She put back her nightgown, which didn't change the fact that she wasn't properly dressed. "I was in the Ironhold castle in my very locked room. How would I have come all the way here?"

He sat and took her hands in his. "Listen to me. Leah, this is real. This is me. I would never have been so forward. Never. But I didn't think. I didn't know! How did you get here?" There was agony in his voice.

"I don't know. I sometimes get trapped in weird nightmares, and I think this is one of them." It had to be, or else she wouldn't know how to deal with the shame.

"It's not. All I know is I almost—" He closed his eyes. His tone turned cold all of a sudden. "Aren't you married?"

She felt a bitter taste in her mouth. "Yes."

"You haven't done this with your husband yet?" He asked the question matter-of-factly. This wasn't dream Fel anymore, and she was starting to get worried.

"No."

"How did you get here?" he insisted. His voice was soft, but his tone was urgent.

"I don't know!" How many times would she have to repeat that? She was starting to think this was indeed real, but then nothing made sense.

He lit a second candle in the room, then his eyes widened when he noticed her hand. "What happened there?"

The burn. She felt ashamed and embarrassed, as if it somehow had been her fault. Embarrassed to confess she was locked into an abusive marriage. "Nothing."

"It doesn't look like nothing, Leah."

"It was an accident."

He looked into her eyes. "Did someone hurt you?" There worry, but also coldness and contempt there.

"Why? Do you by any chance care?"

"No." He looked down and shrugged. Then he added, mumbling, "Doesn't mean I'm not gonna kill them."

Leah shook her head. That didn't make any sense.

He stared at her again. "You made your choice, didn't you? Now why are you here?"

"I don't know! I don't even know if this is real or not. I'm dreaming. Or thinking I'm dreaming. If I were awake and could go anywhere, you think I'd come here?"

He rolled his eyes. "Obviously not."

Her thoughts then went to her parents, and to the threat posed on them. "I need to get back."

He chuckled bitterly. "Well, go then."

"Isofel. I have no idea how."

"The same way you came, my dear Leandra Ironhold. And I do apologize. Truly. I made a mistake. An unforgivable mistake, but please know I'm sorry."

Leah had to go back. She wasn't going to do any of that with Venard, but she could probably convince him to wait or something. Still, he had told her that if she tried to run away, something could happen to her parents. But how was she going back? More and more she was getting mortified by what had passed between her and Fel. So easily, so quickly. He'd probably lost all respect for her. "I thought I was dreaming. I would never have done any of that if I were awake."

"Why?" He crossed his arms. "Am I often in your dreams?"

"No. What about you? Shouldn't you have thought it was a nightmare?"

He shrugged. "It was a regular dream." Was he saying he dreamed about her often? "I should have noticed it was too realistic, for sure, but to my credit, I was half-asleep."

"It's seven at night."

"I've been waking up at three." He stared at her. "Do you understand what happened?"

"I have no clue!"

"Between us. Do you understand?"

Her head was going to burn if she thought about it for even another second. While it had felt wonderful, now all that was left was shame. "I'd rather forget it."

"All right." He closed his eyes and took a deep breath. "We almost had sex, Leah. This is what married couples do, how they make children. I would have gone much, much slower with you, but I didn't know it."

"Because you thought I had done it with my husband?"

"Because I thought you were part of my dream. There are no complications in dreams."

It was awkward but she was glad he was explaining it to her, so she asked another question. "Am I ruined now? Will they notice it?"

"I don't think so. We didn't actually... That's what you're worried about, right? Your husband?"

"I'm worried about so many more things. I need to get back before they find out I'm gone."

He stared at her, an odd coldness in his eyes. "So you were lying down, then puff, you were here?"

"I was dreaming a little before." She then remembered what she knew about Ironhold. "Fel, you have to be careful. Ironhold, they have ironbringers, more than just the royal family. Hundreds. I don't know what they're going to do."

He sighed. "Hundreds? How?"

"They hide them. The princes have... lovers."

"I am actually getting ready to fight ironbringers, I just had no clue it was that bad."

"It is. But they have Ironhold soldiers in Frostlake. I think some of them could be ironbringers. If I don't go back to the Iron Citadel, my parents could be in danger."

"Oh, isn't that a lovely family you picked?" He smirked. "At least your husband has two hands, right?"

She shouldn't have said anything. Of course he was just going to use her words to humiliate her.

He was silent for some time, then said, "Listen. Did someone bring you anywhere, did you see anyone different?"

"No. I was in my room. Alone."

He nodded. "And you're afraid for your parents."

"Yes."

He picked a long brown leather coat that was lying over a chair and threw it at the bed, beside her. "Put it on. We'll need to talk to my father."

The humiliation. The shame. "No. Please. Nobody can know about this." She hated to plead, but she had to.

He walked to her and took her hands in his, which were now gloved, and looked in her eyes. "Leah. It's not your fault. You did nothing wrong. I won't tell anyone what happened in this room, I promise. But I think you might have stepped in the hollow, like a deathbringer. Maybe it's something to do with your necromancy, I don't know. My father has death magic, he can help you. I can't."

If she weren't worried about returning to Ironhold because of her parents, she would want to die right at that moment. Just imagining the humiliation was terrible enough. But she put on Fel's coat, and it was torture because it smelled like him, and it should be a horrible smell, and all it did was make her wish they were still kissing. If he noticed that, he'd probably humiliate her even more.

She looked at him. "Do you promise? Promise you won't tell?"

"I won't. But we need to understand what happened, and my father will need to help hide you here."

"Hide here?"

"If they're threatening your family, you're not going back to Ironhold."

"I have to."

He glared at her. "Let's talk to my father."

He opened the door and checked to see if there was anyone, then gestured for her to follow him. *Hide here.* It could be her escape. It would be her ruin, too. Fel didn't want her. She would be putting her family in danger and ruining her reputation forever. But it could be her way to escape Ironhold —like a coward, only to be shunned and humiliated again, and to put her parents at risk.

They opened a thick wooden door and came to an office with maps on walls and a table with piles and piles of papers on them. King Azir sat behind a desk, across from a guard. Fel stepped in front of Leah, so that she was hidden from view.

"I need to speak with my father in private," Fel said.

"Go," King Azir told the man, who walked away.

When the king saw Leah, he looked between Leah and his son.

"It's not what you're thinking," Fel said.

"You don't even know what I'm thinking," Azir replied.

"Something strange happened," Fel said. "To her magic.

She was dreaming, then she appeared in my room. I think her necromancy might have made her walk in the hollow."

The Umbraar king stared at her. "Is that true?"

"Yes. I have no idea how I got here." And now she was almost completely sure this wasn't some weird dream, which was mortifying.

King Azir kept looking at her, as if seeing her for the first time, then he got up and held her shoulders, urgency and agony in his face. "Are you sure you are a necromancer? Can you talk to the dead?"

Fel pushed him. "Let go of her." His tone was calm, but there was something so terrifying and threatening about his voice that even Leah trembled. Fel and his father then glared at each other. That was quite a disrespectful way to treat a parent, but it was true that the king was being a little too intense. Fel then added, "I saw her revive a rat. Satisfied?" His voice was calmer, but there was still a dangerous edge to it.

Azir closed his eyes and turned to her. "You're absolutely, completely sure you're a necromancer?"

What else would she be? "Yes, I'm sure."

He was still staring at her.

"Dad," Fel said, "I think necromancy works like death-bringing. That's the only explanation."

The king looked at his son, then back at her.

Fel continued, "She's saying that Ironhold has an army of ironbringers. This can't be good. And that she fears for her parents in Frostlake."

It was as if all the air was sucked out of the room then put back at once, but this time heavier and darker. "What?" Azir asked. He turned to Leah. "Is that true?"

He sounded as if he was going to murder her right then if she said yes.

"I don't know," she croaked. "Maybe. There are Ironhold forces in Frostlake, I mean, maybe it's nothing, but I want to go back, just in case. It's just... I don't know how to go back." The words were jumbled, as she felt the tension rising in the room.

The king glared at her. "I'm getting your mother out of there right now. And you stay here."

She felt panic rising on her. "It will only make things worse. And I need to go back. To my husband."

"No," King Azir insisted, and she noticed his eyes were turning black. "You're going to stay here and stay safe."

Fel then said, "If she wants to go back to Ironhold, let her go back. Help her."

The king's eyes became green again and he turned to Leah. "Are you safe there? Are you sure?"

No, Leah wasn't sure, but she didn't want to risk her mother's life, not when she was so close to going back home. "Yes, I'm safe."

Fel then added, "Dad, if you go to Frostlake, it's going to cause an inter-kingdom commotion."

The king waved a hand. "I'm not an idiot. Nobody will even see me." He stared at Leah. "You're absolutely sure you're safe in Ironhold?"

"I'm safe," she insisted, thinking about her parents, thinking that she was so close to returning home and wasn't going to ruin everything now.

Azir took a small communication mirror and gave it to her. "If anything happens, anything slightly suspicious, contact me, and I'll get you out."

"All right." She took the object, surprised that this stranger suddenly cared about her. Then, it was probably because of his son.

"Thank you," Fel said, confirming what she thought. The issue was that Fel only cared about her enough not to want to see her hurt—or dead.

"Can you get me back?" Leah asked King Azir. "And if you go to Frostlake, can you tell my parents to be careful with the

Ironhold retinue, that there might be ironbringers among them?"

The king nodded. "Yes. If that's what you really want."

"I do," she said. "I don't think my parents are in danger, but if I disappear, they might be. I'll contact you if anything happens."

Fel held her arm. "Leah. Are you sure?"

She wished he didn't talk to her like that, she wished he were either cold or sweet all the time, as this back and forth was driving her insane. "What else can I do? What's gonna happen if I stay here?"

"We'll keep you safe." There was no warmth in his eyes, though.

"Until what? Until when?" she asked. "I'm not going to start a war because of a dream turned wrong."

Fel let go of her and sneered. "Fine, then. Go to your dear husband."

"At least he married me."

"Let's go," Azir said. "We're wasting time. Hold my arm."

Like that? Right now? She held it, then barely had time for one last look at Fel before she was engulfed in darkness.

FEL'S THOUGHTS WERE A COMPLETE, illogical mess. And his feelings? Made no sense. *Stay here until when*, she'd asked. The answer was still in his throat. *Until forever. Until we die. I'll honor and respect and love you until the end of our lives.*

If only everything were so simple. If only he knew this wouldn't turn into humiliation, that she would stay, that she would choose him. If only he weren't so weak and foolish to still want her after she'd humiliated him.

Fel was consumed with guilt. Of course he had noticed the dream had been too realistic. But it was like some gift from the gods. How could he have guessed? And yet, he'd almost gone too far. But he was also consumed with shame. She'd seen him as he was; no gloves, no shirt, nothing hiding him. And yet she hadn't seemed to mind. She'd been almost his. So close. And it would have been wrong. It just made him wistful for what could have been. What would never be. Because of her. And then it all turned to anger.

And why was his father taking her back? He'd given her a communication mirror, but was it going to work? Naia's wasn't working. What if Leah was sent back to danger? What if it was his fault? They could have kept her in Umbraar regardless of what she chose. But that would be terrible. If she wanted her husband, they had no business preventing her from returning to him. So much confusion. Driving him insane. No, one thing he knew: the moment she'd been gone, he wished she had stayed. Now he had to regret his harsh words, regret his anger, and live with the knowledge that he had wasted his chance to make things right.

AZIR WAS TAKING Ursiana's daughter through the hollow. Ursiana's daughter, who looked like her mother except for her blue eyes. The necromancer king's eyes. And yet. The girl's magic didn't strike him as necromancy. It opened a locket of forgotten questions.

"You're sure you'll be safe there?" he insisted.

The girl nodded, seeming certain. Azir wasn't going to put Ursiana's daughter in danger, not if he could avoid it. And then, Isofel loved her. The fool. None of his warnings had worked. But perhaps warnings didn't work. His son was going to love this girl until the end of his days. All Azir hoped was that it didn't consume his joy, his life, his dreams. Perhaps Fel would still find happiness despite his broken heart.

She touched her pocket. "I'll contact you if anything happens. Is this normal? I thought you couldn't bring anyone across the hollow." It was as if she wanted to change the subject.

Azir decided to ignore his misgivings about where she was going and answer her. "It's a bad idea. When they don't have the magic allowing them to cross. It's like when you're swimming and you try to drag someone who can't swim. They can pull you into the depths. But you have that magic, so it's different." He took another look at her. "You're absolutely sure you can revive a dead animal?"

The girl frowned. "Why do you keep asking me that?"

"Curious about your magic."

She shrugged. "Well, it's my father's magic."

"Fair." He focused on the paths in the darkness, then traced the steps to the Ironhold castle, this place he hadn't visited in years. The strange part was that the memories were sweeter than bitter, sweet with the memory of the two babies he had taken from that dreadful family. Isofel and Irinaia. Then his breath hitched thinking about Naia. With a fae. Gone. Saying she was spying on them, but what was she really doing? Fel suggested she should still be welcome home, she should be forgiven if she returned. Perhaps he was right.

With his daughter gone, here he was with Ursiana's daughter. Another man's daughter. But that was not the girl's fault. And she wasn't a girl, but a married woman. A married woman who'd just been unfaithful.

"Leandra," he said. "If necromancy is like deathbringing, you need to learn to control it. You will have dreams in the hollow but sometimes they will be real."

"Like what just happened." Her voice was shaky. No wonder. The idea was terrifying. It had been terrifying to him once, before he knew how to control it.

"Yes. You can slip into your dreams. It's rare but it can

happen. Your father never mentioned any of that?"

"He taught me to understand when I'm dreaming."

Maybe necromancy and deathbringing *were* similar after all. "What about walking in the hollow? Has he taught you that?"

"No."

This wasn't good. This was extremely dangerous. "Be careful. There are things out there. Dangerous things. But the biggest danger is not you getting hurt, but unleashing something."

She was quiet for a moment, then said, "How can I prevent that?"

It took a lot of training. Training she obviously had never gotten. But then again, perhaps necromancy was different. It had to be much less dangerous, if her father had never warned her against any of that. Still, he distilled the main idea. "Control your thoughts, control your feelings, control your dreams."

The girl nodded.

They came to the Iron Citadel. A monstrosity housing monsters. What was wrong with Ursiana? How could she have sent her daughter there? But then, King Harold was friends with the necromancer king, and maybe none of that was monstrosity for him. Maybe the two kingdoms were even conspiring together. It made a lot of sense. And the Ironholds wouldn't hurt the sole Frostlake heir. "We won't be seen. Tell me where you need to go."

"It's high up, my bedroom."

He focused and saw the top floor in his mind's eye. Bedrooms and bedrooms. One of them caught his eye. "Is it pink?"

"Yes."

Strange choice for someone with death magic. They usually didn't like bright colors. Then again, he was making assumptions based on deathbringing. Getting inside a closed space was always hard. He grabbed her arm firmly, while he felt darkness pressing on them. "Silence now," he whispered.

When the dark subsided, he was inside a bright pink room. "Is this it?" he asked as softly as he could, to prevent anyone from hearing him.

She nodded, then whispered, "Thank you."

Ursiana's daughter showed no hint of fear, so she was probably safe. The girl was lucky that she hadn't turned out somewhere else, from where she wouldn't know how to return. She should know how to return, but she had obviously never gotten any training. He still had an odd feeling about it. Still wondered... That had to be nonsense.

He nodded and left. For more nonsense. Of course Ursiana was safe. Perhaps she was sitting on a throne with her necromancer husband laughing at the destruction they were planning. Perhaps she was also conspiring with Prince Sebastian, from Wolfmark. Didn't she like him so much?

Azir still wondered how come he hadn't killed the prince. He wondered about it often, but there was nothing to wonder. Murder wasn't going to fix anything. As to Ironhold, there was no fixing. Even if he killed the king, someone else just as awful would take power. They were all poisoned. Except Fel and Naia. And their mother, probably.

But this was not the time to stir the flames of his anger, but to go to Frostlake, just to check if Ursiana was safe. His foolishness still managed to astonish him.

He opened the darkness to see the ridiculous Frostlake castle. What kind of necromancer built a castle that looked like a cake? He closed his eyes to try to look inside. It shouldn't be too much trouble, as it was always easy to see where she was. But before he found her, he saw a corridor—full of blood and dead guards. Frostlake was being attacked. His heart stopped. The world stopped. Everything stopped.

22

FROZEN

Leah was trembling, almost unable to believe she was back in that dreadful room, unable to believe what had just happened, terrified at thinking that she could one day slip into her nightmares. But she was also ashamed and angry at Fel. Why had he humiliated her?

His father had been kind, though. For someone with such a dreadful reputation, he'd been incredibly helpful. And yet. Part of her wished she had stayed in Umbraar, wished Fel had asked her to stay. But that would be foolish. Yes, it would be her much-wanted escape, but what if Ironhold retaliated against Frostlake? Would she bear that blame? And she knew she could make an ally out of Venard, she knew it. And she could wait one day to go home.

More than ever, she was determined to talk to him and postpone their consummation. He was obviously as eager as she was to leave, so there was no point thinking of him as an adversary. It would all work out. Not for her heart, but that had been broken the moment she'd gotten that note from Isofel. Then broken again tonight. She had let Fel smash it then step on the pieces. And a bizarre part of her wished he had taken longer to realize it wasn't a dream.

A look at the clock told her that a full hour hadn't passed yet. She'd been so lucky.

After some time, Venard came in. "I'll turn down the candles. Undress and wait for me." There was something odd, clipped about his voice.

"Venard, no. Let's give it some time. You're my friend, you can wait. We'll rule Frostlake together. We'll have time. Let's get to know each other first, it will be much better. We'll do it when we're away from your family, when there are no threats hanging upon us."

He didn't look at her. "Just close your eyes and relax, all right? It will be fine. Just lie down and relax." There was fear in his voice. Strange.

Leah was immersed in darkness as he left, but she lit a candle right away. If he was more afraid than her, she could use it to her advantage. Venard was a coward, but wasn't cruel. Unless his grandma stood right beside him threatening him, she doubted he'd do anything against her will.

After long minutes, the door opened again. She took a deep breath, trusting herself that she could still convince him, but it got caught in her chest when she saw who came in.

It wasn't Venard, but his brother, Cassius.

BEFORE THE GATHERING, Azir had come to the Frostlake castle a couple times, just out of curiosity, a bizarre curiosity. Still, he didn't know the castle well and didn't know where the royal family would be in an occasion like this. Most castles had a safety vault for the king and queen, but he wasn't sure if it was the case here, and if there had been any time for them to get there.

He tried to feel where Ursiana was, but it was like facing a wall. He decided to remember the gathering and go to the main ballroom. There were Frostlake guards fallen to the ground, but there was no sign of conflict or blood. They were not breathing, though—they were dead.

Who could have caused this? The fae again? His instinct told him that this had been Ironhold's doing, now that they could take control of the kingdom after marrying the Frostlake heir. And if some of the guards they sent were ironbringers... But it still didn't explain how these men had fallen dead without wounds. What Azir had to do now was find Ursiana. He recalled the guest wing and imagined the royal quarters would be near there.

Up in the hallways, he did find signs of battle. Guards and servants were slain with swords—or some other type of cutting object. His experience observing Fel and Naia had taught him that ironbringers could do a lot of damage from a distance. If it had been ironbringers. But he wasn't here to figure out who was attacking the castle, but to get Ursiana to safety—if she was still alive. A heavy weight was settling in his chest as he realized that her odds of surviving this were very slim. Where was she? Faint shouts at a distance got his attention. Azir slipped into the darkness and found himself in a huge bedroom. A corner was covered with some kind of dark vines, which two men were trying to cut.

"Set it on fire," one of them said. He was wearing dark pants and a shirt, and no guard uniform, so it was hard to know where he was from.

"They need her body," the other replied.

"We'll quench it before it burns her."

Azir slipped in the hollow again, then past the vines, where Ursiana was fallen, unconscious.

Something exploded outside the vines, so he grabbed her

in his arms and barely had time to slip away before any fire or heat reached them.

Searching for a pulse, he touched her neck, for a second fearing that she would be dead just like everyone in the throne room. Her heart was still beating, but she was so cold.

Then he looked around and realized his moment of panic had gotten him lost. He could usually see paths ahead of him, like roads on a clear field, but this time there was only darkness. And walls. He was surrounded by them on all sides except one, from where a faint light came. But a monstrous roar also came from that direction. This couldn't be. Of all the times he could have gotten lost, of all the places he could have ended up in, why did this happen now, and why did he end up here?

20 years before

Leaving the crew of the Death Sails was an odd experience, as River felt as if he was leaving friends behind. And yet they were humans, humans who were destroying Aluria, who wouldn't mind seeing the Ancient City destroyed. And now he was in Fernick, a land he knew very little about, without any idea of where to find the dragon lords, dragons, or whatever they chose to call themselves.

He'd always wondered what had happened to the dragons in Aluria and even in Fernick, and now he got his answer and it made his stomach lurch a little. By dragons, he'd always imagined the legendary reptile-like flying creatures. And yet, from some talks with the crew, he learned that dragons were the dragon lords; humans. Magical humans, sure, but definitely not the dragons he would like to see. What a pretentious name, dragons. Couldn't they have picked a humble, realistic name, like Ancients? In a way, it would make his quest easier knowing that he wouldn't have to face gigantic fire-breathing creatures. But he still wished they existed.

Fernick was also the land of many types of fae and elves. He'd always wanted to see faeries with different skin colors, and wondered what it would be like to be blue or purple, or to have wings. The idea of flying sounded amazing, but having fragile wings would make it quite dangerous.

The continent was occupied by humans, like Aluria, but it was huge and had large forests where fae could live undisturbed. But he was here to find the dragons, not other fae.

Moving from bar to bar in the port city of Seminak, it was easy to use glamour to get humans to talk. The hard part was understanding what they said. River used to think he had a good grasp of Fernian, but that had obviously been before he'd heard anyone speaking the language at a bar—or any real conversation, for that matter. The words got all jumbled together in an incomprehensible mush. For him only, of course, as everyone else understood perfectly these mushed words. Here he was: the clueless foreigner, speaking way too slowly. At least there were more humans from Aluria in that port city. The bizarre part was seeing them and recognizing them as sharing some kind of common ground, when they were enemies.

Still, with his dreadful Fernian or talking to humans from Aluria, River gathered information. It wasn't hard to get people to talk about stories, myths, rumors. Humans were fascinated by magic, especially in a land like this, where few of them possessed it. Not even royalty had any magic in Fernick.

And that was how he learned about the dragon lords. Now, this was getting really confusing. Apparently indeed there had been real dragons in the past, and by dragons they meant lizard-like gigantic creatures. By past they meant some five hundred years before or so, which was long enough to make it all sound like a myth. Still, it was a piece of information.

The dragon lords were unlikely to be in the south or near the cities. River's best guess was the mountains. As he got deeper and deeper in the continent, more and more he feared meeting a fae and maybe being exposed. But then he wasn't an enemy here, except that he'd been using his magic to get food and lodgings, and someone would eventually be mad.

Throughout his travel, he'd been looking at his lapse stones. An idea came to him when he was in a small village near the Gray Mountains. The stones could make a circle. Perhaps a circle like the ones in Aluria, allowing him to go somewhere else. He tested it in the forest, in a quiet place. Setting the stones in a large circle, he watched as animals stepped inside it. If it had been a portal, at least some of them would go through, but none did. Eventually, as a flock of birds fought for the corn he'd thrown there, he clapped his hands to shoo the creatures away.

River trembled, unable to believe what he was seeing; the birds had stopped moving. He reached out his hand and touched one creature, and it started to eat again. Then he clapped, but nothing happened. When he snapped his fingers, the birds went back to normal, unfazed, unharmed. This was amazing. That was the lapse that the stones caused, like a lapse in time, except that the time didn't really change. If this magic worked in a larger circle, he knew what he'd have to do to get that staff.

That night, he put the stones around the inn and tested them. They worked. Guests and the owner were frozen in time, as if they were statues, and yet they were living, breathing statues. And River now had access to immeasurable power in the magical objects he had in hand.

It turned out that the dragons were not that hard to find. Once River got to the right valley, the villagers knew where they dwelled. It seemed that the magicians didn't try to hide. What kept them safe was the alleged power they had. If they thought themselves untouchable, that was even better for River.

The Dragon Lair was on top of a steep hill. River placed the lapse stones around it and climbed up, eventually reaching a large marble building. There were no guards by any of the doors, and for a moment he feared the place had been abandoned, but once inside, he saw a group of people around a table. It seemed that they'd been talking. Now they stared at each other, some of them open-mouthed. The security here was crap. He used to think that the security sucked at the Ancient palace, but nothing really compared to this "dragon lair". Unless a real dragon showed up or something. Well, of course not. The "dragons" had been frozen, and they were just humans with magic. A lot of magic, apparently, but it still didn't make them dragons. One day he'd need to find one of them awake and argue about semantics. This wasn't the day, of course.

As he wondered where the staff could be, his eyes noticed that there was something transparent on the wall. Ice. Probably kept cold with magic, since it was summer here. Inside it, there was a metal staff. Great. Right in the entrance hall. Could it be *the* staff? River approached it. He usually could smell magic, it was an odd smell that was always different from natural scents. Of course, he wouldn't sense anything encased in that much ice. But it had to be something pretty important to be there. He could pick the ice until he released the artifact, he could wait until it melted, or—he saw a fireplace on a corner.

Now, this was getting ridiculously easy. But perhaps they counted on the three men and four women around that table to protect it. River took a long log that wasn't deep in the fire, and with it still lit, pressed it against the ice, which melted quickly. River got a handkerchief to take the staff, fearing it could have some protective spell or iron.

Once he wrapped his hands around the magical artifact, cold moved to his arm and then his entire body. Of course, the staff had to be cold, having been there for so long, but this was too much. He dropped the object, which fell on the floor. Ice was forming around him. That had to be a protection spell. Silly River, thinking there would be nothing there. He decided to get the staff and run before the ice encased him, but it was too late. His legs wouldn't move. Or his torso or arms. When the ice covered his head, he closed his eyes. He was doomed.

LEAH REGRETTED at once not having stayed back in Umbraar, having wasted her chance. All because she had trusted Venard, trusted that she was about to go home soon, that they could still be allies. That coward. Now he had let his brother come in.

She made an effort to keep her voice steady. "Wrong room?"

Cassius had a disgusting smirk. "Oh, you can't obey a simple order, can you? You want it with candles lit, want to see it all. I like it."

"I'm waiting for my husband."

He snorted. "You think he's coming? You think he doesn't know about it?"

"I doubt Lady Celia will approve of this." Leah hated that woman, but she didn't think she would stoop that low.

He shrugged. "You think I care? Plus, all they want is a little ironbringer popping out of your cute little belly. You think they'll check whose child it is?"

Perhaps not. Perhaps all they wanted was Frostlake, and considering how they'd been treating her, they weren't at all concerned for her wellbeing. Fear. Fear like she had never felt before settled in. For a moment, it was as if she couldn't see anything, couldn't feel anything, frozen in place.

A horrific laugh came from his mouth and he advanced towards her.

"Help!" she yelled. "Help!" It wasn't brilliant, but was what she came up with.

"I like it." His smirk was a horrific grimace. "Yell some more."

There was no time to reach for the communication mirror to try to seek help from Fel's father. She wished she could disappear in the hollow again, but she had to relax to do that, and right now she was the opposite of relaxed.

"C'mon," he insisted, now right in front of her. "Scream."

There was only a wall behind her, that horrible pink wall. His hands moved to the top button of her coat—Fel's coat. She could still feel Fel's magic hand on her arm, asking her if she was sure she wanted to return to Ironhold. Oh, how proud and stupid she'd been! But then, she had returned to keep her parents safe. Hopefully they were safe now.

Cassius was fumbling with the button, thankfully taking forever to open it. She could try to hit him, kick him. And then what? There was no way she could fight him and win.

He let go of the button and stared at her. "Let's do it nicely, all right? You're a little slut who has had some practice. We all know it. So start by getting undressed. Put on a good performance, and you won't get hurt. See how nice I am?"

At least this would give her time to gather her thoughts, to gain time. Rage was simmering in her as she undid button by button of the coat, as slowly as she could. What did he think he was? What right did he think he had? What right did Venard think he had to give her to his brother? Why did they think they could burn her, hurt her, humiliate her? Didn't they think there would be consequences? Did they think she was so worthless that they could treat her like that? Did they think Frostlake was so worthless that they could risk her parents' wrath? Who did this buffoon think he was?

He had no right to be here, no right to be telling her what to do, no right to want to touch her. All her hurt, humiliation, anger, all the words she had swallowed were bubbling up, threatening to surface. Suddenly Fel's father's words came back to her. *The danger is what you can unleash.* But she wasn't afraid. She wasn't afraid of the dark, slimy feelings inside her. There was no point bottling them in. A strange power was simmering inside her. It was destruction, pain, death. And she welcomed it.

Cassius sneered. "Oh, look. Black eyes. So cute. Is that meant to be sexier?"

Leah smirked. "For me, yes."

And then she felt it. Like a damn being broken. The room was immersed in darkness, even if the candle was still lit. Tendrils of a black, slimy thing were enveloping Cassius. And his expression changed. So simple. So easy. The derision was gone, fear having taken its place.

"Stop this, you witch!"

Leah laughed. "I like it. Scream some more."

He tried to advance on her, but that thing wrapped around his throat and pulled him back. It got tighter and tighter as he screamed for help. It was slow, so that she relished each of his screams. He was so scared, so helpless.

A mirror cracked beside her. Cassius was likely trying to reach for any metal to defend himself, but it would be hard to do anything when he couldn't even breathe.

As he was dying, Leah kneeled beside him. "I promise you that everyone in your family who's humiliated me will see the same end. I want to see you all pay for that. And suffer. Suffer a lot."

His eyes closed, and she felt his life leaving him. It felt

pleasant and satisfying, more pleasant than the best orange cake. So much magic inside her, thrumming with immeasurable power, the power of death.

The door opened, and four guards entered.

"What's happening—" The guard didn't even get to finish the sentence, as they all dropped dead. Death felt so good. She might as well kill everyone in that castle. Everyone in Ironhold. Everyone in Aluria. Everyone in the world.

No. Not her parents. No. What was she thinking? Were those even her own thoughts? There was no time to be horrified at the dead guards, and she still wasn't horrified at what she'd done to Cassius, but she had to escape before more guards came. Unless she could kill them all. *Kill them all, kill them all.* It was as if something was talking inside her head, and it was making her confused. She had to try to go to the hollow, but she closed her eyes and nothing happened. She ran outside, where she was surrounded by some twenty guards. No Venard, no Silas, those cowards.

The first guards fell dead, then she saw a strange blue smoke in the hall, coming from both sides.

The guards panicked and covered their noses and mouths. "Death mist!" one of them screamed. Great. So they were poisoning everyone, including the guards. Including her. There were only two ways out: jumping down or stepping in the hollow. Leah had no idea how to leave that place. And didn't think her odds of survival were good if she jumped. Her odds were also terrible if she stayed and breathed that gas. It was as if she snapped out of that morbid appreciation for death. She didn't want to kill anyone, all she wanted was to survive. The question was how. Trapped, about to be poisoned, how was she going to find a way out?

23
TRAPPED

There was a faint light illuminating the tunnel where Azir was. Ursiana was unconscious but breathing. Thinking back to those vines protecting her in Frost-lake, he realized that she must have used her magic, and an insane amount of it all at once, to have made that barrier. He'd known she was a greenbringer, but had always thought that her magic was dormant. Perhaps it had awoken. Magic acted in strange ways... Like with Naia and her mysterious fire. But he didn't want to think about Naia. At least he still had Fel. But for how long? Would Ironhold move to attack Umbraar too?

Meanwhile, Azir was stuck here, in this hole, while something roared outside. If he was right, the creature waiting for them was a deatheye, and this was one of their traps. There was no stepping in the hollow from here. If he wanted to leave, he'd need to confront the monster—or monsters—waiting for them outside.

For now, all he did was sit against the rock wall and place Ursiana's head on his lap, so that she had some kind of pillow. She'd betrayed him, dishonored him, and yet here he was; worried about where her head was resting. She didn't look that different from almost nineteen years ago. Some lines, maybe, those lines that life marked on people's faces, like his. Perhaps that was why he'd wanted to save her so much, not for her, but for a memory from a time when he'd thought everything could have been different. A time when there was still hope even after so much pain and tragedy, a bright light in a dark world. All illusion, of course, but the reminder was here, as if the dream could become solid and real.

His worry for her was what had caused him to get lost and to end up here. Ironic that he'd wanted to save her so much and yet had ended up dooming them both. Everything so ironic and illogical.

"Azir?" Her voice and her tone took him back to nineteen years before.

But it was her, not a memory. At last, she was awake, and he sighed with relief. Strangely, she didn't stare at him with her usual derision, unless the faint light was tricking him. That thought came too early, as she soon frowned and sat up, as if she'd just realized she'd been resting her head on a nest of scorpions.

"What's happening?" she asked, her voice cold, clipped, and strained, which made sense considering what she'd just been through.

"Your castle was attacked."

"I know that!" She looked around. "What are you doing here? Where are we?"

"I rescued you and—"

Her eyes were wide. "Did you know this was going to happen?"

"I didn't."

"Then how did you—"

"Let me explain. I thought Ironhold could attack, for sure. I would never have guessed they would have attacked their closest allies."

"How did you find me?"

"I..." How was he going to explain this? He didn't want to compromise Isofel. "Received a communication from your daughter. She was worried about you."

"*You* received it? She hasn't contacted me, she's only written strange letters, but she never mentioned anything..."

"She contacted my son. In a dream—by accident." He didn't need to explain how real the dream had turned. "And she was worried about her parents. So I went to Frostlake to check—and unfortunately got there too late. All I could do was take you away from there."

"I didn't ask or need you to save me, Azir. I told you never to touch me again."

"Well, it's done." He shrugged. "But I must say I'm quite glad you don't want to be saved, because I'm not sure I did."

"What do you mean? Wait." She took another look at the cave. "You took me to the hollow? Didn't you say you couldn't take someone else? That it could cause you to get lost?"

Azir was stunned that she remembered something he'd told her so long ago. "Yes. True. I shouldn't try to take anyone across the hollow, but you were surrounded. I..." If there was such a thing as a crown of foolishness, it needed to go on his head. "I forgot."

"Can you get out of here?"

He bit his lip. "There's a deatheye outside. Perhaps more. I'll need to observe them, see if there's a time when they rest, to move past them."

"You can't just... puff?" She snapped her fingers.

"No." He was feeling foolish. "I'm sorry. But I'll try to find a way to get us out."

"Might. You know, of all possible manners of death, being stuck with you is by far a punishment I don't think I deserve. Can't you get out on your own at least? Leave me to my fate in peace?"

"I obviously can't, or I wouldn't be here hearing your voice." It was a lie, he wasn't going to leave her. It didn't mean he liked their situation any more than her. Her presence was like poking an old wound with hot iron.

"You should have left me to die, Azir."

"You unleashed powerful green magic to fight your attackers, Ursiana. That doesn't strike me as someone who's given up on life."

"I hadn't given up. Of course not. But if I knew that the alternative to dying was being stuck with you, I'd obviously would have reconsidered it."

"Why? It makes you feel bad? Maybe you deserve it."

"Fuck you, Azir."

Her tone surprised him. "Using nasty words now?"

"My *feelings* are nasty. There are no words to express them —but some of them come closer than others."

He smiled. "At least your nastiness is surfacing. Better than hiding them under a sweet veneer."

"You're the one who knows all about hiding. Is that why you made this pathetic attempt to rescue me? Can it be that you have some sliver of remorse for what you've done to me?"

"A mountain of remorse and shame, yes. For having trusted you once."

"Trust? You're kidding me, right? You used me and then left me to fend for myself. My fault for being a gullible idiot? Sure. I accept that, I accept my blame. My mistake, for sure. But I can still loathe you for taking advantage of the innocent, hopeful girl I once was."

He rolled his eyes. "Taking advantage... We're past that, aren't we? I see no reason to pretend anymore. Weren't you the one playing me and the Wolfmark prince, Sebastian, at the same time? I don't understand why you didn't marry him. Unless he also knew who you truly were."

"Why? You expected me not to talk to anyone? Not to

dance with anyone? And yet I don't recall ever dancing with him, not that it would have been wrong. Is that your flimsy excuse?" She waved a hand. "Spare me. Just say you got what you wanted and were done. I've made my peace with it long ago."

Why was she insisting on acting innocent? "Ursiana. Please. There's no need to pretend anymore. Not after all this time. I saw you in the garden with Sebastian."

She laughed a bitter laugh. "You saw *me*? You definitely didn't, because I wasn't there. You're either lying for some foolish reason, or your vision was severely impaired."

"I'm not lying. I saw it."

"How could you have seen something that didn't happen?"

"It happened. It was you. I realized you were lying. That was why I couldn't look at you anymore."

She paused, staring at him. "So that was why you didn't propose."

"Yes."

She laughed bitterly. "Fantastic, just fantastic. See, I spent my whole life thinking you're an asshole who just wanted to use me for a good time then toss me. But actually, no. It's a thousand times worse." There was fury in her voice. "You think I have no honor. You think I would be capable of something disgusting like that. I spent the last years of my life hating you. How can it be even worse?"

Her anger almost made him think twice, almost made him believe her, but then, he also trusted his own eyes. "Because it's what I saw."

"Fuck you, Azir. A thousand times fuck you."

He felt something grabbing his foot and dropping him to the hard ground. Then there was something around him. A rope. No, a vine. Then more and more vines were constricting his chest.

"What are you doing, woman?"

"It's my magic. It gets out of hand. Aren't you the most powerful king? Do something."

The vines were making it hard for him to breathe. "What? Kill you?"

"Maybe. Or disappear in the hollow. At least I won't have to hear your rubbish again."

He didn't want to die, but he couldn't slip away, and couldn't kill her either. It took a lot of effort, but he managed to speak even if he was almost being strangled. "If you don't control it, you'll kill me."

"You deserve it." She smiled. "Actually, no. You deserve worse."

The vines got looser, allowing him to catch a breath, but now they were growing thorns.

He was in disbelief. "You're going to torture me?"

"How many times do I have to explain that I don't control my magic? Now, while we're both still alive, please explain yourself. You say I betrayed you. I didn't, but let's assume you really think so. How dare you? How dare you accuse me of that? Three months after the gathering, your children with the disgraced Ironhold princess were born. I know how babies are made—obviously. And I know how long it takes. So funny that some people comment how much you loved Princess Ticiane. Poor Azir, never married again. Poor Azir, risked his reputation for love. Well, no. You betrayed her with me. I was never even your first choice. So don't come at me making up these stupid, offensive excuses. You were lying to me the whole time you were courting me."

"I wasn't lying. I didn't even know Ticiane. That happened after."

"Azir." She rolled her eyes. "Again, we're both adults, we both know how children are made, and we both know how long it takes. Just own it. Say it. Say I was just a distraction.

Don't give this ridiculous 'you betrayed me' lie. You know in your heart it's not true."

Azir closed his eyes. Perhaps he did know in his heart that Ursiana and Sebastian didn't make sense. But the Wolfmark princess had told him... Could it have been a plot to separate him from Ursiana? But then again, he'd seen it with his own eyes. He'd seen it.

"Silent?" Ursiana said. "You can't explain Ticiane, can you?" She rolled her eyes. "I mean, the explanation is obvious."

"It's a complicated story, yes." Way too complicated, and not something he wanted anyone to find out. Ursiana was glaring at him and he decided it was better to try to appease her. "And I'm sorry. If it's really true you were never with Sebastian—"

A vine slapped his face. "*If* it's true? How dare you?"

She *was* furious. But it didn't make sense that she'd never been in that garden. It couldn't be that this whole time he'd been deceived by a lie. It couldn't. The vines were again wrapping him tight. "I guess this is where your magic kills me."

She shook her head. "Hopefully not. Trust me, Azir. I really don't think a fast, easy death suits you."

"Aren't I lucky?" A strange laugh came out of his throat, perhaps because of the absurdity of it all, the absurdity of being stuck here while Ironhold attacked, while his kingdom could be in danger. And yet here he was, unable to do anything, being attacked by green magic from someone he once had loved. Once? Or still? "At least all you do when your magic goes berserk is conjure some cute vines."

"Creepy vines, Azir. Don't insult them or they might get angrier."

"As you say." He didn't think there was anything creepy about her magic—or about her. True that the vine around him was getting tight. "I think it likes me, you know? It's hugging me and won't let go. I mean, if you want to hug me, you can do it, no need to use your vines."

His words did the trick, as the vines receded.

"What about you?" Her eyes were full of loathing and derision. "What does your magic unleash, deathbringer?"

This was not something he wanted to think about. Not in this place. "Let's hope we never find out, shall we?"

LEAH HELD her breath as she watched the guards around her panicking, many of them running away, except that they were falling down, as if that death mist, whatever it was, made them unconscious—or dead. She looked at the railing to check if there was a way for her to climb down, and felt an arrow flying past her. There were guards at the bottom too.

She ran back to her room, now that the guards were dispersing. Her idea was to close the door and put sheets around the cracks to block the gas, to give her some time— hoping there would be time.

Then someone grabbed her wrist. It was a brown-haired young man that she didn't think she'd seen before.

Leah felt darkness closing on them, then she was in an office with some shelves and books, a desk, and two armchairs.

"Believe it or not, I'm here to save you," he whispered. "Don't scream or make any noise."

"Where are we?"

"Still in the Ironhold castle. But they won't check here. Just don't try to go anywhere."

She was about to thank him, when she realized he had horns and pointy ears. "You're fae."

"Oops." He touched his head, then closed his eyes. "Indeed."

It didn't make any sense. "Why are you helping me?"

"Isofel. I had a deal with him."

His words put her at ease. She didn't think Fel would wish her harm, but to make a deal with a fae? It was all strange. "Why would he do that?"

The fae rolled his eyes. "Think hard and deep about it, and I'm sure you'll figure it out. Now, you look depleted of your magic, so rest. Don't try anything or it might kill you."

"Necromancy can't kill anyone." She then realized the nonsense she had just said. "I mean..."

"Look, I won't pretend to be a scholar on human magic, but you seem about to pass out, so rest." He frowned, looking at her. "Are you sure you're a necromancer?"

Again that question. "Why?"

He shrugged. "Nothing. I'm obviously not an expert on human magic, so nevermind. I'll be back tomorrow, then take you somewhere safe."

"Why not tonight?"

He rolled his eyes again. They were not brown, like she had thought at first, but dark red. "As I've told you, you need to rest. Just don't open the door, no matter what happens, and don't let anyone hear you."

She was going to be locked up again, having to trust a fae, of all people. But it was better than being in that hall with nowhere to go. There was just one issue. "What if I need to pee?"

He shrugged and looked around, then pointed to a vase. "There."

"That's disgusting."

"Then keep it in. I don't care."

With that, he disappeared. Great. Now she was making alliances with Fae. No, Isofel was making alliances with them. But why? And why would he ask him to save her? Of course she wanted to think that it was because he cared about her, but she didn't want to deceive herself anymore. And it still didn't answer how come Fel knew him.

Her thoughts then turned to the moments before she'd been rescued. What had happened back there? She'd killed Cassius and a number of guards. Not only killed them, but felt an immense glee, an immense satisfaction in doing it. Now all that was left was regret and emptiness. It was true that she had been angry. But there had been something more, as if death itself had been calling to her, or maybe something else, something sinister, dark, powerful—and terrifying. It was something that had a will, something sentient. Or had it been just her?

This was so strange, so unlike everything her father had taught her. Her father. Leah closed her eyes, remembering Venard's threats. How soon would Ironhold strike? Would they strike? She should have asked that fae to take her to Frostlake. She had to warn her parents, tell them that there could be ironbringers in the Ironhold committee, tell them to be careful. Then she remembered that the Umbraar king was going to Frostlake. Strange that he was worried about her mother. As far as Leah knew, she hated him. Odd.

So much that made no sense. Now she had to figure out what was happening to her magic, and find a way to reach her parents. That was one and the same. If she went home, her father would help her understand her magic—and she would be safe. The issue was getting there. Still, her main feeling was relief, relief at escaping Cassius, and also horror at what had almost happened. The problem was that her actions likely caused a bigger conflict, and she would need to be ready for it.

But she was tired. Exhausted, to be more precise. She lay on a sofa and then felt weariness settling in. As her body relaxed, her thoughts stopped spinning in her mind. And still she worried about Frostlake and her parents. Ironhold would likely strike in retaliation. But something didn't add up. There was something... She recalled what Cassius had almost done, without the slightest fear of repercussion, recalled the way they had been treating her, even hurting her. So many times she had wondered why they thought they could get away with it, and now the obvious answer struck her like a dagger in the chest.

Ironhold had never planned for her to meet her parents again. They wanted to control her, and then control her kingdom. Returning to Frostlake wasn't going to grant her the freedom she wanted. Either Ironhold had already struck, or they were about to strike. That truth settled in with a bitter taste in her mouth. It made sense and was obvious—but horrific as well. She had to go there right now, she had to. But how?

24
ESCAPE

Fel hadn't moved away from his father's office, but it had been two hours now. Two long hours. Something wrong had happened. But what? Could it be that he'd run into trouble while taking Leah to the dreadful iron kingdom? No. That was nonsense. Leah was probably happy there, holding hands with her dear husband. The words sounded wrong. Fel still felt pain in his chest whenever he thought about Leah. It was probably his broken heart. That had to be it.

His father had said he was going to Frostlake. Frostlake and Ironhold were allies, especially now that they were united by marriage. But Leah had been worried about her parents. He kept thinking, trying to understand, and came to no conclusion. There was something wrong happening. The question was what.

With his father gone, the decisions were up to him. He could wait. And yet, he felt that even the air was different. He stepped outside and looked at the sky from the balcony. It was as if the wind itself was bringing a warning of danger. Unless he was imagining it. But he knew Ironhold would attack.

Perhaps they still thought he was dead, but they would attack. In fact, that had been likely the reason they'd wanted to kill him.

Fel took a deep breath. Perhaps it would be brash, hasty. Still, he'd rather be criticized for being too cautious than for getting caught unaware.

He walked to the courtyard and rang the bell twice. Umbraar was going on alert. From here, he would send riders to the biggest villages, telling the commoners to hide. There were shelters underground and by the mountains. Enough for seven to ten days, in case an enemy came in. He felt it in his skin, he felt it his breath, he felt it in his bones. Ironhold was coming.

EXHAUSTION HAD TAKEN hold of Leah. The problem was that as she almost drifted into sleep, her mind kept repeating the image of Cassius in her bedroom, then his life fading away.

Her father had told her that killing was one of the worst things anyone could do; as it wasn't our right to decide who stayed and who moved on from this life. But then, perhaps what Cassius had been about to do had been worse? So much disgust, so much horror. And Venard, where had he been? Perhaps hiding somewhere. Then she remembered the guards she'd killed. Innocent guards, just obeying orders. And yet it had felt so good to kill them, so good to feel the power of taking away a life. Her father wouldn't be proud of her now. What was happening with her magic?

Then Leah was walking in a foggy forest, a horrible feeling of being watched nagging on her. It all felt strange and wrong. She tried to hold her hands together, and instead, they crossed. This was a dream, not whatever had happened that made her do something horrible and shameful with Isofel.

"Leah!"

Kasim's voice. She ran in that direction, and saw him and her father, but they were semi-transparent, as if fading away.

Her father's eyes were sad as he looked at her. "I'm so sorry. I never meant to hurt you. I never should have let you go to Ironhold."

"You couldn't have known." She had been angry before, but now she didn't want him to feel guilty for her. "How are you?"

It was Kasim who answered. "We are fine. But Frostlake isn't. Don't go there now. Wait. Wait until you can save its people. You will always be its true queen."

"What's happening?"

"Don't go to Frostlake," her father said, but his voice was fading away. "Save yourself if you want to save the kingdom."

Then he and Kasim disappeared.

"Dad? Kasim?" She didn't want them to go. There was so much she had to say, so much she wanted to ask. But then, there was so little she could control in a dream.

Frostlake in danger? As she had feared. She thought about her maid Siana, about the people in the kitchen, the guards, about everyone in the city and felt a horrible tightness in her chest. She remembered those training grounds she'd seen, with the ironbringers. What was Ironhold doing to her kingdom?

She felt a bitter taste in her mouth, then breathed some kind of dust.

Leah opened her eyes and realized she was no longer on the sofa, but on the floor, lying on hard wood. At least it wasn't cold granite or marble. But it was... She looked around. It couldn't be. The double bed was the same, but white sheets covered the furniture. It had been her room, her room as a single girl, the room that was no longer hers, but was now a memory.

She was going to try to check if it was a dream, but didn't even bother. It was real. And it was all quiet, so perhaps nothing had happened. She got up, eager to find her mother, her father, to tell them to prepare, to tell them everything. Everything. Except that shameful part with Fel.

As she moved to the door, she heard steps and a stranger's voice.

"Find all the servants. Each and every one of them. We need to know what happened. We need to find out who betrayed Frostlake to the Fae."

So something had happened. Her stomach lurched, together with the hope she'd had. Fae? Could the fae have been involved in this? Well, she had seen a fae—but he'd saved her. And then, there had been the attack during the gathering. Maybe. But it would be a strange coincidence. Why right now? She still didn't recognize the voice, and she knew most of the main guards. But he'd said, "who betrayed Frostlake", not "who betrayed us." It could be someone from Ironhold.

"Find anyone who's hiding," the voice said, now even closer.

Then she heard a key in her lock. Someone was coming. But was it an ally or an enemy?

NAIA FELT as if there had been a glass wall between her and the scene in front of her. What a scene. It was herself, asleep on her bed, and River looking at her. She knew he'd done something: he'd put her to sleep. Naia banged on that glass wall, but it made no sound. Her wish was to cross that glass and slap him for what he was doing to her. This was so wrong.

And yet she paused, noticing the way he looked at her. So much tenderness and care, such a sweet stare. His eyes always got her, but seeing him like this, she could swear he loved the girl he was looking at. To be looked at like that was something she'd always wanted, to have someone looking at her as if she were his whole world, everything.

But he had enchanted her and she didn't understand why. He had hidden things from her, and she didn't understand why. And then all his stare did was make her conflicted. But she had to escape this sleep, had to escape this enchantment. Perhaps she shouldn't be as moved by the way River looked at her. After all, it was very easy to love someone who couldn't talk back. But oh, she was going to break that spell. And then he was going to hear it all. She doubted his look would still be sweet.

20 years before

RIVER ASSUMED this freezing magic was only meant for the dragon lords to catch whoever tried to steal their artifact, and not meant to kill him. Unless they kept a gallery of aspiring thieves, all frozen, ready to be displayed.

Regardless of what they did, they had to be awake to do it. And now, with the lapse stones, he wasn't sure if anyone would find him. He wasn't even sure if anyone could enter the circle and still move.

And now he was stuck to this dragon lair, with no way out. He pushed against the ice, but it was too thick. If only he could produce heat, but that wasn't a type of magic Ancients had.

He didn't want to die. He wanted to see his sister again, wanted to see his father. He did care for his people, he did care for his family, and he wanted the chance to tell them. He wanted to apologize to his brother, apologize even if he thought nothing had been his fault. And more than anything, he wanted to help the Ancients. The humans in Aluria not only had magic, they had weapons with steel, they had fire and explosions, and it wasn't fair. He had to do something—and he was trying.

Perhaps knowing that he died trying would mean something, but then nobody would know about it. And he'd never get the chance to say goodbye, just like he had never gotten the chance to say goodbye to his cousin. River would do anything for another chance. A chance to do it different.

His body extremities were already numb when he saw a light outside the ice—a flame. Perhaps some dragon lord had overcome their spell and was coming. He didn't like that idea, but at least it could mean that he wasn't going to be frozen to death. The person had a torch or something, as they were melting the ice with it. When the last part cracked, he saw that his savior was a young woman with black hair, brown skin, and brown eyes, staring at him in curiosity. River didn't want to owe a life debt, but owing it to such a gorgeous girl certainly wouldn't be the end of the world.

"I... guess you caught me," he said. "Well done."

"I have nothing to do with this..." She looked at the puddle formed by the melted ice. "Very wet spell. I just came to save you." She then glanced at the top of his head, as if surprised by his lack of horns, which made no sense—and was embarrassing.

Yikes. Fine, gorgeous or not, in reality he wasn't in the mood to owe her a life debt. He pointed at her. "That's debatable."

She rolled her eyes. "River, please, let's not start, shall we? It gets kind of ridiculous."

He wondered how she knew his name. And he didn't like being called ridiculous. "You know my name and I don't know yours. We should fix that."

With a stunning smile, she said, "We will." He waited for

her to introduce herself, but instead, she added, "Go. Your stones won't hold the dragons for long."

Great. She knew his name and all about his secret magic. He tried to change the subject. "You do realize they're not real dragons, right?"

"That highly depends on your definition of real. Go."

He glanced at the staff.

She stared at it, her eyes sad. "Take it."

"That's a trick, right? What's gonna happen next? I'm going to be encased in fire?"

"Take it." There was a certain hesitation in her words. "Perhaps it's been meant for you."

"Who are you?"

"Just go. And stop asking questions. Or maybe I *will* encase you in fire."

It was as if his brain melted, thinking about that beautiful girl and a different kind of fire, imagining his lips on hers, his hands on her body, wanting her even more than that staff. He smiled. "Maybe I won't mind it."

She exhaled and rolled her eyes. "I didn't know you were that perverted."

"I'm not... Hey. You shouldn't know anything about me." And yet he still wanted to kiss her. "Are you enchanting me?"

"All right. I just came to save your life, and I had no idea you'd be all weird. I mean, perhaps I should have guessed. Anyway, I'm leaving, River." She turned around and started walking away.

"How do you know my name?" he shouted.

She turned and sighed. "For the last time, go. The dragons are dangerous, even if you managed to trick them. Go, and go as fast as you can."

"Come with me, then."

After staring at him for a moment, she said, "Fine," then took his hand and pulled him.

There was a strange, pleasant energy between them. Soon he was following her, running down a stairway by the hill, a stairway he hadn't seen before.

River was careful not to slip on the small steps. "I still want to know who you are."

"It doesn't matter." She sucked in a breath. "My time's up." Her eyes locked on his, as if she wanted to say something. There was such a mix of emotions there that made him confused.

And yet he felt as if she liked him—a lot. There was warmth and familiarity in those eyes, as if she'd known him for a long time, but it made no sense, and then, at the same time, it explained how she knew his name. River had no time to figure out what any of that meant, as she disappeared, her lips slightly parted, as if about to say a word. But there was nothingness where she had once stood.

River took the stones quickly, knowing the dragon lords would notice the missing staff, but then ran to the village, traded a horse for fake gold and galloped back to the port. He'd need to get in the first boat to Aluria, and quick.

As he left the mountain and the "lair" behind, as the wonder of meeting his beautiful savior faded, his heart sped up, and it wasn't with fear or worry. It was knowing that he had gotten the staff, knowing that it was on its way to its people. For the first time, he'd be able to look his father in the eyes with pride. This was legendary. He was going to save the Ancients.

CROUCHED under a sheet that was covering one of her tables, Leah heard the door open and someone step into her old room. Perhaps she should run to them, tell them Frostlake could be in danger, then run past them and try to find her parents. She just wanted to save her family, to save her kingdom.

And yet here she was, crouching. Her father's words from the dream came to her mind: "save yourself." But she wished she could save everyone. No, she wished there would be no need for any saving.

The steps coming in were heavy, and sounded like boots.

"Empty. No recent fire or candle," a man said.

It wasn't a voice she recognized. She peered from under the sheet and saw the rim of the man's pants. Gray, like Ironhold's uniforms. Probably.

A second man then spoke. "No. We need to find the queen. She could be hiding anywhere."

Find the queen? It meant her mother had escaped. But then, it also meant that they were targeting her.

The man continued, "And any servants who might be hiding. This would be a good hiding place. Search the room."

This wasn't good. Leah could try to pretend she was a servant, but only if people didn't look at her too closely. Few people had both blue eyes and dark skin, so she was too easily recognizable.

The table she'd chosen was small, though, so maybe they would ignore it. The men shuffled curtains, opened the wardrobe, moved the bed, and yet her hiding spot was left alone. She didn't want Ironhold soldiers to find her. But would they even know it was her, when she was supposed to be in their evil castle? Still, she didn't like this.

The steps receded and the only reason she didn't exhale in relief was not to make any sound.

Her plan now was to wait until the hall was quiet, then leave her room and try to find her parents while pretending to be a servant. But they were also searching for servants. That didn't make sense. Why would they bother with that?

Right as these thoughts crossed her mind, she heard steps again, then saw the sheet being pulled.

Leah covered her eyes and trembled, pretending to be scared. Not that she wasn't scared, but she wouldn't normally be covering her face and trembling like that. "Don't hurt me," she pleaded, hoping they would believe she was just a young, scared servant and not look too much at her.

"Oh, would you look at that?" The stupid soldier was mocking her. "What a cute, scared little thing."

Fear became a cold chill running all over her body. His tone reminded her of Cassius, reminded her of what she'd gone through in Ironhold, and she was crouched, cornered, in a position from where there was no escape.

"Let's bring her to the dungeons," the second man said, his tone harsh. That was much better than his companion's lecherous remarks.

"Don't be so boring, a few minutes won't hurt anyone." He chuckled, then touched her face and cooed, "Right? My pretty thing."

Her body was about to turn to ice. Perhaps she could yell for help. There were certainly still Frostlake guards in the castle. But then she would be found out. Perhaps she was overreacting and all the man wanted was to make her feel uncomfortable, to let her know that he had power over her.

No. He wasn't the one with power. Something snapped inside her. Leah opened her eyes, pushed his hand away and glared at him. "Get away from me."

"Oooh, she's got spirit." He laughed. "Or what?"

"Death."

The man smiled, but she only saw his reaction for a couple seconds, as the room soon turned dark. The candle they had brought faded, and even the light from the moon disappeared. All light, all life was being sucked out of that place—slowly. The man screamed and screamed.

"Look, he's got spirit," she mocked.

Yes, that's it. Kill them all. Kill everyone. A voice in her head. Comforting. Empowering. Familiar. She could kill everyone. She should. Kill all the Ironhold invaders. It would feel so good. It was just a matter of relaxing, letting go, letting that power flow.

Then an image came to her: her parents. If she killed everyone, they would die. Not only them, but also Siena, all the cooks, the guards, the castle workers' children.

And so what? the voice said.

Are you kidding me? she replied, still in her head.

The light from the window again illuminated the room. There was a dry branch in front of her. Not a branch. She stifled a cry begging to come out of her throat. It was the man's corpse, dried. She pushed him and got up, trembling.

The other man was crouching, eyes closed, hands covering his ears, his entire body trembling, which meant he was very much alive. Leah was at once relieved and afraid. She didn't want to kill anyone else, but she couldn't let this man tell anyone what he'd seen. That weird death thing was gone. It didn't feel like a power she could use, but rather like something that took control of her. And now it was gone.

Leah had to act fast, as the dead man's screams would have attracted attention.

Out of options, she dashed out of the room, hoping to get to a secret passage before anyone caught her.

25

THE WAVE

20 years before

River made it to the port city without stopping, without sleeping, trading horses on the way, fueled by the excitement and anticipation of getting that staff back to the Ancient City. If this artifact could really counter human magic, it could mean their victory, their freedom.

He would need to find a ship going to Aluria right away, and glamour the captain to let him join the crew. Perhaps he would even glamour them into leaving early. River had looked back a few times, and saw no pursuers. He'd been ready for a fight, or to try to trick the dragon lords, and yet none of them had come. Perhaps it was because he was traveling fast. And yet he had an eerie, ominous feeling.

Could it be that the pretty, mysterious lady had done something to protect him? Maybe. The memory of her had been bothering him too. He would spend the rest of his life wondering who she was, wondering why she had helped him, thinking about her and wishing he could have spent more time with her. The funny part was that he sensed no life debt.

It was almost as if her actions didn't count or, worse, as if she no longer existed, which was an uncomfortable thought.

He'd always thought love at first sight was the epitome of ridiculous. *Well, congratulations, River.* But it wasn't love, it was a yearning, a wanting, something hard to explain. The thought that he'd spend the rest of his life with that wanting unfulfilled didn't make anything better. But he had the staff, and that made everything better.

The sun was rising when he got to the port, rising like his hope. Four ships were docked there, and as a sign of his good luck, one of them was ready to go, a Fernick ship, and River convinced the captain to let him travel with them.

The ship was called *Golden Mountain*, and wasn't decorated with skulls like the Alurian ships, even if they also benefited from the Umbraar death magic allowing them to cross. They left in the late morning, after three tense hours when River had been hiding downstairs, dreading being accosted by angry dragon lords.

When the anchor was raised and he felt the movement of the boat, he barely believed his luck, barely believed he was on his way home, barely believed he had the staff. Perhaps it had indeed been destiny, and destiny was smiling upon him.

His euphoria soon faded, though, as a strong headache took its place. He felt as if someone had a hammer and a stake and was poking his skull. Wait. There was something poking his head all right—but inside out. His horns were coming out, and he bemoaned all the times he had wished for this to happen.

Why did it have to be *now*? He could glamour them, of course, at least in theory, unless pain consumed him, then it was a little hard to keep the glamour on. To make matters worse, since the horns were new, he wasn't used to disguising them. But they were still small, just two little, ridiculous stumps, and if he messed his hair, perhaps he could get by. He lay down on his cot the whole night.

The morning brought fever and shivering, which was something quite rare in Ancients, but happened during the horning. Horning. That was usually a whole event where the young one going through the transition had friends and distant family came by with gifts, food, and comfort. River had spent his childhood expecting this, and now he was having it while on a ship surrounded by humans—right when they were at war with his people.

The captain came down, looked at him from a distance, then ordered him to go to a small storage room on the other side of the boat. They feared he had a contagious disease, which made sense. River carried his cot and clothes with difficulty and complied. At least being alone meant he wouldn't need to glamour himself, and that was a relief. Still, he tied a headscarf around the top of his head, just to be safe. He'd seen some sailors wearing those, and it was the perfect disguise for both horns and ears.

When night was falling, someone opened the door. It was their cook and healer, an old man called Von, bringing him some soup.

River was thankful, but also curious. "Aren't you afraid you'll get sick?"

The man snorted. "I've seen plague come and go. You probably just ate something you're not used to. The body does that. It thinks your food is poison, then fights it. So much fighting." He sighed. "But it's best that you stay here. Makes everyone feel better."

"It does." He tried a smile, despite still feeling like something was puncturing his skull. It wasn't puncturing, but growing from it, which didn't change the feeling. He then added, "And I appreciate the food." This was dangerously close to thanking the man, and River didn't want to be indebted, but he felt it would be odd not to say anything.

Von waved a hand. "It's nothing." He stared at River's eyes for a second too long, a second in which River tried to make sure they looked brown, without being absolutely certain. The man then said, "I'll let you rest," and left.

Hopefully he hadn't noticed what River was. He spent the night fearing not only that the dragon lords would somehow find him, but that the crew of the *Golden Mountain* would come and toss him from the boat, or worse, take him as a prisoner.

The fever and pain didn't subside for the next day, but Von kept bringing him food. On the second night, the old man pointed at his head. "They're showing."

"What?" River ran his hand over the headscarf, realizing the bumps were much larger now. But that couldn't be what the man had meant, could it?

The man shook his head and snorted. "Don't try to fool me. I know what you are. Your eyes turn almost red sometimes, just so you know."

His voice was too calm for someone who knew he was an Ancient. "You mean... I am..."

"A halfling. Got some fae blood in you, don't you?"

River exhaled. Right. There was some inter-mixing in the villages where Ancients and humans lived in harmony. Had lived in harmony. And probably a lot of inter-mixing in Fernick. "Some fae blood, yes. But I'm also human." Just one-eighth human, but still.

"Well, tie that scarf looser so people won't notice it. It's tough for your kind right now. In fact, I don't understand why you're going to Aluria."

"It's my home."

The man sighed and eventually left. A halfling. He'd never thought what would happen to humans who were partly fae. In Aluria, some of these families had moved to the Ancient

City, along with so many refugees, but there were obviously more of them, still living among humans. And yet there was nothing he could do about that. He had to hope the Umbraar king didn't find their city and that his father could use the staff and counter the human magic.

At least they were getting close to Aluria and should be there by the next evening. That night, as he slept, the sound of a rumble woke him up. It was loud, but still muffled, as if far away. It sounded sort of like thunder, but there was no rain.

He closed his eyes again, and was almost dozing off, when the boat turned upside down. He hit the ceiling of his storage room hard, and heard screams above him, on the ship. No, below. The boat had been overturned, and soon water came in through the cracks. He tried to push the door open, but it didn't move, as the water pressed on it. The only thing he had was the staff, which he used to hit the door. When he was already submerged, he opened a hole big enough for him to swim through, and left with the magical artifact. He was almost out of air when he reached the turbulent surface.

The sky was still clear, no clouds in view, and yet, something had turned the boat. Something like a huge wave. At least it wasn't as bad as a sea serpent, and at least the water wasn't cold. There were screams and shouts in the distance, and he hoped the crew had survived. He would need to wait for a boat to rescue him—unlikely—or maybe he'd have to swim to shore.

The problem was that he didn't even know in which direction Aluria was. The ocean was a tangle of dark waves under an eerily calm, starry sky. He found a piece of floating wood and held onto it with one hand, while tying the staff to his belt, keeping his strength for the morning, when the sun would help him find his direction. Perhaps he should have studied the stars, like the sailors, then he would know where to go.

Either way, the ocean had to become calmer for him to advance.

When the sky turned red, waiting for the sun to make its appearance, the ocean calmed down. Overcome by exhaustion, he was almost falling asleep when he saw it—the green sheen of scales. Great. He'd been admonishing his luck, as if things couldn't possibly get worse. It turned out that they could.

Perhaps if he remained quiet, the monster wouldn't see him—or sense or smell him. There were many debris floating on the surface and perhaps that would confuse the serpent.

Then something emerged from the water, and it was the size of a medium boat, but it was just a head. At first he saw the huge green eyes, then the gigantic mouth, which opened, showing double rows of sharp teeth, and uttered a roaring scream.

That was bizarre. He thought that creatures screamed when they were afraid or wanted to intimidate the enemy. There was no possible way River could be any more intimidated than he already was, he who was some twenty times smaller than the creature. Perhaps it wanted to let him know that it was angry. Other than fear, River felt regret. Regret for not asking more about this staff. If it could wield powerful magic, perhaps it could defeat that serpent, except that it was useless in his hand. And he had to bring it to the Ancient City. He couldn't die here, after all he'd gone through. And yet he stared at that huge mouth, unsure what to do.

Huge mouth. He had one shot: jump in it, beyond the rows of teeth, then hurt the creature from the inside. But then a strong flash of light hit his eyes, and he was unable to see anything for a few seconds. When he looked again, the creature had receded, probably also affected by the light. Then there was another sea serpent, smaller, white.

"Don't hurt it," a woman's voice said. Not any voice, the voice of the girl who had saved him. Now, he wasn't sure if she was talking to him or to the serpent. Serpents. He was getting confused. The smaller serpent made an odd, hissing sound, and the bigger one replied, as if they were having a conversation. Perhaps they were debating who was going to eat him, except that he still thought the voice had come from the smaller serpent, which made no sense. Last he remembered, the girl who had saved him had no scales.

But whatever happened, the big serpent swam away, which meant River was safe, at least for now. After another bright light, he did see the dark-haired girl, but she was floating above the ocean, and sort of transparent.

"You saved me again?" he asked, too exhausted to try to pretend there had been no saving.

She tilted his head. "Again? Why? You've been needing more saving than this?"

"In the dragon lair."

The pretty girl shook her head. "It wasn't me."

But she wasn't a faerie, and she could probably lie. He just didn't understand why. But what bothered him most was her eerie appearance. "Are you dead?"

"This is my spirit form, but there are more meanings than death to it."

"If you tell me your name, next time I see you, I'll be sure it's you."

"A name's just a temporary word, given to our mortal form."

"You're dead, then." He sighed. "Maybe you should have let the serpent eat me, then I'd meet you."

She smiled. "Your time's not over yet."

"I'm not even sure I'll make it to Formosa."

"You won't. But you're near Aluria. Vastfield, see?" She pointed, and as he looked in that direction, he did see the outline of the shore. "Not a city, but I think you can find your way from there."

It didn't seem far. "You aren't going to disappear again, are you? And leave me here?'

She had a beautiful smile. "You don't expect me to stick around, do you? Just imagine the awkwardness of it." Her face then turned somber. "But we'll meet again. Be strong. Dark times are upon you. But you... You're good, River. Never forget that."

"I'm pretty good at so many things, you should try to—"

"Shush it." She rolled her eyes. Could vision or spirit forms or whatever roll their eyes? "At least you'll grow up."

"Hey. Did you just call me a kid?"

"You *are* a kid." She sighed. "But it won't last long." There was sadness in her eyes. "Stay strong. And never forget who you are." With that, she disappeared—again, leaving him alone to swim to the shore.

He got to a beach after a couple hours swimming. Vastfield. This kingdom was far from Ironhold, and hadn't been much affected by the war. While the Ancient dwellings had been emptied, some of the fae rings still remained, and River got to the Ancient City by evening. His clothes were tattered, his hair tangled, but he went straight to the grand hall, hoping to find his father.

What he found instead was a celebration. Not a big celebration, just the royal family and their most entrusted ones, but it was still at odds with the war and all the tragedy they'd gone through. There was wine, fruit, meat, musicians, and, strangest of all, there was a lightness and relief in the air, even some happiness, which he hadn't seen in a long time. For a moment he hoped that they knew he was coming and what he was bringing, but since nobody seemed to notice him, he soon realized that was probably not the case.

"Brother! You finally grace us with your presence."

Oh, no. Forest. He was the eldest, but they hadn't spoken for over a year. Perhaps it had been River's fault, but still. He'd spent some intimate moments with a female guard, only later to learn that his brother had been in love with her. The fact that River hadn't known anything did nothing to appease Forest. Or the fact he had been quite young. Love was a tricky thing. Ancients were not possessive by nature, and were prone to temporary flings without attachment. But that wasn't the case with his family, probably due to the human blood. That could cause some problems. And it was as if Forest envied River, which was ridiculous, since he was the eldest and the heir, and always did everything to please their father, even if he didn't have to. It was almost as if he resented River's rebellion and carelessness. To top it all, Forest had the white hair and red eyes of the Ancients, with magnificent horns, and no physical sign of his human ancestry.

River brushed it all aside, actually happy that Forest was speaking to him. "What's the celebration for?"

His brother snorted and looked at him up and down. "Where have you been? Lost in a swamp?"

"Sort of."

"Well. You should thank me." That meant an uncomfortable debt and needed to be for a good reason. "We just had a winning blow against the humans."

This was great news, considering they hadn't had any victory in so long. "Really? Congratulations. What happened?"

Forest smirked. "The Umbraar city, and practically the kingdom, is no more."

He recalled the rumble and the waves, and had a queasy feeling. "What do you mean?"

"Their big city, where they had their castle, their port, it's gone. The royal family is gone. They won't threaten us again." He smiled.

"What do you mean it's gone?"

He shrugged. "Gone. The cliff collapsed on it, buried the city under layers and layers of broken stones."

Formosa. Where a granddaughter had received a gift from Keller, where a wedding had taken place, where many innocent people lived. His brother couldn't be so callous about it, all these people celebrating couldn't be so callous about it. River's knees almost buckled.

But it couldn't be true, it didn't make sense. It had to have been an accident, something else, his brother couldn't have done something so monstrous. "Can we step outside for a moment?"

"River, I'd love to give you my time, but as you can see, this is my night."

"Step outside or I'll talk to you here." He raised his voice enough that other people stared at them.

"Two seconds, then."

When they were on the balcony, River asked, "What magic did you use? Ancients don't have any magic that can break stone."

"I figured something out."

River was disgusted. "And you used to kill innocents?"

"Innocents?" He laughed. "They would kill us all if they could. We were losing, in case you didn't notice. This city won't hold us for long. If they keep destroying Mount Prime, we'll all need to move to Aluria, but that will be impossible if there are humans everywhere. I did something, River, while you did nothing, as usual."

"Nothing?" He was still holding the staff. "Want to guess what this is?"

Forest frowned. "You wouldn't have gotten past the dragons. This is some trick, isn't it?"

"I got past the dragons, and this is their staff. I just got back from Fernick. You didn't have to kill innocents."

"Humans kill innocents all the time," Forest said. "They've wiped entire villages."

"But if we become like them, then what are we fighting for?"

"Survival. I hope you're not stuck in a childish idea of good or evil." He stared at River's head. "Oh, you do have cute little Ancient horns, though, so being childish maybe fits you. You're what? Eight, ten years behind?"

"That's not the point. You don't just destroy an entire city, you don't."

"River. Aluria is too small for both Ancients and humans. It's as simple as that. Only one of us will survive. I want it to be us." He pointed at the staff. "This is really the dragon staff?"

"It was in the dragon's lair, well protected."

"And you took it on your own?"

River smirked. "I also have some tricks you know nothing about."

"You should have taken one of them dragon's hearts."

"They're not dragons, they're magicians."

"Whatever. The hearts have powerful magic."

"Yuck. I'm not taking anyone's heart."

Forest sighed. "Pity. But just the staff is great, and will probably seal our victory. I..." He bit his lip, as if thinking. "Let's forget the past. I say we present it together to our father, to show our union. He'll be happy."

"I don't unite with mass murderers."

Forest grimaced. "You make no sense. Go alone then. You think our father will believe you?"

"Why wouldn't he? I can't lie."

His brother took a deep breath. "I want to help you, make sure he believes this is the staff."

River was still too horrified to walk with his brother, but on the other hand, if they were all celebrating, they were all cold and callous and didn't care. Perhaps many of them could have destroyed a city if they could. Perhaps it was a response to so much suffering, pain, and loss, a numbness that made them monstrous. But if the staff could counter human magic, it was a solution. River had to show it to his father, and his brother's presence would only help.

River nodded. "You're right."

"Let me carry it." Forest extended his hand.

It felt wrong to give it to him, but then again, if the idea was to make his father care, then he wasn't going to overthink it.

They walked into the grand hall. River's father was sitting at the edge of a long table and pretended he didn't see him.

"Father," Forest said. "This is the dragon staff. It can be our salvation."

"Really?"

Forest nodded. "I retrieved it."

That made no sense. It wasn't true. How was his brother even saying that?

His father's eyes widened. "You didn't!"

"I did. It was taken from Fernick before the awful Umbraar city was destroyed."

River turned around. He didn't even want to argue, there was no point. At least the Ancients had a way to win that war, a way that hopefully wouldn't involve killing countless people.

FEL STOOD on the rampart of the fort, watching the forest, wondering if he was stirring up his people and worrying everyone for no reason. The borders were well guarded and the portals even more. And yet his father had not returned. And Leah... Had been sent back to the eye of the storm—where it was calm, though. But only temporarily.

The more he thought back to the moment she had left, the

more he realized he wished he could do it all over again. He
didn't care about his pride, about anything. He'd beg her to
stay here, stay safe. Safe. For how long? No, he'd send her
away to safety, send her to one of the hidden caves, and at least
he would be sure nothing bad happened to her. Now worry
and guilt gnawed on his insides. He'd been trying to tell
himself that she was happy with her husband, but the excuses
sounded weaker and weaker. He'd been trying to believe it
had been her choice, but then realized he had never given her
an alternative, had never truly asked her to stay, still angry
about that stupid note that her mother had probably made
her write.

The sound of fast hooves made him turn and go down the
steps to the court. A young soldier. Fel walked past the men
drawn to the commotion.

"They're coming," the young man said. His voice was weak,
shaky, and he was visibly exhausted.

"Who? From where?"

He shook his head. "About one, two hundred soldiers.
Ironhold. On foot. From the Blue Forest."

That was at most an hour away. Fel trembled. "That can't
be. It's closer than the borders, even closer than the portals."

"Yes," the man agreed.

Fel wanted to run, wanted to hide, wanted to count on his
father to keep him safe. Yes, he had prepared for that, he had
even considered that something like this was about to happen,
and still, learning that it was real felt like more than he could
handle.

He closed his eyes quickly, determined to get ahold of
himself and schooling his features to display calm and
certainty. How could he lead and inspire if he showed fear?
There were ten men surrounding him, and it was time for
action.

"You, take him to the healer," Fel said. "The rest of you are going to wake up everyone in this fort and tell them to get ready. No bells. Not now. Split up." He told each of them to go in one direction, then ran back to his quarters to get his sword. No. He'd have to fight without it. He removed every piece of iron he was wearing, with the exception of his hands, then went back outside.

So far he wasn't even sure if they were coming in their direction, but they were too close and there was nothing else they could be after in Umbraar. If three assassins had found Fel coming out of the fort, of course they knew this was an important place. Perhaps they even knew he was alive and that his father had also been staying here.

Fel looked at the huge iron gates. Why metal? But then, wood could be burned quite easily. So much metal, metal that could be turned against them.

A man came running to him. It was Stan, the commander responsible for this fort.

"Prince Isofel, what's happening?"

"Ironhold is coming to attack us."

The man frowned. "Are you quite sure? How far are they?"

"Blue forest. Too close. We'll be lucky if we're half ready when they get here."

"Where's your father? We should get him here."

"He's not in the manor and not anywhere we can reach him. I'm in charge for now."

"With all due respect—"

"What?" Fel glared at him. "Due respect what?"

"I know these men and this fort." Indeed. And he had trained Fel, who was used to listening to him. But things were different now.

Fel nodded. "That's why I'm counting on you to help us. They have ironbringers among them. And we'll need to act quickly. Get as many men as you can to put all heavy iron equipment in the underground vault."

The man's face was incredulous. "We'll fight them with what?"

"Wood, commander, that's what we'll fight them with. Our bow and arrows and even catapults."

"You can't possibly—"

"Please, Stan. I respect your experience and the years you served our kingdom, but we're outnumbered and running out of time. If they don't have ironbringers, we'll still be at an advantage. We have the walls, we have the upper ground. We'll even have time to take out our metal weapons from the vault. If they do have ironbringers, that gate is not going to stand, and we'll be in trouble soon. Let's not give them even more ammunition. Please do as I say, even if you think it's the most idiotic thing ever. You can scold me later. Acting fast will give us more time than trying to figure out if my decisions are right or wrong. Does that make sense?"

"It does." It was clear that Stan was saying that reluctantly, but it didn't matter. It was good enough.

"Great, then. Get our metal underground."

The man nodded and ran to gather some of the soldiers who were awake and ready. Meanwhile, Fel found some of the men and asked them to build a stone barrier behind the metal gate.

"With what?" a man asked.

"Break the stones of the barracks, and hold them with clay."

"It won't have time to dry."

"At least it's something. Go."

Fel's duty was to stand in his father's place in his absence. Everyone in the kingdom knew that, and yet, they should have practiced it some more. Not only Stan, but some other seasoned soldiers didn't seem too happy to obey him. Perhaps Fel should have let the old commander take over. That was what would happen if he weren't here. But Fel was here—and knew about their magic.

Archers were positioned on top of the wall, and some swordsmen on the ground, in case they broke through the gate or came in by other means. Yes, they had wooden swords and shields.

Fel looked at the sky. He could feel the threat of violence, like clouds before rain. And he dreaded what was coming and the lives that would be lost.

His father's words came to him. *No pity on the battlefield. Put your kindness and compassion aside, or you'll fail.* But what kind of person could strip away their compassion as if it was a coat? And once gone, would it ever come back?

The deaths of the assassins still haunted him, the heavy weight of taking lives. And if he took even more lives tonight, wouldn't that change him forever? And yet, it would be even worse if cowardice prevented him from protecting his people. And then, he could also die tonight.

He regretted not having said more to Leah, having pretended to be indifferent to her. If things had been different, he would have kissed her goodbye, would have promised to come back to her, would know that a part of his heart would never harden, would keep her in his thoughts in the heat of battle. And if he survived, he would go home to her, wherever it was, the happiest man of all. He still loved her, and never had the chance to say so, had never told her that if she wanted, he could forgive her note, her wedding, everything, that he would love her forever if she stayed.

"You're thinking about your necromancer princess," a voice startled him. Arry's voice.

"Why do you think so?"

"You make a face." His friend blinked fast and looked like an idiot staring at the sky. That was obviously a terrible attempt at an imitation.

"Hmm." Odd how his friend knew him, and he hadn't even told him everything. He'd certainly never tell him that she'd been in his bedroom, that they'd almost... This was no time for these thoughts. "Where were you? I thought you had decided to sleep through the battle."

Arry snorted. "Where? Making sure all metal was being put in the vault. I can't believe you truly expected my father to take your orders seriously."

"I asked him to."

"I don't think he understands what ironbringing can do, or even believes they will have magic wielders in their midst. I don't think he's even sure they're going to attack."

"What does he think they're doing?"

Arry rolled his eyes. "Intimidating negotiations."

Fel chuckled. "I never took him for such an optimistic. Let's hope he's right."

"We know he isn't." His expression was serious, tense, then he had a thin smile. "But it will be a pleasure to stand by your side."

Fel stiffened. This wasn't exactly what he wanted. "True. But if I ask you to retreat, retreat. I'd rather you back and safe than by my side and dead."

"If we have to retreat, you're not going to stay and die like a fool, are you?"

"Die like a hero. I will if I have to."

"Oh, stop it. We'll squash them. We have the advantage of our walls—"

"And our strong iron gate. Sure." Fel wanted to strangle his past self for not noticing it earlier. But he had never thought it would come to this.

"Whatever. Don't die. I want to see you stealing a princess from Ironhold."

"She's mine. I won't be stealing." Odd how the words came out, and how they felt like the truth. It was also a decision, and perhaps Arry was right that it made him eager to win, eager to survive, eager to put a dent on Ironhold's power.

"Now that's the pompous Umbraar prince I know."

Fel smiled, but then got serious again. "We better focus. Do me a favor and run through the perimeter making sure everyone's well positioned, and that nobody is wearing any metal, not even rings, chains, nothing."

Arry glanced at Fel's hands. "What about..."

"I can control them. But I can't control all the metal in the fort."

His friend nodded and ran. They were barely prepared—and Ironhold's forces should be upon them any minute now.

26

AWAKE

20 years before

River ended up telling Ciara everything, and at least she believed him. She sat on his bed, as he hadn't left his room since Forest had claimed the staff as his discovery.

Her eyes were kind when she stared at him. "But it makes no difference. What you did will save us."

River shrugged. "I guess."

"You wanted the recognition."

He shook his head. "That would be silly. With everything going on, why care about that? What we need to do is save ourselves, right? Still, it's not fair that Forest gets all the credit, gets everything..."

"He's been working hard. You should put your differences behind you."

"Hmm. And he can lie. How can he lie? Can you lie? Nevermind. It's not a question anyone can answer in a satisfying way."

"You got brown hair and late horns, maybe he got the lying skill."

Late horns. They still looked ridiculous, like a 13-year-old's. "He shouldn't use it against me."

"Maybe he thought it would be easier, I don't know. Or maybe he didn't lie, he just twisted words."

"Great. Now you're defending him."

"No," Ciara said. "I just don't want to see you angry."

"And you think destroying a city is right? You think it makes sense?"

She paused. "Maybe he didn't destroy it."

"Doesn't change the fact everyone was dancing, celebrating thousands of deaths. What's wrong with you?"

"I wasn't dancing, River. But everyone feared the Umbraar king. You have to understand what his death means to us."

"It's still wrong."

"War brings the worst in everyone."

River sighed. "Does it have to?"

Someone knocked at his door. River opened and saw Forest, then pushed the door to try to close it, but his brother pushed it back.

"River, listen. I told the truth to our father. I told him it was you who got the staff. At first I let him think it was me just to help, just so he'd trust it was real."

"Great. Deal with it, then."

"No. It has to be you. You have to use it."

River snorted. "That's why you're calling me."

"I was always planning to say it was you. You should trust me more."

"You're a liar."

Forest frowned. "I never lied. Don't you want this war to end? Don't you want to use the staff? Come on, this is your chance to be our hero, to carve your name among the greatest Ancients."

"You think I care about this nonsense?"

"Everyone does."

"Go, River." Ciara, who had been quiet until now, stood next to him. "I know you want to make things right."

"Of course I do."

He followed his brother into a small room by the Ancient hall. There, he saw his father and Hazela, their most respected magic scholar.

She stared at him. "Where did you get this from?"

"A block of ice in the dragon lords' palace."

The scholar nodded. "It's the one."

His father put a hand on River's shoulder. "You did well, son."

Son. He hadn't called him that in years, and yet, it didn't feel as good as expected. River just nodded.

The magic scholar stared at him. "You'll have to wield it. In one of our circles, at dusk, you'll have to hit the ground with it."

"A circle as close to Mount Prime as possible," his father added.

His heart beat faster. "In Ironhold?"

The woman shook her head. "Wildspring should do. It's still dangerous, but you won't be there for long." She handed him a piece of paper. "These are the words." Old Elvish symbols. "Can you read this language?" she asked.

"Yes." In fact, some of the letters were similar to Fernian, and he knew how to pronounce them even if he didn't understand their meaning.

Hazela nodded. "So it's as simple as that."

River took the paper, an empty feeling in his stomach. "And that will counter the human's magic?"

"It will defeat it, son. It will assure our victory." There was pride in his father's voice, in his eyes. River would be lying if he said he didn't enjoy the chance of being the one to save his people, being the one his father trusted.

"Tomorrow is when you should go," the woman said. "We're lucky the full moon is so close. At dusk. Make sure it's not night or day."

"Can I read it, or should I memorize it?"

She sighed. "Memorize it, but don't say it out loud when you're practicing. Words are powerful. You don't want to waste the spell. And keep it a secret."

That didn't make much sense. "Shouldn't we tell our people? Give them hope?"

His father tapped River's shoulder. "They'll know it when it's time to know."

River walked back to his room, and since Ciara was still there, he ended up telling everything to her.

She was thoughtful. "Why do you think Forest changed his mind?"

"They probably said it had to be whoever took the staff? Maybe he's afraid of being alone in a circle? What do I know?"

"Hmm..." She bit her lip. "Can you check if maybe this is dangerous?"

"Ciara. Even if I die, I'll do this if it means our victory."

She glared at him. "Don't be silly."

"It's not silly. It's the truth."

She sighed. "And what do the words say?"

"I'm not sure."

"Weren't you the language expert?"

He chuckled. "Expert. You should have seen the disaster I was in Fernick."

"I would have liked to. You know what I'm thinking? This would be the perfect opportunity to attack the humans. I don't mean regular people, innocents. But we could storm the Iron Citadel, for example, before they realize their magic is gone."

It made sense, but there was no way something like that could be planned. "Our father doesn't want me to tell anyone."

"That's just silly. If we make the humans lose their magic, we need to move fast."

Maybe, but there was another problem. "Well, no. What if this doesn't work? We can't put our hopes in some old magical books."

"I guess."

"Ciara." He stared at her. "Tell me you're not planning anything."

"Why do you worry so much? You're the one who went on a deadly, hopeless mission. Did I say anything?"

"But that's different from going into Ironhold."

"I just said it was a good idea. Relax, brother."

And yet he couldn't relax, an eerie feeling upon him.

LEAH HEARD steps in the hall, but got into a secret passage before they got to her. Most of the royal quarters had exits, except for Leah's room, perhaps because her mother feared Leah would sneak out. To do what exactly? She then remembered Fel coming to her room. If he weren't able to come in, and if she could go out to meet him, would she have done it? Maybe. Fel. Her heart got tight with worry. But he was fine. He was prepared, prepared even against an army with iron-bringers. And she had to stop thinking about him and focus on finding her parents and helping her kingdom.

She'd been so foolish, returning to Ironhold, thinking it would save her parents. Of course they had already planned all this. If anything, she should have stayed in Umbraar and started planning her revenge. But now she was home—her greatest wish—and yet hiding in a small passage like a mouse.

This passage led to the cellar by the main kitchen. She

wondered if an old drunk king had built this, or if the idea was to go somewhere underground, which offered some degree of protection. When she got downstairs, she listened. Since she heard no steps or voices, she assumed it was safe to open the door.

As soon as she walked out, she saw a young woman and a boy around ten. They both had light brown hair and hazel eyes, which were wide with fear.

Leah raised her hands. "I'm no threat."

The woman looked at the passage, her face overcome with emotion. "Does it... does it lead away?" Her voice was almost a whisper.

It was awful to disappoint her, but Leah shook her head. "It goes to the hallway near the royal quarters. It can work as a temporary hideout, but it's too narrow."

The woman then took a better look at Leah. "Your high—"

Leah interrupted her by shaking her head. "Don't." She noticed that some wooden boxes were barricading them from the rest of that part of the cellar. It was already a special room, separated from the rest, and barricading it would offer even more protection. "Are there more people here?"

With a trembling hand, the woman pointed to the boxes. "On the other side, maybe."

Leah took a better look at her. "I've seen you in our receptions, and around the kitchen, maybe, but I don't recall your name."

"Valeria. I... worked in the washhouse. This is my brother, Lago." The boy was holding tight to the woman and still stared at Leah in fear. Valeria then pointed to the corner, "And my other brother, Sali."

It was a young man, a Frostlake guard, lying in the corner.

"He's hurt," Valeria added.

Leah crouched by the young man and noticed he was

sleeping, but there was some blood on his shirt. "Does he need care?"

"I patched his wound. Just the arm. He's resting now, but he can't be found."

Leah wished she could do something to help him, something to help her kingdom. "I'm so sorry, I..."

The woman's eyes were full of tears. "At least he's alive. So many died."

"Did you see what happened?"

She looked down, and her voice got even lower. "I saw Ironhold soldiers. They were yelling that it was the fae, but... Sali got to our quarters and asked us to hide. He says it was Ironhold soldiers who attacked him and his companions. The only reason he escaped was because he pretended he was dead, then slipped out and found us."

It must have been hard to get across so many soldiers in that confusion, unless... "You used another passage to get here, then."

She nodded.

It could be Leah's way out. "Where does it lead?"

Valeria shook her head. "The servants quarters. They're raiding it. Looking for *traitors*." She rolled her eyes and exhaled in anger.

"Anyone who knows who attacked the castle."

The young woman nodded again.

Leah sighed. "Do you know anything about my mother or father? If they're alive?"

"Oh." Valeria looked down, then, after a deep breath, faced Leah. "You didn't know? They rang the bells and all. I'm so sorry. Your father, he..."

At first the words made no sense, strange words that couldn't be strung together to form a sentence—odd, incomprehensible gibberish—but when the meaning hit Leah, her heart knotted. She felt as if there was no longer any ground beneath her, and covered her face with her hands. Gone? Her father was gone?

Why? Why? Did her marriage into Ironhold cause this? Her stupidity? It couldn't be what she'd done to Cassius, there wouldn't have been time for that. Now she wished she was still in the Ironhold castle, but that she could kill everyone there. And then she realized she should have known her father was gone, she should have known the moment she'd seen him in her dreams, fading away.

"Do you know if my mother survived?"

The woman shook her head and bit her lip. "Sali was guarding the royal quarters, so... But I don't know. We've been here for a while."

Leah recalled that the Ironhold guards had been looking for her mother. It meant she had escaped—at least so far. But her father... She wondered if Kasim had survived, but in her heart, Leah knew he was also gone.

"You're the queen now," Valeria said. "But I heard you were going to arrive tomorrow or today. How did you—"

"I sneaked in early. They can't know I'm here."

"You can't do anything?" Her eyes were pleading, as if looking up to Leah to solve her problems.

That was what a queen should do, wasn't it? And yet here she was: hiding, scared, unsure what to do. She just shook her head, her heart filled with shame. It felt shameful to be weak, not to have a solution.

Leah took a deep breath. She had to think, and at least offer some advice. "I think they want to blame this attack on the fae. They will kill anyone who says otherwise. If you pretend you were just hiding because you were scared, you might get away with it, unless they're killing everyone who was here, but I don't think it's the case. I'm pretty sure many people and guards from Frostlake might well believe it was the Fae and that Ironhold is just helping. But your brother, he'll need to hide. Do you have supplies here?"

The woman shook her head.

Leah swallowed. "Then you'll have to hide him. You can leave him in the passage. You'll have to come out and seem glad that the fae have been defeated. Pretend you were just afraid and that you saw nothing. That's the only way you can survive."

The woman took in a sharp breath and held the boy even tighter.

"Do this in the morning," Leah said, "when more people from Frostlake will be around. They can't go around killing servants and pretend they came to protect our kingdom." It made sense, and made her heart at ease. "Something else: they're more powerful than they seem. Some of them might be ironbringers, and they have some strange magic. An uprising would be dangerous right now. I'll try to leave the kingdom and get help. I'll be back, but I don't know when."

"But how are you going to escape?"

"I'll figure it out."

In reality, Leah had no idea. All she felt was cold and emptiness. All she knew was that she had a strange power that could allow her to escape that castle, but could also kill everyone in it, and that she had no idea how to control it.

NAIA FELT IMPRISONED, not only imprisoned in that house, imprisoned in her dreams. Perhaps River had looked at her with a loving, caring expression, but what kind of care was that? It hurt to know that he'd taken away her freedom, and hurt even more to realize that it was because he didn't want to give her any explanation, didn't want to answer her questions.

She wanted to strangle River, but that would obviously be hard, considering she couldn't wake up.

But she *was* awake—from a certain point-of-view. If she could think all that, if she was aware of what was happening, then she wasn't dreaming. The question was how to be truly awake and in her body.

Fire. The word came to her like a whisper from the wind. Her magical fire could counter the magic blocking the Ancient City, perhaps it could... She lit a flame in her hand.

Naia sat up, her heart racing, and looked around the room. It was night, River was not here, and she had no idea how much time had passed. Days? Hours? Months? She wasn't sure. Perhaps it had all been a strange dream that he'd made her sleep, that he had looked at her with kind, loving eyes. But no, she had asked him about that fae city, had asked what all of that meant, and had gotten no answers. He had made her sleep. Now it was the middle of the night, and he wasn't here.

What part of her thought that living with a fae would work out? He'd said he would declare his love in front of his people, in front of his father. What a joke. That was the kind of fae promise one should be wary of. If his people were all asleep, there was no way that wedding could ever happen.

Naia took the mirror Fel had given her, but she couldn't feel any magic in it. She wondered if her brother was all right, if her father was well. Her father. Now remorse took over her thoughts. What had gotten into her that had made her trade her family for a tricky fae? Now she was here, still without any answer, not any closer to figuring out what was happening than before. And the worst part was suspecting that she was being played by River. But why? Why couldn't he have left her alone? Alone, lonely, and unsure about her future, but maybe it was better than tasting something that wasn't meant to be hers.

Anyway. Whining wasn't going to fix anything. She had to

find solutions, and this time, she was getting to the bottom of this, no matter how long it took. She then recalled getting back from the Ancient City, how River had been distraught with worry, how he had held her as if nothing else mattered in the world. Sure. Then he not only had avoided her questions, he had made her sleep.

Naia got dressed, took a knife, and went outside. Still no sign of River. She'd been under the impression that he would come home every night—like a husband. Well, she'd been under lots of wrong impressions—and was about to fix them and figure out the truth.

With a flame in her hand and fire in her heart, she crossed the thicket surrounding the house and soon found herself walking in the meadow leading to the Ancient palace, only the stars illuminating her way.

At least now she knew she didn't have to avoid being seen, and she also knew she wouldn't find anyone to give her any information, so that was a step ahead of last time. She also knew there was no point asking River about any of that, so that was another step ahead. A painful step ahead, but sometimes you had to wade through pain to move forward. And yet that pain meant she cared for River, which only made her annoyed —and even more hurt.

Naia cared for River, and once she had thought it could work out, despite everything. And yet the reality was that she had no idea who he really was, what he wanted, and what his plans were. She'd once thought they'd share a life together, and yet he'd never shared any of his fears, wishes, and plans with her. And then, he was fae, a race renowned for being untrustworthy. She'd thought she had it all figured out, that she wasn't going to let him trick her, but she'd been tricked and doomed from the moment they had first kissed. Or even from the moment she had first seen him.

Step after step she walked, hoping to reach the city and the castle, not sure what she was about to find, not sure even what she was looking for. All she wanted were some answers. That first little house seemed a lot closer this time, perhaps because she'd been expecting it, perhaps because she wasn't being as careful or slow. This was River's city, and his people. Of course he wanted to save them. The question was: save them from what? And how?

This area had some dry, ugly trees, and it made the landscape spooky at night. If she weren't so angry, she would perhaps turn back and wait for daytime, as the night cast ominous shadows on the ground. But her goal was the city and the palace. Still, she stopped. There was a different sound in the air, perhaps a different feel. Well, it was night, that was what was different. Naia pressed on.

Too late, she heard a set of steps. Far too late. Four fae jumped from trees in front of her, and two more on her back. They were all wearing the uniform she'd seen in the Fae palace, a green tunic with brown pants, and had bows and arrows. Two of them pointed their weapons at her. What surprised her most was seeing anyone alive and moving in this place.

Naia raised her hands slowly. Sure, that movement would only put her at an advantage to set them all on fire, but hopefully they had no idea about it. She wanted to ask them who they were and what they were doing here, but knew that it was better to remain quiet when threatened.

"Who are you?" one of the fae said.

"Oh, I have the same question." Oops, she forgot to hold her tongue. "I mean, I mean no harm."

Guards. They were guards, she realized. The one who'd spoken was a little taller than the others and had hair as white as the snow in Frostlake, with dark red eyes. The two guards with the bows also had snow-like hair, but one had bright red eyes, and the other had pink eyes. The one in the middle had sandy blond hair, and red eyes again. She had no idea what the two guards behind her looked like because she wasn't going to turn.

The fae then asked, "Who are you and how did you come to our sacred city?"

"I'm... a friend," she said. "I wanted to know what's going on. I want to help."

"Help? You're human. You're not exactly a friend of our kind."

"I know River. I'm his... friend." That word sounded awful, but what else was she going to say she was to him?

The guards looked at each other.

The blond guard, who'd been silent until then, stared at her. "We should take her to King Spring."

"She has magic. I can smell it," the other guard said.

Meanwhile, the archers still had their bows aimed at her, not completely taut, to be fair, and she could burn them. But she obviously didn't want to use her fire yet and risk hurting four people. "I'd love to talk to your king," she said.

The blond guard nodded. "Very well. But we'll need to bind your hands." He pulled a pair of shackles from his belt. Brass. Not as easy to work as iron, but she could deal with that too.

Naia extended her arms. The thought of having her hands bound wasn't great, but then, she could get rid of those shackles easily. At least she was on her way to the palace, where the king would shine a light on what was going on.

One thing she hadn't considered was how uncomfortable it would be to spend time walking like that. And how uncomfortable it would be to deal with the curious looks in her direction.

They came across fae—wide awake—all along the way the palace, unlike the previous time she'd been here, which was what? Yesterday? A week before? She wasn't sure. But the feeling wasn't festive or relieved. If anything, what she gathered from the eyes of those fae was fear. Not fear of her, but of something else. Fear and despair, everywhere she looked.

She was going to ask them if they realized they had just woken up from what seemed to have been a long slumber, but then she decided it would give too much away. Instead, she asked, "Did something happen here?"

"You'll talk to our king." The guard's voice was firm, but not harsh.

Indeed. As far as she knew, taking a stranger to the king wasn't something that was usually done, at least not in human kingdoms where they kept formalities. "Do all visitors get that honor?"

The man snorted. "Visitors."

Right. Secret, sealed city and all that. It made sense that they would be wary of her. What didn't make sense was why they were awake now, unless she had previously come during nap time or something.

She decided to be playful and see if she could fish for information. "Aren't you happy to see a new face?"

"Human." There was a warning in the guard's voice. "Keep your words. They'll do you no favors. If you have questions, ask our king."

Human. The derision they used to say that word told her everything she needed to know about them. At least River wasn't like that. Or she thought so. She kept her thoughts to herself, not interested in wasting her precious breath, since apparently it wasn't appreciated.

When they got to the city, more guards escorted her, which made her feel really important. Well, as the Umbraar princess, she was important, it was just that she didn't usually feel it. Perhaps the right word was dangerous, and there was a strange pleasure in noticing that the inhabitants of this city had some fear of her. That was unlike River, even if he claimed she'd almost killed him once. If metal magic itself was deadly to the fae, then she was indeed quite dangerous, and had to remember that. But she wasn't here to threaten or scare anyone, but to talk to them, to understand what was happening.

The palace still looked like a tree—a dead tree—but it felt a lot more grandiose when there were guards standing at its entrance. They took her to a hall with white marble floor and columns, contrasting with most of the wood architecture of the city. She hadn't been here before, as its doors had been closed then. A raised dais had five chairs, and then there were two balconies on the sides, from where more curious spectators could watch whatever happened here. But the room was empty now. And remained empty for many minutes.

In a way, it was embarrassing and slightly humiliating to be brought here in shackles like a prisoner. Perhaps she should have tried to argue more, bargain with them, but then, she'd been so eager for any kind of answer, and the idea of seeing the king had been too tempting. Regardless. What mattered was getting answers.

After a long time standing, a door opened, and five fae came in, two of them guards. Three of them were nobles. One was a young woman with pale hair and burgundy eyes, and the other was a young man with similar features. Then there was another man, somewhat older, wearing a golden circlet. He had to be the king, and Naia had to catch a breath. With light brown hair and brownish red eyes, plus that square jaw with delicate lips, he looked just like River.

27

THE BATTLE

L eah lay down on the cold, hard floor, hoping sleep would find her, hoping her dreams would give her an answer. But she knew the answer. She had to go to Umbraar, to Isofel. Just the thought felt like going home. But it wasn't home. He had rejected her. And yet, perhaps her mother was in Umbraar, and they were the only kingdom standing against Ironhold. And still, part of her was still in love with their handsome prince—despite everything.

She took the mirror and tried to contact the Umbraar king, but to no avail. Something was wrong.

Leah sighed, then tried to relax the same way she'd done when she had ended up in Umbraar. And she kept thinking about Isofel. Isofel kissing her, Isofel's skin against hers. Those thoughts were not helping her sleep at all. And she felt ashamed and angry at herself realizing how much she still wanted him. And yet she had to find him.

Sleep only came much later, after many slow, deep breaths, after Leah tried to think about nothing and bury all her fears and worries.

Leah found herself walking amidst mountains. Oh, no, this

was where that creature had attacked her. She tried to put her hands together—and they crossed. Still a dream. But this was a dangerous place, and she had to leave. The issue was how.

A movement in front of her turned out to be one of those creatures with sharp teeth. Leah heard sounds behind her, and saw two more of them. Surrounded. Great.

"We're not going to eat you," one of the creatures said. "This time. Follow me."

Leah turned the other way and ran, but her arms were caught, and then she was dragged to a cave inside a mountain. The walls had torches with eerie green light on them, and in the middle stood a dark throne, with a woman wearing all black, her face veiled, sitting on it.

"Finally you're here."

Leah frowned. "It helps when your servants don't try to eat me."

The woman chuckled. "Dismissed." The creatures scurried away on all fours, like mice. "Leah, my darling. I have a proposition for you. You can be all powerful. The queen of all Aluria, the entire world. And I can help you."

"I just want Frostlake, but I'm listening. Who are you?"

"Call me the Queen of Darkness. It sounds nice, doesn't it?"

Leah just stared.

"Use the power that's yours. By birthright. Stop with this nonsense of trying to control it. You deathbringers are so boring."

"I'm a necromancer."

The woman burst out laughing. "So silly. You know what? You can be weak, you can be pathetic. But know that it's by choice."

Then the image dissolved. Leah opened her eyes and found herself in the cellar, while someone was banging on their barricade.

Valeria and her brothers were asleep, and she shook them. "Let's hide him. Quick."

The young woman woke up, and she and Leah put the guard in the tunnel leading up to the royal quarters. He was moaning and partially awake, and the tunnel had narrow stairs and wasn't a place where anyone could rest, but it would have to do for now.

A voice came from behind the boxes. "Anyone there? We won't hurt you, we just want your version of the facts."

Leah looked at Valeria. "I'll come with you," she whispered.

The woman pushed Leah. "Hide. I'll come and check on you. Hide him, too." She pushed Lago, her younger brother.

Like that, Leah was in a dark staircase with a wounded guard and a child. She held the boy's hand and whispered, "You'll have to be quiet."

"I know. And if they find me, I'll say I never saw a thing."

Leah squeezed his hand, as if to bring him some comfort.

He then added, "I'm not afraid of the dark."

"You're smart."

Yes, good for him. Leah also used not to be afraid of it, except that now she knew there could be otherworldly things hiding in it. No, that was in the hollow, in the space between worlds, a fissure like an open chasm, from where things looked upon them. A chasm from where horrific power could flow to her.

Leah then added, "Listen to me, Lago. If your sister doesn't come back, and if you feel very thirsty, you'll have to get out."

"I know." His voice was thin, laced with sadness, probably thinking about the worst outcome.

Leah had been rather thinking that his sister could be busy, imprisoned, or something. And yet. Things could happen. She squeezed the boy's hand again, trying to soothe and reassure him, even if she knew that there was no reassuring him, that she could give him no guarantees.

But the superior amount of Frostlake guards should ensure some degree of safety to the castle workers. She hoped so. Valeria's brothers were soon silent again, overcome with fatigue. She was also exhausted, scared, and lost. Her life had always seemed so certain, her mother had always raised her to marry well and become the Frostlake queen, and then this happened. But she didn't think that delaying or waiting would have helped much. Venard and the Ironhold people knew how to pretend to be friendly when they wanted to.

Leah sighed. She had to get to Isofel. Just the mental mention of his name made her heart constrict with worry. So much silly worry. She had to sleep again and try to do whatever she'd done before. As she tried to recall the details as to how she'd gotten to Umbraar, she remembered that she'd seen her dragon. That was what she had to focus on; her magical silver dragon. Perhaps it symbolized her magic, at least the good part of it. It was as if it protected her.

20 years before

RIVER SHOULD BE happy and excited. Instead, there was something nagging at him, and he didn't know what it was. He lay in bed wide awake, his heart beating faster than normal. Perhaps it was still the memory of the Formosa tragedy and the horrific thought that his brother could have done it. But then, what if Forest *hadn't* destroyed the Umbraar city? What if his brother was just taking the credit, like he'd done with the staff? While River would be relieved to know his brother wasn't a complete monster, it led to a worrying question. Who had done it? And why? A cliff didn't collapse out of nowhere.

He took a deep breath. This wasn't the time to worry; he was about to counter the human's magic, and that was good. Iron magic, in particular, was deadly to his kind, and if it could be stopped, it would give his people a chance. Unless the spell was dangerous. But he was willing to risk death to save his people. He wondered if he would find the pretty girl who'd saved him if he passed on to the other side. That was a morbid thought.

Still. There was one thing he could do: translate the words in the enchantment. It would in fact be quite helpful, so that when he said the incantation, he would put meaning into it, he would feel the words. It made sense. With that thought, he took a pile of books on Old Elven and brought them to his room. As he searched each word, compared the sentences, looked at various possible meanings, and tried to make sense of the text, the hours passed quickly.

The sun was already up when he came up with a tentative translation:

By the power of infinity, it's done as I say, covering all this land. I concentrate all the power of the eternal magic to bring change to the non-magical people. Change only to the pure non-magical people, every non-magical person, and as this power spreads, they are changed.

The non-magical people were the humans. It had to be that, because if the magic were to affect only the humans without magic, it would be pointless. *Change* likely meant change in their magic. The original Old Elven, *krittl*, was a tricky word that could also mean *transformation, travel*, or *bridge*. It had to be transformation—or change—in this context.

He left the Ancient City without saying any goodbye or asking any more questions, as he couldn't find his father or the magic scholar. Ciara was nowhere to be found either.

After stepping in the hollow paths, he came to a circle in

Wildspring. There were no more Ancients living in this kingdom, at least as far as he knew. The humans had been coming at his people with steel and explosions, with more and more dangerous weapons that they could never counter. It meant that perhaps blocking their magic wouldn't be the end of the war, but it could do a lot.

This circle was a small one, in the middle of the woods. No human soldiers were around it, at least not yet. River stared at the top of the staff. There was a star and a portal carved on it. Magic as powerful as that could kill the wielder. With eyes closed, he focused. Death wasn't the end of the world, it was just a transition, a passage, and he could accept that. The old books mentioned a bridge or portal to the other world.

He looked at the carved image again. It could well symbolize death. When he was about to perform the incantation, another thought hit him, and a chill ran down his spine. *Krittl* meant transformation, travel, or bridge. All these words would relate to one thing in the Old Books: death. He thought back to the words he had to say, with the new meaning in mind.

By the power of infinity, it's done as I say, covering all this land. I concentrate all the power of the eternal magic to bring death *to the non-magical people. Death only to the pure non-magical people, every non-magical person, and as this power spreads, they are* dead.

Suddenly the words made more sense. A lot more sense. Perhaps this incantation had come from the ancient elves or from dragons, but it should still follow some logic. Fae logic always stated that deals should be clear. Magic should also be clear, not ambiguous or vague. If this enchantment were to bring some kind of change to the humans in Aluria, it should state what kind of change it was. If it was to bring death, there was no need to specify anything.

But it wasn't possible. His father wouldn't... The image of

the celebration of the Formosa tragedy came to his mind. His brother's words, saying that there was no room for both humans and Ancients in Aluria. He looked at the symbol on the staff. As horrific as his conclusion was, it fit.

River recalled when he'd heard his father mentioning the artifact, saying it was a way to deal with the humans. Had he ever stated that it was meant to counter the humans' magic? Or had River just assumed it? It was easy to take isolated pieces of information and build a new narrative.

His heart was speeding up, and dusk was upon him. Killing all humans would save his people. They would be able to leave the Ancient City, repopulate Aluria, make sure the nature in Mount Prime recovered. There would be no more war. But at what cost?

River's hand was trembling as he stared at the magical artifact in his hand. What had he done? Why couldn't he have died on his way to Aluria, buried this dreadful thing in the bottom of the sea? Then he imagined it washing into the shore, ending up in someone's hands, causing destruction again.

Why had the mysterious girl saved him? And twice? She looked human. It made no sense. She should have let him freeze to death. Then her words came to him. *You're good, River. Never forget that.* But what did good even mean? He wanted to be a good son, even when he pretended he didn't, just because trying and failing hurt too much. He wanted to save his people, he wanted to make sure he saw no more senseless deaths, like his cousin's. There was so much he wanted, and using this staff would guarantee all his wishes would be granted. He could bring peace to Aluria.

And yet his throat was thick with tears threatening to come. He couldn't kill thousands and thousands of people, he just couldn't. And he couldn't let anyone else do that either. An object like this was indestructible—in theory. Unless...

River had only a few minutes left, and he changed the words. *By the power of infinity, it's done as I say, covering this staff. I concentrate all the power of the eternal magic to bring death to this staff. Death only to this* staff, *and as this power flows, this* staff *is dead.*

He wasn't sure if a staff could die, but he didn't know the Old Elven for destruction. The artifact started to vibrate, and River held on to it. Magic usually needed a magician, so he couldn't let go. It could well be his death, but if he rid the world of such a dangerous object, it would be worth it.

He didn't let go, even when it vibrated so much that his entire body shook, even when its magic flowed to him, a strange hot wave, painful and uncomfortable, as if he were burning from the inside. He felt death in his hands, and yet kept holding it, determined to destroy that staff, determined to rid the world of such a dangerous object.

THE SKY WAS dark when River woke up. The floor around him was charred and the faerie circle was gone. He'd been unconscious in enemy territory and extremely lucky to have survived. He walked the entire night until he found another circle, and finally reached the Ancient City by morning.

He'd given a lot of thought to what he was going to say. His plan was to say that the staff had been destroyed and that the spell hadn't gone as planned. If he were vague enough, they wouldn't notice the dissimulation contained in his words. That was what Ancients did, they played with words to avoid having to expose themselves. Yes, they only said the truth, but the truth was like a sphere, and it was all about showing the right angle to make it look the way you wanted.

He found his father eating in the meadow, talking to Forest and Anelise.

River approached slowly, but hid behind a tree to listen to their conversation.

"These lesser Ancients have to go," his father said. "No way we can keep them."

Anelise sighed. "But the humans aren't gone. I mean, it's dangerous out there for our kind." It was odd to see her worried about anyone. River had always considered her one of the most ruthless of the siblings, quite different from her twin Ciara.

Forest turned to her. "Well, something went wrong. What do you want us to do? Keep this place overcrowded?"

"Maybe it will take a while?" she asked. "Maybe we could wait?"

They were waiting for the spell River should have done, waiting for all the humans to be dead. He moved beside the tree, to watch them while still unnoticed.

His father shook his head. "The refugees should leave tonight. There's no room for everyone."

Anelise actually looked disappointed.

Forest nodded. "I'll make sure they leave. Any news from River?"

His father had a bitter laugh. "River? How could I have trusted him with anything?"

"Didn't he bring the artifact?" Anelise asked.

His father shrugged. "It must have been a fake or something."

River walked up to them. "I'm here. And the staff was real. Taken from the dragon lords' palace. I almost died bringing it here."

His father frowned. "What happened?"

The spell didn't go as planned was on the tip of his tongue. Instead, he asked, "Would you be happy? If every single human in Aluria died? Pardon, every single *pure* human, otherwise you and all your children would be dead too."

"What kind of stupid question is that?"

"That spell was for death, wasn't it?" He turned to Forest. "And you feared it could kill the wielder, didn't you? That's why you let me perform it."

"Did you do it?" Forest asked.

"No. No." The words sounded right, and all he felt was relief, relief at looking at his father and saying what he truly thought. "A thousand times no. I could go back a hundred times and a hundred times I'd refuse to kill so many innocents."

"What did you do?" His father's voice was calm, but more as if he was struggling to keep it contained. "Where's the staff?"

"I destroyed it."

His father stared at him. "That's impossible. Where is it?"

"Gone. I used its own power against it, and it worked. How's that?"

"Foolish child! Why? We could be returning to Aluria. The land would have been ours. You say you don't want to kill innocents? What about all the Aluria innocents we'll have to send back, huh? What about them?"

"Keep them here."

"There's no room, no food, no resources." His father was yelling, all self-control gone. "Soon there will be no food even for us. You're condemning us to die."

River kept his head high. "No. I took the staff and I destroyed it. We can beat the humans, I know we can, but we're not going to do it through mass murder."

"*You* are not beating anyone." There was hatred in his father's eyes. "River of the Second Dynasty, I mean, River. You are hereby stripped of any claims to my family, stripped of its name. You are condemned to eternal—"

"Father, no," Forest interrupted him. That was surprising. Perhaps he was going to suggest River should be tortured until death instead. River was so angry he didn't care. He didn't care if his father had never appreciated him, didn't care if his brother hated him, didn't care they were upset about what he'd done. He knew it had been the right choice.

His brother continued, "Give him a chance to bring the staff back. Or maybe, if he has so much talent that he can get to the dragon lords' palace, he could bring one of the dragon hearts."

It made sense. Forest wasn't being revengeful or helpful, just strategic, likely thinking that the staff hadn't been destroyed. River laughed. "There are no dragons."

Forest rolled his eyes. "I told you the dragon lords' hearts *are* the dragon hearts."

His father raised a hand. "It's fair. River, you're exiled until you bring back the staff or a dragon's heart."

"Why would I bring anything to you? You think I care?"

"Leave," his father said.

"Great. I'll get my things."

"No, boy. You're taking only the clothes in your body, and consider that a favor."

River wasn't going to owe anyone anything. "I don't need no favors." He took off his shirt, then stopped when he heard a messenger running to them.

"King Spring. Your daughter..."

River could see it in the man's eyes, could see the fear and despair. Not Ciara, no.

The messenger swallowed. "They tried to storm the Iron Citadel last night. Only one of her companions survived."

River fell to his knees, unable to hear the rest, unable to bear the pain. Not funny, sweet Ciara, no. Suddenly his idea of destroying the staff felt stupid. It was his fault his sister had been killed.

Tears fell down his eyes, while he heard his father screaming, "Go! Get out of here. Traitor!"

"It's not going to solve our problem, father," Anelise, his other sister, said, her eyes misty. She'd just lost her twin and River couldn't imagine the pain she was feeling. "River can help us. We need all the help we can get to win this war."

"He's incompetent!" his father roared.

River felt his sister putting something in his hand. He took it, then did as he'd been told, leaving the Ancient City, feeling disoriented, unsure where to go. And guilty. He stood in a clearing surrounded by trees. It was as if it was part of the Ancient City, part of the underworld, but outside its borders. Still in the Ancient realm.

So many things he'd done wrong. Instead of crossing the sea for a trinket, he should have stayed, should have helped them plan and fight. Maybe things could have been different. And yet he couldn't change anything now.

SILENCE HAD SUCH A HEAVY, overbearing weight. Still no enemy in sight, and yet Fel was uneasy. Then he felt it, the magic, as if it called to him. Almost too late he stopped three iron darts from reaching some archers. They had curved over the wall, something an ironbringer could easily do, and something that would make Umbraar soldiers' position precarious.

Nobody had noticed what had happened. Meanwhile, Fel concentrated, trying to find the source of that magic. Then he felt something else, heavy iron weapons approaching the fort. Canons. It was almost as if he could see them, even though they were hidden by trees. But they hadn't been fired yet, and weren't yet in range.

He turned and yelled. "Get cover. Wooden boards or shields behind and above you. They have arrows that can curve over the battlement and reach us from behind. Magic."

"You and you." He pointed to two young soldiers standing

behind him. "Go get as many planks as you can, and bring them to the archers. Fast."

He barely finished saying that, and had to stop two more darts—or metal arrows—from hitting his men.

The canons were getting close. Fel knew that he shouldn't attack if they weren't attacked first, but the arrows were a clear sign of aggression. He reached the thick metal encasing of the canons with his magic—and broke them into thousands of pieces. Screams were heard from behind the thicket, as soldiers were probably hit by the shards. *No mercy, no compassion.*

Still the Ironhold forces hid in the forest by the fort. And there was no denying it was Ironhold, unless ironbringers were now acting as mercenaries, which he doubted. Fel knew where most of their forces stood, he could sense their steel swords at a distance. He didn't want to waste arrows when they were so far, and yet.

"Catapults. I want fire after the first line of trees."

Unfortunately there were only three purely wooden catapults, and using fire with them was tricky, as logs would need to be lit right when they were about to be released, but he trusted his men to do it well.

Some of the logs fell on the first line of Ironhold men. He knew it because he could feel where they were, and he also heard screams. Still, many of the logs got caught in the branches. Some of them caught fire, but it didn't last long, as it had rained recently and the forest was humid.

Five more volleys of curving metal arrows were sent atop the wall, and Fel stopped them. He still couldn't feel where the ironbringer or ironbringers were. If he could, he would eliminate them first, as they were the biggest threat. And yet he felt as if the Ironhold forces were only toying with them, testing their strength.

Fel then heard the iron gate grinding. It was on the opposite side of the fort, not where the Ironhold soldiers were, but he was aware that some of them might have moved to the other side, so that they were surrounded. He focused his magic to keep the gate in place, but it was no use. A lot of magic was acting against his, and he saw it being torn from its hinges and lifted up into the air. At least nobody tried to storm that part of the fortress, but it wouldn't be hard, since the improvised wall was not high.

Outside, in front of him, some Ironhold soldiers were coming and throwing something at the wall, followed by a deafening bang. They had handheld explosives, and would soon destroy all the walls. The archers had gotten two men carrying the bags with gunpowder, but they were still thrown close enough to the wall to be dangerous. Meanwhile, the gate was floating above them. Fel couldn't do much, and didn't understand what they were trying to do. They had to have more than two ironbringers; it was too much power. The gate turned red, and he realized what they were about to do.

"Find cover!" he shouted. "They'll rain molten metal on us." He was unable to stop them, but he could stop the men with the explosives. He felt the swords among the forest, the swords in the hips of so many men. *No mercy.* Fel took a deep breath, and made the swords float up in the air and cut. They should have cut necks, but he couldn't be quite precise.

At that moment, the metal gate melted above them, and Fel was able to take part of it and send it over the Ironhold men in the forest. He could sense the metallic tinge in their blood, and send the pieces, then the swords. He felt like a monster—a monster who had just saved his own men, at the cost of a hundred lives. He felt sick, but the battle wasn't over yet. There were still at least two ironbringers out there, he could feel the magic even if he wasn't sure where they were. He ran down the stairs, jumped the temporary wall, and sped into the forest, searching for the source of magic like his. He heard steps behind him, and saw Arry after him, bow and arrow in hand.

They found two young men running.

"Stop!" Fel yelled. "Stop and your lives will be spared."

They kept running, until one of the ironbringers fell down, and then the other. Arry had hit them with his arrows.

"They didn't stop." Arry's eyes were wide, and he said it like an apology.

Fel nodded. "We'll come check on them later. Let's go back and see if we can take any prisoners, and if the area is safe."

Back in the fort, the healer was taking care of the Umbraar soldiers who were hurt. A few of them had been hit with pieces of the molten gate or curving arrows, despite Fel's efforts. A young man had been strangled with his own necklace.

He wanted to yell and scream. None of this should have happened, he should have protected them better, he should... There was so much that could have been done, such as getting more reinforcements in the previous days, having more sentries. But how could they have known? If anything, Fel had been quick enough to act in the middle of the night, without any forewarning.

There were more horrors for him to face. After gathering a group of twenty foot soldiers, some armed with swords, some with arrows, Fel went to the area where the Ironhold soldiers had been stationed. He wanted to retch, horrified at what he'd done, horrified at so much loss. Perhaps he should have no mercy on the battlefield, but that battle had been over quickly, and now that he was allowed to be human again, seeing the result of his actions hurt.

Arry was beside him. "You didn't have a choice, Fel, they had explosives, they would have torn down those walls and killed every one of us."

"I know." He turned to the soldiers. "If anyone is alive, take them to the prison. We'll treat them and interrogate them. Watch out for any explosives. The others, we'll put them in the open area for a funeral fire." A horrible funeral, without loved ones, without their names being said or honored, but that was war.

He couldn't look at it anymore and was almost dizzy, but it would be a bad example to go back. But then, as the acting monarch, he shouldn't be here in the forest, exposed, where an archer could be atop a tree. He sighed. There were no archers. He had made sure everyone had been killed. Unless Ironhold sent reinforcements, or perhaps one or two soldiers who had ran away returned. No, deserters were cowards.

Still, he had an eerie feeling that this was far from over. Well, it had to be just the beginning. Ironhold wasn't going to quit just like that. And the next time, they would send a much more powerful army. Hopefully his father would be back by then. Hopefully his father was alive, was all right. His sister... It was odd, but he trusted that River wanted to see her safe. He just wished he could talk to her. And Leah... Leah was in the middle of it all, and he hoped she was still safe.

Standing among dead soldiers fallen in battle wasn't something anyone should ever do. What a gruesome, loathsome, terrifying experience. Near him, one of the fallen men moved.

Before calling someone to get him a healer, Fel crouched— and stepped back in horror. There was a soldier moving all right, trying to sit up—expect that the men had no head. Fel looked at the other side, and saw another body stirring. For some reason Leah's voice came to him, even if perhaps she hadn't said it using these words: *Necromancy can't raise a dead army.*

It didn't mean that there was no other type of magic that could: something awful and foul and unnatural.

"Retreat!" He yelled. "As fast as you can. Retreat! Back to

the fort." Still he stood his ground and watched as the men walked back. Walked? "Run! Run!"

"What's going on?" Arry asked in a whisper.

"The bodies are moving," Fel replied quietly. He wasn't sure why he was keeping his voice down. Soon more people would notice what was happening.

"You mean... Necromancy?"

Fel shook his head. "Something much worse." He turned back and yelled again. "We'll need to send fire down here. Get the metal weapons. Run back. Fast. I'll be there in a second."

He focused on the swords lying among the corpses, and levitated them slowly into the fort. If anything, he didn't want living-dead bodies armed. But the time he took doing that was a few seconds too long, as most of the bodies were now standing, some of them putting heads back on their necks. It was almost like the loose pieces of his metal hands, strung together with magic, but this was a strange, unknown type of magic. And then the bodies ran in his direction. They were too fast. Faster than him. He'd have to fight them.

He felt the broken pieces of the canons, pulled them, and made them levitate in a fast circle around him, making an improvised shield. There was no time to try to check if his men had made it to the fort. He looked back and saw Arry still too close to him, too far from the relative safety of the stone walls, so he opened the circle around him and turned it into a barrier, but it did little to stop the corpses, since they didn't mind being hurt. There was no way for example to run a shard through their hearts and stop them. They just kept going, and were now almost on Fel.

He looked back and saw that Arry was now almost in the fort, so he closed the circle again around him, making the pieces turn faster and faster. They should act like the blades of a windmill, pushing away anything trying to get close to him, and still he was hit by an arm and a hand, but kept that circle.

He saw arrows with fire landing by him, but even they did very little. The corpses were like wet branches, hard to catch fire. Some thirty, forty corpses were pressing against his shield, as he stepped back slowly, trying to retreat to the fort, retreat close to where his men could back him up. Back him up with what? Fire arrows that did little to stop these cursed things?

Fel wasn't sure how long he'd be able to keep up his shield, and how long it was going to work. He didn't know what damage those creatures were doing inside the fort and if people were getting hurt. And here he was, unable to do much, feeling useless and hopeless, clinging to his life. Was it too much to wish for a miracle?

He wondered if he could find a way to conjure fire, like his sister. A circle of fire would be much more useful now. But what were the odds that he'd find a way to master it in seconds? And he couldn't let go of the metal magic to try to reach for his fire, or he would be unprotected.

Despair was getting to him, even if he knew he should always hope. He'd never minded dying in battle, but if he did so, he'd like to die like a hero and do something that mattered, not go like that. But it wasn't time to die, but to find a way to live. The question was how. Even his magic was about to fail.

At that moment, when his hope was almost lost, the forest got darker all of a sudden. There was another magic there, a magic he knew, a magic of something more dangerous than even these enchanted or possessed bodies. It almost felt like his father's magic, but it wasn't. And yet, it felt close and intimate, as if it were his own magic. But it couldn't be.

28
THE TRUTH

Azir leaned on the cave wall and tried to listen to what was outside. Two deatheyes, as far as he could hear. He wasn't sure if those things slept, but he was paying attention.

Ursiana was as far away from him as she could, after some convincing that there was nowhere to go. Perhaps he should have let her go outside. Not a single *thank you* for saving her, no. Just anger. He could be endangering his kingdom, being here instead of there to protect it, and he got no thanks for that. But then, being stuck here was his fault. And if he thought about it, he hadn't really saved anyone. Perhaps it was destiny, destiny that he would have a chance to get everything off his chest before dying, because he had a whole ton of things he'd always wanted to say to her. She still insisted she had never betrayed him. But... it didn't make sense. It didn't. Her anger made it seem that she was telling the truth, but many people used false indignation to disguise their lies. But would she do that? That shred of doubt would drive him insane. He decided to focus on what he knew she had done.

"So you decided you hate my whole family?" he asked.

There was more light coming from the opening now and he saw her narrowing her eyes. "Didn't we just agree to remain silent? I prefer it when you're silent."

He chuckled. "Oh, I know what you prefer."

"Fuck you, Azir."

"I didn't mean that, but—" A vine came out of nowhere and hit his face. "Ouch. I said I didn't mean that. Can we stop with the violence?"

"I don't control it." She looked away and shrugged, a sly smile on her face.

"You should try to control it. This is pretty useful magic, you know?"

She was still looking away. "Some silly vines. I can't get a field to grow crops. My magic's just useless poison. Poison and anger, that's all that's left."

That was what had been left for him too. He smirked. "Maybe it suits you."

"It doesn't. It doesn't." She got up. "You know why? I was hopeful, full of joy, full of life. I believed in the good in people. Perhaps I was too innocent. Call it stupid, call it gullible if you will, but I was just a wide-eyed girl full of dreams. And then you ended it all."

"I did? Really?" He snorted and was about to remind her that she'd been happily married, unlike him. As to them, she couldn't seriously be upset at him, when it had been her fault and her choices that had driven them apart. Still, he didn't say anything because he was not in the mood to be strangled by her vines. And it was all so silly and stupid. "Oh, so you were happy? Full of joy? That's cute. So cute. After that dreadful war. Good for you. As for me, I had just lost my family, my home, everything I knew. I was eighteen and couldn't even grieve. Instead I had to take care of a kingdom scarred forever with tragedy and loss. It sounds lovely that you were happy."

She bit her lip and looked down.

Perhaps he'd gone too far. "Sorry," he said. "I know Greenstone also suffered. I know you lost a brother."

"It doesn't compare, Azir."

He sighed. "Loss is loss. Can we really quantify it?"

Ursiana shook her head, and then they were immersed in silence. It was strange how silence could feel heavy, uncomfortable. Perhaps the heaviness were all the words left unsaid, all the words hanging between them.

But there were things that shouldn't be left unsaid. "You have your problems with me and I'm fine with that. But what does my son have to do with it?"

She huffed. "Your son? Nothing." The words came out sharp like a blade.

"Then why..." He closed his eyes and sighed. "I know you didn't let your daughter accept his marriage proposal. Again, I understand you're mad at me, but what does he—"

Ursiana let out a mocking, bitter laugh, so loud that it silenced him.

When her laughter subsided, he said, "I don't understand what's funny."

"What's wrong with you?" She glared at him. "Are you going to tell me you're not only a rake, you're dumb?"

"I'm not a rake." That was an insane accusation, especially coming from her.

"Right. You're dumb."

"Just say what you're getting at."

"I'm getting nowhere. But you can't possibly think Leandra and your Ilofel together would be a good idea."

"Isofel. And I don't see what's wrong."

"You don't see what's wrong? If you aren't disgusted and horrified, you have a problem. Maybe you do have a problem."

"Fine, then." Arguing that he didn't see anything disgusting in his son wasn't going to lead anywhere. He took a deep breath. No, he wasn't going to let it go. "Just so you know,

Isofel is the most honorable young man I know. He has a good heart. Not only a good heart, he has extremely powerful magic. He's smart, gentle and kind. I can't imagine a better husband."

Ursiana sighed, as if exasperated. "Azir. Your beloved, dear son might be the most wonderful human being that has ever stepped foot in Aluria. In fact, it's charming, adorable, how much you love him. Quite something. Now please. We're adults here. We know how babies are made. We both can count months. Don't pretend to be so dim. Oh, maybe you like to pretend it so you don't need to think about what you've done."

"You can't be saying I'm dumb and giving me some cryptic messages. Either I'm dumb and unable to understand anything, or I can guess the meaning of your half sentences. What is it?"

"I don't want to talk about it." Her voice was odd—as if she were crying. In fact, she sat down and covered her face.

He got up, sat beside her, and asked softly, "What is it?"

She shook her head and now she was crying. He'd never seen her so distressed and felt at a loss as to what to do. "Ursiana. I'm here." He reached out and held her hand, which she pulled away.

"Don't touch me." Her words came with difficulty between sobs.

He kept re-reading her words in his mind. Only one possibility came to him. But that didn't make sense. "I'm trying to understand. You can't mean that Leandra is my daughter. She was born ten months after the gathering, premature on top of that. Her eyes are blue like her father's. And she's a necromancer." A necromancer. A necromancer who could walk in the hollow like a deathbringer? "She's not my daughter, is she?"

"I don't want to talk about it," Ursiana mumbled.

"I think I should know."

He stopped crying and glared at him. "Should know? Should know? After using me and tossing me? What should you know? How I managed not to become disgraced, how I didn't become an outcast? Did you care?"

"I saw you with someone else."

"It wasn't true!" she hurled.

"Fine. Now, unless she's a donkey, she can't both be mine and have been born ten months after the gathering, can she?"

"Why? You wanted us to announce her birth on the right date? You don't think anyone would have guessed? You don't think anyone would have done the math?"

Azir was still trying to figure things out, still half believing her words. "Your husband didn't mind it?"

"He helped me! He saved me. And he needed an heir."

Azir swallowed. Too many feelings at once. He had suspected it for a small moment when the girl had shown up in Umbraar, but she had blue eyes... Then, his father had blue eyes too. It was still hard to process. "You should have told me."

"Why? So you'd sneer at me?"

"You betrayed me."

"Oh, that's rich coming from you, who had already been with that Ironhold princess. Now, your twins were born four months after the gathering. There's no way you can say they were conceived after it. It means *I* was a silly distraction. Fine. My fault."

"You were not a distraction. How can you think that?"

"So then the Ironhold princess was a distraction. Or how can you explain not even looking at me on the last day?"

"You betrayed me. Or I thought so."

She rolled her eyes. "Your talk of betrayal when you had already put some children in another woman's belly is ridiculous."

"But I hadn't. I had never met Ticiane. I never had anything with her. I wasn't using you. I was serious."

"Well, explain your twins, especially your boy with green eyes like yours."

"They're not like mine. Different color. And the twins, they're not mine. Yes, they're my children and I love them." Still loved them, even Irinaia. "But I never... I had a vision of this woman asking me to help her kids. She said she was dying."

Ursiana looked incredulous. "So you went to Ironhold and defied them based on some random vision?"

"I know it sounds strange. And nobody can know about this, otherwise they won't be considered Umbraar heirs." He closed his eyes. "Of course I refused at first. I said 'you got the wrong address. This isn't Frostlake, I'm not a necromancer, and, most importantly, I don't care.'"

He sighed. Perhaps it made sense to tell Ursiana all this, Ursiana to whom he'd opened his heart and shared all his grief and fears once. Now he was sharing his greatest secret. "But she insisted. She said all I had to do was go to Ironhold and watch the kids be born. I figured she just wanted witnesses. At the time, Umbraar and Ironhold had good relations, so I ended up conceding. Your husband was there too, staring at me as if I were a criminal."

"He knew what you had done."

"Great. Because I wish I had known it. Anyway, it was princess Ticiane, and she did give birth that day and died. She had asked me to check the babies. It sounded strange, but you won't believe what constant visions and dreams can do to you. Between going to another kingdom to check on a birth and risk being haunted forever, the choice is not that hard. I guess she also visited Frostlake, since King Flavio was there."

Ursiana was paying attention, still with that hard edge in her eyes, but listening. He sighed and continued, "A midwife came out of the room with a little girl, saying that the baby survived, but the mother was dying. Then I heard another baby crying, and asked to go inside. They weren't happy about it, but let me in. A healer was looking at this baby, then saw me and shook his head. I still remember his words. 'Pity', he said. 'What a waste.' Waste. Here was a healthy young baby, and he was calling him a *waste*?" The memory still infuriated him. "And that was when I made my decision. I had already decided never to marry, but I knew that my kingdom would need heirs. And I... I hadn't been well. Then I said the twins were mine. It was really lucky that King Flavio was there. He asked Ticiane who had killed her, and she didn't know or didn't want to answer, but she said the twins were my children. Few people doubt the dead. And so I brought them home. But... I wasn't with anyone else during the gathering. It was only you. I thought it was true. I thought it was forever."

The harshness was gone from her face as she stared at him, but then it returned. "Right. And then you tossed it for some stupid lie, farce, manipulation, whatever. You should have said, 'wait a minute, Ursiana wouldn't do that.' And if you thought I was capable of betraying you, of seeing another man, then you never knew me in the first place."

He sighed. "But who would have created this lie, who would have set up something like that?"

"Half the princesses would have married you. You were a king, not a prince. You think a kingdom isn't something worth staging a lie for?"

"I... don't know."

"Sure. Keep your false story, so you don't need to say you tossed me."

"I would never toss you."

"You did! And I found myself alone, pregnant, with no marriage prospects."

"Well, you found a husband."

That bitter laugh again. "Aren't I lucky?"

He paused. "I'm sorry. I'm sorry I didn't know Leandra was my daughter, but I swear I paid attention. Why do you think I know when she was born? And then she was a blue-eyed necromancer... I understand you did it to fool everyone, and you fooled me."

She was still laughing. "You think Flavio and I actually made a child together?"

"Aren't you married?"

She shook her head. "We're friends. Good friends who love and respect each other, but that's all."

Friends. Interesting. Still, there was something he had to say. "Leandra and Isofel aren't siblings, Ursiana. They weren't raised together, they never saw each other as family, and they don't have the same parents. You should have told your daughter."

"And admit my greatest shame? Easy for you to say it. I thought they were siblings. I wouldn't... I... feel bad for not passing on his proposal, but I thought it would avoid the worst, that was all. And to be honest, I don't think I did anything bad. He was flirting with another princess and in a great mood the next day. I'm not sure he cared."

"Just because he wasn't showing it didn't mean he didn't care. I'm glad they aren't siblings, and I'm not sure your actions would have avoided the worst." In fact, he was pretty sure the worst had already happened, which was terrible in so many ways considering Leandra was married, but he didn't want to say any of that, since it had been neither her fault nor Fel's. "Your—our daughter—can walk in the hollow. I told you she communicated in a dream, but the reality is that she came to Umbraar."

"What? How was she?"

"Worried about you."

"And where's she now?"

"She..." He closed his eyes. "She asked to return to Iron-hold. I... I didn't think she was in danger, and..." He sighed. "I'm sorry. But it was what she asked me to do, so I think she's still safe, and—"

"You couldn't have known they'd become our enemies." Ursiana sighed. "But they attacked us. They kept saying it was the fae, but I saw them."

"I know. They probably want their son on the throne sooner rather than later, and they'll blame the fae. That's why I need to get back to Aluria, to fight them." He closed his eyes. "And you need to tell your daughter the truth. You don't understand what being a deathbringer is like. It's a strange magic, connecting to something else, something dark, danger-ous, something wanting to get out."

"Leah is a sweet, kind girl. She's definitely not going to unleash anything dangerous anywhere."

"She still should know it."

"What about *your* kids? Do they know you're not their father?'

"It's different."

"Different how?"

"The iron princess swore to me that the father wasn't from any of the Aluria royal families. Must have been some guard or something. She didn't want to tell and at the time I wasn't worried about it. But it means they only have iron magic to grapple with."

"It's not shameful for you, though. You should tell them."

"Perhaps I will. Perhaps I'll have to. And why is it shameful for you?"

She snorted. "Don't be ridiculous. Women always take the fall, take the blame, swallow the shame. Men don't need to answer for anything."

"I..." He didn't know what to say. He wanted to tell her she should have told him, but would that have made anything different? What if he'd still been under the illusion she had betrayed him? Funny how he was starting to think it had been a mistake, a stupid illusion, that he'd been fooled by a lie. But he couldn't change any of that now. He took a deep breath. "You're right. I'm sorry."

She got up and looked at the opening. "We need to find a way out of here."

"Let's wait until the sun comes up. They won't be as strong then. Meanwhile, perhaps you should rest."

She shook her head. "When my daughter's in danger?"

"You overused your magic. You need to rest."

"I didn't overuse shit. But I'll lie down and be quiet if my voice disturbs your highness."

"What's with the foul mouth, Ursiana?"

"You got a problem with my mouth? Be glad you can't hear my thoughts."

She lay down on a corner and he sat by her. "If you want to stay awake, we can talk, but I'm worried about you. You were passed out, I was afraid you were going to die. You have no idea—"

"Thanks. I'd rather sleep than hear that shit."

Azir sighed. "I'll let you rest."

He waited to hear some other kind of cursing, but instead her breath was steady, as if she'd fallen asleep already—or as if she was pretending, just so he would leave her alone.

Could it be true what she'd been saying, that she'd never betrayed him? And Leandra, his daughter... A deathbringer out in the world, with no idea about the terrible power she carried. And in love with Isofel, the boy he had raised. That had to be love, to carry her across Aluria to him. Azir would need to get her out of Ironhold. It was too dangerous for her now that she wasn't even a hostage anymore. They had Frostlake already, there was no need to keep her alive. So much for him to do, so much that needed to be fixed.

He looked back at Ursiana. An entire life lost, a heart broken for no reason, an entire life spent with a bitter, frozen heart, when it could have been different. And yet had it been different, he wouldn't have taken in Fel and Naia. Strange destiny.

LEAH WAS TRYING to find her dragon, trying to call him, and soon she was in an open valley, under a heavy thunderstorm. Even with all the noise of the rain, a deafening scream caught her attention. Her dragon was not flying, but lying down, hurt. This time she would use any and every magic in her power to save him, no matter what it took.

Leah ran towards her dragon, but stepped into blackness instead. No. If she truly looked, she could see through it. It was the hollow. And then she saw what she'd been looking for; Isofel, standing in what looked like a small tornado, and then she was standing beside him.

He didn't acknowledge her, but it made sense. It wasn't a tornado, but his own magic, spinning pieces of metal around him, while horrific things, bodies, tried to break his barrier. Fel was in danger. She was in danger with him. No. She knew why she'd come; to save him. If it was a matter of letting some strange power flow through her, she was going to do it. But what if it killed Fel? Perhaps she could try to take him away with her. No, she could barely walk in the hollow alone.

Then Leah remembered the Queen of Darkness. If there was a time to be all powerful, it was now.

"Help me," she muttered, knowing that there could be a high price for what she was asking, but she didn't care.

A dark slit opened in the sky, from where dark things fell

down. No. Flew down. With teeth, claws, and small wings, they attacked those awful animated corpses who were trying to get to Fel, trying to get to his company in the fort. They were vicious things, but she had them under her control, she had them protecting the Umbraar men and, most important of all, the Umbraar prince.

And yet she felt as if her control was slipping, as if it was draining her strength, her life. Death magic. Oh. The Queen of Darkness had tricked her. This was magic that sucked life force. And yet if she let go, she didn't know what would happen, didn't know if these things would make everything worse, if they would attack the Umbraar men. What had she done?

She felt familiar arms wrapping around her, then was leaning against Fel's chest.

"Leah, stop it. Stop it." How could his voice be gentle and desperate at the same time?

"I can't."

"Let go. I think you're dying."

"Escape. Survive." It was even hard to speak.

He held her tighter. "I didn't say it before, and I'm sorry. I love you. I've always done. Let go. I'll figure out something. We'll survive this together. I promise. Let go. Let go of that magic. Come back."

But she was too far gone to stop now, that thing was controlling her, sucking her life away.

The gentle arms around her then turned her suddenly. One of them was now choking her. Everything went black.

So the king of the white fae, or Ancients, looked just like River. Not that he was good looking. There was a certain severity to his features, a frown and a harshness that made his face unpleasant. Perhaps it was some kind of weariness, fear, despair, like she'd seen in this city. Nature was dry and everything was dead, and that certainly didn't make things easy for them. What Naia was wondering was if that king was River's brother or father, and why River had never told her anything about it. Well, he hadn't told her anything at all, so there was no point wondering about any lack of information.

Naia curtsied, even if she knew white fae had no authority over humans, but she did it to show respect and good will.

The king stared at her.

"State your purpose."

That meant she was finally allowed to speak. "I want to understand what's happening here. To help," she added.

"Who are you?"

She sighed and decided to be honest. "I'm Naia Umbraar, and I know River, who said he had no last name. He's worried about you, and I'm worried too."

The king frowned. "And what exactly is your worry, human?"

"It seems you've been in this city for a while, right? And things look a little dead here. I don't know what's happening, but I can imagine that whatever caused this isn't good." She realized that she sounded lost and completely out of her environment, and that her offer to help was laughable at best. "I'm River's friend, so I'm your friend too."

A laugh escaped the king's lips. "Indeed. River is quite friendly to humans."

The girl sitting beside the king then said, "Do you have a message from him?"

"No." She *was* sounding utterly ridiculous and feared these people would think she was a lunatic. "But I know he's worried about you."

The young man sitting beside the king frowned. "Since yesterday?"

The king put a hand on the young man's arm and whispered something to him, who then looked confused and asked, "How long? How long has it been?"

None of the fae said anything, but Naia thought she could give some information. "The war against the humans was almost twenty years ago, and you haven't been seen since then." The two younger fae on the dais shifted and looked at each other. Naia then asked, "Have you been sleeping during this time?"

"We were resting, yes," the king said, without showing any surprise. It was eerie how much he looked like River. He continued, "So you want to help us?"

"If I can."

The king nodded and got up. "Follow me." He turned to the guards and to the young royals on the dais. "You too."

His tone was friendly, but she wished they would unshackle her, not that she couldn't do it herself, it was just that it meant they still didn't trust her, and then, by consequence, she didn't trust them either.

They crossed a door leading to large stone steps going down to a tunnel made of compact earth, with dried roots or vines along it. That place might have been green before, but like all of that city and the surrounding area, was now dry and dead. They wouldn't be able to survive much longer like this, unless they left this place, but she wasn't sure if they were able to do so. She wasn't sure why River claimed he wasn't allowed to get in either. Hopefully a lot of it would be cleared up now.

Something pricked her arm. Naia looked, and saw the young woman with white hair pulling her hand with those sharp claws, but she wasn't staring at her, but at the king, and said, "Father, why are we going to the anti-magic cell? Is there a prisoner there we're going to see?"

So the girl was a princess. *Anti-magic? Prisoner?* But there was nothing threatening in the king's or even the guards' manners.

The king turned and glared at the girl, then smiled. "It's a good place for a private conversation. We don't want to be overheard." He glanced at Naia and gave her a friendly wink.

"We could go upstairs instead. It's nicer," the girl said, then quickly pinched Naia's arm.

That was definitely a warning. But if Naia ran, she wouldn't learn anything. And yet, if she stayed, perhaps they'd want to make her a prisoner. They could even try to kill her. But why? Even the king would certainly want to hear what she had to say. And yet, the girl had warned her.

The first thing Naia did was open her handcuffs, even if she kept her arms in the same position. Could she fight these guards? The ones inside and outside and then get back to the forest surrounding the house? Her chances were slim. She'd need to talk her way out of it.

Naia stopped. "Where are you taking me?"

"Somewhere where we can talk." The king still sounded friendly. "Isn't that what you want?"

"Yes." Naia smiled. Fae could trick with words, but they were also bound to honor them, so she had to try to use that to her advantage. "And I want to leave after we talk. Unharmed."

There was a slight pause before the king smiled. "That's a normal wish."

That pause... And he didn't say anything with his words. Still, she tried not to look nervous. "It is. So just to be safe, can you promise not to harm me, and to let me go when I wish?"

The king shook his head. "I won't harm you." He'd need to honor that. He then added, "You seem scared. Is there a reason for that?"

"Well, the war against my kind is fresh in your memory. But I wish you no harm. If anything, I'd love to help you."

"We'd love that very much."

Everything sounded fine, but they were going down, to a place that was a prison. That couldn't be good.

"Great." Naia's smile had to be forced. "But I'd love to talk upstairs. Outside."

She could feel the bronze swords at the guards and king's hips, the faint traces of iron in the earth surrounding them, but she wasn't sure if she should try to run or not.

The king's lips formed a line. "You surely understand—"

In a split second, Naia made her decision, and pulled all the swords and used them to push the guards standing behind them to the edges of the tunnel, then ran between them.

"Catch her," the king ordered. "Alive."

Naia had never run as fast before. She considered trying to collapse part of the tunnel, but she wasn't sure how much she'd be able to work on the earth, as she had never tried it, and she didn't want to waste time. In retrospect, she should have caught those swords, but it didn't matter, there would be plenty of metal ahead of her, and then there was also her fire.

When she came up to the hall where she had first talked to the king, she ripped part of the bronze door and pushed it back in the tunnel, so as to make a barrier. There were some ten guards surrounding her, armed with bows and arrows. Wood bows and arrows. That was bad. But they weren't shooting yet.

She focused on her fire and managed to make a circle around her. "I could scorch you all to death right now. But I don't want to harm any of you. So let me go."

The king came out the door and waved his hand. "Do as she says."

There had to be a trick in his words, unless the king was in fact friendly and she was over-reacting. Still, she didn't want to take chances and ran out the hall—only to find herself surrounded by some twenty more archers.

Right. The king had ordered only the guards inside to let

her go. Tricky fae. Naia pushed a wall of fire around her that made the archers step back, and then she took the opportunity to run while pulling as many swords as she could, keeping them floating behind her while she ran. It was impressive how desperation improved one's magic.

When three fae appeared ahead of her, she pushed them to the ground using the back of some of her swords. She didn't know how long she'd be able to keep fighting like that, and how far she'd go. The thicket was so far.

Then she felt something on her back, not deep like an arrow, just a prickle. She reached to it, felt a dart, and pulled it out, even if she knew it would make it bleed more. She feared that it had some kind of poison. Naia felt so angry. Why were they doing this to her?

After making another wall of fire around her, she yelled "Stop! I just wanted to help. I'm not your enemy. I'm River's friend."

Her vision was getting dark and her body felt heavy, so heavy. Tiredness overcame her and she fell. Then there was nothing.

FEL HAD JUST SLEEP-CHOKED LEAH, hoping he'd done it right, hoping it would only knock her unconscious and not hurt her. But she would have died if he hadn't done that. He caught her as she collapsed in his arms, just asleep, but still alive.

Those things she'd called, as far as he knew, they were demons. They had been efficient in defeating the corpses—by eating them. And yet, he knew that they'd turn against him and his men soon. Fire. Magic fire was the only thing that could possibly defeat them. If there was a time for Fel to use it, it had to be now. Still, he felt no fire inside him. He wondered if it had to be called with hands, like his sister did, in which case he was doomed.

Fel closed his eyes, holding Leah. Desperation could cause a surge in magic, so this had to be it. If not for him, at least for her. He had to find his fire.

Then his own voice came to him. "Let go. Let go of who you think you are. Let go."

29
HANGING

"I do love you, just so you know." River's words kept repeating in Naia's head. River, who, at least in theory, couldn't lie. River, who had made her fall asleep.

But she had no idea where she was and her body hurt. Right. River's people had made her sleep. Perhaps it was a fae thing.

Naia opened her eyes and realized she was hanging upside down, with her legs tied with strong rope. She could burn that rope easily, but the problem was that the ground was far below her, covered with wooden spikes. Along the wall, near the ceiling where she was hanging, there was a thick glass window, and beyond that, she saw the Fae king, the one who looked eerily like River, except that he was ugly and nasty.

Beside him was the young man. No sign of the princess who had tried to warn Naia. Awesome help. There were three other men with darker clothes, and some ten guards behind them. She could sense no metal, but she wasn't sure if it was because they weren't wearing any or if the wall blocked it. She tried to light flames in her hand, and they were normal, so at least her magic wasn't completely blocked. Perhaps she could burn those spikes or something, she wasn't sure yet.

The king watched her. "Finally awake."

"You said you wouldn't harm me!"

He shrugged. "You seem fine to me. And I never touched you or attacked you."

Of course. Fae's tricky words. He had specifically stated that *he* wouldn't harm her, not that she wouldn't be harmed. It made a ton of difference.

"I didn't do anything. Why are you doing this?"

The king stared at her. "Why don't you ask yourself what your kind did?"

"That was a long time ago. But you also attacked us and destroyed villages and even a city. I think we're even."

The king scoffed. "I'm not talking about humans, girl. Now, I can let you go. Unharmed. But you have to free us."

Free them? "And how can I do that?"

"That's not up to us to know, is it? And perhaps you can't do it, but maybe someone from your kind can."

"I have no idea how or why you're even kept in this city, and I'd sure help you if I knew how. And what do you mean my kind? My family?"

"Dragons, girl. We need dragon magic to free us."

Did she hear it right? Dragons? "I don't know if you've noticed it, but I have no scales. Or wings. Or claws. I mean, it should be quite obvious—"

"Quiet. Dragon lords, dragons, dragon riders, it's all the same. You look human, but you aren't."

That made more sense. And yet it didn't. "I'm an iron-bringer and I have fire magic. I'm not a dragon whatever."

"Perhaps you're not aware of it. We still need to be freed."

"And how is keeping me here hanging going to help?"

"Someone from your kind will sense your distress. Hopefully. And they'll come."

Naia sighed. That meant she was going to hang in there forever—unless her magic could somehow set her free. Or she could convince them. "Seriously, I don't know any dragon lords, and they don't know me. This is not going to work. But if you let me leave, I could try to find them. Sounds more reasonable, doesn't it?"

All the king did was look at one of the fae by him and nod. That was a signal, and probably bad news for Naia. The fae was wearing a hood covering most of his face. She wondered what he could do from such a distance and behind a glass wall, when she felt transported somewhere else.

She was in the garden by her house, and Fel was lying down, eyes wide with fear, blood spurting from his chest. No. Naia took a deep breath. This wasn't real.

Naia then found herself by her father, lying on a bed, pale and sick.

"You left me. You betrayed me," he told her in a weak voice.

She was about to apologize, but then again she had the presence of mind to realize it wasn't real. They were trying to do something to her mind, as if trying to amplify her fears, and while it felt horrible, she tried not to be taken in with these visions, as horrific and realistic as they were.

Naia then was on the bed in River's house, kissing him. The feel of his lips, his hands sliding under her skirt, it felt so real, so pleasant. But it wasn't real, it wasn't... He moved on top of her, and it was scary and exhilarating. It was so odd to both fear and desire something at the same time, but it felt good to get lost in the soft feel of his kisses and caresses, to forget whatever it was that had been nagging her on the bottom of her mind. There was something, something, something she had to remember, but this felt so good.

He took off his shirt, and there he was, like when she'd first seen him, so magnificent, except that he wasn't cold this time, but warm, so warm. His skin felt soft against her hands, and he kissed her again, then stopped and moved back, his hands against his throat, as if being strangled. Not again. She wanted to save him, wanted to undo that kiss, undo the harm she'd done. "River! River!"

And yet her yell made her open her eyes. She sighed in relief when she realized she was still a prisoner hanging upside down and it had been just a vision. It meant River was not dying. It also meant that she was in trouble and probably would die in this place, but at that moment, it was a relief.

The king chuckled. "So the shameful River is mixed up with a dragon. Why doesn't it surprise me?"

"But he's your son, isn't he?" It was a guess, but it was what made most sense.

The man's features hardened. "River's no son of mine anymore."

That was why River had no last name. He hadn't been lying. But it was unfair. "I think he's trying to help you."

"As he should. All of this is his fault. We should have won the war, we should have Aluria to ourselves. And yet, here we are, trapped, dying."

"Let me go. I'll talk to him."

"I want us to be free."

"I'll try to free you. I can even try to find those dragons."

"Trying is not good enough."

Naia was tired of that, and sent a burst of flames to the wall. Nothing happened—of course. Before the weird fae sent her any more creepy visions, she burned the spikes below her, then burned the rope tying her and jumped down. While she managed to land on her feet, she fell right away, her butt hitting the floor hard, having to hear the king laughing from that window.

At least she wasn't in that ridiculous hanging position anymore. But the bottom of that room and the walls were just stone, stone that she couldn't burn. And yet, there had to be something. If she had been brought in then tied, the room had to have some kind of door, passage. This time she would burn any fae standing in her way. If she found the exit, of course.

She moved carefully between spikes then touched the wall beneath the window. It meant that the king and his retinue couldn't see her anymore, and hopefully couldn't send her that weird magic. She still needed to find a way to escape, because she wasn't delusional like the fae and knew that no dragon lord would come looking for her. Not even River could come here, not that she expected him to do anything.

The king then yelled from the window above her, "Eventually you will starve."

"Maybe we'll all starve together. And you're imprisoning the one person who wanted to help you. At least it will be deserved."

Well, no. She thought about some of the faces she'd seen on her way to the castle. They had nothing to do with this. But it was true that she could die here. All because River had never told her anything, because she had to go and look for her own answers while he kept his secrets from her.

Perhaps all of this was because she had decided to follow a tricky fae instead of staying with her family. She wanted to regret it, and then she heard it again, "I do love you, just so you know." But what kind of love was that, keeping her in the dark, keeping her unconscious? And yet she felt something too, and it was more than just enjoying his kisses or being entranced by his looks. But none of that mattered now.

Then pain shot through her body, as if it were burning. So much pain.

RIVER WANTED to get back home soon. His magic had been needed at night, but it was morning now and he wanted to get back to Naia, even if she wasn't likely to care whether he was there or not. He closed his eyes. This wouldn't last long, it was just until everything was settled.

Then he heard it, "River! River!" She was calling him, and he had no choice but to obey her call right away.

An Ironhold and a Frostlake soldier stood by him. Poor Frostlake guys, so convinced it had been the evil fae attacking them. At this point, he doubted any different accounts would be taken seriously.

"I have to go," he said, just to be polite. Then, without even telling anyone else, he slipped in the hollow and walked back to his house.

He rushed up the stairs to his bedroom—and found it empty. He looked out the window at the barrier separating him from his city. She was there, calling him, and yet there was strong magic forbidding him to enter.

Trying to go inside could get him lost in the in-between for years again. Still, he had to try it. No, instead of trying to counter the magic keeping him out, he had to listen to the magic tying him to Naia—and hope it would be strong enough.

20 years before

RIVER WAS STILL within the Ancient's parallel realm, but in an isolated place. Perhaps he could hide here, if the rest of Aluria became too dangerous. He kicked a rock. No. He should be doing something. He wanted to avenge Ciara, wanted to kill everyone in Ironhold, innocents included.

He checked his pocket for what Analise had given him. A scrying mirror to look in the Ancient hall. Great. That way he could know what he was missing, he could look at all the events he'd been cast away from, he could remind himself of all that was lost to him. But she had meant well. And he deserved his exile. He shouldn't have made such a brash decision on his own. River covered his face with his hands. What other decision should have been made? Had he returned to the Ancient City with the staff, they'd try to use it. He doubted even Ciara would approve that. But she had rushed into Ironhold, why? Now she was gone.

Through the mirror, he noticed some odd movement in the hall of the Ancient City. His father had guards around him, as well as his two remaining children. Three strangers advanced on them, wearing dark blue scintillating armor, including helmets. None of the human armies wore armor like that, as far as he knew. And how could they even have found their city? The Umbraar king was the only one who could find it, and he had to be dead, buried under the palace.

"We're here in peace," one of them said, a man. He had an odd accent... Fernian.

They all removed their helmets. There was a woman with fair skin and long blond hair, and a younger man with brown hair and dark skin. The tallest of them, who stood in the middle and seemed to be their leader, was a man with dark brown skin, long, straight black hair, and bright yellow eyes. They had to be the dragons. And yet he couldn't go there and explain that stealing the staff had been his fault, that it had been a stupid mistake for a foolish hope.

His father sat on his throne. "To what do I owe the pleasure of such a visit? Would you like to offer your help?"

"You destroyed a city," the woman said. "You used the Krittl staff to cause death."

Forest got up. "We didn't use the staff. My brother

destroyed it. And we don't have anything to do with the accident in Formosa." Strange. Was he lying now? Or had he lied or twisted the truth before?

The leader shook his head. "This is not what your people say. You celebrated the fall of Formosa."

"They've been killing us!" his brother protested. "Destroying everything in their path. Is it a crime to be happy that there will be fewer of them in Aluria?"

"But you claimed you did it," the leader said.

Forest crossed his arms. "What if I did? What are you going to do?"

"What's your defense? Your justification?" The woman asked.

His father got up. "You don't come into our city, into our sacred hall, and demand answers."

The dragon lords looked at each other. There would be archers in strategic positions right now and he hoped his father wouldn't be that foolish to anger these visitors who had mysterious magic.

"We're not demanding anything," their leader said. "We're here to listen to your side, to give you a chance to defend yourselves."

"A chance?" his father roared. "To defend ourselves? They've been coming at us with fire and steel and explosions, they've been coming at our peaceful folk who'd been living quietly on the land, they've been doing everything they can to get rid of us. Are you going to help us fight them?"

"War is a sad thing." The leader sighed. "It doesn't justify misusing magic, it doesn't justify what you've done. Not only that, we could all have been killed in our lair, when your thief cast their spell on us. Didn't they realize it would have left us all vulnerable? It left us vulnerable for over a day, until one of us found the counter spell."

But it had been just a few minutes that they'd been frozen.

Unless... River recalled he hadn't undone the spell, he'd just assumed that removing the lapse stones would undo it, but apparently it hadn't. It explained how come nobody had followed him, how come only now they were reaching Aluria. They had probably been rescued by someone who hadn't been in their palace.

Forest shook his head. "That was my brother. Take your grievances to him."

His father glared at the dragon lords. "I'm going to ask you to leave. If you, as magical people of this world, aren't intending on helping us, then I don't know what to say."

Their leader shook his head. "You could have taken your grievances to us, and we could have helped. Before."

"It wasn't us!" Forest yelled. "It wasn't me. I don't know what happened in Formosa. I can't lie."

The man stared at him for long seconds. "We'll look into it. Meanwhile, all we ask is that you stay in this city."

River's father snorted. "Who do you think you are? To give us orders?"

"My name's Ircantari, and I'm one of the seven dragon mages." He pointed to the woman. "This is Tzaria, representative of the council for peace, and Risomu, defender of dragons. We will investigate the Formosa accident. And we will return. Your lack of cooperation will be noted."

River's father glared at them. "I'm letting you walk away with your lives. That should be noted."

"Your threat will," the man, Ircantari, said.

River wanted to bang on the scrying mirror. If it hadn't really been Forest who had destroyed Formosa, it changed everything, and his people shouldn't be paying for River's mistake. These dragon lords sure were rigid and thought they knew it all. If they were so worried about justice, why hadn't they come before? Why hadn't they helped them?

As the dragon lords walked away, his father laughed. "Or maybe it won't."

Oh, no. River wanted to scream, but knew he wouldn't be heard. A volley of arrows flew in the direction of the dragon lords—and fell halfway through.

The visitors were not fazed. Ircantari said, "Your pathetic attempt on our lives will also be noted."

River could barely breathe. Would his father order his guards to try to attack them with swords? Perhaps no. One thing King Spring didn't do was repeat his mistakes. The dragon lords were too calm and probably had some kind of magical shield protecting them.

His father laughed. "Let's not be silly. No lives were put in danger here."

Ircantari stared at the king for long seconds, then, as if making up his mind, said, "We will investigate your claims. Meanwhile, you will remain here."

The visitors walked away. River couldn't see much, but assumed they would be leaving through one of the circles. An odd feeling came to him, then, as if something was pulling him into his city. Once exiled, he'd never be able to step into the Ancient City again—unless he brought a dragon heart. There were three beating hearts right in the ancient hall. The view from the scrying mirror got blurry, and River felt sick. *You will remain here.* It hadn't been advice, but an enchantment. The dragons were trapping the Ancients in the city—but that would mean their death, when Mount Prime was being destroyed.

River had to do something. He improvised a ring in that clearing, and then stepped into the darkness of the hollow, determined to find the dragon lords and plead with them. He would even beg if he had to. Hopefully they would understand.

Ironhold. They had just gone to Ironhold, which meant they were quite brave or reckless, or maybe they didn't understand the threat the humans posed. In fact, it definitely seemed to be the case. No, they changed direction. Wolfmark. Almost as bad.

River found them in a faerie ring. "Wait."

Ircantari turned and set his chilling yellow eyes on River. "What are you doing here?"

"*I* was the one who stole the staff. But we didn't destroy Formosa. I got to Aluria *after* the city had fallen, in fact I almost died after the boat I was in turned."

"Go back to your city."

"I can't. You have to investigate the humans. They have magic. The ironbringers also have powerful weapons. They have steel, explosives, fire. Perhaps *they* attacked Formosa." Strange how the thought had only come to him now.

"Why would they do such a thing?"

"Because they're violent? They're insane? I don't know."

"We'll look into it."

"No." Desperation was taking hold of River. "You don't understand. If you leave my people locked in the Ancient City, they'll die. There's no food, nature there is dying, thanks to the greedy humans destroying Mount Prime. They'll all die."

Ircantari stared at River. "It's a temporary solution. Your people won't be stuck there forever."

"But how long? One month might be too much."

"We'll find out what happened, then we'll discuss it again with your king. If you want to help your people, tell him to cooperate with us instead of trying to kill us."

"The people there, it's not their fault," River pleaded. "If you have grievances with me, take them on me, if you have issues with my father, deal with him."

"Go back to your city."

"I can't." The words were said to nobody, as River was knocked back to the hollow. Of course. Knocked back into his city. Now perhaps he'd find out which magic was stronger, his father's or the dragon lords'. Or else he'd be ripped in half.

A last-ditch idea came to him. The scrying mirror could represent a place. Even though River was struggling in darkness, unable to find a circle, he took the object in his palm and placed the lapse stones around it, focusing on freezing everyone within the borders of that city. That way, if the dragon lords took too long, at least nobody would die of starvation. These magicians didn't seem to understand the problem or care about it, and were unlikely to be in a hurry to lift the spell holding the Ancients in their city. If his magic worked, he could save his people, at least for a while, if it didn't... then it was the end.

But he wouldn't know the result of his effort for a long time, as darkness engulfed him right away. Exiled from his city while at the same time ordered to remain there, River ended up suspended in nothingness, frozen in time.

It took him nineteen years to wake up again, hungry, cold, lonely, and disoriented. He wasn't sure if he was dead or alive, or where he was, until he saw a light far away. But there were also eerie growls in that direction. And yet, it was a direction, it was a goal. River fought his way to that light—and passed out.

He woke up in a strange room, still alert to enemies, still trying to fight for his life. But he didn't find an enemy, but his pretty savior—again. Except... she was slightly younger, and looked at him defiantly, not as if she knew him. And she was intent on demanding her due debt for saving his life. He got to kiss her—and almost died with her poisonous iron magic, pushed back again into nothingness.

When River came to consciousness again, he tried to visit his city, but was unable to do so. He considered going to

Fernick again, and pleading to the dragon lords to help his people. But then his thoughts turned to Ciara. Ciara and her words, *let them kill each other*. He could still have his revenge. And if his people were still alive, he could still free them. The only thing standing between him and his plan was actually a person: his beautiful savior, to whom he now owed a life debt.

30
DEBT

Naia lay on the ground, her body shaking. What had they done? She didn't know any magic that could cause pain like that. Illusion. Pain was an illusion, like the visions. It was the weird hooded fae. And yet there was nothing she could do to make them stop other than plead, which she wasn't going to do. Perhaps they truly thought that if they tormented her enough the dragon lords would come. And yet how could she convince them that it was nonsense?

Her hope now was that they would eventually see the futility of their ways and get tired of tormenting her. How long that was going to take was anyone's guess. Meanwhile, she could still try to find an exit. She hated this so much. It felt awful to feel weak and helpless like that. All because she had been careful with her magic when escaping the first time. Had she killed that king, she would be running free. Sure. Right into River's arms. How was that going to work out?

The ground then shook beneath her, and she closed her eyes, bracing herself for more horrors. Instead, she heard, "Naia?"

River was in front of her. A vision, of course. "You're not real."

He held her hand and pulled her up. "I am."

It was him. He'd come for her.

"Father!" River yelled. "Let her go. She's my chosen life companion and I ask you to honor her as such."

"You're not my son. And how did you get here?" the king yelled.

"It doesn't matter," River replied. "Now let us go. I *am* trying to set you all free. But keeping her is not going to help."

River looked at her and pulled her in his arms.

The king sighed. "You know, I gave you one task. I guess you did fulfill it. For once you've done something right. You've brought a dragon's heart."

"She's not..." River frowned, then looked at her and caught a breath. There was fear in his eyes.

"What?" Naia whispered.

He held her tighter. "I'll get you out, I'll find a way." His arms were trembling, though.

The king's voice echoed above them. "You want to be welcome to the Second Dynasty again?"

"No," River yelled. "Just let us go."

Naia wanted to ask him if he couldn't just disappear with her the same way he had appeared, but he obviously couldn't, or else he wouldn't be asking for the king to let them go. And he was afraid.

"Well, that's too bad," the kind said. "Considering you're about to fulfill your word. Get her heart."

River let go of her and stepped back, or tried to, then stopped.

"Run," he muttered. "Away from me."

There were five hooded fae on the window up there, all of them looking at River. She realized they were going to make him do it, make him take Naia's heart. But he didn't even have a knife or anything. He had his nails. And Naia wasn't sure she'd be able to fight him.

There wasn't much space to run, but she stepped back, paying attention not to get her feet in any of the spikes.

River was trembling, his eyes wide in fear, until he had a half smile, as if he'd just had an idea. He looked at her. "Command me. Command me to take you away from here," he whispered.

She wasn't sure why he was saying that, but tried it. "Take me away."

He trembled and stepped towards her. "Com-mand. Order."

"Save me." Her back was on the wall now.

River closed the distance between them, hopefully to get them through the hollow, but he was still trembling as he touched her chest. "Order me."

She remembered then the night she had found him. *Eternal devotion,* she had asked him, but then they had agreed on the kiss instead. But what if? What if he had to do what she told him?

This time she took in the authority of someone who was owned something, as if he were her servant. "Take me home."

There was relief in his face, which she hoped was because her request had worked, and not that he was about to take her heart. Indeed he wrapped her in his arms, and then they were in that dreadful darkness, then in the clearing by his house. *His* house. She had said home, though.

River was still trembling. "I almost lost you, I'm so sorry."

Questions were whirling in her mind. "Don't make me sleep," she said, and only then she realized she had used the same kind of command she had used before.

He stopped hugging her and looked at her. "You know my secret now."

"Not even close, River, not even close. You have hundreds of secrets. Let's go inside. I want to sit."

She rushed into the house, and he followed her. She wasn't sure if she had *commanded* him or not. Exhausted, she collapsed on the pillow on the floor. He sat by her.

She asked, "Did I make you sit, or are you doing it because you want to?"

River got up. "Why? You think I'll only talk to you if you force me?"

"I don't think. I'm sure. Now sit."

He glared at her and sat down. That *had* been a command and she could feel it—and didn't care.

Naia glared at him. "So you owe me eternal devotion? Not sure you've been keeping your part of the bargain."

He looked away.

"Say something."

River smirked. "Something."

"Asshole."

"I just saved you and I wish you'd be slightly more considerate."

"You saved me as part of this weird magic thing."

He rolled his eyes. "Don't be ridiculous."

"Oh, but I want to be ridiculous. How is making me sleep for hours or days or who knows how long eternal devotion?"

He shrugged. "You use ambiguous words, you get ambiguous results." His tone was cold, callous. Was this the real River?

"You're going to answer me now, and not come up with weird word traps. Why did you bring me here?"

"Now? To save you. I apologize if I interrupted your lovely time talking to my dear father."

She stared at him. "I mean before. Why?"

"To make sure you were safe." His tone was clipped, as he was clearly not comfortable being ordered to answer her.

She still didn't care. "Because of the eternal devotion?"

He tilted his head. "Partly. Can we stop this? Talk normally?"

"No. You never talk. Now answer me and don't complain."

He glared at her, visibly hating it.

"Why are your people trapped in the city? Why is everything there dry? Why did you say you couldn't go there and now you just went?"

"The dragon lords trapped them. Everything is dry because the city is connected to Mount Prime. If the nature there is destroyed, the nature in the Ancient City is destroyed as well. I can't go to the Ancient City because I was exiled. It's strong magic. But my deal of eternal devotion to you is stronger. It's stronger than the anti-magic in that room."

"Why were you exiled?"

He closed his eyes and exhaled. "I had a powerful magical tool that would have allowed us to win the war. I destroyed it instead."

"Why?"

"I didn't want to kill innocents. Not even humans."

"That's not a fair reason to exile you."

River shrugged and looked away. There was so much there, so much to understand, so much to unpack, but she decided to move to the questions that had been bothering her the most.

"What are you doing in Ironhold?"

"Creating illusions for them."

"Explain. Explain in a way that I can understand what you're doing there and why you're doing it, and what your goal is."

River sighed. "Let's talk normally."

"I said no complaints."

He rubbed his hand on his face, then glared at Naia. "Ironhold, I think they're worse than they seem. Much worse."

"So you decided to help them. Makes total sense."

"It does. I was alive during the war, and a city in Umbraar was destroyed."

"Formosa."

He nodded. "They say the fae did it. I don't think it was us. I think it was Ironhold. But I need proof. Being there allows me to look. So that's one reason. The second reason is that they killed my sister. She was my favorite sister, the one I most got along with, and they killed her. I'm just one, Naia. All I can do is help them dig their own grave. I approached them and offered to create illusions for them."

"And they said sure, come on in?"

"I used... my powers on their king. And he trusts me now. I am creating illusions, like the one in Frostlake. There was no fae there."

Illusions. It made sense. "Did you create that watersnake that attacked us in the lake?"

He shook his head. "No. I think it was someone from Wolf-mark. A strong wildbringer can enchant a water creature. I didn't know anything about it, but when you told me, I realized you could be in danger. That was why I wanted to take you away."

"So you could help Ironhold and still keep your part of the eternal devotion?"

"Partly."

"So you're creating illusions to make people fear the fae and give power to Ironhold? How's that going to defeat them? And if your people get free, humans will attack them even worse than before."

He sighed. "The illusions are reversible. In six months, people are going to realize it was Ironhold. By that time, I can infiltrate other kingdoms and make them join together to attack Ironhold, which is going to be weakened by then. I am just one person and I don't have an army. This is the best I can do."

"Why didn't you tell me any of that?"

"I didn't think you'd like it, and you had the power to stop me. I mean, you still have it."

"Some villages were attacked. Something mysterious. Was that you?"

He shook his head. "No. But it was Ironhold. They have some strange magic. That was why I thought they could use the illusions instead of killing people."

"Why did you spend a year away from me? How could you even do it, considering your eternal devotion?"

"I got knocked back to the hollow, like I told you. That was months. Then I went on with my plan. I only realized you had power over me in the Frostlake castle, when you called me to your room."

That didn't sound right. "I called you?'

"Somehow you did. And I had no option but to obey."

"Why then did you leave me alone here, when I asked you to stay?"

He shook his head. "You didn't order me to stay, Naia, you just complained I was leaving you."

"Great." She was still trying to trace his steps. "And why did you decide to ask me to marry you?"

"I saw you, and you were so beautiful, and so powerful, and I thought you liked me and you would like that. Maybe I thought we could work, maybe I thought it would be a way to keep you safe. Maybe I thought it was how I would fulfill my duty of eternal devotion. There were lots of things going through my mind. And most of all, I know I'd never want anyone else by my side."

She wanted to believe his last words, and it was tempting to believe them, knowing he couldn't lie. And yet. "Sure. Then you said you'd marry me and you didn't."

"I wanted to get everything settled first. I also knew that one day you would find out everything I did, and you would see me very differently. I mean, if I had married you while still keeping things from you, it would be..." He paused and looked down. "Wrong. I couldn't."

"You said you wanted to declare your love for me to your father, knowing well you couldn't go there."

"I thought I was going to find a way to get back. I think Ironhold is hiding a dragon heart. If I found it, I would be welcome back. Only then, when everything was settled, when you knew who I was, would you be able to say *yes* or *no*. Had I been selfish, I wouldn't wait. I did it to honor you."

"No. You did it because you knew you would make me angry, you knew you were doing things I didn't like, and you wanted to do them anyway, hoping that I would just turn around and walk away at the end, so that you'd feel no guilt."

"Maybe." He grimaced. "Stop it. Stop making me talk."

"Not until I know what I need to know. Why are they saying I'm a dragon? Did you know that?"

"I had no idea, but I should have noticed it. Quite an oversight from my part. I mean, your fire, your brother's bright eyes, your ability to circumvent the magic keeping this house away from the Ancient City..."

"But my father's a deathbringer."

River bit his lip. "I don't think he's your father."

It couldn't be true, it couldn't. It made no sense. "You might be wrong."

"I might. Stop it, Naia."

"No. You're going to tell me what you are avoiding telling me. More secrets. Tell me."

He sighed. "I've met you before. Twice. Don't you remember?"

She shook her head.

"It's what I thought. I sometimes wondered if you were the same person. In the Dragon Lair, you saved me. I... sometimes wish you hadn't. Then on my way back to Aluria. You saved me again, but it was as if you were dead. I... I don't understand it."

"But didn't you spend like some twenty years in the hollow?"

"Yes."

She raised an eyebrow. "Do I really look like I'm forty?"

He shrugged. "I'm just about nineteen. Time acts differently in some cases. The people in my city didn't age either. I don't know, Naia. I never understood it."

"Tell me about it in detail, how I saved you."

River sighed again, then went on to tell her about the war against the humans, then how he decided to get the dragon's staff. Naia was surprised to hear that he had traveled to Fernick. Aluria had been isolated for so long that it felt strange to hear that there used to be boats going to the continent, and a lively city with a port. Of course, she had heard about Formosa, but that was the kind of stuff that sounded like legend, and when he described his trip, it made it seem so real, so tangible. He went on to explain how he'd stolen from the dragon lords using something he called lapse stones, and how she had saved him.

"How could she have been me?"

"She looked like you, Naia. I don't know."

The story didn't end there. He told her how his ship had sunk on his way back, probably because of the tragedy in Formosa. It meant he truly had never had anything to do with it. Then again she saved him, but in some spirit form. Once he was back to the Ancient City, his brother claimed to have destroyed Formosa, but he wasn't sure about it. Then he learned about what the staff did and destroyed it. Except that then the dragon lords came and isolated his city. He used his stones to keep his people frozen in time, but when he pleaded with the dragon lords to free the city, they tried to send him back, and the clash of magic sent him to the hollow.

"I wish I had never stolen that staff. It's what brought the dragons, what made them isolate my city."

"You can't know. If it's a magical instrument that can kill thousands of people, perhaps it had to be destroyed. And maybe the dragon lords would have come anyway, because of Formosa, and would blame the Ancients anyway. The dragon lords... You said one of them was going to investigate Ironhold?"

"That's what he said. I thought it had been a lie, that he had gone back to his land, but now... I wonder." He stared at her.

"You think one of them went to Ironhold... and met my mother?"

"Maybe."

"But what about my father? My real father? I mean, Azir Umbraar?"

"I don't know."

She didn't know anything either, and it was too much to take at once.

"There's more, isn't there?" she asked. "What else aren't you telling me?"

"You'll need to be more specific there." His tone was dry. Of course, he was still under her command. She didn't like what she was doing, but she hated even more everything he'd done, especially because he'd kept it all hidden from her, thinking he would lose her, and he'd done it anyway.

"To me. You made me sleep. Did you use glamour on me? To make me agree to marry you? To make me agree to come here?"

He smirked. "Believe it or not, your attraction to me is your own."

"Asshole. So you didn't do anything?"

He looked down. "I did glamour you. But not to be interested in me. As you well know, such a thing would be completely unnecessary."

She rolled her eyes. "Then what did you do?"

"At the ball. In Frostlake. I made you disappear in the crowd. I made you imperceptible."

Naia wasn't sure if she had heard him right. "You what?"

"I made it so nobody would notice you."

"Why would you do that? Didn't you just say that you weren't interested in me? That you only came to my room because of your eternal devotion?"

"You misunderstand me. I would have left you alone. It didn't mean I didn't find you interesting. It didn't mean I wouldn't try to court you. Properly. Once my life was settled. Once I figured whether you had tried to kill me or not. Either way, going into a human girl's room is not proper behavior. That's why I only went when you called me."

"And yet you wanted me to feel invisible in the ball."

"Most of those princes are horrible people. Then if they saw you, a bunch of them would have wanted to marry you. I did you a favor. To keep you safe."

Naia rolled her eyes. "Umbraar has poor relations with other kingdoms. Nobody would have proposed to me."

"They would. Of course they would. They would talk about nothing but you. I saved you from a terrible marriage."

"For what? So that you could trick and lie to me so much that I would leave you?"

"I was hoping you would understand me. I thought you would. But I had to give you the opportunity to make up your mind about me."

Naia took a deep breath and closed her eyes. "You have to do as I say, right? If I command you?"

"Yes."

Her decision was painful in a way. It meant losing a strategic advantage. As someone who'd always wanted to lead a kingdom, this wasn't a good choice. It also meant perhaps seeing River walk away from her, and the odd thing was that despite everything, she still didn't want him to leave.

He was staring at her. "I'm waiting."

She took another deep breath. "I release you from your life debt to me. You no longer owe me eternal servitude. You don't owe me anything. Did it work?"

"We'd need to test it."

Naia nodded, and realized tears were running down her eyes. "You're free to leave. I'll just ask you to take me home."

"This is your home. That's where I brought you when you commanded me."

"But if it was all because of some stupid magic rule, then it's no more. Maybe I thought it was my home, but I guess it isn't. You were just keeping me here so I wouldn't get in your way, isn't it?" She chuckled. "Maybe I should have asked you that before removing your eternal devotion."

"Naia, that's not right. I told you in many different ways, some of them quite embarrassing and shameful, how much I care about you. I told you I've seen you before. I know that our connection is bigger than what we see. Why would you think I just want you here to get you out of my way?"

"Because you made me sleep. Not to get in your way. Can I ask you not to do that again?" She rolled her eyes. "I should definitely have asked this earlier and made you promise."

"I won't do that. You don't hate me?"

"No. You were trying to save your people, and I can understand that. I don't agree with the way you did things, but I can see where you were coming from. But you know what? I also hate Ironhold. They killed my mother, they might have killed my real father, they might have destroyed Formosa and my grandparents, uncles, and aunts. If you want to defeat them, let's think about this together. I can help you. It's nice that you think I'm beautiful, it's nice that you want me by your side, but you should respect me as a person, not as a pretty object."

"That's not fair. I do respect you." He looked down. "I just... I had to do what I had to do. Once, I ignored my people's needs because of compassion. I got my sister killed. I couldn't let compassion lead me astray again."

"You don't think I can help you?"

He stared at her with his reddish-brown eyes. "I don't want you to risk your life for that. I want you safe."

"I'm not saying I'm going to fight. Let me just understand you. Share your griefs and doubts and fears, otherwise there's nothing between us."

"Well, I had plans and I didn't think you would agree with them."

She snorted. "That's the loveliest part, River, that you were willing to let me go, even if you said you loved me."

"Loving is letting go."

"Letting go." She glared at him. "Not squandering, not throwing things away. You know something? Destroying is easy. Breaking things apart is easy. Splitting is easy. It hurts, but it's easy, it requires no effort. You wanted to go about it the easy way. Getting together, loving, building things, that's messy, hard, that takes work. What do you want to do? Do you want the easy way? Do you want to go about your plans and watch me leave? It's easy. Or do you want to go about it the hard way? Let's plan together, let's find a way to save your city, to defeat Ironhold, let's find a way to get over our differences. It takes work, River. I forgive you because I want to choose the hard way, because I believe in building things. What do *you* choose?"

He stared at her for long seconds, then took her hand. "I want the hard way. With you. And now that you know every-thing about me, and now that I declared my love for you in front of my father, like I said... I need to ask you. Will you marry me?"

She kissed his cheek. "Give me time to trust you, time to think about it."

He narrowed his eyes. "Think? Where is the girl who just said she chose the hard way? Who chose to love, to build things?"

"Hard way, River. It doesn't mean snapping your fingers and getting what you want. You have to work for that. I want to trust you, and I choose to trust you, but you need to do your part. I guess I need to do my part as well, after all, I did disregard your advice not to go in the forest. My actions have put your city in danger. I want to fix it, but trust takes work."

He took a deep breath. "I'll work for that."

Naia smiled. "And we'll work together to defeat Ironhold."

"As much as it's safe for you."

"And for you."

"Fair."

"I still need to go to Umbraar, River. I want to see my brother. Also," she looked down, "I want to talk to my father. Real father or not, I don't like the way I came here without his approval. Would you come with me and talk to him?"

He looked away. "We could wait, right? Until Ironhold is defeated?"

"Are you afraid of the Umbraar king?"

"He is scary, but..."

"River, what is it?"

He looked at her and bit his lip. "Ironhold has just attacked Umbraar."

LEAH HAD trouble opening her eyes, as it was so bright around her. Fel was still holding her, but they weren't by the fort. They didn't seem to be anywhere, or else perhaps she couldn't see because it was all so bright.

"Am I... Are we dead?"

"Not yet." His voice was slightly different, as if he were older, but he looked the same.

"What's happening?"

"You'll soon be back, so I need to be brief. I'm taking you away. To get help. Ironhold, they have more magic than we thought, and they're much more dangerous. We have to find a way to defeat them."

She nodded. "What about my mother?"

"The Umbraar King was with her. We can try to help them later."

The mention of King Azir reminded her of something that had been bothering her, and now had become clear but also terrifying.

"Fel. I think I'm a deathbringer."

"You are."

She swallowed, recalling how King Azir had been so worried about her mother, how much her mother hated him, and her talk about the young lady who had lost her honor. The realization was horrific. "I think we're siblings."

He shook his head. "No. Not at all. Azir is not my father. He could be yours, for sure, but he isn't mine."

"How do you know?"

He bit his lip. "A family resemblance thing. And I don't have his magic."

She took a deep breath. "I... then... I don't understand why you didn't propose. I tried to ask you. I still shouldn't have married someone else, but—"

"It's my fault. I should have spoken to you. Trusting notes that could easily have been tampered with was naive and stupid. And I shouldn't have trusted your mother to pass on my proposal."

His words surprised her. "You proposed?"

"You thought I didn't?"

"I..." She looked down. "But it's too late, right? For us?"

He ran his magic hand through her hair. "I don't mind if you got married, or whatever happened between you and your husband. It doesn't change the fact we belong together." He sighed. "But it is too late for us."

"Why?"

"I don't look the same. In the real world."

There was no change in him now, but this was probably a dream. "Are you hurt? Did something happen?"

He shook his head and focused his beautiful green eyes on her. "Nothing bad. I found my power, that's all."

"But then..." She didn't understand what it could be. Did he think she wouldn't want him? Did he think he was ugly? "I don't care what you look like."

Fel chuckled. "You mistake me. I actually look awesome."

"I don't understand."

He kissed her cheek and kept his face close to hers. "You will. Now focus on defeating the dark forces in Aluria. I'm taking you to Fernick. But I..."

She wanted to ask what he meant, what he was saying, how they were traveling, but she passed out again.

31
GOODBYE

Azir had spent the night awake, mixed-up thoughts going through his mind. At the same time, he paid attention to the deatheyes. There were more than two, and while he hoped they would fall asleep during the day, he couldn't be sure that would be the case.

Either way, he and Ursiana were out of food and water and it would be easier to escape sooner rather than later. The longer they remained here, the weaker they'd become.

He'd thought a lot about what Ursiana had told him. Her version of events made a lot more sense than thinking she'd gone off with some random prince. It had never made sense, and yet he'd believed it like a gullible idiot. All because it was easier to believe the worst in people. Now he was stuck in this awful place, with monstrous creatures outside. More and more he was coming to the conclusion that there was no way for both of them to leave this place alive. He had no doubt in his heart who he wanted to survive.

He kneeled by Ursiana and touched her shoulder.

She opened her eyes, saw him, then sat up, as if scared. "What?"

"You're afraid of me?"

"I hate you. It's different."

"I accept that. I... I thought about what you said." His words came out with difficulty. "And I believe you. You have no idea how hard it is for me to say it, how hard it is for me to admit I was wrong, admit I might have ruined my life and maybe your life because I believed in a stupid lie, but I did. To my credit, I was young. I had nobody to give me advice, nobody to confide in other than false friends. Not that it excuses it. I know it doesn't. I should have trusted you. Or at least given you a chance to explain your side of the story. I never gave you that. But just..." He sighed, words stuck in his throat.

Ursiana shook her head. "It doesn't matter anymore."

"It does. It does because I want you to know it. If ever I believed the worst in you, it was not because I didn't know who you were. I knew it, and I knew it well. But I had just lost my entire family, many of my friends, the very city where I grew up. If I didn't trust you, it wasn't because I thought less of you, but because of my inability to believe that things could be good again. If I didn't trust you, it was because I didn't trust that good things could last. I had just lost everyone and everything I loved, and perhaps it was easier to accept that loving you was a lie than to lose you again."

Her eyes were hard. "Pretty words. It doesn't change the fact that I was the one left alone and pregnant."

"But you found someone who took care of you."

"And if I hadn't? You don't know what happens to us, do you?"

"I can't pretend—"

"Not all families want to live with the shame. A daughter who dies from a strange disease is better than a disgraced daughter with a bastard child."

He frowned. "Your family wouldn't—"

"I don't know. I never asked. Flavio and Kasim rescued me, rescued Leah, but it could have been very different. Perhaps neither of us would have been here."

"You never asked for my help."

She glared at him. "Don't get me started, Azir. Don't."

He nodded. "Fair enough." He sighed. "I... I've been thinking about our escape, and there isn't much we can do, except—" He closed his eyes. "We'll have to wait until they're quiet and run, hoping they'll take long to see us. There should be a corridor leading out of this place. The deatheyes can throw poisonous spikes, and they're deadly, so you'll go in front of me. That way, if any spike reaches us, they'll hit only me, and you'll survive."

She stared wide-eyed at him for long seconds, then, all of a sudden, said, "Fine."

Fine. All right. He hadn't been expecting tears or anything dramatic, but he had been hoping for a slightly stronger reaction than that. After all, he was willing to die for her. Perhaps she secretly thought it was hilarious and was going to celebrate his passing after she got back safely to Aluria. Perhaps he deserved it. Or maybe he hadn't been clear.

"You understand I might die."

She nodded a little too fast, as if nervous. That was at least some reaction. What had he been expecting anyway? She'd always see him as the rake who had taken advantage of her then left her, despite all his apologies and explanations. He'd spent years of his life thinking of her as the cold woman who'd betrayed him, secure in the feeling that he'd never been loved. There was something comforting about hating, it made you much less vulnerable, and perhaps he didn't have the right to take it away from her.

Still, he had things to tell her. "Ursiana, Leah might be in danger. I want you to get her out of Ironhold."

There was fire in her eyes. "You *want*? You have no right to want anything to do with her. You might have conceived her, but she's not your daughter. That said, yes, any idiot will agree she can't stay in Ironhold, and if by any miracle you survive, maybe you should take care of it."

He sighed. "So you agree with me and yet you chastise me."

"Don't you dare act like her father, that's all."

"Great. In fact, it makes sense. Can I ask you a few things? Dying wishes? Or is that too much?"

"Yes. Make your dying wishes."

"I think... If it's still possible, regardless of what happened between Leah and the Ironhold prince, I'd be happy if she and Isofel got together. They're not siblings and they like each other. But it depends on you and her, of course."

She crossed her arms, her eyes distant. "I don't have a problem with that."

"Right. And... try to send a message to Naia. I... I told her she was not my daughter, I... But it's not true. I miss her and I wish we hadn't parted like that. She'll always be my heir. One of my heirs, at least. Try to send her this message, please."

"Sure." Her eyes were still distant, and misty now. She had some feeling, it was just that it was buried deep within her anger.

"It's fine, Ursiana." He chuckled. "Perhaps dying by deatheyes will be deserved."

"It's not funny."

"I... I never stopped loving you. Every day that I thought I hated you it was just a day that I wish I had you by my side. Perhaps I thought I hated you because I thought you took that away from me. I... You went to Frostlake but it was my heart that got frozen, cold, hard, but also frozen in time. I never loved anyone else."

Tears were running down her eyes. "It makes no difference now. We can both survive on our own, and that's what matters, going on, moving on, taking care of our children. The past is gone and doesn't matter anymore. What matters is the future; what can be fixed. That's what matters, not some silly love story from our teens."

"I guess." Perhaps she was cold hearted, but it was better this way. It meant she wasn't going to suffer with his death.

"You know it's true." She was still crying, though.

He wanted to reach out and dry her tears, but perhaps it would only make it all worse. It was time for a final goodbye, not the time to try to rekindle a flame that had been quenched too long ago.

"Are you ready?" he asked.

"Very much." She smiled. "And looking forward to it."

Yes, definitely cold-hearted. At least she would survive his death without any trauma. "I'll keep them busy and you'll run ahead of me. The corridor should be right across from this one."

"Right."

Something in her tone... There was something. No, it was just him being silly and expecting some more sadness. He had no right to expect that.

"Let's go," he said.

Once they were outside, they reached the tunnel leading out, but then she pushed him and formed a barrier of vines between her and him. The monsters were on her side. What was she doing?

"Ursiana!"

"Run!" She yelled. "I can't hold them long."

He wasn't going to run, not with her still here. He wasn't going to leave her. And yet.

"Run," she pleaded. "Please. If I keep this barrier protecting you I can't protect me. I would never survive seeing you die. Please, run. Fix the future. It's *my* dying wish."

There were deatheyes getting close, based on the roars.

He tried to break through her vines but he couldn't, unarmed as he was. He wasn't going to leave her, and yet, if he didn't cross over, they would both die. If he ran, she could use the vines to protect herself, and by staying here, he would only condemn both of them to death. *Run.* What a horrific dying wish.

He ended up doing as she had asked him, even if he hated that, even if he'd been willing to die for her. He found himself on white sands of an unknown beach. Soft waves crashed in front of him. The world crashed inside him. It was all so wrong. He would have given his life to save her, he would have gladly died for her, and yet she didn't even want that. *I would never survive seeing you die.* And why did she think *he* could? *Fix the future.* It was true that he had a lot to do. And yet. If there was any chance that Ursiana was alive, he was getting her out. No matter what it took.

NAIA'S KNEES FELT WEAK. "What? Umbraar being attacked?" She still couldn't believe River's words. "I need to help them now. You knew about it? You didn't tell me? You didn't tell them?"

"Naia, you shouldn't worry." His voice was calm. "The Ironhold forces don't stand a chance against your brother and father. They'll be decimated."

"And you think it's good? To see people killed?"

"They're the enemy. Make up your mind, Naia"

"Take me to Umbraar."

"You don't give me orders anymore."

"River, if you want this to work out, you're going to take me to my kingdom right now. And don't tell me it's dangerous. If the enemy is all decimated, then there's no danger, right?"

"I'd rather be on the safe side."

"Me too, and I want to be near my brother and father when our kingdom is being attacked. Don't take this from me."

He swallowed and stared at her, then took a deep breath and closed his eyes. "Fair enough."

They walked through that strange, dark place, then ended up by the Royal Fort. A lot of smoke was coming from it, and Naia ran towards it—and stopped. There was a pile of burned bodies by one of the outer walls, and some of them didn't look human. River was beside her.

"What happened here?" She turned to him. "What are those?"

He was looking around, frowning, as if thoughtful. "I'm not sure. As far as I knew, all they were sending was a regular army, with some ironbringers, strong weapons, but lots of metal, which your brother probably dealt with quite quickly."

She shook her head and walked towards the fort, now slowly, feeling sick when she saw some of the Ironhold men dead or hurt. She glared at River. He looked different, with his horns glamoured and with eyes brown.

His expression showed disbelief. "I don't understand. They should have been defeated easily."

"Except they weren't."

River paused. "Making mistakes is easy. Fixing them is hard. Let me help you fix it, Naia."

"Let's hope there is fixing."

A soldier came running to her. Not anyone, Arry. He'd often visited their house many years before, when they had been all children. Not so much lately, and Naia had no idea why. She still thought she could consider him a friend, though.

Meanwhile, River put an arm around her, perhaps to console her, but it felt wrong in front of all these people. She wanted to push it away but thought it would call even more attention.

"Where's Fel?" she asked when Arry was fairly close.

He glanced at River, then at her. "Gone."

She felt as if her heart had stopped. "What?"

"No, no. He's alive. But he left." He again glanced at River, as if there was something he didn't want to say in front of him. She'd ask him later.

"What about my father?"

"We haven't seen him since last night. Fel said he was busy somewhere."

She was trying to take it all in. "What happened here?"

"A lot."

PERHAPS LEAH'S talk to Isofel had been a dream, and she hadn't even checked, which was maybe for the best. And yet she couldn't be dreaming if she was thinking all that.

Then she felt as if she was in a black hole, buried in darkness for a long time. Slowly, she felt something warm beneath her, and eventually opened her eyes to see the sun above some clouds, pleasant wind hitting her face. Beneath her, iridescent silver scales shone. Her dragon. She was lying on him, flying above the sea.

She ran her hand over his soft scales, feeling that pleasant texture. This was real.

Finally she had the courage to say what she had been holding back. "I love you."

He slowed down and looked back, one of those huge cat-like eyes on her. Isofel. In his other form.

THE STORY CONTINUES

Naia, Fel, Leah, and River's story is not over yet. Their journey continues in *Iron Hearts and Dragon Magic.*

Find out more at https://dayleitao.com/books/iron-hearts-dragon-magic/

AFTERWORD

Thanks so much for reading this book! I hope you enjoyed it.

If you'd like to know more about me or sign up for free books and news, you can find me at dayleitao.com

Also, reviews are super important for authors and readers, so if you have a minute, please leave your opinion on Goodreads, Amazon, Bookbub or any other site. It doesn't need to be long or eloquent. A short sentence like "this was fun," " I liked this but didn't like that," "good for readers who enjoy...," "reminded me of book so-and-so," is perfect.

Finally, if you enjoyed this book, you might also enjoy my other fantasy series:

Kingdom of Curses and Shadows

Portals to Whyland